DA

BLOOD AND EARTH

THE FIRST BISHOP & POPE NOVEL

STEVE INCE

MILFORD COMMUNITY LIBRARY
Village Hall
2 Park Road
Milford on Sea
Hants SO41 0QU

Copyright © 2020 Steve Ince
All rights reserved.

ISBN: 9798679943278

Imprint: Independently published

www.steve-ince.co.uk

All rights reserved. No portion of this book may be reproduced in any form without permission from the publisher, except as permitted by U.K. copyright law.

Cover illustration © 2020 Steve Ince

To my three sons, Shaun, David and Jason.

For all the love, support and laughs.

BLOOD AND EARTH

Part One

Two Magicians, a Demon and a Pub

BLOOD AND EARTH

The Warehouse

2011, spring

Lizzie's Tea Rooms, a bastion of everything old-fashioned that York seemed determined to cling onto, was hardly a suitable place to talk about the dead body pulled from the river the previous day. But discuss it Bishop and Pope did, albeit in hushed tones. It wasn't as if the corpse was a surprise to them — over many years the two magicians had discussed countless bodies that had met all kinds of untimely ends, from the gentle to the grisly. It was how the majority of their projects — as Bishop liked to call them — began.

"What's taking Dobson so long?" she muttered and fiddled with the teaspoon in her saucer as she watched her friend across the small table.

Joshua Pope appeared to be taking little to no notice of his coffee-drinking companion, more interested in pulling silly faces at the three-year-old girl on a nearby table, but Bishop knew he'd not missed a thing.

"I'm pretty sure a DNA test takes a little time," Pope said without looking away from the girl. "You can't hurry science. It's not magic."

"I meant the name I discovered," Bishop said. "You'd think the police would be able to track down a simple word."

"Maybe the cops aren't as smart as Google and our online search gave us nothing."

"Yes... odd, that." A stray strand of Bishop's dyed, flame-red hair fell across her naturally fresh face and she casually pushed it behind her ear before picking up her coffee cup. She watched Pope and the child through grey-green eyes as she took a sip. Her other hand fiddled, unseen, with a gem in the pocket of her chunky canvas jacket.

The girl was cute, with curly blond locks and sparkling eyes, but she stared open-mouthed at Pope, clearly fascinated by the few remaining tufts of bright colour amid his generally wild hair. Bishop had nearly thrown a party when, a few months earlier, he'd finally announced he was getting rid of the blue Mohican style he'd sported since the early days of the punk movement in the seventies. But now he was growing it out it looked even worse, particularly in combination with his battered leather jacket and the half-dozen piercings divided between his two ears.

The child hovered in that odd little place where she didn't know if she should be frightened by this unusual man or not and her grandparents offered no entertaining distraction. They were long out of practice dealing with such young children and ideas for amusing her had dried up quickly, along with their conversation. The two of them had lost the ability to speak with each other, too. They eyed Pope with a great deal of reservation as he continued to make faces.

He turned to Bishop with a silly distortion still etched across his features and he held it for a moment as he waggled his brows. Then he dropped his voice into a whisper as he leaned a little closer, the daft look gone in an instant. "As soon as he tracks down the name we'll know where the victim was killed. Just..."

"If you say 'chillax' I may well kill *you*."

He grinned, thought about saying something equally

cheesy then shrugged. "Fair enough. Though you have to accept that these things happen at their own pace."

"And if another body turns up in the mean time?" she hissed and glared at him.

"We tried everything we could to find it ourselves," Pope whispered and leaned even closer. "Dobson knows what's at stake — he'll work as quickly as he can." He put on a fake upper-class accent. "Though it may serve you better if you take a moment to ponder on a more soothing train of thought."

Bishop shook her head in mock despair and put her cup on the saucer with a quiet clink. She placed her forearms on the table and leaned towards Pope. "There's something strange going on. I can feel it."

"More so than usual?" Pope asked.

Bishop simply shrugged in reply and leaned back in her chair as Pope returned his attention to the three-year-old, amused by the girl's constant staring, not even taking her eyes away as she comically mouthed for her drinking straw like a goldfish gulping in water. He smiled at her without effect.

Pope had the most genuine smile Bishop had ever seen, which thankfully hid the many layers of his soul, but its charms were clearly not yet working on the girl. She finally captured the drinking straw between her lips and sucked up the fizzy drink with a brief slurping sound. Pope raised his eyebrows and blinked his eyes in pretend surprise, dropping his jaw playfully. When there was still no reaction he stuck out his tongue in a silly manner. The girl finally giggled but her grandmother had seen the exchange and turned on Pope with malice in her narrowed eyes.

"How old are you?!" the old woman hissed haughtily. Her husband looked on nervously, worried that his wife was about to pull him into some kind of trouble. He shifted in his seat like he'd spent all his life avoiding trouble and could do without it now.

When Pope beamed at the grandmother and opened his mouth to reply, Bishop kicked him under the table and whispered firmly. *"Don't* answer that."

He looked at her and grinned as he rubbed at the pain in his shins. She knew him too well, but he turned to the woman and answered her anyway. "Not so old that I've forgotten how to have fun."

Pope's phone was on the table next to his coffee cup and it vibrated for a fraction of a second before the ringtone kicked in. The little girl clapped her hands with glee at the sound and spoke the first words they'd heard: "Piggy, Piggy!"

Pope smiled at her and picked up the phone. He'd thought it funny to use a cartoon pig's grunting sound as the specific tone for Inspector Dobson, their contact in the police. As much as he was taken by the girl's now brightly lit face, Pope cut off the pig sound by answering the call, ignoring the child's calls to play it again.

"Dobson. Tell me you found what we need," he said, his face now serious. He listening for a moment to the information the Detective Inspector relayed to him. "Okay, where is this warehouse?" He drained the remains of his coffee. "Right, we'll meet you there once you've picked up what you need."

Bishop finished her own drink and stood up to pull a tenner from the bottom of her jeans pocket. She dropped the note onto the table and checked the pockets of her jacket to make sure everything was as it should be.

"A gallon of holy water, naturally," Pope continued. He stood up, too, almost pushing his chair into the waitress as she came over to take their money. "What do you mean? You find a priest, of course. Father Grainger is your best bet. You should fetch a couple of silver crucifixes and a string of garlic, too." Bishop shot a look at Pope at the mention of this last item and had to cover her mouth to stop herself laughing.

She noticed the child's grandparents were looking oddly at him and turned to them. "He's a writer," she lied. They nodded as if that explained everything.

"Look, whatever you *think* you know, forget it," Pope continued, playing up the pretence. "*We're* the experts. We'll see you in a couple of hours. No, make it three."

Pope closed his phone as they reached the exit. A centuries-old habit made him open the door for Bishop and she stepped through without comment.

"I presume from that nonsense you spouted we're not waiting for Dobson," she said.

"Hardly," Pope replied as he followed Bishop out. "He's too green to handle a demon."

"He's an experienced cop, Josh."

As Bishop walked along the street she spread out her fingers automatically, drawing earth energy into her. She was near enough to the York ley line to slowly pull in its energy without direct contact with the ground. The action had become a habit over the years and she often topped up her reserves of stored energy without even realising.

"But he's not Tench or Mainbrace," Pope said, squinting against the sun. "Hell, four months ago he never even knew the supernatural existed."

"He's a fast learner..."

"But he's not there yet. If he gets in the way he's likely to end up dead."

"Then we'd better hope we have it all wrapped up by the time he arrives." Bishop was thoughtful for a moment. "You know he'll never trust us again."

"I'd rather piss him off than get him killed." He looked at her. "He's a cop, not a close friend."

Their car was parked a little way down the street in one of the few parking bays in the area and Bishop climbed into the driver's seat. Pope climbed in the opposite side and Bishop pulled out into traffic, nearly hitting a passing car in the process. She ignored the other driver's hand gestures and blaring horn.

Neither she nor Pope particularly liked driving but it was Bishop's turn and she wasn't one to quibble, mostly because it never did any good. However, she was always glad when her driving duties were over again.

Neither had a license — not a legal one, anyway — but they hardly ever used the car and it seemed a little pointless worrying about such a trivial thing. Strictly speaking, the car didn't even belong to them but to Maggie Trimble, the woman who'd kept house for them for more years than she'd like to admit, but as they'd bought the vehicle, paid for it to be regularly serviced and always made sure there was money in the fuel jar, they felt entitled to use it now and again.

Progress was erratic in the slow-moving traffic and Pope cringed every time Bishop changed gears. She seemed determined to grind the cogs down with every shift. Even so, she was still a better driver than him. In spite of the way he always embraced change and progress, driving was something he really struggled with.

"What's the name of the warehouse?" Bishop asked, fastening the seatbelt she'd forgotten when she'd climbed in, using her knees to steady the steering wheel while she groped with the catch. "Where are we going?"

"Pascoe and Saige," Pope replied. "Near Newton-on-Ouse."

Bishop nodded. "That explains why the body was in the river. Must have been dumped in up there and carried down to York with the flow."

The corpse the police had fished out of the river the

previous day was strange by anyone's standards, which is why Bishop and Pope were consulted. They were never brought in for anything normal, but the instant they saw the body they knew this was even further beyond ordinary than even their more regular projects.

The victim was male but so badly bruised and swollen that identification and cause of death would likely take a lot of work to confirm, but the deep claw marks that ran from neck to pubis were a likely safe bet for the latter. The sight of the wounds made them grimace, but the symbols carved into the victim's back gave them real cause for concern.

Demonic in origin, the context of the gory inscription was all wrong. Carving protection symbols on a body that was already dead was pointless. The action had presumably been designed to intrigue any knowledgeable finders and announce the presence of a demon in the vicinity of the city. The demon might as well have sent out a formal invitation, but the creature would have found no fun in that. A dead, mutilated body was as formal as demons got and with far more impact than a calling card.

Bishop and Pope had a somewhat significant reputation in the supernatural community, following many decades of dealing with the kind of paranormal cases that never made the media or appeared in court, yet were still common knowledge in the circles in which they moved. Because of this reputation, the message had been clearly intended for the two of them. Even with the limited knowledge Dobson had, he'd at least known to bring them in immediately and let them examine the body.

Using the earth magic she practiced, Bishop had managed to draw out a trace of vestigial memory from the corpse's brain. Although it had been in the water for too long to get more than a superficial read, she'd gained the strong impression the man had been killed in an old building. There was a glimpse of a name, too — Saige. An odd spelling, but Inspector Dobson had at last tracked it down as an abandoned warehouse near the river.

"It's outside the walls," Pope said, caution in his voice. "We'll have about three hours to get this done."

"You've used up seven hours already?" Bishop turned in her seat, taking one hand from the steering wheel. "When?"

"Keep your eyes on the road, Faye!"

Bishop swerved as she corrected the car's drift. She could never get the hang of not facing the person she spoke to. "Well?"

"I fought that werewolf last week," Pope said. "He knocked me off the wrong side of the wall. I must have been out cold for seven hours. Still haven't figured out why he didn't kill me."

At well over two thousand years of age, Joshua Pope generally survived on his wits and a natural ability with blood magic, but sometimes a little luck came in handy. Half human, half Shadow Dweller, his appearance was that of a man in his mid to late thirties, though he often acted like he was sixteen. He'd roamed most of the known world for fifteen hundred years before a spell had been placed upon him in the fourteenth century — a curse that has trapped him within the ancient walls of York for all the years since. He and Bishop had tried to reverse the spell on numerous occasions, but so far each attempt had ended in failure. In spite of the curse, however, the entrapment was not total and he was able to go beyond the walls for a total of ten hours each lunar month.

"Will three hours be enough?" Bishop asked.

"Yeah, just get a move on," Pope replied then

immediately regretted his words. Bishop's driving got worse with speed and she gripped the wheel as if trying to throttle a ghoul.

As they passed the York Theatre Royal and the line of the city's ancient wall, Pope felt the passage through the curse's barrier like a sudden drop in pressure. Momentarily giddy with the effect of it, his subconscious began counting down the time.

Bishop glanced at him for an instant. He didn't show any outward signs but she knew the time limit always made him nervous, mostly because he hated to be outside the walls when his free time ran out. The curse wrenched him back to the city in an agonising manner, his insides tumbling cartwheels as if being turned inside out. She felt his concern almost as deeply as he did, she knew him so well.

It was to be expected, of course. When two people have been friends for nearly four hundred years, the wrinkles and creases of each other's personality can offer up little in terms of mystery. Each of them had far greater insights into the other's idiosyncrasies and foibles than they could ever have about their own. The marks left by the passage of time were purely internal, of course, for they both looked far younger than their true ages. Almost youthful, an observer might say.

Faye Bishop had no restrictions on the way she moved about the world but, having lived for more than four centuries, her friendship with Pope was a rock to which she anchored herself. There had been periods when she'd had to move away from the house they shared for the sake of her sanity, but she'd always come back, finding that she missed his company after just a few months.

Although they never mentioned it these days, she still felt she owed him a debt she'd never be able to fully repay. He'd saved her from being burned at the stake back in 1630, which was not the kind of thing any grateful person would ever forget. Pope had made no big deal about the rescue, but he'd continued to help her afterwards by encouraging her to build up the strength of her earth powers and the skills that went with them. Drawing energy from the strong York ley line, she'd soon learned to use it in all kinds of ways, including the constant regeneration of her body to keep herself young, maintaining her physical appearance in line with a woman of about 30 — young enough to satisfy a small spark of vanity but old enough to match her mind's image. Slowly, over many decades, she became one of the foremost earth witches in the land. She'd not previously known that such possibilities existed.

The two of them had very different magical specialities. While earth and blood magic didn't normally mix well, nor their practitioners, they'd learned how to make those differences complement one another and, on important occasions, combine them to powerful effect.

As time passed, the pair had fallen into dealing with supernatural events on a regular basis, along with threats from all kinds of uncanny creatures, in order to keep the mostly unaware citizenry from harm. Now they were heading out of the city to deal with one such beast.

Fifteen minutes after leaving York, Bishop pulled the car into the top of a narrow lane then immediately stamped on the brakes. The wheels slid on the grassy gravel — access to the lane was barred by an old, overgrown gate. It looked like it was only held together by the mass of ivy and brambles covering it, but it was substantial enough to damage the car if hit.

"Ready?" Pope asked, studying the overgrown mass.

Bishop took a nervous breath as she cut the engine. "I've been expecting something to happen. It's been a slow month." She climbed from the car and checked her pockets again.

"You got everything?" Pope asked as he got out.

Bishop nodded, pulled out a bright green gem and hung it about her neck by the chain to which it was attached. She slipped it inside her T-shirt for good measure. Such a gem was her way of storing additional earth energy if she depleted her normal store or a particularly powerful spell required it.

Pope walked to the gate and pulled out a small but incredibly sharp penknife He unfolded the blade and sliced at the ivy and brambles in a few key places before kicking at the gates with the flat of his boot. One of them twisted on one of its rusty hinges but the other came free completely and collapsed to the ground. Pope put his knife away and beckoned to Bishop by cocking his head.

They stepped over the gate and walked quickly along a lane made narrow by untended trees and hedges, whose stretching, reaching branches formed a shadowy tunnel of spring growth with a sense of foreboding constriction. The silence was almost complete, broken only by their footsteps and the nearby river, currently hidden behind the dense hedgerow. Birdsong and the buzzing of insects were eerily non-existent.

The end of the lane turned into a large open area in front of the warehouse they were looking for, on the front wall of which was, very faintly, the word "Saige", the paint having almost completely flaked off. "Pascoe" had vanished years earlier.

Bishop and Pope strode across flat, overgrown ground, paved with large flagstones that were clearly visible between the grass and weeds. The remnants of an old steam engine rusted in a far corner, almost completely hidden by burgeoning brambles.

The building itself was a combination of stone and brick, much of which was water damaged and beginning to crumble. Its windows and doors had been boarded up a long time ago, judging by the look of the sun-bleached wood, streaked with dried tears of nail rust.

Two sets of large loading doors were each fastened tight with heavy timbers bolted across them. A smaller entrance looked more promising as a way in. At the worst, it would be less difficult to break down.

The old, weathered door actually pushed open easily at Pope's touch. Suspiciously so. But he paused for just a moment before stepping through the entrance and into the dusty gloom inside. Bishop followed quietly.

As soon as they were clear of the door, it slammed shut behind them with a thunderous echo and the entrance sealed itself completely. They turned around and could see no sign the door had ever been there. The wall looked old and in need of repair, but solid nonetheless.

"We're caught," Bishop said as if stating the obvious would make it less so.

"Yeah," Pope whispered as he and Bishop took in their surroundings. "But we knew it was a trap from the symbols carved on the corpse."

Bishop moved cautiously then crouched down to put the flat of her right hand against the stone floor. She closed her eyes and sent her magical senses through the earth, feeling her way along filaments of natural energy, reading the subtleties of its texture, feeling the way it permeated the old building.

"It's dark here, Josh," she whispered and Pope knew it wasn't a reference to the low level of light. "I don't like what I'm feeling."

Using earth magic in this way was incredibly valuable when she had a very specific focus, but most of the time it simply indicated the broad shape of things or confirmed that a particular presence was in the vicinity. This time her search had a significantly different outcome.

In a blast that lasted a tiny fraction of a second, a surge of earth energy slammed into her. Totally unexpected. Very powerful. Hitting with the force of a steam train, it knocked Bishop into the air a few feet. When she came down on her back the impact blew the breath from her lungs. The shock-wave from the blast caused Pope to stagger and he only just remained upright.

"Faye!" He moved to her side but she was already sitting up, sucking in lungfulls of air. She reached for his hand and he pulled her to her feet.

"The demon's definitely here," she said between gasps, "But I triggered some kind of earth magic defence." She sighed and put her hands to her face then stopped, suddenly frozen in place.

The silence was complete until broken by Pope calling her name again. She screamed as if seeing him for the first time and jumped back, looking about with wild, darting eyes.

"Faye? What is it?!" Pope grabbed her by the shoulders but she acted as if totally unaware of his presence. He shook her a little and her roaming eyes found his face but struggled for recognition. Then they slid away again, the task of remaining in place too much of an effort for her. Here body sagged and Pope lowered her to the dusty ground, supporting her head and shoulders. Her behaviour was like that of someone suddenly drugged.

"Faye!" She gave no indication she even heard his shout let alone responded to it. "Faye, fight this. It's some kind of enchantment."

Bishop stared with a hint of recognition but it was short lived. She closed her eyes and began to gently snore. Pope laid her down completely. As powerful as the two of them were, it was easy for any magician to get caught off guard by a low-key spell.

Pope pulled a small carpet tack from his jacket pocket and pricked his thumb on it. He always carried a tack because they were viciously sharp and perfect for when he needed some blood in a hurry. Squeezing a good drop from his thumb, Pope smeared it onto Bishop's forehead and muttered a few words in the ancient tongue of the Shadow Dominion.

"*Braench ach mentum fo lictach*," he said, attempting to unlock something in Bishop's mind. "Faye, someone's cast a spell that's confused your mind and made you drowsy. You can't give in to it. I don't want to interfere with your mind more than I have to."

Bishop squirmed on the filthy floor and reached up with her hands as if to claw at her own face. Pope knelt over her and grabbed her wrists, holding them away from her face, struggling against her increased, unconscious strength.

"Faye! Listen to me. Resist the spell."

She snarled like a captured beast and snapped at the air as if trying to bite Pope's face. Then she tuned her attention to Pope's right hand around her left wrist and almost sunk her teeth into his thumb.

"*Braench ach mentum fo lictach*," he repeated, this time with a little more of his will behind it.

Bishop stopped her raving and her eyes flew open — Pope's spell working at last — but she glared at him with a mixture of fear and indignation. Then she twisted her wrists around inside the sleeves of her jacket so her palms now faced Pope. Just as he realised what she was doing,

Bishop blasted him with a controlled burst of earth energy and he flew off her like he'd been struck by an elephant.

Pope's back slammed high against the wall behind him and he dropped to the ground instantly, his fast reactions gathering his legs beneath himself just in time to cushion the fall. He rolled to one side then sprang instantly to his feet and saw that Bishop was upright, too.

"What have I told you about using blood magic on me!" she screamed, holding her hands ready to strike again.

"I had no choice, Faye."

"You always have a choice."

"Spare me the cheesy philosophy. You'd fallen under a spell and it was the only thing I could do."

"What?!" Her anger quickly dissolved into confusion. She looked down at her hands and sought her recent memories to make sense of the situation. Pope watched her cautiously and fingered the tack in his pocket in readiness.

Bishop felt her eyelids getting heavy again. "No!" She clenched her fists by her side and forced her eyes wide. "No, no, no!" She pressed her right fist to her chest and clenched her teeth as she whispered a brief phrase to help her focus her magic.

"Earth, brace my mind!"

For a moment there was a green shimmer in the air surrounding Bishop, which dissipated quickly and left her looking eager and alert once more. She licked the fingers of her left hand and wiped the smear of blood from her forehead.

"You okay?" Pope asked.

"Yes!" She hissed then took a deep breath.

Pope relaxed slightly but still looked worried. "You said Earth magic."

She nodded. "My own type of magic is being used against me."

"You're not the world's only earth witch." But as soon as the words left Pope's mouth he realised what they implied.

Demons practically never controlled any kind of magic but their own and then rarely with any kind of expertise. But this spell would have involved a high level of earth magic proficiency and this conclusion shocked them both.

"I hope we can stop this monster," Bishop said.

Demon Hunt

"We've faced worse than a lone demon," Pope said. "This'll be a breeze."

In spite of his apparent bravado, Pope wore an expression of concern — he'd learned to trust Bishop's judgement over the years. If she was worried, they had good reason to expect serious trouble.

Bishop spoke through clenched teeth. "If this demon uses earth magic like this, how much power does it wield?" She looked around the gloomy interior, struggling to make out any details in the darkness. "It could be a kind we've never dealt with before."

Pope shrugged. "We'll scale that wall when we come to it."

Bishop brushed herself clear of dust and nodded to Pope that she was ready to continue. He led the way, not through any misplaced chivalry but simply because the Shadow Dominion heritage from his mother's side meant his eyes had a natural ability to to see in very low levels of light.

The large space they crept through had once been the building's main loading area, back when the warehouse had been in use. Old hoists and pulleys were attached to the heavy ceiling beams; trolleys and handcarts were scattered about; hooks, chains and ropes lay discarded randomly. Everything was stricken by rot or rust. The decaying leather and green brass of a horse harness hung on one wall. A few huge bundles took up a large part of the far end of the room, some of which had split open and their contents burst out — woollen fleeces, filthy with years of damp and dust.

A rat scurried along an old workbench and into the mass of wool. A single creature was of little concern but the thought of an established nest inside the fleecy pile made Bishop uncomfortable. She shuddered at the thought, made worse by the chilling sound of the breeze whistling between the planks at the boarded up windows. Those same, narrow openings were also the room's only source of light, little though it was.

They made their way to the only staircase they could see and when Pope reached the stone steps, set against a dark back wall with no windows, he paused and made sure Bishop was ready to ascend to the first floor. It was his turn to check his jacket.

Three of his pockets contained vials of blood, two of which had been taken from his arm earlier in the day but the third was an extremely rare sample of dark demon blood he'd obtained decades ago. Other pockets contained his sharp knife, a length of fine iron chain, a child's water pistol and the carpet tack he'd used earlier. Satisfied, he was about to start climbing the stairs when Bishop grabbed his arm.

"Wait," she whispered.

She crouched down and brushed a patch of dust from the bottom step with her left hand then pressed it flat on the stone, worn smooth over many years by the countless footsteps of many workers. Bishop closed her eyes as she pushed out her senses again.

Old stone always gave her a good connection to the earth forces she used, but it also captured traces of those who passed by, building over time into a sensory fog that could get in the way of a clear magical search. For those with limited ability and lack of experience, these traces could be overwhelming.

Bishop pushed through the fog with an ease from her many years of experience then spoke with her eyes still closed. "The demon's been here for quite some time."

"Really? Yet we've only just found out about it?" Pope looked up the flight of steps towards the floor above, now a little reluctant to ascend.

Bishop peeled her hand from the stone as if removing it from a sticky surface then stood up again, rubbing her eyes open. "There are no traps on the stairs."

"Where's the demon?" Pope asked.

"It's up there, all right, but I can't pinpoint it exactly. It's masking itself against my senses."

"Typical. Demons always like to piss about."

Pope climbed the stairs cautiously with Bishop following a little way behind. Dust billowed with each footstep. The wooden handrail was frail and looked like it would crumble if they breathed on it too strongly, so they hugged the wall and Bishop kept her magical senses alert.

Pope reached the first floor and sniffed. "Sulphur."

As she climbed the last couple of steps, Bishop kept her fingers in contact with the brick wall, more for reassurance than support, but it meant she detected the rise in magical activity as soon as it began.

"Move!" she shouted.

She leapt onto the creaking boards of the first floor, taking her own advice instantly. But in her haste she missed seeing the thick layer of coarse plaster dust that covered the floor boards around the top of the stairs. Her left foot landed in the middle of it and shot out from under her. Bishop's backside hit the top step and she fell backwards.

With a reaction speed that gave no time for a thought

for the consequences, Pope leapt toward her, grabbed hold of her jacket's lapel before she tumbled down the stairs then heaved her up and across the floor. They cleared the area near the steps just as the ceiling directly above gave way and collapsed into the stairwell, blocking it completely. The route back to the ground floor was cut off by a pile of wood and rubble.

"Thanks, Josh." Bishop took a few gasping breaths as the dust settled, taking a moment to let her racing heart calm down, trying not to think about nearly being crushed. It was all very well being a powerful witch, but all the magic in the world couldn't help if there was no time to cast a protective spell.

Pope shrugged and grinned. Near death moments always gave him a buzz once they'd passed. There was a time when he'd actively sought out extreme danger just to feel that buzz, but he'd managed to overcome this habit nearly two millennia ago. Sought-out danger was never quite the same as the totally unexpected.

Pope let go of Bishop's jacket and brushed some of the dust from it just as a hissing, guttural laugh caught their attention. They shot a look towards the new hole in the ceiling and saw the demon gazing down at them. Its wide grin showed matching rows of blade-like teeth and gaping nostrils flared in time with the strange flapping of its huge ears. The world's ugliest bats were cute in comparison.

The demon cackled again and disappeared in a silent implosion that left behind a small column of smoke. The noxious smell of burnt sulphur drifted down to them and Bishop coughed.

She and Pope quickly positioned themselves back to back, expecting the demon to appear nearby, but their level remained clear. After a few moments Bishop's concern turned to anger and she moved towards the wooden stairs at the opposite end of the floor, determination stamping out in every stride she took. Pope followed her in silence, his eyes and ears alert for the slightest sign of attack.

This floor was laid out differently to the one below, separated into a number of large storage bays by wooden partition walls, designed to organise stored goods into whatever system had been in place at the time it was last used. A couple of them contained remains of woollen bundles like those on the ground floor, while others contained goods that had shrivelled into piles of unrecognisable, decayed matter.

They were halfway across the creaking floor when, like a sinister whisper, the sound of high-pitched chittering rose from somewhere below. They stopped and turned in eerie synchronisation and stared towards the wreckage-strewn stairwell. A dark mass emerged from the debris and swept towards them.

In the low light it seemed that deep shadows had come alive with murder in mind, but it quickly became clear — the approaching horror consisted of hundreds of scurrying rats that had found their way between the fallen timbers and rubble. They now headed towards the magicians with malicious intent, driven by forces over which the creatures had no control.

"Run!" Pope shouted and immediately took his own advice without checking to see if Bishop had followed suit. He ran like lightning and reached the stairs well ahead of her, but instead of racing upwards he stopped at the foot of the steps and turned to face the rats. He took out a vial of his own blood and poured the liquid into his cupped hand.

As Bishop raced past him and up the stairs — unconcerned by the poor state of the wood from which they were made — Pope waited, letting the rats come closer. He could have attacked them in the instant he first saw them but he wanted to be sure they were all swarming towards him before using his valuable blood. When they were close enough he quickly muttered his spell in the ancient tongue of the Shadow Dominion then threw the bodily fluid in an arc towards the vermin.

For a moment the droplets of blood appeared to hang in the air as the teeming mass of rodents drew closer. Then they ripped through the rats like a fan of shotgun pellets, suddenly accelerated by Pope's blood magic. The majority of the creatures were torn to shreds and those fortunate enough to escape the evisceration halted their charge to feed on their fallen kin. The attack was over and the forces controlling the rats were neutralised.

Pope wiped the remaining blood onto the leg of his jeans and returned the empty vial to his pocket. He jogged up the stairs to join Bishop, who had her hand on the wall of the next level, searching with her earth senses again.

"I still can't pinpoint it, Josh." She removed her hand from the wall and frowned at him. "The demon could be anywhere."

"We'll find it," Pope said and took in their new surroundings.

They stood in a corridor, off which were various workshops and offices, separated from each other by half-glazed partition walls. Although the warehouse had been out of use for decades, most of the glass remained intact, although dusty and cobweb-ridden. The low but disconcerting sound of live rats eating dead ones drifted up from below.

Pope shook his head. "This is the top floor. Maybe the demon can turn itself invisible."

"Josh!" Bishop snapped. "We have enough to worry about without your jokes. It's probably hiding in one of these rooms."

"I wasn't joking. This demon's really pissing me off."

Pope took out another vial of blood from a pocket and held it up to a dusty ray of light streaming through one of the gaps between the window planks and the dirty office glass. He wanted to be sure he had the right vial before he broke the seal. Demon blood was blacker than a new moon midnight and reminded Pope of a glass of Guinness, but with none of the tasty appeal.

Satisfied it was the blood he needed, he broke the wax and unstoppered the vial then poured a little onto his index finger. He stooped down to draw a circle on the floor with the dark blood. There was a faint hissing sound as it touched the wooden boards but Pope ignored it, continuing quickly while the blood's power remained.

"*Braench al deffer tan al demondac*," Pope chanted and, as he did so, tipped a single drop from the vial so it fell into the middle of the circle.

The drop hit the floor, but rather than splattering, it instantly turned into a ball of mist that shimmered and played tricks on the eye. A moment later it transformed again and took on the shape of a gossamer ribbon that would, hopefully, lead him to their quarry. Pope normally used his own blood for locating others but this one was skilled at masking itself. However, the demon couldn't hide his location against the additional power of a spell cast using the blood of its own kind.

At first the misty gossamer struggled to find any direction so Pope repeated his words with increased determination. The ribbon of black blood mist shimmered before groping for its focus, slowly working its way down the corridor, wavering from side to side as it did so, still not fully certain of the correct direction to take. Then it abruptly shot away from the two of them, down the full length of the corridor and through one of the office doors at the far end.

Pope hurtled after it with Bishop close behind and the demon grinned at them from the opposite side of the office as they pelted through the doorway without pausing.

But then it was gone. Everything was gone.

They were falling down a dark shaft.

A trapdoor in the office floor had sprung open the moment they'd stepped upon it. If the fall was too great there was every likelihood they would die.

Pope quickly grabbed Bishop as they fell and hugged her to him.

"What?!" she asked.

But Pope had no time to respond. He'd just managed to twist around in mid air, to get himself below Bishop, when the bottom of the shaft abruptly stopped their descent with the kind of resounding crack that came from a painfully breaking bone. Pope screamed in agony as he passed out.

Although Bishop's impact had been cushioned by Pope's body, she was also rendered unconscious when her temple collided with the point of his chin.

The Cellar

Pope awoke first in complete agony, his leg twisted beneath him, Bishop still unconscious on top of him. He had no idea where they were for the darkness surrounding them was complete and even his eyes couldn't penetrate it.

He rolled Bishop off him and lay her down by his side on the cold, stone floor. The action shot stilettos of agony up his leg and he clenched his teeth fiercely before continuing. He had no time to take things easy and straightened out his leg, almost vomiting from the pain.

Pope groped for Bishop's face and slapped it lightly to try and rouse her. When that failed, he pulled the water pistol from his pocket and shot a single squirt over her upturned face. She breathed in suddenly with the shock of the liquid and Pope could hear her sit up and take a few deep breaths.

"Josh? What...?"

"We fell down a shaft."

Bishop felt the ground at either side of her, one of her hands brushing Pope's leg as she did so. He winced but waited for Bishop to use her senses.

"We're in a cellar," she said, spreading her magic outward. "I can feel the earth beyond the walls and beneath us. Its power is strong, undisturbed, yet..."

"Are you all right?"

"Bit dizzy, but yeah."

"My leg's bust." Pope sucking in the air between his

teeth. "How about some light? Even my eyesight can't cope down here."

Bishop stood up then drew on her stored earth powers and willed a small, magical light into the space above her upturned hand. It illuminating their surroundings with a piercing glare it was wise not to look at directly. With another gesture it rose a little higher.

The cellar was large, the walls and floor of a stone construction with a low, vaulted ceiling, barely two feet higher than Bishop's head. The evenly spaced support columns cast black, contrasting shadows. Old, unlit torches in sconces were set at regular intervals along the walls and on a number of the columns, suggesting the cellar was far older than the warehouse above. Bishop moved the light sphere around the grim room with her will and the shadows swept dizzyingly in the opposite direction. But the glowing ball revealed no immediate sign of escape from the cellar. There was no sign of the demon, either.

"We've got to get out of here," Bishop said.

"Some help with my leg would be good."

Bishop turned and dropped to her knees beside his legs, pulling the magical light closer as she did so. "Sorry, Josh."

"It's my shin. The right one."

Bishop looked at his legs. "There's no sign of blood — the bone can't have broken the skin."

"Should be easier to mend, then." He winced as she probed.

She unbuckled his belt then pulled his jeans right down his legs to his ankles, which cause him even more pain. "How long were we out?"

"About an hour and a half." Pope looked down to where Bishop was examining his leg. The break in his shin was visible as a lump beneath the badly bruised skin.

His natural toughness had prevented the injury being much worse. "I only have an hour and twenty minutes left."

"Are you sure?" Bishop rested her hand on the injury and pain shot through Pope's body again.

"Of course!" Pope snapped, his discomfort affecting his normally cool demeanour. Over the seven centuries he'd been trapped within the walls of York he'd developed the ability — with the help of a little blood magic — to know exactly how much time remained of his monthly ten hours of freedom.

Bishop took hold of her earth gem with her free hand and drew on some of its power, channelling it through her body and into the injured part of Pope's leg, guiding the power with her mind, helping it straighten and knit the bone rapidly. Pope grimaced — he could have ground rocks with his teeth he clenched them so hard.

Then the pain was gone and only a slight sign of bruising suggested there had been anything wrong with the leg. Bishop quickly got to her feet but swayed a little, her magical light dimming for a moment. She took a deep breath, the light returned to normal and she faced Pope's look of concern. "I'm okay. Just a little light-headed."

Pope got to his feet and pulled up his jeans, testing out his leg as he did so.

"I do wish you'd wear underpants," Bishop said. For a brief moment Pope looked embarrassed, a once in a century rarity.

"We really need to get out of this cellar," he said. "And fast. We can't let the demon call the shots any longer. What about a portal?"

Over the years, Bishop had developed a powerful ability to create gateways to other places at will, as long as she could form a clear image of the destination in her mind and had the magical reserves to open one. It always took a lot of stored energy to generate a portal because the route between the two locations passed through a limbo realm that existed between realities, a potentially dangerous place for the unwary.

"I could open one to take us home," she said, "but we came here to deal with that demon. I'd rather we looked for another way out of this cellar."

"We don't have time to waste."

"No, *you* don't have time to waste." Bishop folded her arms and glared at him. "I have all the time in the world."

Pope glared back for about ten seconds then turned away. He could never stare her down. "Fifteen minutes! If we haven't found the demon by then we use a portal to get out of here."

"Whatever..." Bishop moved her light ball around the room, between the columns, looking again for signs of a way out.

Abruptly, the torches all burst into flame and the demon appeared before them, smaller than a person might expect, being at least six inches shorter than Pope, but its large ears and wide, square jaw made its head look huge and out of proportion. It's skin was pale and translucent, made grey by the black blood flowing through its veins.

"What do you want, demon?" Bishop asked, putting out her magical light now the cellar was illuminated by the smoky light of the torches.

She and Pope stepped back a little — it never paid to remain too close to such a creature. She prepared her earth energy again and Pope held ready the vial that contained the last of his blood.

The demon laughed.

"Do I see before me the renowned Bishop and Pope?" it said in a hissing, guttural voice laced with sarcasm.

"Warlocks of earth and blood — a rare partnership, I understand! Exorcists, too, by all accounts, both fair and foul. Yet hardly so humble you'd not regard yourselves as champions of lost souls."

"You forgot demon killers," Pope said. Bishop glanced at him. He could never resist goading an opponent if the opportunity arose. More than once it had nearly gotten him killed.

The demon spread its hands wide in a strange kind of shrug. "If such a maid or man would truly believe that demonkind are wont to shuffle off the mortal plane."

"What the hell does that mean?" Bishop asked.

The demon shrugged again and laughed.

"You're just pissing about with us," Pope said. "Why?"

"Such is the depth of my boredom, I fear for the sanctity of my mind." The toothy grin turned into a snarl and the demon's face became truly monstrous. "Years have passed since I was graced with any form of entertainment."

"What do you want?" Bishop asked again.

The demon paced towards them and stopped ten feet away. "Ah, but what in all the world's darkness would *you* want with such as I?"

"We've come to avenge the poor guy you killed and dumped in the river." Pope tried matching the demon's snarl. "You think we'd ignore your written invitation?"

The demon was taken aback momentarily. "You lie! I am fully trapped within these walls and have been for several decades! The last creature of Earth I killed was a mere pigeon six weeks ago."

For a few seconds, Bishop and Pope looked at each other; unexpectedly a little unsure.

"As if we'd ever believe a demon," Pope said, although his sense of conviction wasn't complete.

"Who are you working with?" Bishop added.

The demon's muscles rippled with rage, his nostrils flared. "Would that I had an accomplice, for then I might yet escape this foul trap."

"We've seen no sign of a demon trap," Bishop said.

"Then your eyes are decidedly feeble."

"Just tell us," Pope yelled. "Who's pulling your strings?"

The creature stepped forward and hot breath moistened Pope's face. "I dance to the tune of no puppeteer."

"A fool, then," Pope said. "Stupid enough to fall into a simple trap."

The demon narrowed its eyes. "Is that your best, pathetic human?"

"I'm half Shadow-Dweller," Pope said.

"Your look does not support this claim."

"I'm fixed in human form. But even so, my magic is just as powerful and we will still beat you." Pope glared at the demon.

"Silence!" The demon roared with such formidably deep undertones that the two magicians felt the sound pound at their chests. Then the monster moved swiftly forward and grabbed both their throats with its mighty hands. "Not one word more of this nonsense."

Bishop beat at the demon's arm holding her while trying to bring her magic into use. Using earth magic took strong concentration, even in an ideal situation; being held in a demon's death grip made matters much worse.

Although he was unable to breath, Pope didn't fight; he simply pulled the water pistol from his pocket and in one swift movement shoved the barrel up the nose of the demon and squeezed the trigger. He was in the process of squeezing it a second time when the demon released his grip on Bishop and Pope and pushed them away.

Pope was ready for the sudden thrust but Bishop staggered back and nearly fell to the floor.

"Thank god he had short arms," Pope said. Bishop took no notice of his quip — she was too busy gulping air through her bruised throat but she shot him a questioning glance. He grinned slightly. "Holy water."

The creature put his hands to his head and screamed so shrilly and loudly it pierced their eardrums. Sulphurous smoke poured from its nose and mouth, black blood ran from its ears and its eyes burned. It tried to back away but found itself too weak and disorientated to retreat. In agony it fell to its knees.

Pope moved closer, squirted the demon with more holy water and it's pallid, grey skin immediately blistered and burned, creating more of the repulsive smoke. Bishop put her hand over her nose and mouth as she backed away. Pope emptied the water pistol and turned away from the creature.

"Run!"

He and Bishop fled as quickly as they could towards the far side of the room, their feet skidding with each step, threatening to upend them. They almost reached the opposite wall.

The demon's head rippled like the surface of a thick porridge simmering in a pan, then it exploded quite abruptly, scattering blood, flesh and fragments of skull across the floor in a pattern that any worthwhile forensics analyst would investigate with fascination, given the chance to do so.

Although the two magicians were far enough away to escape most of the gore, Pope flinched as a piece of the burning flesh hit the back of his hand and stuck there. He shook it free and wiped the remaining gore on his jeans before it did any permanent harm.

"Thank god for that!" he exclaimed.

"Your hair's smoking," Bishop said.

He leaned forward and over to turn his head upside down then rubbed at his tangled mop with the sleeve of his jacket, which rid him of the small piece of smouldering demon brain that had lodged in his hair.

"Thanks, Faye."

Bishop gave a slight nod and started looking for a way out but Pope grabbed her arm.

He smiled cheesily. "I have less than an hour to spare."

Bishop looked at him and nodded. With their task complete there was no point wasting any more of Pope's available freedom.

Avoiding the gory spatter, she laid her hands to the stone floor and pulled more earth energy through it. The area was relatively untouched with plenty of earth energy available. After just a couple of minutes she stood up looking somewhat refreshed. "Home it is."

She raised her hands in front of her, palms facing out, then closed her eyes to concentrate her energies and picture the location in which she'd open the target portal. She had to be very clear in her mind where she wanted to go, but as she'd done this hundreds of times she opened her eyes again after just a few seconds.

The air at her fingertips began to shimmer and a grey oval formed just beyond the plane of her hands, a couple of yards in height. It gently glimmered with a pearlescent sheen.

Bishop stopped manipulating earth energy, reached for Pope's hand and pulled him through the portal after her. It swallowed them up without sound or disturbance.

Complete silence filled the cellar for just a brief moment until the sound of Bishop's shrill, terrified scream escaped back through the portal and echoed around the stone walls of the cellar. A fraction of an instant later, the portal completely vanished.

The torches went out and the cellar was plunged back into darkness.

The Golden Woolsack

Bishop stepped through the portal and stumbled on the thick pile of the recently laid carpet, almost falling into the fire in front of her. If she hadn't been holding Pope's hand she would have landed among the burning logs, but even so, she got far closer than she liked and screamed like a banshee.

Pope immediately pulled her back, away from the hearth, and tried to draw her close and hug her to him, but Bishop had other ideas and she squirmed in his embrace. The scare from the unexpected fire sent her mind back to a time nearly four hundred years earlier when she'd been tied to a makeshift stake, flames burning fiercely around her, on the verge of death.

With no control over her magic, her portal swiftly dissolved. She shrugged herself free of Pope's restricting arms, scurried across the room and pressed herself against the wall. She covered her head with her arms as if trying to keep out the whole of the world, looking like she'd collapse at any moment.

Pope stared at her for a few seconds, swallowing hard. "Faye...?"

He stood, rooted to the spot, half reaching out, concern and fear on his face. He'd been in this position with her a number of times before and it was rarely a good idea to interfere. He dropped his hand and sighed, then looked around the room and though confused he recognised his surroundings.

Pope knew the pub well — he'd been a semi-regular since it opened centuries ago — but they were supposed to going home to their shared house. The Golden Woolsack was situated inside the old York walls but Faye had missed her target by a good half mile, something she'd never done before, which was why he was confused.

As far as he could tell the place appeared to be empty, if he discounted the ghost standing by the bar — a former employee whose spirit hung about the place, visible to those attuned to such things.

There also appeared to be no immediate danger, so with narrow, concerned eyes he turned back to Bishop. "What the hell happened, Faye? Why aren't we at home?"

Bishop whispered something but the sound was inaudible, coming from behind her arms as it did.

"Faye! What in Shadow's name is going on?"

She didn't moved but she now spoke much louder. "Leave me alone!"

"Why are we here?"

"I don't bloody know!"

Pope opened his mouth and spread his hands helplessly before spinning on his heel in exasperation and taking it out on one of the small bar stools, kicking it across the room with the toe of his boot. If Bishop didn't know why they were here, it meant they were in danger and someone intended them harm. With the demon dead it was likely some other magical creature.

The sound of the stool crashing into one of the tables made Bishop flinch and her knees weaken further. She dropped into a nearby chair set against the wall, shaking almost uncontrollably, dry-heaving with remembered pain and fear. Then her whole body went into a relaxed slump as her eyes rolled upwards and she lost consciousness.

"I be afraid. What is this place?" The eerie, child-like

voice coming from Bishop's lips did so without any other part of her body moving, as if the words originated from her dreams.

"Bloody hell, no! Not now." Pope stood over Bishop, uncertain. "Faye! Wake up!"

"Oh, my Josh, is that you?" Bishop didn't open her eyes but they moved rapidly under her lids. "Take me home, my love. This be a dark place."

"I can't." For a moment, Pope's voice became a little softer. "And it's too dangerous here for you." He looked Bishop up and down. Her facial features appeared to soften. "I'm sorry."

"Dangerous? I be fearful, my Josh."

"Go back, then. I need Faye to help me keep you safe."

"Oh goodness, no! The bad man be here again."

"What bad man?" Pope asked, gripping her shoulders. "Tell me!" But the strange voice was gone and Bishop's eyes fluttered open.

"What's happening?" she asked, looking about the room with fearful eyes.

"You passed out. Your fear of the flames."

She gave him a dark look and tried to shrug him off but he held her tightly and she winced a little. Her teeth chattered with the fear that still had control of her.

"Faye, you've got to calm down," Pope said. "You'll kill yourself if you don't."

It was true. Crow's feet were already encroaching at the corners of her eyes as four centuries of ageing, held back by her natural magical abilities, threatened to unleash itself upon her. She licked her lips, feeling them drying out rapidly.

She glared daggers at Pope, even though she realised what he was trying to do and the help he was offering. She almost lost it with a series of short, juddering gasps but fought to calm herself, pulling herself into a more comfortable sitting position. She placed her hands on her knees and looked into Pope's eyes again before clenching her teeth and nodding to him.

He let go of her shoulders and she began a practiced mental routine she'd developed over many years, designed to get such panic attacks under control, however few and far between they might be. Pope noted her shift in mood and relaxed a little. He could do nothing else but leave her to it.

Pope stared at the pub's windows and what he'd initially taken as the darkness of night was actually an unnatural, too-deep black. There was no sign of the city lights coming through the glass from outside. Something prevented the light from entering and, most likely, from leaving, too.

However, what really made the least sense was why they had really been brought here. In all their dealings with malevolent, supernatural crazies, not one of them had brought Bishop and Pope to a warm and friendly pub. Which meant that something about the old drinking establishment was significant.

The Golden Woolsack had a reputation for being the most haunted pub in the whole of York and it was certainly one of the oldest. Previous owners had even laid claim to it being the most haunted in Britain, but such a thing was highly contested by other pub owners up and down the land, particularly when the potential benefits of increased tourist custom were at stake. Thoughts that such monetary considerations coloured the plausibility of those claims were not without merit.

Of course, the general public didn't object to this kind of embellishment and rather liked the idea of the pub being referred to as "most haunted". All the same, none of them really believed any of the old tales of ghosts and malevolent spirits, which was more than a little amusing to the few people who knew that ghosts did, indeed, frequent the establishment, particularly those spirits in need of regular company. It was true what they said — you spend a long time dead. And it never took long for a ghost to get lonely.

"Is there anything I can do to help?"

Pope turned at the sound of the voice and looked at the ghost. "How can you help, Archie? You don't have enough substance."

Archie Morton, sporting an old-fashioned mode of dress and mutton-chop whiskers, looked indignant. "An offer of aid doesn't have to be restricted to the physical." He sniffed in a disparaging manner. "I've been a resident here for more than a century, after all."

Apart from Malcolm, a ghost he'd known for centuries, Pope had had little to do with the departed over the many years of his life and he looked at the spirit a little quizzically. He'd seen Morton plenty of times over the years and even knew his name but that was as far as his familiarity went.

"Okay..." Pope considered his words for just a moment. "Tell me who set the trap and how they did it."

"Well, I'm afraid I don't actually know that."

Pope shook his head and began to turn away.

"My conscious existence in this plane isn't completely continuous, you know." Morton rested his hands on his hips. "Whoever managed to trap the two of you must have done so between my manifestations." He paused for a moment then continued. "If I may be so bold — considering the reputation you and Miss Bishop both enjoy, your foe must be someone of substantial magical ability. Dare I say it? Formidable, even."

Pope nodded. "That sounds pretty accurate, Archie. What about you? Can you leave the pub?"

"It's difficult for me to travel much beyond the building's walls as it is, but even that kind of short excursion is out of the question at the moment. I fear I am as trapped as you."

"If you've already tried, that means the barrier was in place when we arrived."

"Indeed so. I'm unsure exactly when it occurred but the other gentleman has been trapped her since yesterday."

"What?" Pope looked around the bar again. "There's no one else here."

"Ah..." Morton looked around, too. "He was here a few moments ago. You don't think he's escaped the trap do you?"

"Of course I haven't escaped, you idiot," came a voice from behind Pope.

He froze for a moment, performing an almost comical double-take, but then his face split wide and he laughed out loud before turning to face the voice's owner.

Emerging from the back of the pub was a huge man, well over six and a half feet tall with a physique like a power-lifter. Although his face was in shadow and he was silhouetted by the light of the corridor behind him, the way he carried his large bulk would have been unmistakable to Pope even if he hadn't just heard him speak. His continued delight turned his whole face into an expression of genuine pleasure.

"Ah, here's the chap," Morton said. "Allow me to introduce..." The ghost's words petered out as it quickly became clear that the two knew each other well.

"You old tosser, it's been too long." Pope stepped up to his large friend, clasped the other's plate-like mitt and tussled with him for a moment in a friendly, guy-thing way. He slapped him on the shoulder with his other hand for good measure, an action not unlike smacking the powerful haunches of a prize bull.

The big man grinned. "It's good to see you, Joshua."

"You too, Sam."

Samuel Finlay slapped Pope's shoulder in return and nearly knocked him off his feet. The two laughed again then Finlay led the magician to a table on which was an empty beer glass. He looked a little uncomfortable as he sat down.

Morton hovered nearby as the two men took seats across the table from each other. "I didn't realise the two of you knew each other."

"Archie, clear off for a bit, will you? And let two old friends catch up with each other," Pope said. "Keep an eye on Faye for me, okay?"

Morton paused for a second then moved away on silent footsteps. Pope watched him go and looked over to Bishop, still a little concerned by her earlier reaction, but she was oblivious to her surroundings while she dealt with the situation in her own way.

"What's the matter with Faye?" Finlay asked, noticing her for the first time. "Is she all right?"

"We materialised too near the fire. Scared the shit out of her."

Finlay nodded. He'd been a friend of the two magicians for decades and knew all about Bishop's pyrophobia. "Can I help?"

"Just give her time to handle it, Sam," Pope replied. "You know she likes to deal with this in her own way."

They watched her in silence for a moment before returning their attention to each other, chatting about the years since they'd last seen each other.

Bishop's practiced routine quickly stabilised her initial shock. She used a little earth magic to overcome her fears and calm her mind then returned her internal rhythms to normal, checking each of her organs, before closing her eyes and letting the tension fall from every muscle in her body.

She knew the others watched her but ignored them to concentrate on using her magic to explore her surroundings. She pressed her hand to the wall beside her and pushing out her senses once more, spreading them like feelers probing the structure of the building, looking for anything that would reveal more detail of their current situation. She tried reaching out beyond the building, through the cellar walls, down into the earth...

"Bloody hell!" She jumped up from her chair looking bewildered and Morton stepped back in surprise. The other two rushed over and she stared at Pope with wild eyes. But her expression wasn't like the fear the fire had instilled in her; this was a dread of a much deeper kind. "Josh! There's a really dark power at work here."

"Tell me the obvious, why don't you." Pope was nervous, too. He'd been trying to ignore a grim feeling since they'd arrived but Bishop's intense tone of voice pulled it into the light.

In spite of the pub's cosy appearance, especially compared to the warehouse they'd just visited, the danger felt much greater here, even though he couldn't pinpoint it. Something seethed — waiting patiently — but for what, he had no idea. Judging by Bishop's expression and body language, she felt it even more acutely.

"We need to go," Bishop said. "Now!" Her voice cracked with an disconcerting edge. "I can't connect to the earth!"

She made for the door and pulled so hard on the heavy brass handle she threatened to wrench her own shoulder. But not only did it fail to open, it didn't even rattle in its frame. Held tight by something completely unnatural, fed by magical forces the nature of which she couldn't yet sense, it pulled at the basest level of her senses.

Pope quickly joined her, pricked his thumb on the carpet tack in his jacket pocket and smeared a drop of blood on the door. It burned up before he had the chance to recite one of his ancient incantations and he pulled his hand back as if he'd just stuck his thumb into an electrical socket. Bishop wrenched at the handle again then gave the door a frustrated kick.

"I already tried," Finlay said, his clenching fists bulging the muscles in his arms in frustration. "Even I can't pull it open. We're trapped pretty damn tight." His face was set in a dour expression.

"Samuel!" Bishop said, noticing him for the first time. She rushed to him and he leaned down so she could put her arms around his neck in a warm hug. For a brief moment, the pleasure of seeing an old friend fought with her worries. "We've missed you."

"Well..." He blushed.

To Bishop, Finlay was a man who looked like he could wrestle bears for fun but worry that he might hurt them. He appeared to be in his mid-forties but he'd known the two magicians since they'd met him in the period between the wars nearly ninety years ago. Although he'd happily tell the casual enquirer that his physical prowess and longevity was down to good food and healthy living, those close to him knew it was mostly due to the troll blood in his veins.

"We'll catch-up once we're out of here, okay?" Bishop said, her urgency to leave returning once more. Finlay nodded and sat down at the table again.

"Can you make another Portal?" Pope asked and her eyes became a little vacant.

"I don't know if I dare," she said, gesturing at the pub, reminding him that her last attempt hadn't been a success. Her hand trembled as she reached towards the earth gem that still hung about her neck. She didn't quite touch it.

Pope gripped her shoulders gently and looked into her eyes. "Tell me what happened."

"I..." Bishops hands shook more and she grasped Pope's jacket tightly to stop the tremor getting worse. "We should have appeared in our kitchen. Something..." She breathed deeply for a moment. "*Someone* brought us here. They took control of my portal away from me!"

Isolated

"How is that possible?" Pope asked.

"I wish I knew!" Bishop was scared and snapped at her friend. "I understand how portals work but I wouldn't know how to do something like that."

Pope searched her face for signs she was going to fall apart again. He'd always admired her toughness, but even she had her limits and he needed to give her some focus to keep her mind occupied. "I still think it's worth trying, Faye."

She looked at him intently, her breathing still rapid, her heart racing, but she worked to get herself under her own control again. She nodded and let go of Pope's jacket.

Grasping the earth gem around her neck, Bishop took a deep breath then concentrated on the space in front of her, raising her hands and closing her eyes as before. When nothing happened after a few seconds she gritted her teeth and reached into the depths of her magical powers, hoping to pull the portal into existence by her strength of will. Her whole body tensed and the cords in her neck stood out with the effort. It didn't take her long to realise she was unable to create the magical doorway. She opened her eyes and shook her head.

"No good," she said, her eyes darting about nervously, tinged with panic. "Whatever holds us here has cut me off completely. I couldn't even squeeze a pea out of here, let alone any of us."

"It's okay, Faye," Pope said. "You can't do more than try your best."

Bishop stared at him for a moment, blinking, then gave a little laugh. "You're so full of crap you should write greetings cards."

"Wouldst thou have me converse in a higher tongue, fair damsel?" He gave a slight flourish and a bow to match his speech.

Bishop smiled for a moment then her frown returned.

"I know," Pope said. "We need to find another way out of here."

"It's impossible to leave," Finlay said and leaned heavily on the table in front of him. "I've been here more than a day and tried everything I could. And speaking of peas, the Gents is bust and I really need one."

"Use the Ladies, you brickhead," Pope said. He looked askance at his friend.

"Get lost, I'm not a pervert," Finlay snarled with a sudden change in mood. His eyes bulged and he grabbed the edge of the table in a grip so fierce the wood fibres splintered with a gentle crackling sound. In spite of his generally calm nature, he could turn scary when anger clouded his judgement.

"Oh, Samuel," Bishop said with a forlorn look on her face. "It's only a toilet. Do you have 'his' and 'hers' loos at home?"

"I don't have people round." Finlay's statement came out as if it was a challenge.

"Still?" Pope rolled his eyes. "You may not be a pervert, but you're bloody weird." Bishop almost said something but moved away and started pacing the room, avoiding the fireplace. The big man eased his grip on the table and looked about, suddenly feeling a little guilty.

Growing up with unnatural strength had been a problem for Finlay. While his mother wouldn't normally have cared about him breaking the bones of his human school friends during play, as a Fae living on Earth she had to make sure they drew no attention. There was no telling what would have happened if his teachers had discovered he was part-troll.

While it might be seen as particularly insightful of his mother to raise her son this way, her actions were actually dictated by a very strict set of guidelines for those creatures of Faerie who wanted to live on Earth. Even a half-troll such as she had to adhere to them. Unfortunately, being a particularly low-watt bulb, her entire approach to keeping him in line consisted of making him ashamed of who he was and letting him know what would happen if he showed her up in even the smallest possible way.

Finlay had grown up with such an intricate list of what he could and couldn't do, always fearful of giving his nature away, that he had serious difficulty knowing how to behave in a world that changed far more rapidly than he could hope to keep up with. It wasn't that he was slow or stupid, just that he liked things to stay as they were so he could get used to them.

He shifted in his seat in an attempt to alleviate the discomfort in his bladder. "What's Faye doing now?"

Bishop continued walking around the room, pausing in different places, touching the walls here and there. She shook her head regularly and had the look of one who was lost.

Pope stared at Finlay. "Being cut off from the earth and the energy she draws from it makes her jittery."

"You'd feel jittery, too," Bishop said, "if you had your arm cut off or your eyes gouged out."

"What?" Finlay looked at Pope.

Pope shrugged. "That's what it feels like, apparently."

Bishop rolled her eyes and slunk into a chair,

dropping her head into her hands and resting her elbows on her knees. Although someone had once likened it to coming off drugs cold turkey, the similarities were modest at best. On the few occasions she'd been cut off from the earth in this way, she felt like part of her had died.

Pope sat down, too; in a chair across the table from Finlay. He looked at Morton who'd been watching the three of them with intense concentration. However, under Pope's gaze he turned away and walked over to the bar, taking up station behind it.

Over a hundred years had passed since Morton was the pub's cellar man, priding himself on keeping a well-stocked cellar of finest quality beers and ales. Now, he looked lost, unable to undertake the trade he loved yet stuck here for all eternity, seemingly. He looked up and down the length of the bar and sighed.

"Cheer up, Archie," Pope called. "I'm sure the trap isn't designed to harm a ghost."

"Really, Mr. Pope?" Morton said. "What makes you so sure you know the true nature of this trap and whether it might be harmful to someone of the spirit world?"

"Do you?"

"Alas, no." Morton sighed again. "My restricted movement gives me little opportunity to avail myself of that kind of knowledge." He turned away from the others as if indicating an end to the conversation.

Pope shrugged and turned to his friend with a warm look on his face. "How long's it been?"

Finlay's eyes lost focus for a moment as if counting. "Fifteen years..."

"Seems like yesterday."

"It would. To you."

Pope frowned. It was the first time he'd known Finlay show even the slightest sign of bitterness over Pope's apparent immortality. Perhaps the big guy's one hundred and seven years were beginning to take their toll.

An unfortunate disadvantage of living a very long time was the large number of friends a person would outlive. No matter how full a life they enjoyed, eventually they passed on. If Finlay's mother was anything to go by, he probably had another fifty years or more in him, but even that amount of time would flash by way too quickly to someone like Pope. Even so, the big man's friendship was something he cherished, even when he thought him weird.

Bishop, too, was far older than Finlay. Her use of powerful earth magic had had an unexpected consequence — the ability to regenerate her body's cells and keep herself young. But it wasn't something either of them had foreseen when Pope had saved her life the first time. Now she was the longest lived of all the friends he'd known over the last two millennia. Although those from his home in the Shadow Dominion were equally long-lived, he didn't count any one of them as friends.

"We need to find a way out of here," Pope said, repeating himself. There was nothing he could do to prevent the eventual demise of his friend, so it was simply best not to dwell on it. That way lay madness. "Do you have any idea what's happening?"

Finlay raised his brows, surprised that Pope would ask him such a thing. "The pub's a magical nexus," he said, as if that was all he needed to say.

Pope nodded and looked over at Morton. A powerful nexus made the ghosts look more solid to those with the ability to see such things.

Nexuses were always associated with old buildings, particularly those situated near ley lines. Time has a way of capturing low level energies from the unwary, using the stones and brickwork of old buildings to leech it from them. Ghosts would draw on that energy to manifest a visible form. But other things could use that energy to act as a catalyst or give focus to a specific spell.

Finlay leaned forward and lowered his voice. "But where are the other ghosts?"

Pope blinked. "Good point. I know of at least six ghosts that regularly frequent this place."

"Twenty seven," Finlay said with the authority of a very regular customer. "Someone's used the power of this nexus to trap us and it's keeping the other ghosts out." He shrugged. "I have no idea why."

"Really? You discovered nothing since yesterday?"

"I tried everything I could, but I have such little magic. All I found out was that it's impossible to break free." Finlay stood up. "Sod it, I'm gonna get myself a beer."

Pope looked surprised. "I thought you were dying for a pee. There must be a limit, even for you."

Finlay stood still for a moment, indecision halting his progress midway to the bar. Pope rose from his seat and walked across the room. "Get the beer in. I'll fix the Gents."

Finlay went behind the bar, ignoring Morton completely, while Pope moved through an archway that led to the back rooms of the building.

In the small corridor that let to the toilets, he tried the door to the Gents but it was locked and someone had taped a hand-written sign to it: "Out of order." Pope pricked his finger on the carpet tack and squeezed some blood into the keyhole. He held his hand over the lock and muttered more unearthly words under his breath. The tumblers turned and the lock opened easily — modern locks hardly took any manipulation at all.

Stepping inside, Pope wrinkled his nose at the smell and had a quick look around before spotting the small window set high in the wall above one of the two stalls. It had been propped open and had escape potential written all over it. He lowered the toilet lid, climbed onto it and examined the opening. The window was small, but large enough that he might be able to squeeze through if he didn't mind landing on his head at the other side.

He tried reaching through the open space to get a grip on the outer sill, but his fingers met an unyielding, invisible barrier. The magical force that trapped them here completely surrounded the building and even this open window gave him no means of escape.

He squeezed more blood from the small wound he'd just created and flicked it at the invisible barrier. It flared with a burst of energy that suggested a conflict of magical properties. It was instantly followed by a backlash that shot a small bolt of electricity at his still outstretched finger.

"Agh!" he yelled and pulled his hand back so quickly he fell off the toilet lid and crashed into the side of the cubicle, only staying upright by grabbing onto the toilet roll holder. "Bugger!"

He left the cubicle and examined his injury. The finger was burnt at the very tip — a small blister a few millimetres across — and he sucked at it in the hope of relieving the sharp pain. He glared at the small window and stomped out of the toilet with no intention of fixing whatever problem had caused it to be closed. As the door closed behind him he removed the makeshift sign and crumpled it into a ball.

Back in the bar, Finlay placed the first of three pints on the counter just as Pope returned and put the ball of paper into an empty, used glass.

The magician was just about to say something to Finlay when he had an idea. Pulling the remaining vial of his blood from his pocket, he took out the stopper and poured the liquid into the palm of his right hand. He strode down the room and halted when he was about ten feet from the front windows.

He threw the blood at the windows at the same time as he spoke his ancient tongue.

"*Braench fe taro ach velostic.*"

The blood shot like bullets towards the windows and shattered them instantly, wrecking a large part of the wooden frames in the process like a strafe of machine gun fire. The instant he let the blood go and cast his spell he leapt to one side and only just dodged the intense lightning bolt that blasted back at him. As it was it singed the sleeve of his jacket.

The beam of energy zapped down the corridor behind the bar, passing between Morton and Finlay with barely any room to spare. It hit a door at the far end, blowing it off its hinges. The sound created by the whole sequence was frighteningly loud in the confines of the room and Bishop jumped like the world was ending.

"Bloody hell!" she said. "I wish you'd warn me before you did that kind of thing."

Pope looked at the damaged window in close fascination. Whatever force had trapped them in here now held most of the broken fragments in place like a supernatural flypaper had been stuck to the outside of the window. He picked up a chair and pushed it against the pulverised debris but it didn't give way. There was no sign that his action had affected the spell that held them prisoner.

He put down the chair and looked at Bishop. "Look, I had a theory, all right?"

"I think you mean," Morton interrupted, "that you had an untested hypothesis."

"No one likes a smart arse, Archie." Pope glared and the ghost chuckled.

"Or is it that no one likes to be wrong, Mr. Pope?"

Pope scowled and rested his hands on his hips.

Bishop jumped in. "Perhaps a wise man would know when there's enough fuel on the fire?" She glared at Morton and, with a gesture of her head, indicated that he should move away.

Watching Morton head through to the back, Pope walked over to the bar, picked up one of the pints and realised that Finlay was looking at him hopefully.

"Oh, sorry, Sam," Pope said, halting the glass just before his lips. "The Gents is okay to use."

Finlay almost dashed off but halted in his tracks. Although there was no one around to ask him to pay for the drinks, he pulled a tenner out of his pocket and put it next to the till before rushing to the toilet.

Pope smirked as he swallowed a mouthful of beer — he loved the big guy's little foibles.

Part Two

Changeling

A Message

Monday, 10th June, 1957

"Samuel! Wake up!"

The voice startled Finlay. He was sitting in the shade of a half-built wall with a mid-morning mug of tea, avoiding the direct sunlight to keep cool rather than resting from any exertion. The delivery of sand that, according to the foreman, should have been here over an hour ago still hadn't arrived so he'd taken his break in a quiet spot away from his workmates. He'd closed his eyes to listen to the birdsong and had dozed off without realising.

He looked over to the hut at the other side of the building site and as far as he could tell the bricklayers were still inside. Without the mortar Finlay mixed for the crew they had nothing to occupy their time except to drink tea and prattle on about women, beer and football. He had nothing against any of the men and got on well with them, but today he wasn't in the mood for chat. Whoever had called out his name, it hadn't been any of them.

"Samuel!"

He couldn't get a bearing on where the voice originated and he began to think he'd imagined it when he spotted a face peering from behind one of the trees at the edge of the site.

"Malcolm?" Finlay wasn't entirely sure it was him.

He could only just make out the faint image in the bright daylight, even though the ghost was only twenty yards away.

"Come quickly, Samuel. As always I have little time, as well you know."

Finlay drained his tea, put down the mug and walked over to the tree. He rather liked Malcolm, in spite of the fact that he only ever saw him for a maximum of five minutes every once in a while.

"What d'you want? This is where I work."

"Indeed." Malcolm smirked — he wasn't going to be put off by Finlay's abruptness. "'Tis fortunate that you appear to be taking a moment to quench your thirst. Doubly fortunate that your place of toil is close to my route or it would have been a difficult task for me to deliver my message."

Finlay raised a brow in surprise. Using a ghost to deliver a message was a little unpredictable at best. There was always the chance it would never get passed on.

"Who sent you?" Suddenly suspicious, Finlay looked around cautiously.

Malcolm wrung his ghostly hands, a serious weight settled about his spiritual demeanour. "I've been charged with the task by your old Mam, Samuel."

"I've not spoken to her for more'n ten years," Finlay said and began to turn away. "I'm not interested."

"Wait, my friend." Malcolm spoke quickly. "She's not in the least bit well, if you take my meaning. Your good mother desperately needs to speak with you and pressed upon me the urgency of the matter. I ask that you honour her request."

Finlay turned back to face the ghost. "I don't believe you. She's half-troll and as strong as a team of oxen."

"The Fae may be immortal," Malcolm said, "but any progeny of mixed blood are not blessed in such a way.

Did she not teach you of your heritage?"

"The only lesson I learned from her was to distrust everything she said. It's probably just a way of wrangling some gin money from me."

"A ghost always knows when a person's end is nigh. Whatever past transgressions she may have been guilty of, on this occasion she is genuine. Even her brother has travelled to these shores from the land of the Norse."

Finlay clenched his fists and ground his teeth with a force that caused the veins on his neck and forehead to stand out and throb with each frustrated heartbeat. For a moment it looked as if they might burst.

"All my life she treated me like something she scraped off her shoe. Why should I visit her?" Finlay forgot himself for a moment and tried to grab Malcolm. His hands went through the ghost and he nearly overbalanced, but grabbed the tree in time to steady himself. He gestured in exasperation. "I'll be glad when she's gone."

"I missed the passing of my own mother while delivering turnips to Hull," Malcolm said, his presence beginning to grow more transparent. "She was two days cold and six feet beneath the sod by the time I returned to hear the sad news. To this day I regret not being there when she passed on."

"If you feel so strongly, *you* can sit with the old cow while she dies." Finlay folded his arms in and glared at the ghost who now faded steadily.

"I would if I wasn't forced to..." His voice trailed off as he disappeared completely. The curse Malcolm had been under for centuries took him off to the next way point on the old route he'd travelled between York and Hull and back when he'd been alive in the sixteenth century.

Finlay stared at the spot where the ghost had stood as if willing him to return. Although he didn't move from his position he couldn't stay still; unfolding and folding his arms, clenching his fists and fidgeting with his feet. He even opened and closed his mouth a few times.

Then, in an abrupt explosion of bellowing rage, he launched himself at the tree, pushing against its trunk as if he wanted to topple it over. Its branches shook with the force he exerted, his face turning red with the effort. For a moment it seemed like he might just do it, but his well-scuffed boots slid backwards on the dusty, dry soil and he collapsed to his knees. He threw his head back, still holding onto the tree, and wailed.

"Bugger, damn, blast!"

He lurched to his feet, grabbed his jacket from the shade he'd just been sitting in and strode towards the site exit just as the bricklayers came out of the hut in the hope of resuming work. Smedley, the foreman, saw where Finlay was heading and dashed over, grabbing his arm when he reached him. Unfortunately for him, Finlay didn't stop and the foreman was pulled off balance and fell to the ground.

As angry as he was, Finlay couldn't leave Smedley like that, it wasn't in his nature. He turned and picked the man up by the armpits as if he was a small child and deposited him back on his feet. Although he'd only run a short distance Smedley was wheezing badly.

"Where the hell... do you think you're... going?" The foreman coughed, spat on the ground then coughed some more. Finlay waited for him to finish before replying.

"I'm leaving," he said. "My Mam's dying and wants to see me."

"What?! How did you find that out? Has someone been on the site without permission?" Smedley looked around for signs of a visitor. He pulled out a tobacco tin and began rolling a fresh cigarette almost absently while he talked.

"I got a message from the afterlife." Finlay gave a look that dared Smedley to disagree with him.

"If I find you're lying, you'll not work here again. About your Mam, I mean."

"Get lost, Smedley. I do the work of two men - I could get a job with any crew I wanted." Finlay strode off without giving Smedley the chance to say anything more. The foreman opened his mouth as if to shout after the big man but knew he'd be wasting his time.

He thrust the finished roll-up cigarette into his mouth, lit up and drew in an angry chestful of the smoke. Then he coughed like his lungs were trying to escape the torture he constantly put them through.

Finlay stood outside his mother's house for ten minutes before his uncertainty spiralled so tightly in his mind he was forced to knock on the front door just to avoid his head exploding.

It was late evening and he would have arrived much earlier if the fight he'd had with his feelings hadn't delayed him. He'd spent the last few hours drinking solidly, but with his constitution it was hardly enough to dull his anger and overcome his urge to flee, but he'd come anyway.

In his nervousness he knocked a little too hard and the grimy brass door knocker hung a little askance after he's done so. Through the pair of frosted glass panels set into the door, he saw the fuzzy shape of a large man hurry up the passageway and wrench it open.

"Oh, it's you," he growled. The big man filled the narrow hallway like a small elephant. There weren't many people in the world who could make Finlay look small. "I should have known *you'd* knock loud enough to wake the dead."

"Ever tactful, eh, Uncle Sean?"

"What...?" For a moment Sean Malloy's face went through a few shades of puzzled before it shifted with a glacial grind of comprehension. "Oh..." Being half-troll like Finlay's mother, not only was he bigger and stronger than Finlay, he was also much slower in the head.

"Well?" Finlay asked and cocked his head on one side. He glared at his uncle.

"You shouldn't even be here," Malloy replied, not moving an inch. "Walking out on your Mam like that."

"Dad's death was the last straw. I couldn't stay."

"You know full well that was an accident." Malloy folded his arms and his shoulders almost touched each wall of the passage.

"Maybe so, but she should have taken better care." Finlay looked away, a slight glazed look to his eyes. "She was too demanding on the old man."

"That's thirty years since, boy. Forgive and forget."

Finlay glared at Malloy. "I'm here aren't I?"

"So?"

"Just let me in, will you? She wants to see me."

"May sent the ghost a week ago and it's taken that long to come to see her?"

Finlay hung his head and sighed. "Malcolm only found me today. I nearly didn't come at all."

"Then why not just piss off?"

"Because I want to annoy the hell out of you." Finlay tried to grin scathingly but it collapsed before it formed. "Just let me in. Mam invited me here. It's her house."

Malloy looked at Finlay through narrowed eyes that reflected the workings of his mind. With little forthcoming he tried to step to one side to let him in but his bulk was too great. He was forced to move into the house to let his nephew in. Finlay stepped inside, closed the door behind him and walked down the hallway. At the bottom of the stairs he paused and half turned to the older man.

"She in bed?"

Malloy nodded and Finlay mounted the stairs, which creaked with every step. Malloy followed him up and Finlay looked over his shoulder at him, raising his brows in an unspoken question. Malloy ignored him and continued to follow — he wasn't letting his nephew out of his sight.

Finlay entered his mother's bedroom and was immediately struck by the smell of urine and faeces, along with a strong hint of gangrene, even with the window wide open. All doubts about the genuine nature of his mother's illness evaporated in that instant. While she'd never been prone to unnecessary concern over hygiene, she'd never let herself get in this kind of state without good reason. For a brief moment it saddened him.

May Finlay almost filled the double bed, even seriously ill she gave the impression of a blanket-strewn hillock. Her feet stuck out from under the bedclothes and rested on the battered, old ottoman at its foot and it was clear that this was where the gangrene smell came from. Her left foot was badly necrotic and Finlay grimaced when he saw it.

The floorboards creaked heavily as he approached the bed and May's eyes fluttered open in a delicate fashion that belied her heavy build and strong, square face. A weak, happy smile spread her lips across her face.

"You came," she whispered and turned to Malloy. "He came, Sean. See?"

"Yes, May." Malloy sat in a plain wooden chair by the door, which looked more like a child's seat against his huge bulk. He wiped a tear from his eye and cast a nervous glance at Finlay.

"You came, Sammy." Her grin grew stronger and there was a hint of the old light in her eyes. "You came to see your old lady."

"You wanted to see me, Mam." Finlay forced his voice into a monotone to prevent it betraying his feelings.

"I did?" She looked confused for a moment then remembered. "I did, Sammy. Give your old Mam a kiss."

"You wanted to see me just for that?"

"Course not, you daft sod. But can't a dying woman have a kiss from her only son?"

Finlay sighed, but bent down to give his mother a brief peck on the cheek before sitting on the room's other chair by the bed side, it's re-glued joints complaining at the load.

"I should be grateful for what I can get, I suppose." Disappointment flitted across her eyes.

"What do you want, Mam? Malcolm said it was urgent."

"Your mother dying not urgent enough for you?" Malloy asked. Finlay refused to register his comment.

May grasped her son's forearm and in spite of her poor state of health she still had a grip like a vice. "Ignore him. You're here, Sammy, that's what matters."

"It's not just because you're dying, is it?" Finlay patted her hand absently while trying to read her expression. "There's something else going on."

"Sean?" She flicked her eyes over to Malloy and the big man left the room, closing the door behind him. Only when the sound of him descending the stairs had finished did she continue.

"I had a vision, Sammy!" May's weak voice broke up a little with her excitement. "I knew I had it in me. Didn't I tell you?"

"Yes, Mam. Forty years, since."

"But why did it choose now of all times to come? Why so late in the day?"

"Maybe if you'd kept off the gin...?"

"I know, I know... But I don't have time to dwell on regrets. The vision... I..." Tears came to her eyes and the joy she obviously felt transformed her, for a fleeting moment, into a resemblance of the younger half-troll he'd known as a child, when Dad had been there to temper her rages.

"Tell me what you saw, Mam."

"A changeling!" she gasped. She was clearly thrilled but Finlay was puzzled.

"Is that all?"

"The exchange will happen in a couple of weeks. Midsummer's Eve." She bit her bottom lip with nervous joy. "There hasn't been a Fae changeling in over a century."

"I don't understand, Mam. Why is it so important?"

"Changelings are always important."

Finlay searched his memories but all he knew was that a Fae child would be swapped for a human one. He'd never been taught the significance of doing so.

"It's a time to celebrate, Sammy!" She smiled again and gripped Finlay's arm even tighter. In spite of her impending death, he couldn't remember ever seeing her so happy. "Having troll blood in you means you're part Fae. You have an important part to play."

"Me?" Finlay was taken aback. "What's it got to do with me?"

"The vision was very clear." A look of pride came upon May's face and her eyes filled up again. "Without you the changeling's welfare is at risk."

"What? How? It's only a dream." Finlay became a little dismayed. He'd been humouring her so far but now it felt a lot more real than he'd have liked it to be. He sensed his mother's claims were in earnest.

"No, Sammy, not a dream," she said. "A vision. Sent by the Fae Lords themselves. They knew I'd get the message to you. You're going to make the family proud and I can die happy."

"I don't understand, Mam. What is it you think I'm supposed to do?"

"Your friend... the nice one... Mr. Pope."

"Joshua? Nice?"

"He's lovely he is." For a moment May's mind wandered and she eased her grip on Finlay's arm.

"Mam?"

"Yes, very lovely. Well, he's going to try to prevent the exchange and he'll ask for your help. It's your job to stop him."

"What?!"

"The exchange — it must take place, Sammy. You have to stop Mr. Pope."

"And if I refuse? The Fae have done nothing for me." Finlay pulled his arm free of his mother's grip.

"Sammy, you can't let the family down." The sudden fear on her face made it look like this big woman would burst into tears of a different kind. "Lord Ealvun will be furious. He'll torture you in his dungeon for ever."

Finlay stared in disbelief and slumped back in the chair. His insides wrenched at him and his hands began to shake. Pope hadn't lived for over two thousand years by allowing people to stop him doing what he wanted.

Midsummer's Eve

Sunday, 23rd June, 1957

The living room door flew open then slammed closed. In between the two actions Faye Bishop swept into the room with seemingly murderous intent.

"Bloody hell!"

She clearly wasn't happy and wanted the world to know. Or at least the part of the world that included Joshua Pope who'd been asleep on the sofa but no longer was, thanks to the noise she'd just created. She threw herself into an armchair and glared at his prone form. In spite of the commotion she'd made he hadn't budged an inch. She rolled her eyes, clenched her teeth then increased the intensity of her stare once more.

"Do you ever do anything but sleep?"

Pope opened an eye and rotated it in Bishop's direction. "How else would I maintain my naturally good looks?" He closed the eye again. "But it's a hard fought battle when you're around."

"Pig!" Bishop threw a cushion at him and he sighed when it bounced off his head. He opened both eyes and turned to face her more fully. For a moment he considered her appearance then smiled.

Pope was still getting used to Bishop's new look, which was a little drastic, even for her. The bleached blond hair and summery dress gave her a vaguely Marylin Monroe appearance, but it was the petulant pout that made her more like a spoilt film star than she'd probably intended.

"Well?" she demanded.

"All right, I'll bite." He paused a further moment to tease her a little more. "What's got you in such a state?"

"Felthrop Market!"

"It was open on a Sunday?" Pope's eyes widened in genuine surprise.

"It *is* Midsummer's Eve."

"I was trying to ignore that, thanks." Pope closed his eyes and rubbed his face with his hands. "There's always some fool trying to make a big deal out of nothing. Midsummer brings out all the cra-azy people."

"Not funny, Josh," Bishop said and drummed her fingers on the arm of the chair. "The market hardly had any of the ingredients I need to renew the protection wards on the house." She looked hard at Pope who was trying to sleep again. "There's been a run of Fae buying up everything they could lay their hands on."

Pope sat quickly upright. "What?! Since when have the Fae needed the kind of magical ingredients you'd use?"

"I know. Weird, as well as annoying."

Pope stood up and walked about the room. He was now wide awake and a little on edge. His clothes — a pair of dark jeans with the bottoms turned up and a white T-shirt — were both crumpled and in need of a good wash. He stopped pacing and ran his fingers through his greased-back hair, originally inspired by James Dean a couple of years earlier but now a little on the long side. "Do you think there's a connection to all the Fae activity in the city lately? It's more than we've seen for over a hundred years. Even Sam acted all arse-about when I saw him last week."

"His mother's just died, Josh," Bishop said. She sat

forward in the chair and clasped her hands together.

"It was more than that." Pope leaned his hands on the windowsill and pressed his forehead against one of the cool panes of glass. "He really hated his mother."

"Doesn't matter. It still affects us when they die." She paused. "Probably more so. There's extra guilt to deal with."

Pope went silent for a moment. He'd never known his own mother — she'd died in childbirth — but from what he'd learned he doubted they'd have had a loving relationship.

"Finlay was quiet, even for him. Acting like he had a secret to keep from me, or waiting for something to happen." Pope pushed away from the window and turned to Bishop. "I think the Fae are up to something."

"You could be right." Bishop's face shifted from a look of annoyance to one of concern. "The power in the ley line has been erratic for weeks, probably disturbed by the coming and going of the Fae. What the hell could they be doing?"

"The last time we had this kind of extended activity it involved human sacrifices on Clifton Moor." Pope scratched his chin and squinted against the low evening sunlight streaming through the window.

Bishop fiddled with the green gem around her neck. "Whatever the Fae have planned, we need to stop them before they pull it off."

"How?" Pope turned away from the window. "We have no idea what they're doing and we don't have much time to find out. I presume it has something to do with Midsummer and there are only a few hours until midnight."

Bishop perched on the edge of her chair, resting her forearms on her knees in thought. Pope moved away from the window and paced the length of the room a few times. Bishop's earlier frustration was catching.

"We can find out," she said and got to her feet. "But we'll need to combine our talents."

Pope nodded. "Blood and earth."

They both set about gathering the materials they needed. Bishop climbed the stairs to her rooms and Pope went through to the kitchen.

He entered the walk-in pantry and removed a jar of blood from one of the shelves. The small room had been cleverly constructed to stay cool even in the middle of summer. Being a blood magician, he always kept a supply of blood handy, usually it was some he'd recently taken from his own arm. He closed the pantry door and set the jar of blood on the kitchen table.

Bishop entered the room a moment later carrying three things - a small sack of earth, a small pouch made of blue velvet and a large, shallow, home made bowl. The last item had been constructed from a mixture of clay, dug up from a location on the nearby ley line, and Pope's blood. The bowl had then been fired in a ceremonial, makeshift kiln out in the woods. They only ever used the vessel in rare times when it was important to combine their different strands of magic.

They sat across from each other with the bowl resting on the table directly between them. Pope raised his eyebrows in question and Bishop nodded her readiness. She grabbed a handful of earth from the sack and lay it in the bottom of the bowl, loosely levelling it out. Pope took the lid from the jar and poured a thin stream of blood over the earth in a spiral pattern that began at the outside and swept towards the centre. He stopped when the blood reached the middle and sealed up the jar again.

From the velvet pouch, Bishop took out a small pewter snuff box she'd once bought from an antiques shop. It didn't contain snuff but something she liked to call Faerie Dust. It was actually dried mud she'd once scraped from Finlay's boots when he'd returned from the Faerie realm one day twenty years earlier. She'd had no idea if it would ever come in useful but it was always better to have such things than not. Now was her chance to combine it with the earth and blood in the hope of enhancing their magic and give focus to the combined spell they were about to cast. She sprinkled some of the powder over the contents of the bowl and put the snuff box away again.

"Mmm... Bloodmud pie," Pope said but became serious again after Bishop glared at him.

The two of them linked hands across the table, encircling the bowl, and stared at its contents in heavy concentration. After a brief pause they each began to chant at the same moment as if given a cue of which only they were aware.

"*Braench ach to am mey tally saren,*" Pope said, his mouth forming the guttural words of his ancient language with ease. "*Braench fo palen te feerten kach al.*"

Bishop's chant was something she made up on the spot. It was entirely likely she'd have been able to cast her spells through strength of will alone, but the impromptu verses helped to give the right kind of focus to the power behind her earth magic.

"Mighty Earth, bestow clear sight,

"Show the Fae who plans tonight."

As they repeated their chants, the words fell into a shared rhythm that helped combine the power of their two very different types of magic. They fused and became almost one. The mixture in the bowl churned, stirred by some unseen force, and a vapour filled the bowl to the brim. The smell became strong — compost, loam, rotting flesh and something indefinable, likely caused by the "faerie dust". Bishop's nose wrinkled with the urge to sneeze but she didn't falter.

Their chanting gradually gained pace and the bowl of mist swirled like a tiny storm, complete with miniscule sparks of lightning. Then it abruptly became still and changed form, a dull shimmer played across it like the surface of an autumn pond. Reflections shifted and changed. For a moment it seemed as though they stared at the surface of a mirror before the reflectivity vanished and it became the window they were hoping for.

Through this magical opening they gazed down upon a stone floor in a location with an altogether unfamiliar quality of light. They each stopped chanting the moment the image became clear and stared at the limited view, made somewhat interesting by the shadows that moved across the floor.

"A Fae Lord," Pope whispered as a slender but powerful man stepped into view. Adorned in fabulous clothing decorated with exquisite embroidery and gems, he gestured and talked to others outside their narrow field of view.

"You and you!" He stabbed with his index finger as he spoke, his eyes narrowed. "I give you a final opportunity to redeem yourselves. Fail yet again and your only reward will be banishment for the remainder of your existence."

Bishop and Pope saw movement in the shadows on the floor and it was clear that the two figures casting them were bowing their acknowledgement.

"Now, begone," the Lord said. "The hour grows short and I can sense the hand of others coming into play."

The two shadows left the scene, to be replaced by another. The Fae who cast it was a man armed with a sword at his belt.

"My Lord..." The new shadow's owner spoke from out of view but the Fae Lord lifted his hand for silence.

He cast his gaze about, searching for something that

niggled at his senses like a gnat in a stuffy room. He cocked his head on one side and listened, moving his hand to rest on the pommel of his sword as if in preparation for an attack. Then he spun his head and shot a look directly at Pope and Bishop.

"Begone, mortal interlopers!" he commanded and spread his right hand out towards them. There was an abrupt explosion of light and sound, made to seem worse in the confines of the kitchen.

As well as being momentarily blinded, Bishop and Pope were flung away from each other and over the backs of their chairs, hitting the kitchen cupboards heavily. They both cried out in pain, less from the impact with their surroundings than from the backlash of the Fae's magic. It had burned their hands where they'd made contact with each other.

"Bloody hell!" Pope said. "He knew we were watching."

"I don't think he saw us; he just sensed that we were spying on him." Bishop moved into a cross-legged position and placed her blistering hands onto the stone floor. The coolness was soothing but she was really using the contact to draw on the earth energy to heal the burns.

Pope stood up and looked at his own hands. The pain had been pretty intense but there was only a slight sign of burning. His mixed parentage gave him a toughness humans didn't have and he was thankful for it. His hands were sore but not so bad it would concern him overly much.

He moved to the table — the bowl had shattered and the mixture was smoking, singeing the wooden surface where it had spread across the table. It smouldered with an unpleasant sulphurous odour, which was odd considering there had been no sulphur in the mix. But magic crossing the boundaries between Earth and the

Faerie realm often resulted in the stench of brimstone.

"That could have gone better," Pope said.

"At least it proves the Fae are up to something." Bishop stood up and flexed her fingers. The rapid healing left them tingling. "The ley line is damaged - I could barely pull in enough power to heal a few blisters. It will take months to return to normal."

"Did the Fae do it deliberately?" Pope tossed the broken pieces he held back onto the table.

"I'm not sure. We should talk to Malcolm — he usually knows what's happening when the Fae are on Earth."

"We don't have time to wait for him to appear. Whatever the Fae have planned it'll take place tonight. I'd almost stake my life on it."

"Any ideas?" Bishop looked a little disconnected, moving her head like she was trying to recall where she might have misplaced something.

"We should split up. I'll visit Sam and see what he's been hiding."

Bishop nodded. "Good idea. Just don't get drinking with him."

"There'll be no time for that." Pope started towards the door then paused. "What's your plan?"

"I may be able to use the broken ley line to follow this up." Bishop spoke through clenched teeth. "If it was disrupted on purpose the Fae may have left a trail."

Pope thumped on Finlay's door for a good two minutes before admitting that the big guy probably wasn't home. Most likely he was already celebrating Midsummer's Eve. For Finlay that meant trying to drink some pub dry, but finding which one he'd chosen was the trick.

Pricking his finger on the carpet tack in his pocket, Pope used the blood to cast a location spell and began by drawing a circle on the pavement. When he squeezed out another droplet and let it land in the middle of the ring, it turned into a sphere of mist as usual, but didn't create the ribbon-like trail it should have done. Instead, the mist simply swirled around a number of times until the energy contained in the spell expired in a tiny explosion that sounded like a bubble-gum burst.

Pope rose from his squatting position and scratched his chin. Something magical had blocked his spell but he had no idea if it was some kind of general Fae interference or a specifically targeted ward designed to prevent him finding Finlay. If it was the latter, it meant the situation was far more serious than it had already seemed. He'd have to search for the big guy the hard way — by checking all the nearby pubs his friend normally frequented.

The Landsman, just around the corner, was his first port of call. It was busy and smoky but there was no sign of his friend, so Pope walked a brisk fifty yards to the next pub, the Golden Swan. The bar was half full of men with a few women scattered amongst them and the room was noisy with chat and again murky with smoke. Pope looked over to the landlord and raised his eyebrows in question. The landlord inclined his head and gave an upward, sideways jerk towards the door at the far end and Pope waved his thanks. This wasn't the first time he'd been in here with his friend.

Finlay was the only occupant of the small snug, a room served by a small hatch that looked through to the area behind the bar. He was sitting in the opposite corner to the door, hunched over and cradling a nearly empty pint glass. The number of glasses on the table gave the impression he'd been there all day but the pub had only been open an hour. Although he was quiet by nature, it wasn't like him to isolate himself from the other drinkers in such a way.

He didn't look up as Pope entered but he sniffed gently. "Get lost, Josh."

"What sort of a friend would I be if I didn't offer to share your troubles?" Pope sat down on a small stool across the table from Finlay. "It is Midsummer's Eve after all and you should be celebrating."

Finlay lifted his head a little and peeked under his brow with narrow eyes before finishing off the remains of his beer. "You've been a good friend, I'll give you that. And that's exactly why you shouldn't have anything to do with my troubles."

"Let's assume I want to help you anyway."

"You can't. Not with this." He pushed the glass across the table's surface and it clinked against the others. He avoided eye contact.

"Maybe that's so, but do you think I wouldn't try?" Pope leaned forward and rested his arms on the edge of the table but Finlay wouldn't raise his eyes. "You're a fool, Sam."

"What?! I..." Finlay bit off whatever he was going to say but his breathing picked up its pace and he clenched his fists. Pope's eyes took in every detail of his friend's posture and expression — he may well regret what he was about to do but time wasn't on his side and he was getting a little desperate.

"Only a dim-witted troll would think he could hide his problems from me."

"Bugger off!"

"I thought you were smarter than this, Sam," Pope said. He readied himself and shifted in his seat. "I thought you had at least half a brain."

"Watch your bloody mouth."

Pope knew he was pushing the right buttons; Finlay hated being called stupid, mostly because trolls were not known for their intelligence. "If you're not smart enough to take my help when it's offered, you can't be much of a friend."

Finlay stood up and threw the table to one side as if it was made of balsa, taking the glasses with it. The whole lot hit the wall with a might crash that instantly brought the landlord to the open hatch. He watched the two closely without saying a word.

Finlay looked fully into Pope's eyes for the first time. "You don't know how much of a bloody friend I am! Warning you off is the best thing I can do for you, but you can never let anything go, can you?"

"I was wrong. I can't help you because your problem isn't anything but your own stupidity."

"Because no one's ever as clever as you, right?" Finlay stepped closer and looked down at Pope. Buried resentment burned in his eyes.

"You have it arse-backwards," Pope said, glaring up at the big man, trying not to show any of the fear he felt. "No one's ever as stupid as you."

Finlay picked up Pope by his shirt front and snarled into his face. "Do you think I want to stop you? Do you think I wouldn't do anything else but? I don't have any choice!"

Pope's eyes lit up a little and he couldn't prevent a half smile twitching at the corners of his mouth. Then he took hold of himself and pressed on with the advantage.

"You couldn't stop me in a million years," he said. "I'll do whatever it takes and sod the bloody Fae!" Because he knew the Fae were up to something, this wasn't much of a gamble, though he had to make Finlay think he knew more than he did. Judging by the big man's reaction he was close to hitting the nail on the head. "Midnight's not far off. I'll stop the Fae if I have to fight every last one of them."

"I can't let you, Josh," Finlay said, his grip increased, pulling the shirt material tightly across Pope's back. "The exchange has got to take place and there's nothing you can do. You can't save the—" He stopped and stared at Pope's now hopeful face. "You tricked me!"

Finlay pushed Pope away and the latter staggered back across the small room and against the wall. Finlay scooped up the only unbroken beer glass and threw it at him. It shattered against Pope's left forearm, raised in defence, and cut the skin in a few places.

Trying to dodge a stool that suddenly flew at his head, Pope lost his footing and sprawled across the floor. Although he immediately tried to get to his feet, Finlay was on him before he could and the part-troll rained a number of blows on his face with such force that Pope was sure he was being hit with a sledgehammer.

Pope didn't defend himself against the blows but dipped his right forefinger into the blood oozing from his arm and smeared it on Finlay's forehead.

"*Braench ach mentum fo lictach*," Pope said, managing to get the words out around the blows. Something unlocked in Finlay's mind and he stopped punching. Pope pushed him off and the big man sat on the floor with a thump and a blank look on his now peaceful face. Pope crouched beside him and wiped the blood flowing from his nose, but otherwise ignored the pain from his injuries.

"Now, Samuel, tell me exactly what's going on tonight."

"Tonight..." Finlay paused, unsure.

Pope grabbed his friend's shoulders and shook him

gently. "What have the Fae planned for tonight, Sam?"

Finlay looked at Pope with glassy eyes. "At midnight tonight, the Fae Lord Ealvun will create the first changeling for one hundred and seventy-three years. The exchange must take place. I am to stop you from interfering. My Mam had... a vision..."

He stopped speaking, as if these last words had triggered something inside of him, and shook his head. He stared at Pope, his eyes still glassy but with a wild fury building inside. He was desperately trying to fight his rising anger but his expression suggested it was a battle he was rapidly losing.

Pope leaped to his feet and grabbed one of the stools. He stepped around and swung it with all his might against Finlay's head. There was a sharp crack so loud Pope knew instantly it would be of no further use. The stool, that is. Finlay simply slumped to the floor unconscious.

The landlord leaned through the hatchway. "Mr. Pope, will you be paying for the damage or shall I send the bill to Mr. Finlay?"

Pope grinned then winced with the pain of doing so. "I'll settle up with you tomorrow, Will. If I survive the night."

In the Crypt

As soon as Pope left the house to look for Finlay, Bishop changed into something more practical — linen trousers and a blouse. On top of this outfit she added a light jacket because she needed something with pockets. Although a bag would have given her more space, she liked to avoid carrying one if she could, ever since she'd nearly hung herself on the strap of one when it became snagged on a protruding piece of the city walls. The chasing golem had nearly grabbed her but thankfully Pope and Finlay had arrived in time to destroy it.

Bishop had no idea what she might encounter this evening, so she grabbed a couple of earth gems from her magical workshop and stuffed them into her pockets. She left the house and stopped in the middle of the enclosed private courtyard in front of it, where she squatted down and placed her hands onto the flagstones, still warm from the day's sunshine. She pushed her senses into the earth, reaching for the nearby ley line again.

Being outside normally gave Bishop a more direct connection to the earth but something interfered with the link. Although her hands still tingled a little from the healing it didn't hamper her magical ability, yet she still couldn't hook up to the full power of the earth. The obstruction of the ley line from the high level of Fae activity made it impossible for her to do so.

Bishop stood up again and looked over the rooftops to where the York Minster poked its old stone tower into the air, catching the rays of the evening sun. She needed to go to where the power of the ley line was at its strongest in the hope that some of the power remained and that meant going inside the ancient building.

Ten minutes later she made her way through the echoey interior, moving as quietly as possible and hoping not to be seen. A midsummer service was under way, so getting inside the building had been easy, but now she needed to descend into the crypts in order to get as close as possible to the focus of the earth line.

As usual, the gates at the top of the crypt stairs were locked, but Bishop had been here many times before and knew exactly how to draw on her stored earth magic to work the tumblers of the lock. A moment later, following a quietly muttered spell, the gates swung open with a gentle, but slightly resistant, metallic whine. She walked through and descended into the gloom of the crypts with a quiet tread.

On previous visits she'd used her magic to light her way, but up ahead was a glow she'd never seen before and the reflected light was enough for her to see the way. By her reckoning the source of the glow came from the approximate position of the ley line's focus, which was located directly beneath the cathedral's main tower. Whatever generated the glow, she instinctively knew it formed a connection to the earth power's disruption.

The whole of her body began to tingle; it always did whenever she came down here. The excavation into the ground, the ancient masonry all around her, the earth deep beneath her — all had soaked up the power of the ley line focus for centuries. The ley line itself may be disrupted but the residual energy here was strong. And very primal.

Bishop had to focus her mind or the elemental, ancient energy flowing around her would excite the animal lust within. It was the kind of powerful distraction she didn't need.

It was difficult not to think about the passions of the flesh in the crypt and Bishop occasionally wondered what would happen if a child was conceived down here as a result of the coupling of two earth magicians. Of course, it was unlikely to happen in her case — most earth wizards she'd met were so full of their own perceived importance she'd never touch them with a cursed rod. But swamped by the vibrant power of the focus, there was always the chance she'd succumb to passions she had no control over.

This evening, though, the power was erratic and the waves of lustful emotion that swept over her were manageable, though nauseating and in danger of making her physically sick. She drew on some of that energy to calm her nervous stomach and clear her mind, ensuring that she channelled the power in the right manner.

But speculating about offspring brought Bishop's mind around to thoughts of her daughter. Although it was sixteen years since Catherine had been killed, aged forty-eight, she still missed her. Deeply. Now she found herself breathing heavily as the emotions from those days came back to her, cranking up her heart rate to maximum. There was nothing she could have done to prevent the death but she still felt like she'd failed her child.

Bishop's breathing began to run away with itself and even though she feared it might give her away there was nothing she could do but ride out her emotions. But then she was sick; throwing up against the wall she stood beside as her memories collided with the disrupted waves of earth energy. Thankfully, she had the presence of mind to keep the volume down on the vomiting noises.

"Forgive me, Catherine," she whispered, then pushed

her daughter from her mind.

Wiping her mouth, she listened for any sign that she'd been heard but there was no indication of that so she continued towards the light.

The glow spilled around the corner at the end of the passage and as Bishop drew closer she began to hear voices. Two of them. But even straining as hard as she could she was unable to make out what they were saying for one spoke in a mutter, the other a whisper. She crept a little closer and peered around the corner.

The area was illuminated by a lantern that hung from the end of a long brass rod, the top of which was bent over in a hook, and the whole thing appeared to stand without support — clearly through some application of magic. However, as unexpected as the magical lantern was, the real surprise was the pair of individuals who continued with their subdued conversation.

Two Fae males were positioned a short distance from the lantern, dressed in light leather and silk with sheathed swords at their belts. Their bored manner gave the impression of waiting for a bus that was long overdue. Bishop smiled and thought of Waiting for Godot, which she'd seen the previous year and wasn't sure she'd liked.

The two men were patently uncomfortable with their surroundings but they really should have been in agony. Consecrated ground was not only extremely painful to the Fae, it would kill them in time. How was it possible for the two of them to even enter the church let alone remain here for so long? They seemed to be immune to its effects. More Fae magic, no doubt.

Bishop pressed her hand against the wall corner around which she was spying and cautiously reached out with her magical senses, slowly spreading them outward, inch by inch, making sure she disturbed the underlying energy patterns as little as possible. She didn't want the two Fae to be alerted to her presence before she'd got the measure of them. No one ever won a battle by being unprepared, should the situation develop into that kind of confrontation.

As her earth sense touched the closest of the Fae, ethereal tendrils exploring with the lightest presence possible, she sensed a magical signature that reminded her of something familiar; a snippet of something she almost recognised...

Her mind, filled with four centuries of memories, thoughts and knowledge, wasn't always the easiest to navigate. Older recollections could take long seconds to pull from the depths of her brain. Although she still dug into things long unremembered, this memory already sounded warning bells in spite of not yet becoming clear. It called to her... from...

Bishop's mind was abruptly transported back to the seventeenth century, to the time she and Pope had helped Malcolm the ghost in the smith's old store room, fighting against powerful magical forces and combining their magic for the first time. It had been both scary and exhilarating, but it had been important to remove the curse.

Then she was back in the here and now and knew this Fae male had been the one who'd laid the curse upon Malcolm. A curse so powerful that anyone who'd cast their gaze upon him had instantly been struck blind. It was going to be a pleasure to deal with this Fae and his friend. Perhaps the second man was the one who'd cast the other curse; the one that caused him to travel between Hull and York constantly for all eternity.

Bishop pulled back her senses, stepped around the corner and strode purposefully towards the two men. As soon as they saw her they started visibly, taken aback at the confident way she approached. They glanced at each other, unsure of what to do, then returned their attention to her.

"Leave now, woman," Blind Curse said to her, but the command he'd hoped his voice would convey failed him and the words sounded weak.

"That's funny," Bishop replied. "I was going to say exactly the same to you." She stopped about ten feet away and folded her arms.

"It would serve you best if you kept to your own business, lest we should be forced to kill you," Travel Curse said.

Bishop laughed. "Are you so inexperienced you would dare threaten an earth witch here, at one of the most powerful sources of earth energy on the planet?"

"Under normal circumstances that would be true, but not at this moment."

"You may have disturbed the line's flow," Bishop unfolded her arms and spread them wide, "but this is the heart of its power. It undulates around me, fills me to the brim with primal energy."

"You scare us not," Blind Curse said and put his hand on his sword. "You cannot grasp the scale of power behind Fae magic."

"Yet I know that, centuries ago, the two of you cursed a poor traveller," Bishop said and smiled at their nervous, surprised reactions. "One a curse of never ending travel, the other with the power to blind onlookers." She pointed to each of them in turn as she spoke, which increased their nervousness.

"How is it you know such things?" asked Travel Curse.

"I'm the witch who removed the blinding curse."

His mouth fell open in surprise. "That was..."

"Nearly three hundred years ago, yes." Bishop put her hands on her hips and her smile grew wider and distinctly wicked. "Just imagine how powerful I have become in thirty decades."

She'd never seen two Fae look so fearful, but in spite of the pleasure it gave her she turned serious. "Inexperience or not, you are disrupting the power of the ley line. Is there a point to that or are you simply causing mischief?"

"That is not something we are willing to discuss with you," Blind Curse said. He was clearly taking the lead and Travel Curse was happy to let him do so, drifting to a position behind his friend.

"Yet I know you cannot tell a lie."

"Still, one does not have to always give the truth."

Bishop nodded and narrowed her eyes. The Fae were probably schooled in this from an early age and wouldn't tell her what she needed to know directly. However, the truth sometimes lay buried in the phrasing of an answer or in what was not being said.

"Do you truly possess the power to ward off the influence of the consecrated ground the Minster sits upon?"

Blind Curse's eyes glazed a little as he thought of a response but Travel Curse absently fingered a delicate crystal that hung about his neck on the finest silver chain she'd ever seen. Now Bishop's attention had been drawn to it she could see they both wore one. She reached out with her earth magic and sensed the Fae power the gems contained.

"Never mind," she said. "I can see for myself that you have charms of great power hung about your necks. Is it true that such gems are incredibly rare?"

They each grasped their charms protectively, as if fearful that Bishop would try to steal them for herself.

"Don't worry," she said. "Although I would love to own such magnificent prizes, stealing them would likely make my life forfeit. It does, however, explain why the ley line power has been so disrupted. Which also suggests the two of you have been here for some time. Days at least."

She began slowly circling the two men, strolling around with her arms behind her back as if taking a walk in the park. Although it may have appeared that her concentration had moved away from the two Fae, she kept her focus on them through the corner of her eye.

"But my question still remains — is there a point to what you do?" She stopped walking again, nearer to the lantern that illuminated the area, and saw that its supporting rod was not held in place by any magic, but thrust into a gap between the flagstones of the crypt floor. Bishop turned to face them again.

"It is Midsummer's Eve, yet you stand here, where it's so dangerous to your kind, instead of revelling with other Fae." She smiled at the look on their faces. "Something is clearly going to happen this night and it's important to your task that the city's earth power is as disrupted as possible."

"Why pose such questions if the answers are already yours?" Blind Curse said.

"Because, until you just spoke, my comment was simply a guess." She smirked as they looked at each other again. "Perhaps the cathedral authorities would be very interested in what their crypt contains."

"We cannot let you leave, whatever your reason," Travel Curse said. "We have been instructed to deal with the Bishop of York."

"You'll find he's an Archbishop, actually."

"Our orders are clear and you will not stop us." They each shifted their stance in readiness.

Bishop pointed at them. "You have no real task and are nothing more than a distraction. Two complete buffoons would never be trusted with anything remotely important."

Blind Curse held up his charm smugly. "Would two buffoons be entrusted with these? Lord Ealvun has given us the chance to redeem ourselves."

"Artill, you fool! We were forbidden from mentioning the Lord's name."

"It matters not, Cerrin. We will not let her take this knowledge from here."

Artill abruptly cast a glamour and became invisible, which was followed by the sound of his sword being drawn from its scabbard. A moment later Cerrin did the same. While Bishop had been expecting an attack since she'd confronted them, she hadn't counted on them being so devious. Underestimation was always a dangerous thing and she'd allowed her confidence to get the better of her judgement.

She drew on the energy within her and used it to cast a quick spell directed at the lamp, which extinguished immediately, plunging the crypt into complete darkness. Now none of them could see.

She put her hand into a pocket and pulled out the piece of chalk she kept there. She tossed it into the darkness and it made a gentle sound as it hit the floor thirty feet away. Hoping it would give her a few moments of distraction, she pulled off her canvas shoes one at a time and thrust each into a pocket of her jacket. She crouched on the floor as low as she could get and spread her hands on the flagstones.

She drew on the power of the ley line and, in spite of its disruption, she had to be careful not to take too much, too quickly. Without due caution, it could be like opening a sluice gate fully while standing in the water channel it opened onto.

Replenished, she sent a wave of earth power across the floor and it sparked when it encountered the Fae magic of the two glamours, showing their positions as lightly glowing footprints only she could perceive. The trail indicated that they had moved away from her position, drawn by the sound of her distraction.

Taking up a little more of the ley line power she sent out another wave. She set up a rhythm and saw that they were moving about a little aimlessly, not knowing where she was but clearly not daring to talk to each other for fear of giving themselves away.

But what should she do? It would be easy to take them out or simply render them unconscious, but she needed more information from them. She needed to understand why they were here and what their intention was tonight.

Then Bishop noticed something unusual — the charms the two Fae wore glowed ever so slightly in reaction to the earth energy she sent out every second, faintly shining through the glamour. She could use these to her advantage and muttered a spell so quietly she could barely hear it herself. When it was complete the two charms flew toward her open hand, torn from the necks of the two men, the silver chains snapping in the process.

Artill and Cerrin instantly screamed and their glamours dissolved. No longer protected by the priceless, magical gems, the power of the consecrated location reacted with their Fae nature and they writhed in agony.

Bishop stood up and created a small sphere of light. She moved it over to where the two Fae writhed in pain. "Tell me why you are here tonight and what it is your Lord plans for the Archbishop! Tell me and I will give you back your charms."

But instead of answering, Artill gestured with his hand to cast a spell that abruptly filled the crypt with dazzling light, far outshining the small glow Bishop had conjured. For a moment Bishop was blinded. She feared that they would attack while she had no defence and worked her healing magic swiftly in the hope of clearing her vision before they did so.

However, it became obvious that their only interest was to escape. They dropped their swords with a clatter before dashing over to a nearby wall where Artill drew, with a piece of red chalk, an image of a door on the stonework. As soon as the rectangle was complete they pushed against the stone and opened a magical door, through which blazed an unusual blue light. Artill and Cerrin dashed across the threshold immediately.

Bishop's eyes were healing rapidly and she could make out the glowing rectangle of the doorway and the blurry silhouettes of the two men fleeing. With no hesitation whatsoever, she followed after them and only just made it through the already closing door. Then, as her eyes cleared completely, she realised she may just have made a huge mistake.

She was in a large room with stone walls, of an architectural construction that looked more organic than designed by a draughtsman. A few feet away Artill and Cerrin were sprawled on the floor, their skin badly blistered and covered in erupting boils. Also in the room was the Fae Lord she and Pope had seen through their scrying magic, but this time he was flanked by a couple of efficient looking guards.

"Well done to you both," the Lord said, addressing Artill and Cerrin. "You have truly excelled yourselves and redeemed your previous actions. Rest and recover. It will not be long." He turned to Bishop.

"Lord Ealvun, I presume," she said.

Ealvun bowed slightly, in admission rather than respect. "I am pleased to meet you, Bishop of York."

"Ah..." Realisation dawned. She'd been fooled by a

couple of fools. "I thought they were simply a distraction."

"Which is exactly what I'd hoped for. Sometimes the most sluggish of wit delivers the best results." Ealvun beckoned his guards over. "Now I insist you stay as my guest."

"Not a hope, my friend."

Bishop drew on her stored power and pictured the kitchen at home, using this mental image to quickly open a portal. Only, there was something strange about this place and the portal wouldn't form easily. She would need more time to manipulate the energy she needed.

Lord Ealvun waved his hand and cast a spell that confused Bishop's mind. She blinked and gasped, her mind reeled like that of a drunk. The struggling portal collapsed and vanished and she fell into the grasp of the two guards.

"Make her secure," Ealvun said as he left the room. "I have other matters to which I must attend."

Race Against Time

With a bucket of cold water dumped on him, Finlay came round suddenly and bellowed, pulling savagely at the heavy brass chains that secured him by his wrists and ankles to the large steel ring embedded in the floor. Pope laughed at the unexpected sound — he'd never actually heard anyone bellow before, but the seriousness of the situation quickly quelled the amusement.

"Calm down, Sam," he said.

Finlay tried to get to his feet but the chains were too short to give him enough freedom to do so.

"Let me go, Joshua!" He pulled at the chains again but there was no give whatsoever, which was hardly surprising considering that the big man had been the one who'd installed them for occasions when his rage got the better of him. These were the times he hated being part troll the most.

Pope had borrowed Tim, the pub landlord's son, to help carry Finlay back home. Although they'd travelled no more than a hundred yards, they'd had some difficulty doing so because of the dense nature of his bone and muscle. Once inside his house, they simply threw him down the cellar stairs rather than struggle down the narrow fight of steps.

The big man had crashed into a heavy work bench at the bottom, part of which broke on impact, and a number of bottles that had been sitting on the top of the bench were dislodged. A couple of them had rolled off and smashed on the floor but Finlay had been oblivious to the commotion, unconscious and snoring throughout.

Pope and Tim had dragged him into the centre of the room where Pope had chained him up to the steel ring before giving Tim a ten bob note and letting him leave.

Now that Finlay was conscious again, Pope crouched down in front of him just beyond the reach the chains allowed and looked him over. Although he was tough, he'd still have some nasty bruises the following day.

"Do you remember what happened?"

"You tried to mess with my mind," Finlay replied. "You said you'd never do that."

"And I really meant it." Pope paused and sighed. "But situations change and when we have no other choice we're forced to do things we'd rather not. You can't blame me for wanting to obtain that information."

Finlay slumped to the ground knowing he was at the mercy of his friend. "The Fae Lords will kill me for telling you about the changeling."

"I think not," Pope said. "You didn't give up the information of your own free will; I had to force it out of you."

"You think that will make a difference? The Fae are crazy."

Pope laughed. "Yeah, but how will they even find out? Are you going to tell them?"

Finlay fell silent for a moment then lifted up the chains towards Pope. "Whatever you plan to do, you've got to leave me chained up. I've been compelled to stop you."

"Yet you just volunteered that."

"I..." Finlay frowned, baffled. It didn't make any sense. The compulsion should have prevented him even mentioning it.

"You already told me what's going to happen," Pope

said. "But I need you to help me, Sam."

"Don't you think I want to help?" Finlay began breathing heavily again. "The thought of exchanging kids makes me feel sick. I'm going to have to live with it, not you."

"Then fight it, Sam." Pope grabbed Finlay's shoulders. "Fight the compulsion and stop them with me."

Finlay shrugged off Pope's hands and hung his head. "Go..."

"No. I need to know which child is the target."

"Go, Josh! I've done all I can." He ground his teeth and pulled at the chains again.

Pope rose and moved towards the cellar steps then turned back to his friend. "I'm sorry I had to chain you up, but I'm going to stop the exchange even without your help."

Finlay nodded and a flicker of a weak smile passed over his lips. "Good luck," he whispered as Pope climbed the steps, pretending he hadn't heard those words. It was difficult not to like the big man.

Out in the street Pope breathed in the night air and immediately set off for home at a fast run. He didn't have much time and if Finlay couldn't help him he needed Bishop by his side.

Unfortunately, the house was empty and Pope realised she must still be searching for information from her own angle. He had no idea if she'd discovered anything, but now he knew about the Fae plan for the changeling he had to find her and bring her up to speed.

He used a little more of his blood to cast another location spell and for the second time that evening the blood failed to give him the location of his target. It was unlikely that Fae magic hid Bishop from him; more probable that something serious had happened to her. Whoever had dared harm her...

Pope quickly pulled his anger under control. He didn't have time to waste thinking about vengeance, particularly when it might not yet be warranted. He had a child to find and save and, if what Finlay had said was right, he had to do so before midnight or it would be far too late.

In his bedroom, he took hold of a large bookcase and heaved it out of the way, swinging it to one side by pivoting it on the leg at the bottom left corner. Behind it a hidden alcove was revealed, in which stood the smallest refrigerator he'd been able to buy. Hardly anyone in Britain owned a fridge but he'd bought this one eight years ago for one specific purpose.

He opened the door and the cool air wafted out. Sitting in the middle of the fridge was a wooden rack that contained about fifty glass vials of differing sizes, stoppered with corks and sealed with wax. In each vial was a measure of blood, ranging from the relatively ordinary to a handful of rare specimens. Among the latter were samples from a vampire, a werewolf and a Fae. It was this last one Pope was particularly interested in.

He removed it from its place in the rack, closed the fridge door and pushed the bookcase back into position. Holding the vial up to the light, he looked through the glass at the liquid inside. It was such a dark red it was almost black and there wasn't very much of it.

Pope cleared a space on his desk, broke the wax seal and unstoppered the vial. He poured a little of the blood onto his index finger and used it to draw a circle on the desk's surface, speaking his spell as he did so.

"*Braench al deffer tan* Ealvun," he said and let a single drop of blood fall from the vial and into the circle.

The blood droplet fought against the power of the spell and even as it turned into a mist it shimmered for a moment. It seemed that nothing was going to happen so

Pope repeated the words of his spell, putting more urgency into them. The mist instantly formed into a fine ribbon and led a trail out of the door. He replaced the stopper in the vial and put it into his pocket.

Pope quickly pulled a scabbarded sword from a nearby umbrella rack and buckled it about his waist as he followed the trail out of the room, down the stairs and out of the house. Although he set off running again he wished to himself that he'd had time to don some armour, too. Dealing with the Fae was always more dangerous than he liked.

Running through the streets of York late on a Sunday night while wearing a sword was hardly the best course of action, but thankfully the pubs had been closed for a little while and although he passed a couple of people, both of whom gave him strange looks, he didn't meet any police and reached his destination without any trouble.

The trail ended at a fairly ordinary terraced house in a smarter part of the city and Pope paused to suck in as much air as he could. His breathing recovered quickly and he walked up to the front door then began beating on it. He looked at his watch — ten minutes to spare — but because the blood trail had led him here it meant the Fae must have already arrived, preparing for the exchange.

The door opened and a wiry man stood at the other side of the threshold in his vest and trousers with a pair of braces hanging loose. He looked angry.

"What on Earth are you playing at?" he snarled. "It's nearly bloody midnight and I've got work in morning."

Pope didn't give him a chance to say anything further and pushed past, along the narrow passage and straight up the stairs where the blood ribbon led him.

"Hey, you!" he shouted. "Where the bloody hell do you think your going?" The man chased after him, taking the stairs two steps at a time and caught him on the landing, slamming Pope against the wall.

His wife, Ethel, came out of the living room, scared by the commotion. "What's going on, Morris?" she screamed and ran up the stairs, too.

Pope tried to push at Morris's face to get him out of the way but the sprightly man dodged like a boxer and followed it up with a left hook to the magician's jaw that connected with enough force to make him see stars after the injuries he'd received earlier from Finlay. Morris followed it up with another blow to the face with his right hand and Pope's lip split against his own teeth.

"Shit!" Pope said, spitting blood.

Ethel rapidly climbed the stairs. "Morris, what's he doing in here?!"

"Whatever the hell it is, he's leaving."

Unfortunately for Morris, the brief pause he'd taken to chat to his wife gave Pope's head enough time to clear so that he was able to knock the man to the floor with a blow from his elbow.

Pope immediately kicked open the child's bedroom door, drawing his sword as he did so, causing Ethel to scream in horror and Morris to jump to his feet again.

The blood magician was confronted by a Fae swordsman, the same person he and Bishop had seen earlier through the scrying spell — Lord Ealvun. Behind him were two more Fae, both women. The one dressed in a red robe stood with a Fae child in her arms and the other, in green, stood poised to snatch up the human infant.

Pointing his sword at the Fae Lord, Pope's voice dripping venom as he spoke. "Leave now, Lord Ealvun. I'll not let you take the child."

"Do not interfere, mortal..." Ealvun paused. "Ah, I see who you are, now. But in spite of your ancestry and power, you have no right to interfere."

Behind Pope, Morris and his wife were initially stunned by the sight they beheld in the room then tried to push past Pope to reach their baby, only to find they could not enter the room — an invisible barrier prevented them from doing so.

"No!" Ethel screamed. "Leave Arthur alone!"

Morris grabbed Pope's sword arm and his throat, pulling him away from the doorway. He pushed him against the landing banister. "What in bloody hell is going on? What are they doing in our son's room?" His words were barely audible above his wife's screaming and yelling.

"They intend to swap your child for one of their own," Pope replied, shrugging off Morris's hold with some difficulty, though not taking his eyes from the Fae Lord. "But not if you let me do my job."

Ethel pushed repeatedly against the invisible barrier and screamed at the Fae inside the room. "If you harm my son I'll bloody well kill you. Let me in!" She turned to Pope. "What's stopping me? What are they doing?!"

"Move out of my way," Pope said, pushing past Ethel. "I need to get in there if I'm to save your child."

Ethel screamed with frustration, her fists clenched tightly, her eyes streaming with tears. "It's impossible! You can't get in there."

"You cannot, but I can."

"Can you really save him?" Morris suddenly looked a little helpless as he realised their only chance was to trust a man who'd just forced his way into their home. Pope didn't answer but turned to the doorway with determination.

Leading with his sword, Pope pushed it through the doorway, feeling the resistance of the charm the Fae Lord had placed upon it. Although Ealvun had taken the precautions he thought reasonable, the iron in Pope's steel sword pierced the barrier, allowing him to follow it through like squeezing through a split in a sheet of rubber.

"Finlay had orders to stop you coming here," Ealvun said.

"Believe me, he tried," Pope said and gestured at his now swollen face. "Where do you think this came from?"

He stepped fully into the small room and Morris tried to follow him in but the barrier was complete again. The man snarled with the frustration of being kept from his son. Ethel's desperate wailing continued, though muffled somewhat by the barrier.

Pope lunged at the Faerie man and with lightning speed Lord Ealvun drew his own sword and parried the thrust with ease. Fae swordsmen were difficult to beat when it came to swordplay, such is their power and elegance in brandishing their light but resilient weapons. However, Pope never intended to play entirely by the rules. He followed through the lunge with a shoulder charge that slammed the tall but slender man against the bedroom wall, winding him a little. He grabbed Ealvun's face with his free hand and slammed his head against the wall for good measure.

Pope turned to deal with the other Fae, knowing that he had little time in which to do so. Through the wide open window came the sound of the first of the midnight chimes from a nearby church clock.

Lifting his sword to strike at the red robed Fae woman, Pope heard Ethel let out a little squeal from the landing. He whirled around and only just caught Ealvun's sword on his own but managed to land a blow in his attacker's face with his elbow. Unfortunately, his desire to strike put him off balance and he fell to the floor.

Almost immediately he was back on his feet. The seventh chime sounded as Ealvun lifted his free hand towards Pope, the palm outward, and cast a Fae spell on him. Pope staggered, his mind befuddled for a moment, but although it cleared quickly, it wasn't swift enough. As the confusion lifted from him, the final chime struck and it was midnight.

The Fae in green snatched up the human child and moved rapidly towards the window as her counterpart in red placed her child into the baby's cot and followed her.

"Stop!" Pope yelled and lifted his sword to attack once more but the after-effects of the spell caused him to stumble and he only just prevented himself from falling to the floor.

"No!" Ethel screamed, watching the rapid exchange without being able to do anything to help her baby.

With his companions clear, Ealvun made for the window himself. As he turned his back to climb through, Pope lunged with a little more surety and the tip of his sword sunk into the Fae's calf. Ealvun screamed — less at the direct pain of the injury than at the touch of the steel sword. He shot through the window as if pulled by an elasticated cord. When Pope stuck his head through there was no sign of any of them.

Pulling back into the room he looked at his sword — the Fae blood was blackened and smoking. A moment later it was gone, leaving a nasty stain on the metal. Pope sheathed it and turned towards the doorway.

Morris and Ethel almost fell into the room as the ward charm vanished, and Morris grabbed Pope's shirt front and pushed him up against the wall.

"What the bloody hell are you doing in my house?" Morris demanded.

"You saw what I was doing," Pope replied. "I tried to save your son."

Morris looked over to the cot where Ethel was lifting the Fae child protectively.

"Look! There's nowt wrong with him. Are you mad? Have you escaped from a mad house?"

Pope stared in amazement. "That child is not yours; it's not even human. Your son has been taken by one of the Fae Lords."

"You *are* mad," Morris said and Pope knew in an instant that the two were under a charm.

"Shh..." Ethel soothed the baby, which made gurgling noises through a set of wickedly sharp teeth. "Don't you listen to the nasty man."

"Can't you see that he's not yours?"

"Of course he's ours," Ethel said. "A mother knows her own child."

Pope's look of astonishment turned to one of anger. The parents' acceptance of the Fae child was clearly part of the changeling magic. How else would parents accept a baby that was so obviously not theirs?

He looked at the child and a shiver ran down his spine. It grinned at him wickedly, as if knowing that the other Fae had beaten Pope and the infant was glad to be a part of that scheme..

Faerie

Pope grabbed Morris's wrists and pulled the man's hands free of his shirt. He pushed away from the wall but kept hold of the other man in spite of Morris trying to free himself.

"Look at the child again," Pope said, pulling Morris close and staring hard into the man's eyes. "He's not yours. Your son has been taken to the realm of Faerie."

"You think this is a fairy tale?" Morris wriggled more fiercely and Pope let go of his wrists. "You're a bloody loony. Now get the hell out before you upset Ethel and the baby even more."

"If only…" Pope mused, taking little notice of Morris's order.

"What?! If only what?"

"I have a friend who would lift this glamour from your eyes; if I could just find out where she is."

"I don't know who you are, mister," Ethel said. "But we want you to leave. Please go."

"Pope. My name's Pope," he said a little absently.

He strode over to Ethel and grabbed her shoulders. She drew the child closer to her, protectively, and Morris grabbed Pope's arm to pull him away from his wife but he ignored the tugging. He looked intently into Ethel's eyes.

"Look at the child. Please."

Ethel gazed lovingly at the infant in her arms, though her eyes flicked about with overtones of nervousness caused by Pope's proximity.

"Think of how you carried your son for nine months inside of you," Pope urged. "Think of how you suffered the pains of labour to give birth. Picture the first time you laid eyes on your beautiful baby and the delight it gave you. Remember that instant where you connected with your wonderful bundle of joy." He paused. "Now tell me if this is that same child."

Ethel's eyes glazed over and she did as Pope asked. The memories of pain and delight worked across her face in turn. As she regained focus there was a very brief moment where it seemed she didn't recognise the child she held. Then it was gone.

"This *is* my baby, Mr. Pope," she said. "The one I gave birth to. Now please leave us be!"

Pope released Ethel and stepped away from her. "Do you know Father Martin?"

"We have nothing to do with Catholics," Morris said, pulling at Pope's arm again. "No offence."

"Martin will tell you everything you need to know about changelings."

"What the hell's a changeling? And why would we need to know about them?"

"Just remember, Father Martin," Pope urged.

Pope touched his finger to the oozing blood on the split lip Morris had given him. He smeared a single stroke on Morris's forehead before the man had the chance to back away.

"*Braench ach mentum fo lictach,*" Pope said and the man became docile. "Contact Father Martin after I've gone. He's at St. Michael's church."

He quickly turned to Ethel who was already backing away after what she'd seen Pope do to her husband. But he grabbed her, smeared blood on her forehead and chanted the same, strange words.

"This is not your child," he said. "Give him to me."

Ethel almost dropped the child, such was her hurry to pass him over. While it probably would have done little harm if she'd done so — Fae children being so tough — Pope's natural reaction was to save it from crashing to the ground. He swept it into his arms and scurried from the house before either of them could recover from the spells he'd just cast.

The Fae baby looked at him with malice in its eyes and began to scream.

"You have a baby!" Finlay said as Pope returned to the big man's cellar. He was still chained to the floor, just as Pope had left him, but his demeanour was now much calmer.

"Nothing escapes you, Sam." Pope seated himself on the floor and tried to ignore the child's spooky stare. Although it had stopped screaming pretty quickly once it realised the noise had no effect on Pope, its alert, knowing eyes were too advanced for a child of such a young age.

Finlay grinned at the baby. He managed to get his hands close enough to stroke its chin in a friendly way and the child bit him, though the sharp teeth did little harm to his tough hands.

"He's cute!"

"For a Fae child."

"What? Oh..."

"I didn't stop the exchange taking place, Sam. Faye's missing and you were indisposed." He hung his head. "I couldn't do it on my own."

The chains rattled as Finlay buried his face in his big hands and began to weep, his whole body shaking with the sobs that racked his body. "I'm sorry, Joshua."

"It's not your fault, Sam."

"Yes it is. A baby's gone and I'm to blame."

"Then help me put it right." Pope looked at his friend hopefully.

"How? I was commanded to stop you."

Pope looked suddenly thoughtful and the passing of a thousand ideas traced their way across his face. "Who commanded you?"

"Lord Ealvun." Finlay looked up for a moment and the dirt from his hands was now streaked across his teary face and it made him look like a little boy who'd hurt himself playing in the woods.

"Exactly what did he say?"

"I had to make sure that you couldn't stop the exchange."

"Just that?" A hint of a smile tugged at Pope's lips. "Nothing else?"

"No..."

Finlay paused to run through the implications of Pope's question. He smiled and wiped his face. He knew the direction of Pope's train of thought and he was already on board. His reasoning made perfect sense.

Pope put the child on the floor and stood up. "So there's nothing to stop you helping me now the exchange has taken place."

He unlocked Finlay's chains and the big man stood up, too. He held out his hand and the two of them shook.

"Forgive me?" Finlay asked.

"There's nothing to forgive, Sam." Pope picked up the infant again, which started screaming once more as they headed for the stairs. "Let's go save that baby."

At the top of the cellar stairs Finlay paused. "Wait here a moment."

He disappeared into another room and emerged a

short time later with a large battle mallet in his hand. Made of dense, heavy wood and carved with symbols that looked Nordic, the striking faces of the mallet were plated with iron, fixed in place by large nails with spiked heads.

"It was my Dad's," Finlay said. "He could barely lift it but he needed it to keep Mam in check at times."

Pope nodded. He'd known Finlay's parents when they'd both been alive and his mother was a woman who needed keeping in check, being half troll. He'd never quite understood why they'd stayed together for so long or how his father had survived to old age.

"Where is the nearest Fae gateway?" Pope asked as they left the house. He looked up at the stars and took a deep breath.

"The side of the hill at Clifford's Tower."

"But that's a man made hill."

"Fae made. The best kind for a gateway." Finlay looked at Pope as they walked. "Fae craftsmen were involved in the building of the hill and the tower."

"Why?"

"The Fae need an anchor point in York." Finlay set off with purpose. "This city is a powerful focus for all kinds of magic."

A large man wielding a battle mallet with another holding a child and wearing a sword at his waist may have looked rather formidable as they marched swiftly through the silent, night streets of York, but as a force to storm the Fae realm they felt a little inadequate and wished they were greater in number.

Minutes later they reached the hill Finlay mentioned, on top of which sat the ancient Clifford's Tower. Finlay walked back and forth along its base on the eastern side near the steps, to get a sense of where he needed to concentrate his efforts. After a few moments he seemed pretty certain that he'd found the spot. He crouched down, pressed his hand to the base of the artificial hill and closed his eyes.

A gap formed in the side of the hill about twelve feet tall, spilling out a glow the colour of bright moonlight. The gap widened, the turf of the hillside peeling open, seemingly forced apart by the Fae moonbeams, revealing an opening in the process. A magical Fae gateway.

The two men peered through and into the realm of the Fae. The enchanting quality of the light made it look more real than the world in which they stood, somewhat like a large photo that has had its detail and contrast enhanced beyond what is regarded as normal.

Pope followed Finlay through the opening and stood for a moment taking in his surroundings. Behind them the gateway closed and all that remained was a hill, the counterpart of the one back on Earth.

A bright moon hung in the sky, too large to appear entirely natural, but there it was anyway, immense and more than a little threatening. However, in spite of this, it illuminated the landscape with a beauty that sparkled and Pope looked over rolling hills, fanciful forests and rippling, silver rivers.

"Now that we're here, where do we start looking?" Pope asked.

Finlay lifted his head and sniffed the air, turning to face in different directions before finally lifting his arm and pointing. "There."

Behind the distant hills they could see the towers and roofs of a castle, barely visible in the moonlight, and Finlay set off running towards it.

"Come on," he urged. "We've a lot of ground to cover.

We must return the human child before dawn or the exchange will be permanent."

"Now you tell me," Pope said, breaking into a run, too.

Escape

Bishop woke and immediately threw up on the floor beside the bed on which she lay. The second time tonight — not good at all.

With her eyes closed she groped for the drawer of the bedside cabinet, where she kept a number of handkerchiefs, but when her hand only found empty air where the piece of furniture should have been, her eyes flew open and she looked around. In spite of the gloom she immediately remembered where she was and what had happened.

She sat up, swilled some saliva around her mouth and spat on the floor beside the patch of vomit. The taste remained but it would have to do. She always reacted badly when Fae magic was used to overpower her.

The room in which she was imprisoned was somewhat basic — stone walls, bed, bucket, reinforced door — but at least it wasn't damp or particularly unpleasant, if you discounted the smell of her own vomit. However, it was still a cell and she was still a prisoner.

The only illumination was a single beam of moonlight shining through the small, barred window, but Bishop was able to take in her surroundings and tried to get the measure of her prison while she thought about her predicament. She had no idea why the Fae Lord would want to capture her, but it wasn't much of a stretch to figure that it had something to do with the recent Fae activity in York. And their Midsummer celebrations.

She didn't know how long she'd been out but she was determined to do something about her situation.

Stumbling to her feet, Bishop felt pretty woozy as she forced herself upright. She made her way to the door and had to put her hand on the wall to steady herself. That simple touch gave her a shock like a slap in the face.

The stone blocks were dead. Not lacking in warmth, but actually dead. There was no earth energy here in the Faerie realm, which explained why she felt so bad. Being cut off from earth power so totally, her heart suffered an agony like the tearing of barbed hooks and her lungs the torment of a giant's crushing fists.

Bishop was used to magical energy coursing through everything that surrounded her, mostly in miniscule, unusable amounts, but even hewn and sculpted masonry bore the life of the Earth. Simply being in this realm made every action she took a major undertaking. Which was probably why Ealvun had brought her here — to keep her off her game.

Her head was taking time to clear and the tight feeling in her chest reminded her of the time she'd been sat on by an ogre, which had been on a Midsummer's Eve, too. "Come and watch some Shakespeare outdoors," Pope had said. "It'll be fun." It turned out to be fun in the same way a steak dinner is fun, for the cow.

Bishop shook her head again but there was no sign it was going to fully clear and she didn't want to use up her valuable, stored earth energy to do so. There were going to be more important things that needed her magic. She knew she had to escape but it would be impossible to bring forth a portal the way she felt right now. Maybe it was for the best. If she didn't discover Ealvun's interest in her, there was no telling what greater trouble might lurch her way further down the line.

She still had a little stored energy inside of her and —

she checked her pockets — the earth gems were still there. How odd of her captors not to have taken them. She crouched by the door and studied its lock and looked into the keyhole; even better, the key was still in the lock. She was sure she'd be able to use her magic to unlock it.

Drawing on the last of her stored energy she pushed her power through the door and used it to grasp the end of the key as if reaching out with an invisible hand.

"Grant me strength, Earth." She willed the brass key to turn but it proved harder than it ever had with locks on Earth.

Closing her eyes, she pictured the key in her mind and used her earth power to feel its shape, then did the same with the pattern the tumblers made in the lock. But in spite of this clear, mental picture she still could only turn the key a quarter turn in one direction before it reached a hard stop without turning any of the tumblers.

Bishop was not yet ready to give up and decided to explore the lock mechanism in more detail, sensing its shape and the way the tumblers were arranged. She'd studied numerous locks but this one was distinctly different. Then she saw the shape more clearly, grinned and took hold of the key with her power once more.

After she'd rotated it the quarter turn, she pulled it towards her, further into the lock — a person using the key from the other side would push in the key — before turning it further. There was a clear click of the mechanism and Bishop was now able to turn the key the rest of the way and unlock the door.

It opened outward, into the corridor, and because she'd been leaning against it while performing her magic manipulation, she fell forward unexpectedly and sprawled across the stone floor.

By using up the last of her stored energy, the spell had really taken it out of her and for a moment she thought she might just lie there and take a nap, such was the nature of complete energy withdrawal. A lesser witch would likely have succumbed but Bishop had centuries of experience that pushed her into action.

She dragged herself upright by using the handle of the door as an aid, but as soon a she let go she swayed and had to lean heavily against the opposite wall. She was a little surprised that guards hadn't heard her shenanigans. Perhaps they'd planned on locking her away and forgetting about her. More likely they were busy celebrating Midsummer.

The corridor was surprisingly clean for a prison, but only dimly lit by a small number of globes attached to the walls at distant intervals. They gave off a weird, greenish light that made the place feel more dead to her than it already did. Other cell doors ran along each side of the corridor, offset so they didn't face each other. From where she stood, the corridor looked the same in either direction and her muddy mind had trouble deciding which direction to take.

Bishop was taken with how silent the place was and as she strained to listen the faint sound of trickling water came to her ears. She was suddenly aware of how dry her mouth felt. If nothing else, the thought of quenching her thirst and washing away foul taste that coated her tongue gave her the direction she needed.

She closed the cell door, locked it again and removed the key. It would be difficult to check on her cell if the key wasn't in the lock.

Using the wall as occasional support, Bishop made her way along the corridor towards the sound of the water. After about fifty shaky steps the corridor turned a corner. Another twenty paces later it opened into a junction of four corridors, just large enough to hold a small fountain in the centre that ran with beautifully clear water.

Checking in each direction first, Bishop drank her fill from one of the spouts then plunged her head into the cold water rippling in the fountain's basin, holding her breath for quite a while.

It was much more refreshing than she'd anticipated and very different to the brain-freeze effect she'd expected. Her mind cleared, she felt completely refreshed and invigorated but also a little embarrassed that her mind hadn't been clear enough to use her earth magic to heal her befuddled state. She would have happily kept her head under the water all day it felt so good, but she withdrew it quickly when her lungs demanded air.

She squeezed out the majority of the water from her hair as she drew in a series of deep breaths. Although she now knew she'd be able to open a portal, fleeing wasn't going to get her the answers she needed and she was eager to find them.

The sound of approaching footsteps caught her attention and she snapped her head in that direction. A number of light boots marched along the stone floor of one of the corridors and were rapidly getting closer. Bishop crouched down and hid behind the base of the fountain, waiting for the advancing Fae.

The marching feet entered the junction from one corridor and left down the adjoining corridor, shifting their direction through a right angle, cutting the corner opposite Bishop's position. She risked a look over the lip of the fountain and saw two guards escorting a Fae woman dressed in a red robe. She moved reluctantly, her mind elsewhere, and they pushed and dragged her constantly to keep her moving in the direction they wanted.

At the second cell along the corridor they stopped

and one of the guards unlocked the door. The woman registered her surroundings for the first time and immediately shrank away from the cell door with horror, looking around wildly, fearful of the guards, trying to twist away from them.

"Why am I being imprisoned?" she asked.

"You questioned the actions of Lord Ealvun," the guard holding her replied.

"I only wanted to know the fate of my child."

"The exchange is concluded," said the other guard, swinging the door fully open. "It is an honour to be the mother of the changeling."

Bishop's eyes widened and she had to put her hand over her mouth to stop herself from gasping. Things began falling into place in her mind. There hadn't been a changeling for more than a hundred years — no wonder they wanted her out of the way.

"You were ordered to forget about your child," the first guard added. "Why do you persist in questioning the Lord's will?"

"I know not why," the woman said, her eyes darting from one to the other. "I had little feeling for the boy until I gave him up. Alas, it was too late. I thought Lord Ealvun would bestow upon me the task of caring for the human child."

"Enough!" The second guard grabbed her arm and his companion firmed his grip at the other side. They threw her into the cell in spite of her attempts to resist but she immediately tried to flee it before they could close the door. They grappled with her for a moment before carrying her into the small room.

Bishop immediately dashed along the corridor, ignoring the sounds of the woman being slapped, then slammed the cell door closed and twisted the key in the lock. She paused for a moment, thinking of the woman in the cell with the two guards, but when they began pounding on the door she removed the key and stepped away. They all deserved imprisonment. The woman had been part of a plan to steal a human child after all.

One of the guards pushed his face to the small grille set into the door. His anger briefly replaced by surprise as he caught sight of Bishop glaring at him. "Release us, mortal! The Lord must not be disturbed until dawn."

"Anyone who steals a child doesn't get to choose," Bishop said. "You can all rot in here for your part in this."

She closed the small hatch and walked away, ignoring the muffled shouts from the cell, the laughter of the woman. Now she knew what the increased Fae activity had been about.

Bishop headed in the direction the trio had come from. The corridor led, via a number of twists and turns, to a locked, brass gate; the exit from the dungeon. Through the bars was a modest room and she could see a low table and a couple of chairs. There was no sign of any other guards, but across the room, opposite the gate, was a spiral staircase leading up.

Bishop tried each of the keys she carried but neither of them opened the gate. She crouched down and looked into the lock — she'd have to manipulate the tumblers directly this time. Reaching into one of her pockets, she took hold of one of the earth gems and drew on a little of its power. She didn't want to use too much in case she needed it later. Still invigorated from the fountain water, it took less than a minute for her to unlock the gate, cross the room and start climbing the stairs.

At the top, the spiral staircase opened onto a wide corridor and she nearly rose into the view of a pair of Fae; a willowy woman of almost unimaginable beauty and, in complete contrast, a huge troll. Thankfully, they appeared to be distracted and she was able to duck back out of sight before being seen.

The troll sniffed the air and his stomach rumbled long and loud. "I thought we'd left the infant behind, but human smell is everywhere. It's making me hungry."

"Control yourself, you imbecile," the woman said. "At the moment of dawn, my Lord will consume the child alive and we will begin our orgy." She became a little thoughtful and licked her lips as she smiled wickedly. "It's been so long since our last changeling, the two of us may well re-define the meaning of wanton lust." She grinned wider still and shuddered with anticipation, which only enhanced her beauty further. "I must get to my chambers to prepare."

"Lady Calista, about Lady Florienta..."

"You think I wish to discuss a love rival before taking part in a changeling orgy? We shall talk about it after."

"But..."

The two disappeared around a corner and their conversation became unclear then eventually inaudible, which allowed Bishop to leave the stairwell and continue. She took the direction from which the two had first approached. She didn't know how long it was until dawn but she had little time to save the child.

The corridor ended in a pair of ornately carved double doors and Bishop pressed an ear to them. Either there was nothing to hear or the doors muffled any sound extremely well.

The doors were unlocked and she opened one of them a crack, the heavy wood moving easily on perfect hinges, and held her breath. The hint of a familiar smell, just at the edge of recognition, drifted through as she pushed one eye to the opening and looked into the room beyond. What she could see of the chamber suggested it was empty so she pushed the door open wider and stuck her head inside. When she saw it was empty of any Fae, she slipped through and closed the door behind her.

There was a large fire pit in the centre of the room, surrounded by a variety of sofas strewn with cushions and throws. Gold and silver inlays adorned every decorative feature, as did jewels and gems in a multitude of hues. Unfortunately, however, the decor appeared to have been put together by an interior designer with no sense of design, taste or colour. What should have been an ostentatious delight looked garish and cheap.

Bishop looked around quickly then moved towards an archway to her right. As she did so she caught another whiff of the familiar odour. This time it was stronger and she identified it instantly — the unpleasant, milky smell of an infant's vomit.

Hurrying through the archway she found another door and pressed her ear to the wood. The gentle sobs of a baby brought a slight lump to her throat at the thought of what it had endured.

The door opened easily on her touch and she stepped through.

The child was in the centre of the room and lay in what appeared to be some kind of ceremonial crib; a design in gold that resembled a woven basket. Next to this was a sharp ceremonial knife and a large, ancient bowl of dark, beaten gold. Bishop shuddered at the sight and tried to stop her mind thinking the thoughts the items suggested following the words of Lady Calista.

She moved closer and peered at the poor mite. His distress had gotten the better of him to the point where his wails had given out and fallen into simple sobbing. His primitive emotions were torn between hunger and exhaustion.

As much as Bishop would have liked to do so, she was unable to feed the child. Instead, she removed the fully charged gem from her pocket and draped its chain around the child before wrapping his blanket tightly once more, hiding the gem from view. She picked him up to comfort him and spoke a brief chant.

"Earth Spirits, shield this child."

Almost immediately the baby stopped his sobbing and fell asleep. Although not nourished by the gem he was made comfortable by the earth energy that now diffused slowly and warmly through him.

A wave of longing washed over her and Bishop hugged him to her breast as if she didn't want to let go. She closed her eyes and rocked him gently, soothing herself as much as the baby, and deep within her something began to stir. Bishop opened her eyes wide, sudden concern flitting across them.

"Baby..." A child-like whisper in her mind. "Baby, beautiful baby..."

"Not now!" She spoke aloud through clenched teeth.

"Our baby!" the voice responded and for a moment Bishop was sure she was going to lose control.

Calling on her earth energy, Bishop forced the waking essence within her back into slumber and knew she had to hasten in case it began to wake once more. Reluctantly she placed the infant back into the crib, took the remaining gem into her hand and drew on every last drop of its power.

Spreading her arms wide she created an image of her home in her mind and linked the earth energy directly to it. She then pushed out that energy and used it to form a portal large enough to step through.

With a huge sense of relief, Bishop turned to pick up the baby again and found she couldn't move, frozen in a pose in which she had begun to reach for the baby. Out of the corner of her eye she could see that Lord Ealvun had entered the room and must have cast a spell on her to hold her rigid. The muddiness had returned to her mind but less extreme than it had previously been. She had to keep it clear for the child's sake and breathed deeply, though it was a struggle.

Ealvun walked around to where she could see him properly and he folded his arms across his chest as her regarded her.

"Did you think I wouldn't know when you interfered with the child?" he asked. "Do you regard your trinket as a match for the magic of an immortal?"

Being immobile, Bishop couldn't answer, so she ignored the question and desperately tried to hold open the portal, hoping for the chance to gather up the child and whisk him away from here, but it was rapidly becoming impossible to do so. She looked down at the baby and used its innocent face as a focus while fighting against her magical restraint. But no matter how she tried it was to no avail and the portal vanished, taking the last of her earth energy with it.

With the portal gone Ealvun released his hold on Bishop and she nearly fell over. She caught herself and immediately picked up the child, pulling it close to her.

"By all means comfort him, for all the good it will do," Ealvun said. "You are in my home and come the dawn you will relinquish the child so I can feast."

"I know the Fae stoop pretty low, but harming a child simply for pleasure beats everything in the depravity stakes." Bishop glared at him and he laughed.

"What does one child matter?" he smirked. "Humankind has done far worse to its own people, children included."

"I agree, but that does not mitigate your intended action in any way." She seethed as she spoke. "He has parents who love him."

"We left a substitute in his place."

"A changeling!"

"Indeed so! A very fair trade."

"A baby that will tear at its new mother's breasts as no human child or even beast of the field would do. A child that will grow up different and outcast, shunned so badly it will develop into a bully and likely turn into a tormented killer."

Ealvun nodded and smiled, lightly stroking his chin with the tips of his fingers. "I never realised you knew us so well."

He strode to the window and looked out at the moon, his hands clasped behind his back, almost tempting Bishop to attack him.

"Everything you say is true," he said. "But do you know the most wonderful part?"

Bishop looked daggers at his back but said nothing.

Ealvun turned very casually and laughed. "There is nothing you can do to stop it happening."

Assault the Castle

Pope and Finlay were making surprisingly good time, covering the ground faster than Pope could have hoped. The castle loomed closer with every passing minute; spookily so.

"How are we travelling so fast, Sam?" Pope asked as he ran.

"Distance is a bit subjective here," Finlay replied, his mallet held over his shoulder carefully so the iron didn't touch him. "Ten miles can become one and vice versa. We're lucky this is Midsummer. If it was the other end of the year we'd take forever to get there."

Pope ran with the baby nestled inside his shirt and supported by his left arm. He wouldn't dare run like this with a human child but Fae children were much tougher. The little blighter had even bitten his chest a few times and drawn blood. He was tempted to give it a rock to chew on.

They crested a sharp rise and were suddenly assaulted by a raucous sound that rose from the valley between them and the castle gate, now just a half mile away.

The whole vale was filled with Faerie folk of all kinds, celebrating Midsummer. They were illuminated by moonlight, light globes of all colours, candles, bonfires and lanterns. They ate and drank, made music and love, danced and cavorted, laughed and fought. There were clothes in a mixture of fashions, from simple tunics to flowing silk robes embroidered with gold and studded with gems. In equal measure, there was also the most basic of attire — sheer nudity.

The people of the realm were out in force and partying in a manner that assaulted the senses in every way imaginable. Satyrs and centaurs drank together, pixies rained magical dust as they flew here, there and everywhere, trolls arm-wrestled with ogres or took part in dwarf-tossing contests and woodland spirits spread their bounty wherever they walked, saplings springing up in their wake. The valley was carpeted with a magnificent display of wondrous creatures.

"What was that about luck?" Pope asked.

Finlay shrugged.

"Is everyone in Faerie gathered here?"

"Just those who live on Ealvun's estates."

"Can we go round?"

"We don't have time," Finlay replied. "Follow me and keep the child hidden. At least the castle will be empty."

He strode down the hill, his long legs covering the ground quickly and Pope could barely keep up without running. They were soon in amongst the partying creatures and judging by Finlay's body language and determined stride, Pope realised his friend wasn't going to pause or deviate from his direct course to the castle's gate.

A pixie flew close and prepared to spread dust over the pair but Finlay batted it away with the back of his free hand as if the creature was simply an annoying wasp.

Many of the creatures moved out of the way of Finlay's determined march but a number of them were either preoccupied with other matters or refused to do so. Most were dealt with by stepping over their bodies or pushing them out of the way, but a couple of times Finlay was forced to trample on a few creatures in order to continue his progress and Pope was given no option but to do the same. In spite of the danger he was enjoying himself.

With just a hundred yards to go to the castle gate, a troll wandered directly into Finlay's path and spread his arms wide, a big, broken-toothed grin on his face and a huge mug of ale in one hand. He was a good foot taller than Finlay and almost twice as broad.

"Samuel," he bellowed.

Without breaking stride, Finlay let the battle mallet fall from his should and used the momentum of its descent to swing it back and then round in what seemed to Pope to be a very casual manner. His timing was perfect and as he reached the troll the mallet made a resounding contact with the side of his head and knocked him ten feet to one side. All of those nearby creatures who saw the action burst into laughter then carried on with their partying as if the blow had simply been another part of the fun. The troll was only stunned but the side of his face was already blistering where the iron-shod mallet had made contact.

"Do you know him, Sam?"

"My grandfather. We don't have time for a family reunion."

"I guess not." Pope was amazed at the blow Finlay had delivered and looked over at the big troll. He'd landed on a slender looking dryad who was now having difficulty extricating herself from beneath his huge bulk and screamed in indignation.

A few moments later they were clear of the mass of partying creatures and standing before the bridge that crossed the huge moat surrounding the castle. Barring their way was a tall but slender swordsman wearing studded leather armour and thigh-high boots; everything was highly polished and glinted in the moonlight.

"I am Kealin, Lord Ealvun's champion. Neither of you

may proceed any further."

Finlay turned to Pope. "I cannot fight Kealin. If I defeat him I will become Ealvun's champion and that's not something I want."

"I understand," Pope said. "Leave him to me. Here, take the child."

Finlay took the Fae infant from inside Pope's shirt and was surprised by how much blood his bites had brought forth. Pope shrugged and gave Finlay a look he hoped showed confidence. Finlay nodded.

Pope turned to face Kealin and they both drew their swords. The Fae's blade was little more than a rapier and looked to made of silver. Pope swung his own blade around to demonstrate its superior weight and size. Kealin smiled and lunged.

Their swords clashed in earnest and Pope was surprised at the force with which the small blade impacted his own. He'd expected the Fae sword to buckle under the weight of his own, but instead his whole arm tingled from the shock. He knew that he couldn't handle too many blows of that nature — the fight had to be won quickly.

He pushed in closer and the champion brought his sword swiftly around, but Pope caught the slender blade on his own. The tip of the silver weapon nicked Pope's shoulder, drawing a little blood and Pope cried out in pain at the touch of the silver. As the simple touch of iron pains the Fae, so does the touch of silver to those from the Shadow Dominium.

The Fae's eyes widened with delight, his confidence rising further. Pope had made this sacrifice deliberately and used his opponent's momentum to twist them about, pivot his weapon against the other and bring the flat of the blade against Kealin's face.

The Fae champion screamed at the contact of the iron

in the sword and pushed Pope and his weapon away from him. Pope used this momentum to slide his sword back along the length of the Fae blade and, twisting his hand awkwardly, sliced into the back of Kealin's hand with the keen edge of the sword's tip. He screamed again and dropped his sword.

Pope stepped forward and stamped on the silver sword but Kealin gestured towards him and a magical force knocked Pope backwards off his feet. He managed to land without skewering himself on his sword but looked up at the Fae swordsman and scowled.

"Very well," he said. "You changed the rules and the gloves are coming off."

Using his free hand, Pope scooped some of the blood that oozed from his chest wounds and flicked it into the face of his rapidly approaching opponent. "*Braench ach fo margant.*"

Kealin screamed and his head whipped backward as if he'd suddenly been struck by a large roof timber wielded by a giant. Each droplet of blood on his face had been pushed into the flesh by Pope's magic. It was like being poked in the face with the ends of numerous steel rods of different sizes, the finest of the droplets piercing his flesh like needles. As he tumbled backwards his own blood began to flow down his face, black and viscous.

Pope leaped to his feet and prepared to swipe at the downed Fae but the champion had trained himself well over the countless years of his existence and was quick to deflect the thrust. The steel sword gouged a large chunk out of the wooden bridge beside the man's head.

Using Fae magic again, Kealin knocked Pope's sword from his hand and swept his own sword at the blood wizard's head. Pope ducked, rolled to one side and onto his feet in a single, smooth movement. Kealin followed swiftly, preventing Pope from regaining his weapon. The

Fae champion advanced with a snide grin upon his face — there was nothing Pope could do.

"Josh, catch!"

Pope looked towards Finlay and saw that the big man had thrown the battle mallet to him. "Bugger me." He knew he'd only have one chance at this before he'd be skewer meat for the Fae.

As the mallet flew towards him, he snatched the handle out of the air with both hands and used its momentum to spin around in a complete circle and connect the heavy weapon with the champion's sword arm. Not only was Kealin knocked to the floor, his arm was paralysed and his rapier fell from his grasp. Pope dropped the mallet, pounced on his own sword and raised it above his head to plunge into the injured Fae who appeared to accept his fate. He waited for the blow with honour.

However, an inch from the champion's face the tip of the blade stopped. In Pope's mind he was suddenly thrown back to a time over two thousand years earlier when his sister had urged him to deliver the killing blow in a similar situation. He'd refused then, too.

"Do you agree that I have defeated you in combat?" Pope asked, pushing the memory away.

"Indeed so," said Kealin. "Now deliver the killing stroke."

"There is no need for further bloodshed, providing you agree to leave me to my business while I'm here in your realm."

"You make no claim upon my champion status?"

"I have no interest in doing so."

"Then I agree. I give you my word."

Pope removed the sword from Kealin's face and helped him to his feet. Behind the champion, Finlay picked up his mallet and hit the Fae on the head knocking him out.

"He gave us his word, Sam," Pope said, astonished.

"He gave *you* his word. I'm taking precautions."

"Fair enough."

Pope sheathed his sword and ran into the castle with Finlay. They paused just inside the main doors and Finlay used his nose to pick up the human baby's scent again. He set off at a run and Pope followed once more.

The castle was a warren of corridors and rooms but Finlay guided them through, following the scent easily. How they'd find their way out again, Pope wasn't so sure.

They burst into the child's chamber and immediately came to a halt, taking in the room and its current occupants.

"Faye!" Pope exclaimed, drawing his sword and turning his focus to the other Fae in the room.

"How did you get here?" Bishop asked.

"Sam knows a few tricks." Pope grinned. "We're going to do a reverse changeling."

"Never mind that," Finlay said. Lord Ealvun and his two guards approached them with swords drawn.

"Did you best my champion?" Ealvun asked.

Pope shrugged. "We had a little confrontation and he's now taking a nap."

Finlay gave the Fae child to Bishop and turned to face the two guards, swinging his mallet as he did so. The guards stopped their advance and watched the big weapon nervously.

Pope saw the choice his friend had made. "Thanks, Sam. Take the easy option, why don't you."

Ealvun lowered his sword. "This course of action will be rather unwise on your part. I suggest you take the changeling and return home. Forget the human child — its parents have already done so."

"Of course, silly me," Pope said. "We didn't really

come all this way to save the baby." He rolled his eyes in a pantomime fashion to drive home his sarcasm. "Tell me, Lord Ealvun — why would we do that?"

"I would imagine that even you would prefer to avoid an incident between Faerie and The Shadow Dominion."

Pope laughed. "The Dominion disowned me over two thousand years ago when I refused the urging of my sister to take a life."

"Do you expect me to believe that this has remained an undiscovered fact until now?" The scorn on Ealvun's face was tinged with doubt.

"Looks like your intelligence gathering needs some improvement." Pope smiled with a clear thought flitting across his face. "I'm a free agent, Ealvun. And as such I declare myself the child's champion."

"You will fight me for a mere child?"

"Don't give me your false surprise. You knew from the outset that I would stop you."

"I knew that you would try," Ealvun said. "You have yet to do so."

"If I defeat you," Pope said, his eyes narrowing. "You will allow me to return to Earth with the human child and no repercussions."

"I agree. But if you fail to accomplish this before dawn the child will remain mine to do with as I wish."

"Big mistake, my friend." Pope glared and swung his sword in readiness. "That's exactly the encouragement I need."

Ealvun raised his own sword and shifted the balance of his weight. He had a feline grace and a calm body language that Pope knew would be difficult to read. They circled each other in a clockwise fashion.

Meanwhile, Finlay approached the two guards and dispatched them quickly with the mallet, taking a couple of blows from their swords in the process.

With the swiftness of a big cat striking, Ealvun lunged. But as Pope made to block the blow the Fae altered the direction of his sweep and avoided Pope's sword altogether, hacking at his side. Pope had been expecting some kind of feint and grabbed the Lord's wrist with his free hand. The Faerie sword still hit Pope but not with the force Ealvun had intended. It cut the fabric of Pope's shirt and broke the skin. The wound was superficial, although the silver in the sword caused it to burn like fury.

Blocking out the pain, Pope pulled Ealvun's sword arm to the side and made to strike with his own blade, but the Lord grabbed his wrist in return, gripping much harder than his build would suggest. They looked into each other's eyes and Ealvun grinned like he'd just got the very thing he wanted. What was going on?

It struck Pope like a blow that the Fae didn't need to win outright, he just needed to keep him busy until dawn broke and he'd walked right into the Fae's planned stalemate. He couldn't release Ealvun's wrist for fear of a killing blow and the Lord wouldn't let go for the same reason.

"Sod this," Pope snarled and brought his knee swiftly up into his opponent's groin. Immortal or not, a swift blow to the nether regions would always bring a man down.

Ealvun collapsed to his knees gasping for breath and leaning on his sword as support. "You play dirty, Pope."

Bishop had watched the brief battle closely and was outraged. "You steal a human child with the intention of consuming him and you think Josh plays dirty? Get some perspective."

Ealvun began to recover so Pope swapped his sword to his left hand and punched him in the face. He fell back a little so Pope punched him again and he sprawled on the floor. Pope kicked him in the chest for good measure and in spite of the Fae's toughness he heard the snap of a rib or two.

The blood wizard pressed his booted foot on Ealvun's neck and raised his sword, aiming it for his head, but as he brought it down the Fae grabbed the blade in both hands and screamed. Not only did the sharp edges cut into his flesh, the iron burned him badly. But he couldn't let go.

"You win," Ealvun gasped. "Take the child."

Pope had other plans and pushed down on the sword with his weight behind it and the sword's tip moved closer to Ealvun's face.

"Josh!" Bishop yelled. "Leave him!"

Pope paused reluctantly then pulled his sword away from the Fae Lord who released the blade, his hands a bloody, burning mess. Pope bent and wiped the blade on Ealvun's tunic.

Bishop looked at Pope. "Should we take both children?"

"That's not a good idea," Finlay interrupted, walking over. "Lord Ealvun would put a price upon your heads."

Bishop nodded. She understood that the Faerie idea of justice and fair trade was weird at best, so swapped over the children, placing the Fae child into the crib and lifting the human child in her arms. However, the instant she did so a shriek of horror sounded from elsewhere in the castle.

In her rooms, Lady Calista screamed. "No!" The sound echoed all the way down the corridors to the Lord's chambers. "No, no, no!"

Echoing her horror at this sudden reversal, knowing the changeling ritual was being undone, the partying creatures in the valley outside also sensed the change and bellowed their outrage as one. The noise of their anger assaulted the castle, followed in turn by a powerful wave of emotion that swept over the three like a tsunami. Bishop and Finlay staggered and Pope winced at the intensity.

On the floor, Ealvun laughed. "Good luck getting to the gateway before dawn."

"You bastard!" Bishop said and kicked him in the head.

"Faye, you can open a portal," Pope said. "You can get us back in no time."

"I can't, Josh. I've used up all my earth energy and have nothing left." She looked forlorn. "We're trapped here."

Transfer of Power

Bishop and Pope stared at each other a little helplessly. Had they come so close only to run out of options? Finlay walked over and pointed at the baby. "What's wrong with that one?"

Bishop looked — the earth gem she'd hung around the baby's neck had slipped from the child's blanket and was clearly in view. "I set a spell to protect him. It can't be removed for seven days."

"What would happen if you did?" Pope looked at the child and scratched his head.

"The energy would be released in a single burst. I dread to think what would become of the poor thing if that happened." Bishop hugged the baby even closer.

"You're the smart ones," Finlay said. "Think of something!" He looked towards the doors nervously. Through them the sound of an approaching horde was growing steadily louder.

"Bar the door, Sam," Pope said. "The arrival of dawn isn't our only worry."

As Finlay moved over to the door, Bishop paced back and forth. The child began to whimper, sensing her unease. "I'm so cut off from the Earth's energy, here. If we could only find another source of it we'd be free. I don't even have enough to heal you and stop your bleeding."

Pope's head shot up and he looked at Bishop with enlightenment spreading across his face. For a moment there was hope. Then it was gone and his mood was worse than before. "Damn!"

"Josh, what is it?" Bishop was puzzled.

Pope watched Finlay bar the door then turned back to her. "I could transfer blood energy using my magic, but the only way to make it work here is to use Fae blood."

Finlay stepped over to Ealvun and grabbed him roughly by his finely embroidered tunic. "We have plenty of Fae blood here."

"No good, Sam. It needs to be freely given."

Dropping the Fae Lord again, Finlay approached Pope and bared his arm. "Take mine. I'm part Fae."

Pope looked at Bishop and then back at Finlay. "It's too dangerous, Sam. Because the Fae in you is three-quarters diluted I'd need buckets of the stuff to make the spell work."

"So? This is my mess to put right." Finlay clenched his teeth, breathed deeply and looked at Bishop. "You'd better heal me fast when we get back."

"Of course." Bishop smiled warmly at Finlay. He had a heart that more than matched his size.

Pope set about it in an instant. He grabbed the ceremonial knife and bowl then cut into the vein in the crook of Finlay's left arm. The blood flowed swiftly and Pope held the bowl beneath Finlay's arm to catch every drop.

In spite of a good flow, the bowl seemed to take an age to fill and they were all aware of the rising noise — the party crowd were getting closer. They could do nothing but stare at the bowl and will it to fill more quickly.

They each jumped at the sudden loud banging on the door of the chamber — the general sound of the mob hadn't seemed close enough to have reached the chambers. Although the door had muffled the chants and threats, direct pounding on it had sounded loudly.

"Let me in, you vile mortals!" Calista screamed. "The child cannot be returned, he's ours."

Pope looked at the bowl then at Finlay's face, which was becoming a little ashen. "We need to do it now. Sam, bend your arm tight and take the baby from Faye."

Finlay rolled his shirt sleeve down until it reached the incision then bent his arm to wedge it in place and staunch the bleeding. He swayed a little but caught himself and planted his feet as if trying to grip the floor with his toes.

Bishop looked at him warily but passed the baby over very carefully, knowing that she had no other choice. She knelt before the bowl that Pope had now placed on the floor.

"Put your hands in the blood."

She did what Pope said and the blood almost rose to the brim. She felt a slight tingle from the unpleasant energy it contained — blood magic generally gave her the creeps. Pope closed his eyes and began to chant.

"*Braench delan fo ree calcen.*

"*Braench as mel ach fortisc.*"

He repeated the chant over and over but nothing appeared to happen. Bishop felt a slight increase in the tingling but the transfer of power didn't take place. She jumped again as an even greater pounding sounded on the door.

"Let me in, humans!" It was the troll Bishop had seen earlier with Calista. After getting no reply he beat on the door with more ferocity and, although strongly barred it creaked on its hinges.

Pope opened his eyes without breaking the chant but looked at Bishop with a worried expression. Even though Finlay's blood was only a quarter Fae there should still have been more progress. The troll outside the door pounded harder and Pope knew he had little time to complete the transfer.

"Hurry, Josh," Finlay said and slumped to one knee in order to keep from falling or dropping the baby. He was fading fast.

Then Pope's eyes lit up as he continued chanting. He drew a vial from his pocket that contained the remainder of the Fae blood he'd used earlier. There was little remaining but they had nothing to lose. He pulled the stopper from the vial and poured it into the bowl, shaking every last drop from the tiny bottle.

Acting like a catalyst, the pure Fae blood triggered a visible reaction in the red liquid and Pope closed his eyes again, building up the rhythm of his chant with urgency and increased passion.

The surface of the blood rippled with peculiar standing wave patterns and the red liquid retreated a little from Bishop's wrists, resisting her natural earth aura before embracing it and flowing up her arms, coating them with dark red.

Bishop felt the energy enter her body. It was like nothing she'd ever experienced and it immediately fought for release. It was alien and exotic. It filled her with dread yet gave her a high she struggled to keep control of. It made her happy but caused her to weep. It rushed from head to toe and back again, flowing around her body, following the paths of her circulatory system like an express locomotive. It filled her to excess and still it came.

Her body gorged on this new energy, consuming it, changing it to the kind of natural energy she was used to, charging every cell of her body with an earth energy flavoured with the tang of iron.

She shrieked with pain and joy. Her teeth ached and her legs spasmed as if wanting to dance all night and she immediately knew she'd taken enough of it.

She pulled her hands from the bowl of blood and leapt to her feet just as the door to the chamber began to splinter and a large fist punched a hole through it. When the troll pushed his face through the hole Pope picked up Finlay's battle mallet, ran to the door and smacked the creature with as much strength as he could muster. It's nose spread across its face and it screamed from the touch of the iron.

Pope stood by the door and yelled at Bishop. "Faye, do it now!"

She raised her hands in front of her and created the portal in an instant; far more quickly than she'd ever done before. The strange energy had unlocked something new inside of her.

Grabbing the baby from Finlay she urged him to his feet. He was weak and could barely stand but all he had to do was get through the portal with her.

Ignoring the pain he was in, the troll at the door reached through the hole and groped for the bar that kept it closed.

"Josh, come on!" Bishop shouted.

He brought the mallet down on the trolls fingers for good measure before legging it over to the portal.

The door behind him flew open, but as soon as Pope grabbed Bishop's arm the three of them, along with the baby, stepped through the portal with the troll racing towards them.

For a moment they hung in the void between the place they'd left and their destination, stepping through in apparent slow motion.

Bishop had never experienced anything quite as prolonged as this before. She'd always known the void existed but even at the slowest of times it had only ever been a fraction of a second. Now it felt like it was going to take forever. Had the strange, blood-earth energy caused this effect, or was it down to the fact that they were travelling between Faerie and Earth? But as much as she'd love to know, now was not the time to ponder such matters.

The troll reached into the portal, hoping to grab the baby from Bishop's grasp but his huge hand also moved in slow motion as it passed the portal entrance into the void. Yet in spite of the slowness it was getting closer, reaching for the baby. Grasping closer still...

Then the three, along with the baby, abruptly stepped into one of Bishop's rooms at home and their motion returned to normal. She closed the portal immediately and the troll's hand thudded to the floor, severed at the wrist, leaking its tarry blood onto one of the rugs, still twitching. Finlay collapsed into a chair and fell unconscious.

"Josh, take the child home," Bishop said. "Samuel needs me to heal him."

She held out the baby and most of the blood that had been on her arms had been transferred to the child's blanket. Pope grabbed a towel from a nearby pile of clean laundry that hadn't been put away.

"I can't take him like that. Let's swap."

They juggled the baby carefully and soon had the infant looking more presentable.

"Don't forget," Bishop said. "He must wear that gem for seven days.

Pope nodded and cradled the infant as gently as he could then left the house without further hesitation.

Bishop quickly washed the drying blood from her hands in the bathroom next door then returned with a look of concern for her big friend. She grabbed another gem from her now low supply and drew on the earth energy within, enjoying the comfort of its familiarity. It was like she'd moved back into her proper body once more, her heart and lungs free of pain and pressure.

Kneeling on the floor in front of Finlay's chair, Bishop grabbed hold of his hands and began the work of healing the incision and helping his body replenish its supply of blood. The former was a moment's task but the latter was much more difficult — not only was he a big man, his Fae heritage resisted her earth magic. She was forced to constantly counter his natural defences as she healed him, thankful that he was only part troll.

Ten minutes later he opened his eyes.

"I'm hungry," he said and Bishop smiled.

"I'll get you something." She rose from the floor and left the room.

"Something big," Finlay called out.

Pope turned into the street that housed the child's home and immediately saw the police officer stationed outside. The parents had obviously called the police when he'd taken the Fae child they mistakenly thought was theirs. It was only to be expected.

The child was getting restless and Pope needed to place the young boy in its crib very quickly. He could have done without the complications of the police, who would insist the child was taken straight to the hospital.

He turned about and entered the narrow alley that ran behind the houses, parallel to the street. It wasn't difficult to find the right house — it was the only one burning lights at this early hour. He quietly lifted the sneck of the back gate and entered the small garden, planted with a mixture of vegetables and flowers.

The back door of the house was locked but Pope still

had enough blood oozing from his wounds that it was a simple task to open it with one of his spells.

Through the kitchen he crept and into the narrow hallway that led past the open door to the living room. Pope peered around the door frame and saw two detectives talking to Morris and Ethel. He recognised one of them as Roland Tench, a man he and Bishop had once worked with and recently promoted to Detective Sergeant. The other looked green — fresh out of training, probably. Under normal circumstances he'd have gladly entered the room but time was of the essence.

Standing to one side was a Catholic priest, Father Martin, at whom Morris cast resentful glances. The priest was the only one looking towards the door and he almost called out before Pope silenced him with a finger to his lips. The magician took his chance to sweep past the door and up the stairs as quickly and quietly as he could.

There was no illumination in the child's room but the light from the landing was enough and Pope laid the baby down in his crib, smiling as he did so. The child seemed to sense that it was home and gave a satisfied gurgle before falling straight to sleep.

For a moment the crib was lit by a glowing sphere that spread out from the child to a size just large enough to encompass him fully. Pope fancied that he sensed the breaking of a powerful connection and a calm settling on the city like the sudden passing of a storm. The Fae presence in York was gone in an instant and the sphere faded to nothing.

Pope was about to leave the room when he heard the detectives enter the narrow hallway and open the front door. They promised they would do everything they could to find the baby. Then the door closed with a bang behind them.

In his crib the child jumped at the noise and began

crying. His parents immediately thundered up the stairs and into the room, followed after a moment by Father Martin. Ethel immediately went over to the crib and picked up the child, hugging him tightly to her breast. Morris switched on the light and both parents looked at Pope nervously, particularly with the state of his bloody shirt and the wounds beneath. Morris's anger was building, as was Ethel's fear, but Father Martin stepped up to them with a consoling word and a comforting hand on each of their shoulders. The tension fled immediately but Morris shrugged off the priest's hand.

Ethel looked at the baby then at Pope, her eyes filling with tears. "You were right. Now I can see that other child wasn't ours."

"I said I'd bring him back," Pope said. He watched Morris who was uncertain what he should do and the poor man looked a little helpless.

"We can't tell you how grateful we are," Ethel said.

"Did you call the police?" Pope asked.

"I did," Father Martin said. "I've known DS Tench for some time and thought he might help. Seems that the child was in safe hands."

Pope nodded and looked away.

Morris groped for the right words to say. "I don't understand. The cops seemed to know what was going on."

"The world is stranger than many realise," Martin said. "Some officers in the force are familiar with matters of a more peculiar nature."

Morris looked bewildered for a moment then stared directly at Pope. "Thank you, mister." The words caught in the young man's throat and he fought back tears of relief. He moved over to his wife and child and hugged them. The weight of the world lifted from his shoulders.

"What really happened?" Ethel asked. "It all seems

such a blur."

"I saved your child from some nasty people," Pope replied. "Let's leave it at that." He looked through the window and saw the first light of dawn.

"What about the other baby?"

"Unfortunately, he's been returned to where he belongs."

Ethel nodded then looked adoringly at her baby. "Our little darling is back. That's what counts."

"Father Martin explained everything, but it must be impossible," Morris said. "It feels like the world's gone mad."

"Not mad," Martin said. "Just different. I'm always available if you need me."

"We're not Catholics," Morris said.

"That hardly matters."

"Is there anything we can do to thank you?" Ethel asked of Pope.

"That's not necessary," Pope replied. "He's a child who's back with his mum and dad. There is nothing else."

"But you're bleeding."

Pope waved his hand dismissively. "I'll live."

Morris grabbed Pope's hand and shook it vigorously. "Thank you again, Mr...?"

"Just call me Joshua."

"We're Morris and Ethel Drax. And our son is called Arthur."

"A grand name, Arthur Drax," Pope said and stroked the child's face tenderly. He made to leave the room then turned around in the doorway. "By the way, it's vital you leave the gem on the child for at least seven days. It will protect him from further harm."

"Will they come back?" Ethel was suddenly horrified.

"Not if you keep the gem on him," Pope replied. "It contains protective magic. Beyond a week and they cannot return."

Pope left the house quickly and didn't look back. He'd even make sure he avoided this area of the town for a while. But as he walked down the street he began to whistle. Then he had to stop doing so when a broad smile split his whole face in two.

The following night, Ethel sat in a rickety old chair beside the baby's cot watching him sleep until tiredness overtook her and she closed her eyes with her head slumped on her chest. Morris had gone to bed hours earlier.

Arthur opened his eyes and giggled. Upon his forehead a previously invisible Fae symbol flared into green luminescence, a glow that was echoed in his eyes for a second. In the Fae realm, the would-be changeling infant, now in the care of a reluctant goblin wet-nurse, bore a duplicate of the symbol on its own forehead, its own eyes aglow with an eerie light. For a moment the two babies, separated by the gulf between the two universes, gurgled and moved as one. Then Arthur's small hand grasped the gem that hung about his neck and the power it contained surged into his body in a single, steady discharge.

For a few minutes his tiny body spasmed and shook, his eyes screwed tightly closed, his mouth pulled wide in a toothless grimace. Whatever strange sensations coursed through his body, pain wasn't amongst them. The cot rattled lightly with the motions of his body and his little feet kicked off the blanket that covered him.

Then it was over, his body relaxed and his eyes opened again, glowing brightly still for a few seconds before fading to normal. The Fae symbol on his forehead disappeared, too, leaving no mark visible to the human eye.

As if from nowhere, a disembodied voice, not unlike that of the Fae Lord, whispered to the child. "Sleep well, Arthur Stuart Morris Oswald Drax."

Part Three

Close Friends

Kitty Spender

2011, spring

In the Golden Woolsack, Bishop watched Pope take a sip of his beer and shook her head in annoyance. A situation was never so bad that he couldn't waste time having a beer. The fact that there was a drink for her, too, was doubly annoying.

She turned her attention to the pulverised window and stared hard. In spite of the force with which Pope had blasted it, there was hardly any debris on the floor or on the nearby tables and chairs. It clung to the barrier like a high-speed snapshot taken mid-blast.

Bishop moved closer. Slowly. Something about the way it remained in place bothered her. A shiver ran up her spine — she couldn't help feel it was some kind of booby-trap waiting to explode back at them. In spite of this she moved closer still.

She stopped a couple of feet away and reached out her hand towards the window debris. She stopped short of touching it by just a few millimetres and wriggled her fingertips gently.

"I can feel something," she whispered and Pope turned nervously towards her. In the otherwise silent pub, he had no trouble hearing her words.

"It's alive..."

Pope frowned, his eyes narrowing. "The barrier's some kind of being?"

"Not quite, but it's active rather than passive." She moved her fingers a little more, trying to use her magical senses in the lightest way possible. "It's feeding on energy to keep it locked in place." She pulled her hand quickly away in sudden shock and pressed it to her chest. Her other hand went to her mouth.

"Faye?" Pope said. "What's wrong?"

"The power feeding it..." Bishop turned to face him. "It's earth magic."

Pope raised his brows and silently urged Bishop to continue, needing her to clarify what she'd said. But she didn't take the hint.

"So we're dealing with a really powerful earth wizard?" Pope asked. "Or a witch of course."

"Maybe. Or at least a practitioner who's managed to devise a particularly powerful spell." Bishop became thoughtful.

Generally speaking, powerful spells went hand in hand with magicians of a similar calibre, but it was possible for a magician to craft a strong spell without necessarily possessing the raw power. It wasn't always about the amount of energy commanded by the user, but how that energy was used and replenished by the spell itself.

"Can you find out which kind it is?" Pope asked. "Maybe it'll help us break out." He took a long pull from his pint then put the half-full glass on the bar.

"I'll do what I can," Bishop replied. "But don't get your hopes up." She turned back to the window and reached out once again, using both hands this time. As before, she stopped short of actually touching the broken fragments or the barrier itself.

Curiosity getting the better of him, Morton wandered over to watch but Bishop stopped what she was doing, lowered her hands and bowed her head. Her shoulders became tense as she spoke without turning.

"Back off, Archie! I don't want you looking over my shoulder."

Both magicians glared at the ghost with dark intent and Morton walked away with a shrug.

Bishop lifted her arms once again and closed her eyes. With just the lightest of touches she reached out her senses to feel for the barrier, probing its nature with a hint of her magical energy.

For a number of minutes there was almost complete silence and Pope clenched his teeth as he willed his friend to succeed. He'd watched her use her magic on countless occasions but there was always an element of backseat driving about doing so. Not that he could have even begun to do the kind of magic Bishop wielded — blood magic was too different in nature — but he empathised with her every twitch and gesture.

Then, without any warning, a startling flash of energy flung Bishop backwards as if she'd been hit by an ogre's club. She landed on her back fifteen feet away and the wind was hammered out of her. Pope rushed to her side as she gasped to draw air into her lungs.

"Faye! Are you all right?" he asked.

"Just feeling a bit stupid," she said, getting to her feet. "I should have seen that coming."

"Did you find out anything?"

"Yeah... I think we're screwed."

"That powerful?"

"Without a doubt." Bishop moved her neck as if loosening a few knots in the muscles. "Nothing is going to shift that barrier. I tried drawing on the earth energy feeding it to weaken its hold. That's when it blasted me."

"Wow."

"Exactly." She stared into Pope's eyes. "The barrier spell has defensive spells layered on top. Whoever set it up thought of everything."

Pope's eyes went a little vacant while his mind ran through a number of ideas. "We could try a sacrificial ritual," he said.

"We're not harming Sam!"

"No." Pope looked a little uncomfortable. "Stupid idea. I just..."

"I know," Bishop said. She had long experience of Pope's tendency to run through all kinds of possibilities, whether they were practical or morally viable. "What about...?"

Whatever Bishop had been about to say, she was interrupted by the sound of the Gents' toilet door slamming open and closed, followed by Finlay thundering along the corridor towards them.

"Can you feel it?" he blurted out. "Something's coming."

"What?" Pope asked in return.

The big man shrugged a little helplessly. "I don't know, just... something. I sensed it." He grabbed his pint from the bar and downed it in a few seconds of gulping.

Pope scratched his head but Bishop already had her eyes closed and reached out with her senses, hoping to discover what Finlay meant. She slowly turned on the spot like someone trying to pinpoint a sound. A few seconds of this and she stopped turning, but moved her head from side to side, fine-tuning a final confirmation of the location. She opened her eyes and pointed to the area of carpet in front of the fire.

"There," she said.

When nothing happened straight away, Pope gave Bishop a quizzical look and took another mouthful of his beer. She glared back. "Can't you feel the energy building?"

Pope held out his left arm and watched the hairs on

the back of his hand prick up. He nodded, drank a little more and set his glass down again. Finlay looked at the remains of the pint and licked his lips. Pope nodded to him with a wry smile on his face and Finlay finished off the beer in less than a second.

Pope, Bishop and Finlay moved to stand around the area Bishop had indicated, hoping to be ready for whatever was coming. Bishop breathed heavily, Pope fingered the carpet tack in his pocket and Finlay cracked his knuckles, a sound not unlike Chinese fireworks going off.

The area in front of the fire remained still for a few moments longer but their noses sensed an ozone tang in the air from the build-up of power. Then the empty space warped and twisted, pulling at the eyes like a migraine sufferer's worst nightmare. At some hard to pinpoint moment, a middle-aged woman appeared as if she'd slunk into the room by some means of misdirection, defying even the most perceptive analysis. She wore an eye patch, a broad-brimmed hat and old, rugged clothing. Her good eye blinked as though trying to clear her vision.

As soon as she realised there were others in the room, and in spite of her disorientation, she drew a knife from inside her short coat and lunged at the person directly in front of her. If Pope hadn't been waiting expectantly, she would likely have gutted him with a quick thrust of her sharp blade. As it was, he simply grabbed her knife wrist and grappled with her. She went for his testicles with her other hand and missed the mark with her first attempt. She swung her fist again but her blind rage was abruptly halted by a shout from Bishop.

"Kitty, stop! It's us."

She whipped her head around and the blind rage cleared from her single good eye as she recognised Bishop. She looked back at the man she was trying to kill and his features became familiar, too. Kitty's surprised turned into a grin and when she tried to step back Pope released her.

"It's good to see you," he said and grinned back, though without humour. "Pity the circumstances aren't better."

"Trap?" Kitty asked. Pope nodded. "Bugger!"

"It's been one of those days," Bishop said. She moved forward to hug her friend and their embrace lingered until Kitty pushed Bishop away so they could look at each other.

At fifty one, Kitty Spender looked twice Bishop's age, even though the latter was over three and a half centuries older. The grey in Kitty's hair was mostly hidden by regular dyeing, though the few wisps at the temples showed that her roots hadn't been done for a few weeks at least. She bowed her head to try and keep her face in the shadow of her broad hat.

Kitty moved away a little further and began to turn around but Finlay stepped forward, spun her around and picked her up like she was nothing. He hugged her like he would never let go. "Missed you," he said.

"We've all missed you, Kitty. Where have you been?" Bishop's concern was echoed by Pope and Finlay put the woman down so she could talk again. Kitty checked her ribs and gave Finlay a wry smile.

Kitty shrugged and lowered her head once more before lifting it self-consciously, not because of the eye-patch over her left eye or the scarring on that side of her face, for her friends knew those full well, but for the recent age lines that now added unwelcome detail to her countenance. She shrugged and the grin faded.

"Here and there," she said. She didn't elaborate.

"We thought you were dead. We haven't heard from you in years. No one has." Bishop took her hand, felt the dry, weather-beaten skin.

"You know how it is, Faye," she said. "The years catch up with some of us."

Kitty stared at Bishop with a hollow loneliness in her one good eye in which the magician was in danger of becoming completely lost.

Bishop broke the shared look and glanced around the room with awkward, darting eyes. In nearly four hundred years, signs of age had never once marred her thirty-year-old looks. "Sorry," she said and cautiously looked at her old friend again.

Kitty glared more strongly with her single eye than most people could with two. "After Paris, I just didn't need the reminder."

"Oh, Kitty..." Bishop was at a loss for words. No matter how often it happened, she was never prepared when her friends started getting old. Not for the first time she wished there was something she could do to prevent Kitty ageing.

Kitty rubbed at the scars on her face with more than a little regret in her expression, then pulled herself out of it, grabbed Bishop and gave her another hug. Bishop paused, then hugged back, increasing the embrace further after a moment.

The two of them had been friends for thirty five years, since the magician had come across Kitty stealing from a magical shop Bishop used to frequent. Kitty had been homeless, in her teens and a little wild. Though she had no magical ability of her own, she'd hoped to sell the items on the black market. How she'd even known about the shop was a mystery until, over tea and a bacon sandwich, she'd explained that she'd followed Bishop one day and saw the secret entrance. Bishop had taken her under her wing and tried to teach her magic, but unfortunately Kitty had no natural magical ability.

Instead, she learned how to tap into the power of magical symbols and took up martial arts to help handle her youthful frustrations. She became an investigator of the supernatural, scraping a living as best she could with guidance from her friends.

Bishop broke the silence. "I wish I—"

"Don't!" Kitty interrupted. "We've been over this old ground too many times. There's no fountain of youth; no magic to turn back time; no undiscovered secret..." They broke their hug and regarded each other solemnly.

Pope and Finlay fidgeted as they stood, waiting for the two women to have their little moment. Finally, Kitty turned and smiled.

"Some reunion, eh?" she said. "Do you have any idea who trapped us?"

"Not yet. A powerful bastard, though." Pope gestured towards the damaged window.

"Our captor did that?"

"No, the damage is mine," Pope admitted. "But the barrier around the building is holding it in place."

Kitty stared for a moment longer then looked about as if trying to get a sense of the scale of it.

"Don't worry, Kitty. We'll figure it out." Finlay looked awkward and bashful as he spoke to her.

She smiled at him warmly. "Thanks, Sammy."

"Perhaps you'd be good enough to make an introduction?" Morton had silently crept over to the group and his interruption surprised them a little.

Kitty glared at him and almost yelled but Pope raised his hand and she gave him a questioning glance before looking away. She angled her head to dip the brim of her hat again.

"He's just one of the pub's ghosts," Pope said.

"Whatever," Kitty said, becoming serious again. "Can we concentrate on getting out of here?"

"You think we haven't tried?" Pope asked. He again gestured to the window. "We just haven't found the right approach."

Kitty looked at Bishop who said, "Or how to discover who's behind it."

"I can't imagine it's going to be a long list." Kitty thrust her hands into her jacket pockets and became thoughtful. "What branch of magic?"

"Earth," Bishop said. She watched Kitty's eye open wide with a scary thought she immediately dismissed. "None of the local magicians are powerful enough."

"Unless they teamed up," Pope suggested.

"I've met some of them," Kitty said. "They couldn't agree on the colour of a tangerine without a B&Q colour chart."

Bishop chuckled and Pope gave a wry smile, but it was a full twenty seconds before Finlay got the joke. Kitty squeezed his arm in a friendly, if slightly patronising, manner.

"Ah, sod it!" She said and delved into the bag slung from one shoulder and across her chest, pulling out a lighter and a pack of cigarettes. She put one of the cigs into her mouth, ignited it and drew heavily on the smoke before letting it out slowly, making sure she exhaled away from Bishop. Kitty looked away from her friend's disapproving eyes. "Three hours without one, okay?"

Bishop sighed. "I thought you'd given up."

"I should really. Mother died of emphysema, apparently." She looked at her cigarette for a moment but continued smoking anyway.

Kitty waved her cigarette around as she spoke and Bishop tried wafting the fumes away. Kitty turned to her. "Sorry, Faye."

She threw the rest of the cigarette into the fire then linked arms with Bishop and drew her off towards a corner alcove to continue their catch-up.

"Are you okay?" Kitty asked. "You and Josh look exhausted."

"It's been a long day," Bishop replied. "A stray demon, then this trap." Kitty nodded as if it needed no further comment.

Pope shrugged and walked back to the bar. For a moment Finlay didn't know who to follow but shortly decided the bar was the better option. The two of them leaned on the counter.

"Didn't you have a thing with Kitty a while back?" Pope asked.

Magic Symbol

Finlay looked down at his feet. He never liked being put on the spot, even by his friends. Then, in spite of the beetroot red his face had turned, he grinned and looked at Pope.

"Still do," he said. "Kind of."

"Kind of," Pope repeated, nodding his understanding. "Kitty's not the settling down type."

"You're right there, more's the pity." Finlay hung his head, pausing before continuing, his whole body sagging. "I think she's beginning to resent me."

"That's a load of crap. She thinks the world of you." Pope gave him an encouraging slap on the back but he didn't react. Instead, Finlay's voice dropped to a low rumble.

"It's not like she, well, means to." He lifted his head and stared into Pope's eyes. "Look at me. I'm well over twice her age but I look ten years younger."

"So?"

"So, who can blame her for resenting me?" He glared at the empty pint glasses on the bar top. "I'll probably outlive her by a good fifty years."

"If we escape this trap."

"Yeah. There's a bright thought." He reached over for the lemonade pump and filled up his glass, the fizzy liquid overspilling the rim and soaking the bar towel.

"I thought you lived on beer and chicken pies." Pope rubbed idly at a smear of blood on the back of his hand.

"And cheese-and-onion crisps." Finlay downed the lemonade in one huge gulp then gave a belch that shook the glasses on the shelves behind the bar. "I was thirsty. Besides, we should keep a clear head."

"What?" Pope was astonished. "I've seen you down a dozen pints and still have a clear head."

Finlay looked sheepish again.

"Oh, I see," Pope said. "It's Kitty, right? She's got you under the thumb."

"It's not like that."

"She's hog-tied you into submission." Pope dodged as Finlay swatted at him with the back of his hand. "You gotta be faster than that, man." He raised his arms in a mock-boxer pose.

"Leave him alone, Josh," Kitty said. "If you want to help, figure us a way out of here."

She and Bishop had emerged from their quiet corner and the latter's dark look only enhanced Kitty's admonishing tone. Pope shrugged in mock innocence.

"Hey," he said. "What if we tunnel out of here. Sam and I can take it in turns to dig."

"Huh!" Finlay snorted. "I know what your idea of taking turns means."

"Well, you're built for it, man."

"He's not a work-horse to be exploited!" Kitty snuggled up to Finlay and put her arm around his huge waist as far as she could reach; the top of her hat well short of his massive shoulder. He went red again.

"We all have our strengths," Pope replied. "Sam's is his... strength."

"It wouldn't work anyway," Bishop said. "I can't connect to the earth so the barrier must reach completely under the pub. Breaking the spell will be the only way out, but I have no idea how to do it."

"Have you tried symbols?" Kitty asked. "I discovered

some pretty powerful ones in China about three years ago that go back a few centuries at least. They mostly protect against magic, but some were designed to break magical seals."

She delved into one of the pockets of her jacket — Kitty always wore jackets and coats with plenty of pockets, even if she had to sew extra ones in herself — and pulled out a seven inch touch-screen tablet.

"Something new?" Bishop nodded to the device as Kitty switched it on.

"My old paper notebook got too large and started falling to bits," she said, scrolling through virtual pages with a familiar ease. "This can store a hundred times as much and I've set it to back up to the cloud twice a day."

"Cloud?" Finlay looked puzzled. From the expressions on Bishop's face she was just as much in the dark. Pope's poker face covered up his ignorance better; he'd been doing it for so much longer, after all.

"Online digital storage on remote servers. Saves me the pain of keeping a computer."

"Are you on Facebook?" Pope grinned.

"Like you know what that is." Kitty raised the eyebrow on her good eye and it made her look a little comical.

"He actually has his own Facebook page," Bishop said. "Calls it The Oldest Living Man. Everyone thinks it's a spoof page."

Pope shrugged. "Hide in plain sight."

Kitty stopped flicking through her stored pages. "Got it." She turned it to show them. On the screen was an image of an old piece of parchment scanned from the original document. In the centre was a single, very complex symbol. The brushwork clearly gave it a far eastern look, but that's all they could tell. None of them were experts like Kitty — she'd made magical symbols her life's work.

"Will it work, Kitty?" Finlay asked.

"I hope so. Never had a chance to actually try it out yet." She looked at Bishop. "Do you still carry chalk around with you?"

Bishop pulled a piece out of her pocket and tossed it to her friend. "Of course." It was actually a stick of home-made pastel, created to her own recipe.

In spite of only having one eye, Kitty's coordination was still good enough for her to snatch the short stick out of the air. She headed for the door, studying the image on her tablet as she moved, playing a voice sample that spoke a Chinese phrase.

Pope, Bishop and Finlay followed Kitty but left her enough space in which to work. They couldn't crowd her in case it affected her task but they had to be ready in case something untoward happened.

She knelt on the floor in front of the door then stopped the voice sample playing. She propped up the tablet so she could see the symbol clearly then paused for a moment before drawing the symbol on the door with the pastel.

Kitty worked slowly but surely and, in spite of never using the symbol before, it gradually appeared in a series of confident strokes. As she made the final mark, the door rattled a little, which was more than even Finlay had been able to do. She spoke the Chinese phrase from the voice sample at the same time as touching the centre of the symbol with her finger tip. Although she had no magical power of her own with which to infuse her drawing, this action had the effect of switching on the symbol's innate power.

The door rattled again, harder this time. Kitty tossed the pastel stick back to Bishop, grabbed her tablet and stuffed it in an inside pocket before standing up, her arms by her sides in readiness. She sensed the others behind her were doing the same but she didn't dare take her eyes off the door.

The door rattled more ferociously and the slender gap around the edges began to glow, quickly brightening into a piercing light that burned into the retinas of anyone looking directly at it.

Kitty stepped forward, reached out her right hand and wrenched the door open with a single tug on the handle. It flew wide more easily than she'd expected and caught her a little off-balance. The light now filled the whole of the open doorway with a brightness akin to a door-sized strip from the surface of the sun. There was no heat but it was far too painful to look at.

Screwing up her one good eye as tightly as possible and keeping a hold on the open door, Kitty stepped towards the dazzling rectangle but she met a resistance that felt like walking into a strong headwind. Her hat was whipped from her head and her red hair, gone grey at the roots, billowed out behind her. She pushed forward slowly but steadily, ignoring the whipping of her jacket, reaching with her left hand towards the plane of intense light.

The moment her hand made contact, the glowing rectangle exploded, blasting Kitty backwards with such force that if Finlay hadn't been behind her, ready for such an eventuality, she'd have been slammed into the wall and killed. As it was, her momentum, combined with the force of the blast, was enough that Finlay's huge bulk was lifted from the floor. He'd barely had the chance to grab her before he hit the wall ten feet behind him with a mighty impact that stunned him for a moment. He dropped Kitty and slumped to the floor.

The open doorway turned instantly black, plunging the pub into relative darkness following such intense illumination. The door slammed shut and the pastel of the drawn symbol could no longer adhere to its surface. It drifted to the floor in a line of fine dust.

Bishop and Pope blinked through the after-effects of the bright light and picked themselves up from where the edge of the blast had deposited them. They rushed over to their two friends — both were unconscious but Finlay was already showing signs of coming round. Kitty was more of a concern and Bishop cradled her head in her arms, stroking her long hair. She adjusted the eye patch so it was seated properly over Kitty's empty socket.

Pope lifted her clear of Finlay with Bishop still cradling her head and set her on the floor so the earth magician could tend to her. He then slapped his big friend's face to bring him round properly. As Finlay returned to consciousness, he grabbed Pope's wrist to stop the slapping and squeezed a little more forcefully than he'd intended.

"Agh! Careful Sam," Pope said, trying to get his wrist free. The big man was still dazed and a little confused but he let go of Pope and scrambled to his knees when he saw Kitty being cradled by Bishop.

"No!" he shouted and shuffled to her side, wanting to touch her but, without knowing how she was, afraid of hurting her. "Is she...?"

"She's just knocked out. I think." Bishop placed one hand over Kitty's forehead and used a very light touch of her magical senses to see how she was doing. After a moment she removed her hand and smiled at Finlay. "She's okay. No major injuries."

Finlay expelled a huge breath in a gust of relief and sat back against the wall. A tear squeezed out of the corner of his eye. Pope dropped into a squat beside him and squeezed his shoulder in a reassuring fashion.

Bishop was still stroking Kitty's hair when the latter came round, her eye popping open suddenly filled with fear. She looked up at Bishop as if she'd not seen her before.

"What the hell are you doing?" she asked, pushing Bishop's hand from her hair. She got to her feet on unsteady legs, with hands raised to ward off further help. "Stop treating me like a child." She turned to each of them. "Why do you all do it?"

Bishop stood up and reached towards her friend, concern and uncertainty on her face. Kitty pushed her palm outward as if it was a shield.

"No," Kitty said. "Don't. Just don't."

"Kitty, it's not like that," Bishop said. "We..."

"Then what is it like?"

Bishop tried to find the words but struggled to do so. She'd never seen Kitty like this before.

"Do you think I want you pawing at my grey hair with a look of pity stamped across your face?"

Bishop put her hand to her mouth. "Oh, my god."

"Kitty..." Finlay said, his arms open wide in a helpless gesture.

She rounded on him. "Even you, Sammy. It's like I'm a delicate flower you tread carefully around in case you shake my petals loose. I'm still the same person I was thirty years ago. I still do the same stuff, even if I don't have the speed and agility I once did. I..."

"Bloody hell, woman," Pope said. "What is wrong with you?"

"Josh!" Bishop snapped, but he spun to face her with a face filled with fury.

"No, Faye, don't try to stop me. This is exactly what she means and you can't be like this." Pope paused and Bishop struggled with herself for a moment. In the end she gave him a slight nod and he turned back to their friend.

"You're right, Kitty, we have been guilty of treating you wrongly." His eyes searched her scarred face. "What I don't get is why you didn't just bloody well tell us."

Kitty opened her good eye wide, her mouth hanging open.

"We're not perfect," Pope went on, "but we're not stupid. And we'll always be your friends."

Finlay and Bishop nodded their agreement with Pope's words. For a moment the tension between them teetered on a delicate balance but no one attempted to speak before Pope continued.

"If we've done anything to push you away, tell us so we can put things right. We all need a slap on the face from time to time." He stepped a little closer, wanting to hug her but stopping himself from doing so. "Running away like you want nothing more to do with us doesn't solve the problem."

"Look, I may have been a little distant lately, but... Oh, shit. I don't know what it is." Kitty paused and looked at each of them in turn. "Sometimes I get so scared and lonely..."

"That's why you have us," Bishop said.

"Kitty..." Finlay held his hands by his side, his fists clenched like he wanted to pull apart the world. He couldn't find the words.

"Sammy, it's okay," Kitty said. She took a deep breath then looked at Bishop and Pope. "The thought of dying terrifies me."

Her three friends were momentarily dumbfounded. She'd always been so tough and forceful. Considering her lack of natural magical abilities, she'd never backed away from fighting the supernatural.

"Look, you know I think the world of you guys. Without you I'd have been dead long ago." She looked away from their collective gaze. "But sometimes you remind me that my death is so inevitable."

Part Four

Killer

BLOOD AND EARTH

The Coven

Midsummer's Eve, 1978.

Five young women chanted in unison, holding their hands aloft, fingers spread wide, their voices echoing around the dark, old church hall, now no longer in use.

"Be with us this night and guide us!"

They each stood behind one of five candles placed at the points of a roughly constructed pentacle and were dressed in home-made shifts, fabricated from white cheesecloth, covering them from shoulders to the ground but leaving their arms and heads free. Hanging around their necks on black leather thongs were chunky copper pentacles, connecting them to the larger symbol on the floor.

"Hail to the ancestors and welcome."

They had gathered in the hall once a week over the past two months in preparation for this night and earlier in the day they'd created the large pentacle on the floor, positioning it just in front of the small stage. Dry, powdery earth had been poured in a circle and bleached, bone-like branches had been arranged within it as the spars of the pentagram. Together they combined to form a powerful, magical symbol.

With a diameter a fraction over twelve feet, the simple pentacle would have seemed innocuous in the large hall without the presence of the women, the candles and the strange mass that occupied the pentacle's central space — something of a dark and formless appearance; difficult to make out in the dim, flickering light.

"Hail and welcome! Guide us this night, we beseech you."

The women's voices continued, edged with a mixture of nerves and excitement and they closed their eyes in concentration, pushing thoughts of their mundane university lives out of their minds.

Even Sarah, the physics student, bullied into joining the coven by her friends, now accepted that things were possible for which current science had no explanation. But rather than feeling directionless at this revelation, for the first time in her life she felt she belonged to something much greater than herself. Carole, Shirley, Monica and Jilly — all doing arts-based courses — had become closer than her family had ever been. Sarah's hands shook as she breathed in the dusty air; she could barely contain herself.

Moonlight struggled through a couple of the grimy windows, occasionally darkening as fleeting clouds blocked out the rays. An involuntary shiver passed through the group but they held their concentration. Outside, faint remnants of light still touched the northern horizon, but midnight was rapidly approaching — the climax of their ritual.

"Guide us as we endeavour to enhance your power."

The hall rumbled gently, shaken by the forces of a soft, localised earthquake. A framed picture, left on the wall when the hall had been closed up, fell to the ground with a nerve-jolting crash. Sarah gasped in surprise, the candle by her toes guttering for a moment. The others glared at her, particularly Jilly, but she recomposed herself quickly.

The rumbling died away to be replaced by a whispering from the dark form in the centre of the pentacle. The women took their cue to chant with additional enthusiasm.

"Earth goddess! We ask for your blessing and humbly request that you anoint us with your power."

The group's timing was perfect, for in the distance a clock struck the first of its twelve midnight chimes. Two bare arms, unnaturally thin, shot out from the black, formless robe that had, until now, disguised the man crouching in a tight ball beneath it.

Although his whispered chanting built in volume, it remained difficult to make out his words. For a few seconds he stayed still, the candlelight revealing the rough, cracked skin that covered both hands and arms, more closely resembling a dried riverbed than human flesh.

He stood up swiftly, raising his hands to the ceiling, matching the poses of the five women, the large hood of his black robe hiding his face.

"Be with us this night and grant us your power!" the women cried, then opened their eyes wide, focusing their attention on the figure in pentacle.

They thrust their arms towards him before dropping their hands to their sides momentarily. Spreading their fingers, all five raised their arms once more, palms upward, as if lifting something invisible from the earth, offering it to the man in their midst, as if making a gift of this unseen force, driving it his way.

"Be with us this night."

The man lowered his own arms and reached towards the floor, fingers cracking as they spread impossibly wide, bowing his head as he did so, hiding his face further.

"Hail and welcome!" The pitch and volume of the women's voices increased again.

The chimes of the clock reached ten and the man's whispering switched to a deep chant.

"Grant me time everlasting," he said.

"Grant us time everlasting," the women echoed.

The eleventh chime sounded, seemingly closer now. Earth energy shot from the ground, into the hands of the man. Lightning-like tendrils played back and forth between the ground and his fingers, yet he was not burned nor did he feel pain. Similar branching strands leapt from the women's hands to the man's body. All but Jilly stared wide-eyed at this unexpected development, their hair standing out, filled with static charge. Sarah gave out a small whimper then clamped her mouth shut when it was clear she was in no pain. Power flowed with such volume the man levitated a few inches above the ground, held in place by the net of energy like a fly trapped in a web.

Then, on the exact stroke of midnight, the lightning ceased, all forces stopped flowing and the man dropped the short distance back to the ground, cushioning the impact on his toes, bending his knees, holding himself hunched over. The women's triumphant smiles quickly faded into uncertainty as the dark-robed form remained motionless for what seemed like forever. Jilly gave reassuring glances to the others, gesturing them to wait patiently.

Then, with a strength that defied his frail physique, he leapt into the air, his scrawny right arm and hand pointing directly at Sarah's head. She drew in a breath of surprise but before she could release it he rapidly spun in a complete circle, still in the air. A blinding orange disk of immense power exploding out from him, intersecting with each of the women at neck height, decapitating them instantly with cuts so clean their heads and startled expressions remained momentarily in place.

Although instantly dead, their bodies stayed upright, held in place by magical forces while the man drew on the last dregs of earth energy he'd stored in their bodies in the week leading up to this ceremony. As the power roared into him, the cracked skin on his arms swiftly healed and the muscle tone returned to normal.

The hall shook again and small chunks of plaster fell from the ceiling. But the quake was over as quickly as it began and the five women crumpled to the ground as the man released them. He smiled to himself beneath his hood, watching their heads roll away on impact with the ground, leaving bloody trails across the dusty floor.

The candles guttered and extinguished as a sudden gust of wind moved through the hall but the moonlight was enough for the wizard to admire his bloody handiwork. The women had served their purpose well, although not in a way any of them had expected. They'd been easily fooled into thinking that a portion of the Earth power would be theirs, but he'd never intended to share it with anyone.

He bowed his head in concentration for a moment then simply vanished.

Detective Inspector Tench parked his car beside a number of other police vehicles outside the old church and switched off the engine. He paused before pulling the key out of the ignition — whatever was inside must be pretty bad for his sergeant to pull him out of a morning meeting with the superintendent. The call had been vague — multiple bloody murders — but Tench preferred it that way and Sergeant Mainbrace knew his boss well. Tench liked to form his own opinions of a crime scene without too much prior editorial.

He got out and locked the car door. It was a habit

that came from growing up in an area where, in the post-war years, nothing was safe; an area in which his family had been treated oddly for having law-abiding standards. As he walked towards the church hall, the building to the right of the church, Sergeant Peter Mainbrace strode over to meet him.

The younger man was fairly tall at a smidgeon under six feet but Tench beat that by a good couple of inches, and whose wiry frame made him appear taller still. Mainbrace, though, had a broad build to go with his height, which made him a stone heavier than the Inspector. None of that weight was fat, though and he played regularly in the local force's rugby team.

"Morning, boss," the sergeant said in a tone that suggested it was anything but good. His notepad was gripped tightly in his big hand and his face filled with relief now that Tench had arrived.

"Peter," Tench said by way of greeting. "How many?"

"Five women, all decapitated," Mainbrace replied, walking alongside his boss.

"The weapon?"

"No sign, sir." Mainbrace paused. "It's like…"

"Not another word, sergeant."

"Yes, sir." He sighed. "I don't understand this one."

Tench raised his brows as he looked at Mainbrace without breaking stride. His curiosity now truly piqued, his pace increased.

Although Mainbrace had said practically nothing, Tench still didn't like the sound of what the sergeant's few words implied. He reached into the inner pocket of his jacket to check the device he'd been given years earlier was still there. He always transferred it from one jacket to another, almost without thinking, but it paid to be sure.

They passed a number of uniformed officers who

stood outside the hall looking a little useless and Tench glared at them. Mainbrace pulled open the door for his superior who stepped lightly over a fresh patch of vomit on the threshold. The sergeant followed him in.

Forensics personnel were already doing preliminary work at the far end of the hall, taking photographs and measurements of key pieces of evidence and their relative locations. The two detectives approached with their footsteps echoing slightly.

"Excuse me," Tench said, loudly enough to draw the attention of the team. "Could you please step back a moment so I can see the whole scene for myself?"

The forensics people — three men and a woman — stood up without a word and moved over to a position behind the detectives. Tom Parker led the team and nodded a greeting to Tench; the two had previously met on other cases. The detective moved around the perimeter of the area, taking care not to disturb any evidence.

"Who discovered the bodies?"

"A guy employed by the church to check on the place once a week." Mainbrace looked in his notebook. "A Mr. Robinson. Took one look and threw up."

"Ah, the mess on the doorstep."

"Yes, sir. Thankfully away from the scene itself."

Tench rubbed his chin then folded his arms. "What comes to mind, Sergeant?"

"At the risk of sounding ridiculous," Mainbrace replied. "It looks like there's been some kind of ritual."

"Indeed." Tench walked around a little more, very slowly. "Last night was midsummer's eve."

Mainbrace wrote a note in his book then watched as Tench crouched down to look closely at one of the severed heads. In spite of the daylight streaming through the broken windows, the Inspector pulled out a small torch and shone it on the surface of the cut. He stood up again and waved over one of the forensics team.

"Have you had the chance to examine the wounds?" he asked the woman who came over, Hilary Quinn.

"Only a very cursory inspection," she said. "Why?"

"Would you say that the cuts are unnaturally clean?"

"I wouldn't say unnatural, sir," Parker said as he stepped up beside them. "But whatever cut through their necks was incredibly sharp and must have moved very fast."

"Thanks. Carry on."

They returned to their work and Tench turned to Mainbrace. "Do you know if there's a coven in the area?"

"Of witches, sir?"

"What else?"

Mainbrace hadn't expected such a question and stared at his boss blankly before gathering himself. "There were rumours a few months back but when we investigated it was just a group of students with too much time on their hands." He chuckled. "You don't think this is real magic, do you?"

"I do hope not."

Mainbrace dropped his voice into a whisper. "I'm sorry, sir, are you saying there's such a thing as magic?"

"That's right, Sergeant," Tench muttered. "Just don't go telling that to the general public."

Mainbrace stared again. He opened his mouth a few times as if to speak but couldn't find the words to comment on his boss's revelation. He would have thought the Inspector was making fun if only he'd told even a single joke in all the time they'd worked together. Tench gave him a flat smile, patting him on the shoulder as he did so, a gesture of reassurance he'd only used twice before. However crazy it seemed to Mainbrace, Tench was convinced of the reality of magic.

Tench knew that he should have had a talk with his Sergeant long before now, but without a case that involved magic or the supernatural in general to back up the idea of such things being real, the Sergeant was likely to have remained unconvinced. Without the proper context, talking about such things with a trained sceptic had all the appeal of broaching the subject of sex education with a teenage son you barely connected with.

"So the coven wasn't just a bunch of students playing silly buggers?" Mainbrace asked.

"The likelihood is that they probably were, but you never know. When these women are identified, check if they were part of the coven."

Mainbrace nodded, wrote in his book then gestured towards the dead bodies. "What was this about then, sir?"

"Perhaps they tried to cast a spell that went wrong," Tench said. "Equally, one of them could be a delusional psychopath who decided the best way to fulfil a disturbed fantasy was to behead these women. Or it could be a drug-fuelled suicide pact dressed up to look like a ritual."

Mainbrace's hand hovered over his notepad for a moment before he flipped it closed, clicked off the pen and stuffed them into his inside jacket pocket. He didn't know whether to believe his boss or simply humour him until he could apply for a transfer.

"Which do you favour, sir?"

"Too early to say." Tench peered at the centre of the makeshift symbol, where the overlapping branches formed a rough, five-sided shape. "Is there a void in the blood spatter over in the middle, Peter?"

Mainbrace placed his feet carefully between blood drops and leaned in a little closer. "Certainly looks that way, sir."

"I'm willing to bet good money that a sixth person

stood there when this took place."

"So he decapitated them with some kind of weapon then fled."

"From the centre of the circle?" Tench sighed. "If it were only that simple."

Mainbrace looked at Tench a little confused, hoping the Inspector would follow up with further explanation without additional prompting. That clearly wasn't going to happen.

"Sir?"

Tench didn't respond but reached into his inner pocket to pull out the object he'd checked for earlier.

Wrapped in a small piece of worn, faded blue velvet, Tench removed a disk about the size of a pickle jar lid, handling the object as if it were highly valuable and extremely delicate. However, the device looked more like something a child would make in craft class than anything of significance.

The disk was made of blood-red clay, with strange symbols and markings pressed into the earthy material when it had been soft, along with six small, differently coloured gems that looked more like pieces of cheap costume jewelry. The whole thing had been hardened rather than properly fired, which is why Tench held the disk carefully in the flat of his hand as he drew in his breath.

"Pattarocht," he said, slipping his tongue around the strange word with relative ease. The disk immediately trembled, which spooked him, just as it had on each of the previous three times he'd used it. Mainbrace almost jumped out of his skin.

The cheap-looking gems began to flicker like the lights of a Christmas tree, seemingly at random, then one by one, their shine dimmed until only the orange gem still glowed.

"Bloody hell!"

Mainbrace was so taken by the operation of the disk, he almost missing Tench's profanity. The Inspector so rarely swore on duty it always meant trouble when he did so and Mainbrace glanced at the older man a little worriedly.

The gem's brightness increased to become almost blinding, heating up at the same time. Tench drew in a harsh breath, his hand in some pain. "Pattakacht"

The light vanished and Tench quickly wrapped the disk up again before returning it to his pocket. He looked at his sergeant who tried to pull himself together.

"What was that thing, sir?" Mainbrace asked. He looked between Tench and the rustic pentacle on the floor. The rules of the world had suddenly changed to include things he knew nothing of.

"It's a magic detector," Tench replied.

"Is the colour of the glowing gem important?"

"It means I have to visit some people." He sighed. "You keep an eye on things here a while, Peter. Tell forensics to do what they can but don't let them move the bodies until I say so. Get the uniforms to canvas the area. Meet me at the station in a couple of hours."

The sun in the courtyard was too beautiful to resist; even Pope had dragged himself from his bed to sit outside in a faded, well-worn pair of jeans and a ragged cheesecloth shirt. He loved the feel of the rays on his skin but he never tanned due to the toughness he inherited from his mother's side. He had no idea what he'd inherited from his human father as he'd never been able to learn anything about him, even his name. And with his hateful mother dying in childbirth, it had been impossible to ask her.

He was brought out of his reverie when Bishop gave him a playful slap on his shaved head. "Earth to Joshua, come in Major Josh."

"What did I miss? Something exciting?" He looked around but the courtyard was as quiet and still as it always was. Just the way he liked it.

Of the four buildings that defined the courtyard, theirs was the only one that looked onto the irregular rectangle of ancient flagstones; the others showed only blank, mediaeval brick walls topped with roofs. The three mostly featureless facades were broken in only one place — the narrow alley at the opposite side of the private space. The whole construction, which Pope had manipulated hundreds of years earlier, gave them a level of privacy most central city dwellers could only ever dream of.

"No. Not a blessed thing," Bishop said. "Isn't that brilliant?" She wriggled down into her chair and enjoyed the tingling sensation as the sun reacted with the earth energy stored in her body. She wore a sleeveless T-shirt and cut-down pair of jeans so her arms and legs were absorbing a lot of the sunlight. She's been sitting or working outside a lot in recent weeks and her naturally red-brown hair had a number of golden highlights, which made her look younger than usual. "Maggie just asked if you wanted a drink and I chose for you. You were in another world."

"Just thinking of years past. Family..."

"Never a good idea, Josh. Not for us."

"I know, I..." Pope's voice faded and he shrugged.

Bishop grabbed his arm in a friendly, supportive way and smiled at him. He patted her hand in thanks and grinned back.

"I might get another tattoo," he said.

"What for? They only ever last five years on you before they grow out."

"That's the best part. I'd never get one if I had to live with it for the rest of my life."

Because his body was very efficient at regenerating, another gift from his mother, Pope had lived for over two thousand years. In the Shadow Dominion, people usually met a violent death before they ever reached old age, so no one knew if they were truly immortal or simply long-lived. One advantage Pope had by being exiled to Earth, was that he'd already lived longer than most Shadow Dwellers and showed no sign of growing old. So far.

He glanced at the only true friend he'd ever had, still surprised that their friendship had lasted for nearly four centuries. However, in spite of their closeness, he'd never been able to bring himself to tell her the reason for his exile back in the iron age.

Bishop looked at Pope. "You know yesterday was Midsummer's Eve, right?"

"Don't spoil the morning," Pope said, a little more angrily than he'd intended. "I've been trying not to think about it."

"I only mention it because we managed to get through the whole night without incident for once."

"Stop. Right now. We don't need to discuss it any further."

Bishop was about to continue when Maggie Trimble brought out a tray holding three large glasses and set it on the old wooden table, ignoring the sudden halt to the conversation.

"Fabulous!" Pope said, relieved at the minor distraction. He grinned at the woman who'd worked for them so long she felt like family.

Maggie always made her own version of lemonade —

a mixture of freshly squeezed lemons and tonic water poured over ice. It was as sharp as hell but incredibly refreshing.

She grabbed one of the glasses and took the remaining chair. "I'll deal with the kitchen when I've had this."

In spite of the insistence from Bishop and Pope that she should approach her work as she saw fit, Maggie always liked to justify any break she took. Even though her employers were the last people to be hung up about schedules, regarding her as a friend they paid to help, she couldn't let go of this urge. Now it had simply become one of Maggie's endearing foibles.

The sun was beautiful, the buildings surrounding the courtyard shielded them from most of the city's sounds and the three of them relaxed without speaking.

Bishop felt the tingling of her skin increasing. She rarely suffered from sunburn because her earth energy protected her, but yesterday she'd topped up her stored energy to the limit and now the strong sunlight was making her feel a little antsy. She knew that she wouldn't be able to sit for much longer without succumbing to the urge to do something physical and burn off the excess, so she was a little pleased when their peace was interrupted by an unexpected visitor. However, she would have preferred someone who tended not to bring trouble with them.

Inspector Tench emerged, stooping, from the small alley opposite and brought himself back to his full height as he strode across the courtyard with uncertain determination. His face didn't carry the look of a happy man.

"I thought I smelled something fishy," Pope said and grinned.

Tench rolled his eyes. He must have heard this same

joke from Pope at least a dozen times in the last fifteen years and it never put him in a good mood.

"Faye. Joshua," he said curtly, then nodded to Maggie.

"Inspector, it's always good to see you." Bishop smiled. "I don't think you've met our friend, Maggie Trimble. Maggie, this is Detective Inspector Tench."

"I've heard stories about you, Inspector," Maggie said. "It's good to put a face to the name."

"Likewise." Tench almost smiled at her then turned to the other two again. "Why do you make this damn place so hard to get into? It's taken me over an hour to find the amulet I need to gain entry."

He always felt a little uncomfortable when dealing with the two magicians, but he fidgeted more than normal and found it difficult to stand still. He liked to be in control of a situation but always told himself that, no matter how they looked, Bishop and Pope would never be normal people. They had a command of powers that scared him more than any of the hardened criminals he regularly dealt with.

Bishop watched the Inspector for a moment. "We like our privacy. Let's just leave it at that."

"Do you have something to hide?" Tench's voice had a sharp edge to it.

Pope bristled and Bishop tried to rein in her feelings. Normally she quite liked Tench but he was in a strange mood today and one she wasn't particularly taken to. She'd never known him get stroppy with them before.

"Can I get you a glass of lemonade, Inspector?" Maggie asked in an attempt to diffuse the situation. "I make it fresh to my own recipe."

Tench put a finger in the collar of his shirt and pulled at it, as if the mere mention of lemonade was making him hotter. "As tempting as that is, Mrs. Trimble, I'm going to decline. I'm not here to socialise this time."

He looked at Bishop and Pope with an annoyed expression on his face. "I need you two to come to the station and help us with our enquiries."

After a short moment's pause, both magicians burst out laughing. Tench stood in front of them with his look of annoyance setting in more firmly.

"Good one, Tench," Pope said when his laughter died away.

"It wasn't a joke."

"No, I can see. Look, if you need our help, why not just talk about it here?" Bishop asked.

"Because it's more complicated than that." Tench put his hands in his trouser pockets but it didn't give him the more relaxed look he'd intended.

"You think we did something," Pope said. "You think we were involved in a case you're investigating. And judging by the look on your face, you probably think we committed a murder."

"How perceptive of you," Tench said. He tried to look nonchalant, but it seemed to be a police thing where nothing ever looks less casual than trying too hard.

"Why would you think that?" Bishop asked. "We've worked together in the past. You know us."

"Even so, I would be failing in my duty if I did not investigate the evidence that presented itself."

"You think you have evidence that we were responsible?" Bishop smiled. "Interesting."

"You're not taking me in, copper," Pope said in a mock cockney accent.

Tench hardened his gaze. "That's where you're wrong."

Pope stood up and stood with his nose a couple of inches away from that of the detective. "Actually, that's exactly where I'm right."

"Josh..."

"I can always return with a warrant and a couple of dozen uniformed men." Tench leaned in closer still. "We can tear the place apart and see exactly what secrets you're keeping in there."

Pope ground his teeth. "I'd like to see you try."

Kitty and Art

Kitty Spender looked at the four sheets of paper for the tenth time, shuffling them back and forth, feeling as if she was back in junior school working out problems involving men digging ditches.

She was sitting on the low wall outside the university library, considering her options for her second year. Although the end of year exams had only just finished, her tutors were keen that she should make a decision as soon as possible in order to set a reading list for the summer vacation. She never thought that studying the history of myths and legends of ancient cultures would throw up more options than she had time for. Like always, she wanted to do everything but knew she'd never fit it in.

Pulling at one of the additional, pointless zips that she'd stitched to the legs of her black canvas trousers, Kitty moved the tag of the fastener back and forth subconsciously while she tried to make a decision. She wasn't exactly enamoured of Punk music but she liked the rebellious look of the clothing. Her hair was dyed an orange-red, shaved at the sides, and her scruffy, white T-shirt bore an image of the flag of the Japanese Navy on the front — a design favoured by many of the Punks. On the back was a symbol she'd painted herself. To the untrained eye it looked suitably anarchic, but it was actually a magical symbol of protection.

Pulling a notebook from her bag, Kitty began

scribbling rapid thoughts and ideas, circling key words and linking important elements with emphatic arrows. It wasn't that the available choices were particularly complex, she simply wanted to devise a schedule that enabled her to maximise her tuition, keep up her already advanced martial arts training and still work on the merchandise she sold in Felthrop market. And that wasn't counting the time she spent with Bishop and Pope as they taught her everything they could about magic.

Not that she was any good at it. If someone had a talent that was the opposite of magical ability, she was that person. She understood how magic worked, how spells were cast, how elemental magic energy could be absorbed into the body then used, but none of that theoretical learning made a difference — she had no magical ability. She was a non-conductive material when it came to magical energy.

Kitty was a dab hand at charms and protective wards — minor stuff, mostly — but that was because such things worked from the power inherent in the materials from which they were constructed, bound and activated by the symbols used to decorate their surfaces. These were the kind of objects she made and sold at the market.

She'd also become fascinated by the underlying ideas, which had inspired her to take on a study of ancient cultures as the main thrust of her university course. At the heart of it was a hope that she'd be able to uncover secrets of ancient amulets that had been lost for centuries, perhaps even millennia. There were people in the wider magical community who spent a lifetime trying to locate lost magical artefacts, but if she could find the means of actually making items that had similar properties she would bypass the need to find the real thing. To some people that was kind of missing the point and she could see why they would think so, but discovering the knowledge and principles behind the artefacts had to be of better long-term value to everyone. Besides, she also hoped to use the knowledge to make a comfortable living.

Kitty shook her head — she'd become lost in her thoughts again, which wasn't surprising considering how she was going around in circles. She sighed.

She nearly jumped out of her skin when two hands pressed lightly over her eyes, totally unexpectedly, and she reacted as anyone trained in martial arts would when an attack was sprung — by grabbing the thumbs and twisting them viciously.

"Aagh! No, no, wait! It's me, Art." The young man behind her yelled at the pain she inflicted.

Kitty stood up, still holding his thumbs and her papers fell to the ground. She turned around to face him, forcing his hands and arms into shapes they struggled to maintain.

"Let go!" Art yelled. "You're going to dislocate my thumbs."

"Tell me why I shouldn't do exactly that, you creep." Her reflection stared back at her from his mirrored sunglasses

"Because you're a kind, forgiving person?"

"A smooth-talking creep." She held on for a few seconds longer before giving a final little twist and releasing him. She stepped back a pace and took a martial arts stance. "Don't ever do that again, you bloody idiot! Who the hell are you, anyway?"

"I just said. Art." He rubbed at his thumbs and checked they still worked in the way they were supposed to, moving them around in circles. Kitty hadn't quite dislocated them but they were still as sore as hell.

"Like that's supposed to mean something to me?" She continued to scowl at him and looked like she might launch an attack at any moment.

"We met a couple of months ago at that guest lecture on ancient pagan rituals." He tried to hook his thumbs into the pockets of his tidy jeans then winced and thought better of it. "We chatted in the bar afterwards."

"Ah, now I remember..." Kitty relaxed a little. "I didn't recognise you in your shades."

Art removed the sunglasses and placed them in the breast pocket of his shirt, revealing dazzling green eyes that seemed a little unreal with their intense colour — Kitty found them almost captivating. However, eyes aside, he had the look of someone trying too hard to be cool but without the first idea how to do so. He was handsome enough with his strong jaw and noble nose, it was just his sense of fashion seemed to be struggling to keep pace with the passage of time. He looked sheepish. "Sorry."

"Yeah, okay." She watched him rub his thumbs again and became thoughtful. "You know, I don't think you told me your name when we last chatted."

"Probably not. I'm pretty good at forgetting to do so." He smiled wryly. "Not that you gave much chance to get a word in. You got pretty worked up and inspired a new line of research for me."

"That doesn't make us friends."

"I guess not, no."

"Let me give you a tip — get to know someone better before you pull a trick like creeping up behind them." Kitty folded her arms with serious intent in her stance. "I could have killed you."

"Believe me, I won't make that mistake again," Art said. "You're full of surprises."

"What does that mean?" Kitty wasn't sure she liked that comment.

"When we chatted after the lecture, you told me that

everything the speaker said was wrong."

"I remember what I said."

"Then you explained what it was really like, as if you'd actually been there."

"I got a little passionate." Kitty looked down and shuffled her feet.

"Do you have a time machine or something?"

"I'm Doctor Who's assistant, didn't you know?" She risked a grin and Art couldn't help smiling with her.

"Then you left before we had a chance to talk any further," Art said. "I wanted to ask how you knew that stuff."

Kitty looked him over suspiciously again. Even though it had been three years since her days of living on the streets, she couldn't shake off the feeling she should question everyone's motivations. "I have good research sources."

Art narrowed his eyes. "Better than the leading expert in the field?"

"Something like that." Kitty put her hands on her hips and took on an intense expression that suggested there was no more to say. In spite of this, her eyes twinkled in her fresh face in a way that almost invited the strong of heart to be more curious.

They stared at each other for a short while before Art looked away from her penetrating gaze, not rising to the unspoken challenge. Kitty bent down to pick up her papers and stuffed them into her bag before hanging it over her shoulder and standing up again.

"Trying to decide my options for next year," she said, tapping her bag. "Hey, weren't you about to sit your finals when we last talked? How did you do?"

Art shrugged. "A two-one."

"Pretty neat." Kitty nodded in admiration. "So how come you're hanging about round here?"

"I, um... had some books to return to the library." He jerked his thumb over his shoulder. "Bloody fines!"

"Well, it's been good chatting to you again," Kitty said and began to move away. "Sorry about your thumbs."

"Do... do you want to go for a drink?" Art blurted, his confidence sliding away from him a little. "I'd like to chat some more."

"Are you sure your thumbs are up to holding a glass?" She edged away a little further.

"I could use a straw. Or..." He mimed picking up a glass between the palms of his hands.

Kitty stood still, cocked her head on one side as if weighing him up, then folded her arms and narrowed her eyes. When the lost look on Art's face got the better of her she burst out laughing, went over to him and linked her arm in his, which caught him a little by surprise.

"Come on, then," she said, pulling him along. "You can pay."

"Hey, now wait a minute," Art responded as he let himself be led. "I'm a firm believer in Women's Lib."

They both laughed as they walked down the street.

Police Enquiry

"No biscuits?" Bishop asked. She smiled up at Tench as he put the chipped cup and saucer on the table in front of her. It rattled cheaply.

"Don't *you* start," Tench said, sitting opposite her. He straightened his tie, pulled a pen from his jacket pocket, before opening the manila file in front of him.

Bishop looked at the drab, blue crockery with disdain. There were stains that hadn't been washed off from the last dozen times it had been used and now she regretted asking for the drink. It wasn't that it was likely to kill her as much as the thought of all the unpleasant mouths that had been there before.

She'd been waiting in the interview room for half an hour, convinced that the delay, the drab decor and, now, the unappealing tea, were designed to have a psychological effect on interviewees. She was on the verge of opening a portal to go home when Tench had returned.

"Thanks for getting Mr. Pope to see sense, Miss Bishop."

"How formal."

"This *is* formal." Tench leaned forward to emphasise the point. "And highly serious. The fact that I already know you has no bearing on the matter at hand. I have to conduct this interview like I would any other — in a professional manner."

"The way you picked us up was hardly professional."

Bishop narrowed her eyes. "If the posturing between you and Josh had gone on much longer, I'd have had to hose down the urine."

Tench rolled his eyes. "*Can* we continue? I can't be held responsible for the actions of Mr. Pope."

"Oh, come on... you were both to blame for the way things escalated. If I hadn't been there..."

Tench waved his hand dismissively. "Be that as it may, you're both here, now, and I have a murder investigation to conduct."

"Whatever you think Josh has done, he's no murderer." Bishop picked up the cup, took a sip and pulled a face. It was worse than she'd expected. "He didn't commit this crime."

"Actually," Tench said, "it's you I'm interested in."

"What?!" She put the cup down sharply and some of the liquid spilled into the saucer. "You think I killed someone?"

Tench ignored the question, closed the file and moved it to one side so he could write on the notepad that lay beneath. Bishop noticed the name on the manila folder for the first time.

"Why do you have a file on me?" Bishop looked sharply at Tench.

"The police have been keeping tabs on you for nearly a hundred years. Not that it has any relevance."

"For the government?" Her eyes narrowed — she thought they'd been able to keep below the radar for the most part.

"For our own purposes. Governments come and go." Tench's face became hard. "Death and destruction are never far away are they, Miss Bishop?"

He clicked his pen a couple of times as he looking intently at her. She slumped in her chair and stared back through cold eyes. She could see why he'd gained such a strong reputation as a detective.

"Where were you last night, Miss Bishop?" Tench's pen was poised to note down her answer.

"At home."

"And can anyone—?"

"Josh, of course."

Tench nodded, considered writing something on the pad then changed his mind. "Would you say that Joshua Pope was... trustworthy?"

"Without doubt," Bishop said. "I'd trust him with my life."

"And is the reverse true?"

"Definitely!" Bishop narrowed her eyes further, her face a picture of caution.

Tench scribbled on his pad. Bishop tried to read it but his handwriting was too spidery for her to make it out upside down. It struck her as a little odd that someone so fastidious would have such poor handwriting.

Tench looked up. "Would you kill for him?"

Bishop glared and sat up straighter. "I don't like the way this is going."

"Just answer the question." Tench leaned in and frowned deeply.

"Not when it feels like you're trying to put words in my mouth."

"Are you refusing to answer the question?"

"I'd like to know what the relevance is," Bishop said. "Ask me specific questions. Don't ask me about hypothetical matters or I'll demand to see your superiors."

"You think a feeble threat will work?"

"It's neither feeble nor a threat. Josh and I are known to the Chief Superintendent."

Tench tried to hold her stare, but after a moment he looked away. Bishop had nearly four hundred years more practice at staring people out.

"Very well." He paused then drew a deep breath. It was time to show the thickness of the cloth. "I have good reason to believe you killed five women, using magic, at the old church hall on Silvergate."

"Your belief is irrelevant — there's no hard evidence because I didn't do it." Bishop paused to calm herself and soften her tone. "What is wrong with you, Tench? You know us; we've worked together..."

"Earth magic was used to kill the women." Tench let that little nugget settle for a brief moment. "You're the only person I know who's powerful enough to do it."

"I know of at least four earth magicians in the area." Bishop smiled sarcastically. "Strong ones, too. Perhaps you need to update your files."

"Do any of those magicians have the ability to decapitate five women at the same time?" Tench leaned forward intently, this time holding Bishop's gaze until she looked away. As the impact of Tench's words sunk in, she began to realise how serious they were.

"Five killings would take considerable power and a substantial amount of evil intent." Her eyes flicked about with concerned calculation as she considered the scale of the magic involved. "I doubt I have the former and I certainly don't have the latter."

Tench scribbled some more, paused to obliterate a couple of words with quadruple lines, then continued with his scrawl.

"Wait," Bishop said. "How do you know Earth magic was used? You're not a magician."

"I have a device," Tench replied, still writing. "A magical item Mr. Pope gave me. It detects the type of magic that's present."

"Show me."

Tench looked up, fought her gaze for a second, then

sighed, pulled out the device he'd used at the murder scene and held it in the palm of his hand. He peeled back its velvet covering quite methodically.

"*Pattarocht,*" he said. As before, each of the gems lit up then, one by one, they winked out until the orange one glowed brightly on its own. Bishop reached towards the device and the light of the gem shone more intensely, fading back when she moved her hand away again.

"*Pattakacht,*" Tench said and the glow vanished.

"You're linking me to the murder based on that?" Bishop smiled, a little perplexed. "That's like blaming someone for wearing the same perfume. It'll never stand up in a court of law."

"The same orange glow was present at the crime scene."

"That's not evidence, it's coincidence. You need to refine its use to get more detail." She stretched her had out for the device but Tench pulled it out of her reach. She took her hand back and clasped both of them together on her lap. "Very well, I won't touch it."

Tench held it out again. "What are you trying to do?"

"Watch." She closed her eyes for a moment, trying to remember the exact phrasing she needed. "*Pattarocht kinal.*"

The light sequence the gems went through was similar to the previous time but when it had settled down the orange gem didn't glow on its own. The red gem held a faint light that flickered in a hesitant way.

"What does that mean?" Tench asked.

"Most magicians have a trace of at least one other type of magic within them," Bishop explained. "Mine is predominantly earth magic, but I have a little blood magic mixed in, too. Earth and blood. Look closely and you might also see a faint suggestion of air magic."

Tench cupped his free hand around the gem to put it

into shadow and saw that the clear gem gave forth a subtle luminescence, barely detectable.

"If you check the murder scene you'll find a different signature."

"You're sure of that?" Tench looked dubious.

"Absolutely! I already told you I didn't do it."

"Damn! Every time I get mixed up with you and Pope I have to learn something new." Tench slouched back in his chair and stared at the object in his hand. It was the first time Bishop had seen him sit so casually.

"I have tons more experience than you and *I'm* still learning," Bishop said. "Magic is scarily complex."

"*Pattakacht*," Tench said and put the object away. He looked at Bishop thoughtfully. His eyes narrowed as he brought his steepled fingers to his lips.

"I think you need our help," Bishop said.

"Or perhaps I was right all along and you are still responsible." He breathed deeply and sat erect again. "The different pattern of lights could just be a trick to throw me off."

"That's true." Bishop shrugged. "But how would you prove that? Sometimes you have to take things on trust. We've never given you any reason to doubt us."

Tench stood up. "This doesn't mean you're off the hook."

He walked over to the door and opened it, holding it wide for Bishop who got up from her chair and walked over. She smiled and shook her head before exiting to the corridor. Tench followed, closed the door behind him and called out loudly.

"Mainbrace!"

The sergeant entered the corridor from another room, a little too quickly, and almost bumped into his superior. He looked a little dazed.

"Fetch Mr. Pope," Tench said. "We're returning to the

crime scene."

"But, sir..." Mainbrace looked at Bishop and then back at Tench. "They're our main suspects."

"Indeed. But they may also be the only people who can tell us what's going on."

"Excuse me, Sergeant," Bishop said. She licked her thumb and wiped a smudge of blood from his forehead. "You'll probably find he's not in the room."

"What?!" Mainbrace threw open the door of the room he'd just left and was astonished to see that Bishop was right — there was no sign of Pope. "But I was just interviewing him."

"Do you still profess your innocence?" Tench barked.

"Josh won't have escaped. He's just having a little fun."

Tench strode into the main squad room and shouted again. "Daniels! Get me..." His order was cut off by laughter coming from a group in the far corner.

Pope had been telling jokes to a small group of detectives and uniformed officers who now split up and moved to their desks when they realised Tench was in the room.

"Sir?" a young detective asked.

"Never mind, Daniels," Tench said and waved the now confused man away. "What did you do to my sergeant, Pope?!"

"Nothing long lasting," Pope replied. He grinned wide when he saw how angry Tench was. "Look, I got bored, okay?"

"This is serious, Josh," Bishop said. "I think we're dealing with a powerful earth magician."

"How powerful?" Pope turned solemn.

"More powerful than me. Maybe."

Pope raised his eyebrows. "I find that hard to believe."

"Just because we haven't come across him before, it doesn't mean it's not possible."

"Him?" Tench asked.

"Five women brutally killed — it's more than likely to be a man. Women tend to kill differently."

"That shows you don't know my sister," Pope said. "She once killed a man by ripping open his chest and crushing his lungs." Bishop glared at him but he simply shrugged. "It's true."

"Until we know it's a man for definite we should keep our minds open," Tench said. He walked towards the exit. "Follow me," he called over his shoulder.

Bishop followed straight away but Pope casually put his arm around Mainbrace's shoulder in a mock-friendly way. "I hope we get to drive with the siren on," he said.

"I think that's enough levity for the moment, don't you?" Mainbrace said, shrugging off Pope's arm and following after his boss. Pope waved at those who remained in the room.

"See you," he said. "Gotta go catch the bad guy. You take it easy."

As all four climbed from Tench's car, the Inspector became instantly more intense. "This is a crime scene, keep your hands to yourselves!"

"We know the drill, Tench," Pope said. His flippancy had been discarded like an old raincoat and he donned a more solemn cloak; it was time for business.

"Josh and I should stay here for now," Bishop said and leaned on the car. "You wouldn't want us to contaminate the magical aura in there."

Tench looked a little uncertain but Pope looked

baffled. However, Mainbrace had taken on a seemingly permanent look — that of a fish stranded on the river bank.

"Go in on your own," Bishop said to Tench. "Use the device as I did and you'll get the killer's signature without picking up ours."

"Ah..." Pope said, now understanding. "I'd forgotten I'd given you that little magical widget. Faye's right, you don't want us clouding things. Give us a shout when you're done."

Tench nodded then turned to Mainbrace. "Stay here, Peter. Watch them." He lifted the police tape and entered the church hall.

The forensics team was still working at the far end where the bodies lay. They worked in a silence disturbed only by the buzzing of the flies that were already gathering. One of the team looked up as Tench approached.

"When can we move the bodies, Inspector?" Parker asked.

"Soon, Tom."

Tench pulled the magical device from his pocket, ignoring the curious look of the other man, and spoke the strange words. *"Pattarocht kinal."*

As earlier, all the gems began to glow before some of them faded completely. This time, however, as well as the continuous brightness from the orange gem, there was a regular, strong pulse from the green gem and a slight flicker from the red one. From his understanding, this meant the main power used had been earth magic, but there was also a strong vein of Fae along with a hint of blood magic. He had no idea of its significance.

"What the hell is that?" Parker asked, his curiosity getting the better of him.

Tench stared at him for a moment, lost for an

explanation that would satisfy a scientist. He turned away without speaking and walked out of the hall with the device still activated. With anyone else Parker would have taken offence, but he knew of Tench's peculiarities.

Outside, he showed it to Bishop and Pope. "What does this mean?"

"Jesus Christ!" Pope exclaimed.

"Your killer is definitely a powerful magician," Bishop said. "You can see how bright the earth gem is."

"But look at the power undertones." Pope looked at Bishop but gestured towards the device.

Bishop nodded slowly, her distant expression an indication of the thoughts racing inside her mind. She bit her lip nervously.

"What's the significance?" Tench asked.

"A lot of magicians have a hint of blood magic, but such a strong strand of Fae magic is unknown. Only the Fae themselves are imbued with their kind of magic."

"That's true," Bishop said, recovering a little. "And many of them don't have this much magical power."

"Fae are... fairies, right?" Mainbrace asked, desperate to get involved and understand what was going on.

"The Fae come from the realm of Faerie," Bishop replied. "They are not the fairies from children's stories."

"Can the Fae use earth magic?" Mainbrace spread his arms and shrugged when the others looked at him. "I'm just asking."

The two magicians looked at each other and thought it over before Pope shook his head.

"I doubt it," he said. "The Fae would find it almost impossible to connect to the Earth. Just as we'd find it difficult to connect to the Faerie realm. This is something new."

"Do you have any idea who he is?" Tench asked.

"No, but I might be able to find out," Bishop replied

and pointed at the ground. "Put the detector down on that patch of earth."

"Sir...?" Mainbrace's uncertain voice questioned the idea that these two should give orders.

Tench gave him a look that suggested they were both out of their depth, then did as Bishop asked. The patch of earth should have been a grass verge but numerous feet walking over it every day had rid the border of any green.

Bishop squatted and put her hands flat on the compacted soil on either side of the device, making sure not to touch it. She closed her eyes, drew on the residual energies of the ground then sent her senses through the earth and into the object, which vibrated as she did so. A swirling orange glow formed around it, looking very much like the contents of a small, smoke-filled goldfish bowl.

"Earth spirits find the magic caster, thereby helping avert disaster," Bishop chanted.

The sphere expanded rapidly and the two detectives flinched as it reached them, expecting the spherical surface to have substance to it, though they actually sensed nothing of its passage through their bodies. They looked at each other a little embarrassed but neither magician took any notice as the sphere expanded and attenuated to the point where it disappeared entirely.

Pope watched Bishop intently, his whole body alert should he need to move quickly. Bishop was completely motionless. She'd even stopped breathing while she awaited the outcome of her spell. The others held their breath, too, as if caught up in the magic.

Abruptly, there came a strange reverse sound, like a recording of crashing cymbals played backwards. The ground beneath the detector and Bishop's hands exploded upwards, knocking her a few feet onto her back and hurling the device into the air.

Pope stepped forward and grabbed it from the midst of a shower of soil before the hardened clay and gems could shatter on the ground. He then quickly crouched by Bishop's side.

"Faye! Are you okay?" He didn't touch her in case there were any residual effects.

Her hands and face were covered with flecks of the dry earth and she was breathing heavily. "Yeah. More shock than harm."

Pope offered his hand — if she took it there would be no lingering energy. She grabbed it and he helped her to her feet. She brushed herself down before taking the device from Pope's hand. The clay looked like it had been in a fire and the orange gem had exploded out and was now useless.

"Whoever the killer is, he's put a defence in place for this kind of spell," Bishop said, poking at the few tiny fragments that were the remains of the orange gem. "And before you ask, Tench, it's definitely a man. I was able to sense that much."

She gave the device back to Pope. "You'll need to make Tench a new one."

Pope pocketed it. "His use of power and the planning behind it... Hell, why have we not heard of this guy before? Why haven't you sensed him?"

Bishop shrugged a little helplessly.

"We need to find him before he kills again," Pope said.

"Do we have the strength to take him down, Josh?"

Pope clenched his fists and almost snarled. "Strength or not, we have to do it."

Fear crossed both their faces even as they tried not to focus on the negative, but at least they were of the same frame of mind. It was a strong part of what kept their friendship going through four centuries where lesser individuals would have gone their separate ways long ago. Bishop had only ever wanted to help others with her magical ability, in spite of nearly being burned alive by those she'd tried to serve. She'd been saved only by a last minute intervention by Pope, whose urge to do the right thing was ingrained much deeper. In part it came from his upbringing, but also from a determination not to be defined by the dubious morals of the Shadow Dominion half of his ancestry.

They both stared at Tench in earnest and the detective's manner changed. Although there was a look of guilt in his eyes, he nodded his understanding but didn't say anything. He shouldn't have suspected either of them but he'd gone with the evidence his limited knowledge and and understanding had provided. He held the tape up for them and the trio entered the hall while Mainbrace remained outside.

The old church hall was much cooler than it had been outside, a breeze blowing through the length of the echoey room. As soon as Pope stepped inside he paused and sniffed the blood on the air before continuing with Bishop and Tench on either side of him like they were making a movie entrance. All they needed was a slow motion and dramatic music.

They'd only walked a short way down the hall when Bishop's legs began to tremble. She was forced to hold onto Pope for support. He put his arm around her and tucked his hand under her shoulder to take some of her weight.

"What's wrong?" he asked. "You've seen dead bodies before."

"It's the residual earth magic..." Bishop struggled to breathe for a moment and she clutched at her chest, her legs almost completely giving way. "Dark... Darker than I've ever known. Malevolent..."

Pope led her over to an old, dust-covered wooden chair that stood by the wall and lowered her onto it. "Wait here, Faye. Take your time."

Bishop closed her eyes and nodded. Pope rose slowly then, satisfied she was okay to leave, walked with Tench over to the scene. He breathed deeply.

"Blood magic?" Tench asked. The forensics team pricked their ears at this but continued their work in spite of their obvious surprise.

Pope shook his head. "No. There's a lot of blood here, but none of it's been involved in casting spells. It was definitely earth magic the guy used." He took in a deep breath again. "I'm trying to get a sense of what happened."

"Can you?" Tench was briefly hopeful.

"Unfortunately, nothing more than you can surmise from simply looking at the scene."

"We believe the victims were all killed in the same instant," Tench said.

"That makes sense." Pope looked around at the bodies. "If you want to kill five people, you can't do it one at a time and hope they all stand still for you."

"Could they have been drugged or hypnotised?"

"I'm sure your forensics team can tell you about any drugs when they test the blood." Pope scratched his head and looked around. "I don't think we'll ever know if they were hypnotised."

Tench fidgeted — he didn't like being unable to bring regular police procedures to bear. He'd managed to embrace the idea of magic fifteen years earlier when he'd first met Bishop and Pope, mostly because he couldn't deny the things he'd seen, but he didn't enjoy the feeling of losing control of a case.

"Do you know anything about the victims?" Pope asked.

"They may have belonged to a local coven." He looked uncomfortable saying such a thing out loud in the presence of genuine magicians. "We'll check it out when we've identified them."

"Can I try something?" Bishop said, approaching them cautiously, fighting the rising dread caused by the tainted residual energy. She trembled noticeably as she moved and swallowed as if trying not to puke.

"By all means," Tench said. "But try not to interfere with the scene too much."

Bishop approached the nearest body and took hold of the lifeless hand lying at the young woman's side. She closed her eyes and used her senses to reach into the lifeless form. It was difficult to do so with the interference from the killer's spell, but after just a moment she stood up again.

"They might have imagined themselves witches but I don't think any of them had magical power," she said. "Certainly this one didn't."

"So why were they here?" Pope was puzzled.

"I think they were used as storage for earth energy."

"Like batteries?" Tench asked. Bishop nodded.

"Can they do that without magical ability?"

"No, the killer must have done it to them," Bishop said. "When they were killed, all that energy would have been released, absorbed by the killer."

"That's a frightening level of power to control," Pope said.

"I don't think he had complete control." Bishop tapped her finger on her chin and Pope shot her a questioning glance. "If he had better control there wouldn't be so much residual energy."

"A new wizard would explain why we've never heard of him." Pope folded his arms thoughtfully. "But a new wizard with this level of power...?"

"Exactly!" For a moment Bishop wobbled again. "We have no idea what we're up against."

"And you can't track him down?" Tench asked.

"The more powerful a magician is, the harder they are to find," Pope replied.

"We'll figure it out," Bishop added.

"I may know a way," Pope said. "But I've only tried this once before."

"Is it dangerous?" Tench looked around the room. There were people in here he couldn't put at risk.

"No, but I'll need to use some of this blood."

Tench became thoughtful and turned away from the two magicians. Although he ought to be concerned with preserving the evidence, the need to apprehend the killer before he struck again was more important. He turned back. "Do it."

Bishop looked at the forensics team then spoke to the Inspector. "Do you want them to see this?"

Tench sighed. "Tom, can your team wait outside a while, please?"

"They can go, but I'm staying," Parker replied. "I can't let you compromise the scene."

Pope waited while three of the four left the building then crouched down and touched a finger to one of the pools of blood. He began to chant in the strange tongue of the Shadow Dominion.

"*Braench fo an ta tempastach revut.*"

He repeated the phrase slowly, over and over, as he willed his blood magic to work. For a couple of minutes nothing happened, then a faint red mist rose up from the blood and hovered about a foot above the hall floor.

Bishop whispered to Tench. "You might want to get your guy to take pictures of this."

"We could never use it as evidence," Tench mumbled in return.

"So? We're trying to identify him."

"Will it even work?"

Bishop shrugged in a doesn't-hurt-to-try way and Tench signalled to Parker, miming taking a photo. The scientist stuck up his thumb nervously in acknowledgement and grabbed a bulky crime scene camera.

Although he'd worked some of Tench's peculiar cases, nothing in his training, or the wider world of science, had prepared him for what was happening. There was no scientific explanation, yet the evidence of it actually happening was right before his eyes. Documenting it with photographs might help the team make sense of it.

As Pope continued to chant, the mist began to undulate, rising and falling. Strange shapes shifted in and out of existence, indistinct at first but they quickly became much clearer. The forms stabilised, matching the outlines of the heads and bodies of the victims where they had come to rest. The magical mist had replicated them a foot above where they currently lay.

Nothing further happened for another two minutes then things moved very quickly.

The red mist outline of a man in a hood and cloak abruptly appeared above the centre of the pentacle, his face masked by the hood of his robe. He raised his hands high in the air in a strange, reverse action.

"It looks like a film running backwards," Tench whispered, while Parker snapped away with his camera, his fascination and scientific curiosity overcoming any fear he felt.

The scene playing out above the crime scene gained momentum. Red mist heads rolled towards their respective bodies, coming together to resume an upright position as the five falls reversed direction and paused for a moment. The insubstantial nature of the mist made it difficult to see clearly, but a disk of some kind shrunk back towards the man's outstretched hand as he rapidly turned in a complete circle in the air. Mist heads became securely attached to mist bodies.

The tenuous recreations of the women appeared to be chanting but no sound came forth and it was impossible to read their lips in this backwards fashion. The unknown man now floated a few inches above the mist floor.

Parker crouched down and used his flash to take a picture looking up at this figure and for a fraction of a second the image of the man's face was faintly shown, then it was gone.

Abruptly, the mist dissipated and Pope fell over, unconscious.

Bishop rushed to his side and put her left palm on his forehead. With her right hand she pulled a gem pendant from inside her shirt and absorbed the earth energy it contained.

"Shall I call for an ambulance?" Parker asked.

"He'll be all right," Tench replied and watched Bishop.

Bishop used her senses to reach into her friend, searching for whatever had gone wrong while Pope had performed the spell. She quickly discovered that he'd merely over-extended himself, passing out through rapid exhaustion. An unfamiliar spell could drain a person's natural resources if not controlled properly; in the heat of the moment Pope had simply not prepared himself fully. He was not injured so it only took a few moments for Bishop to replenish his energy, then she slapped his face to bring him round.

Pope sat up and rubbed his face. "Bloody hell! Wow!"

"What happened?" Bishop helped him to his feet.

"It just... took me over." He rubbed his face. "I can't remember the last time that happened."

"Take it easy, Josh," Bishop said. "You'll be right as ninepence, shortly."

"What in God's name is *that*?!" Parker exclaimed. All eyes shot first to him, then to where he pointed.

A section of blank wall between two windows had developed a crack that hadn't been there a moment ago. It now grew, spreading vertically with a sound of shattering plaster and brick, clearly no ordinary break. But the light pouring through the narrow gap was even more disturbing, for it clearly didn't match the quality of illumination coming through the windows, the feel of it entirely different, as if originating in a different part of the world.

When the ends of the split reached the floor and the ceiling, it stopped, but just for a moment. The light spilling through grew even brighter then the wall began to peel back from the split, curling on itself at either side like two enormous Swiss roll cakes. The bricks and mortar seemed to be made of mattress foam. The light that shone through came, not from the outside of the building, nor from another part of the world, but from another place entirely — the realm of the Fae.

Bishop and Pope knew this instantly, for standing just the other side of the opening was someone they'd had dealings with in the past — twenty one years earlier, to be precise — Ealvun, one of the Fae Lords. He was an important individual in the Faerie realm and not a person to be taken lightly.

Parker staggered at the sight before him, his legs weak from the shock of this impossible scene, and he could do nothing else but sit on the floor, unable to think of whether doing so would affect the crime scene. For a moment he retched but managed to control his urge to be sick.

Tench, to his credit, handled himself much better.

But although his previous experiences with the supernatural prepared him, he still looked pale. He breathed heavily in an attempt to calm himself.

Lord Ealvun stepped through, into the church hall and winced with clear discomfort. Although the hall was not on actual consecrated ground, the connection with the old church was enough to give him considerable distress, though he did his best to ignore it. Eight of his guards followed him through, fully armoured and with swords drawn, and from their facial expressions felt the pain far worse than their lord.

Bishop knew that whatever they had come here to do, they probably didn't have much time in which to do it. She helped Pope to his feet slowly, hoping to prolong the visitors' discomfort with the delay but Tench stepped forward to face the newcomers, his shock already abating.

"Who on Earth might you be?" he demanded. "This is an active crime scene."

Ealvun smiled icily at the detective. "I am Ealvun, a Lord of the land of Faerie. If you know what's good for you, you'd be wise to kneel before me, mortal."

"As an officer of Her Majesty's police force, I must ask if you have leave to venture onto British soil."

"Leave it to us, Tench," Pope said. He and Bishop stepped in front of him, hoping to protect him from the Fae's anger. "What do you want, Lord Ealvun? We're actually rather busy with our own problems to get involved with yours."

"I understand, Prince. Your problems are the reason I need you to come with me to Faerie."

"Prince?" Tench asked, staring at Pope, but no one took any notice.

As a son of the previous Queen of the Shadow Dominion, Pope was entitled to be addressed in such a way, but rarely did anyone take such a formal approach.

Certainly, Pope never regarded himself as royalty, particularly as the Shadow Dominion had cast him out when he was still a child.

"You know something about our killer?" Bishop asked. She moved toward the Fae Lord in her eagerness then caught herself and moved back to Pope's side.

"Not here." Ealvun looked around, worried. "I cannot stay within these walls for long."

"We'll not come with you unless you guarantee each of us safe passage back before sundown." Pope folded his arms and planted his feet in a firmly defiant pose.

Ealvun nodded. "I agree. If you come with me to Faerie I guarantee you a safe return before sundown."

"Now, wait a minute," Tench protested. "We have an urgent murder case to solve and I'm not letting them out of my sight."

"He's right, Ealvun," Bishop said. "The three of us are working together."

"Very well," the Fae Lord sighed. "He shall come, too, and the guarantee of safe return extends to him."

"I have work to do!" Tench protested.

"This *is* work, Tench," Pope said and grabbed his elbow.

They followed Ealvun and the guards through the opening and the wall unfurled and closed behind them, sealing itself up as if it had never been opened.

"What the bloody hell was that?!" Parker asked but there was no one in the room to answer him. As he climbed to his feet he looked at the camera sitting on the floor beside him, completely unused throughout the whole arrival of the Fae. "Damn!"

In the Pub

"What do you call a man with his head in a bucket of water?" Art asked and smiled.

Kitty grinned widely but looked thoughtful as she did so, trying to work out what the answer could be. She took a sip from the glass of lager on the table in front of her then shrugged. "I don't know," she said.

"Anything you like, he won't be able to hear you," Art said and Kitty laughed.

"I don't know why I'm laughing — that one's really bad," she said.

They'd been sitting in the pub for over an hour, telling each other dreadful jokes, but because they were intentionally bad they found them funnier than they should have been. At least Kitty did. Art seemed to tell and receive the jokes with good humour but rarely burst out in rib-shaking laughter. Kitty had surprised herself — she rarely got on so well with someone this quickly, but Art had been pretty cool from the moment they'd bumped into each other earlier.

"What do you call a gorilla with a machine gun?" Kitty asked.

"You already told that joke."

"It's a different gorilla."

"And a different machine gun?"

"Of course," Kitty said. "They don't share."

"Okay," Art said, then sighed. "What do you call a different gorilla with a machine gun?"

"Copycat."

"What?!" Art frowned but laughed a little anyway, which set Kitty off again.

"Okay, I fluffed it," Kitty said after a moment. "I'm not cut out for telling jokes."

"Me neither," Art said. "I remembered all mine from old copies of *The Beano*."

Kitty looked at her watch. She wasn't normally one for drinking in the middle of the day, but it had seemed like a good idea when Art made the suggestion — it was an excuse to put off her need to make next year's course choices. It wasn't that she didn't like a drink, but her life was so completely full of all the other things she did that drinking was a low priority.

She became a little thoughtful and tried to remember something important that slipped away from her mind. Art fell quiet, too.

At the opposite end of the pub's main room, the door swung open with a slight squeak and Samuel Finlay walked in, ducking his head slightly to keep it clear of the top of the frame. He made straight for the bar without looking around and rested his forearms on the counter while waited to be served. He made the nearby drinkers look small in comparison.

"Two pints of bitter," Finlay said when the man behind the bar nodded to him. "Please."

"You must be thirsty," the barman said.

"Yeah," was all that Finlay cared to say in return, showing his complete lack of interest in small talk. He paid for his beer then downed one of the pints in a swift gulp that drained the glass in a few seconds.

"Bloody hell!" the barman said. "Did that touch the sides?"

The big man ignored the remark, leaned on the bar and took a sip from the second pint big enough to take the level down by an inch. It had been an early start and eight hours of work without a break. He desperately needed something refreshing.

Art, who was facing the bar, had seen what happened and nudged Kitty's arm, dropping his voice into a whisper as he spoke. "That big feller at the bar just downed a pint in about three seconds flat."

"What big...?" Kitty turned around in her chair to see who Art meant, then squealed with delight when she saw who it was. "Sammy!"

Because Finlay was an old friend of Bishop and Pope, Kitty had come to know him well since she moved in with the two magicians three years earlier. She thought the world of the man, in spite of his taciturn nature, and didn't have the slightest care that he was part-troll. To her, he was simply a good friend and one she was sure she could always trust.

She leapt from her seat and ran over to Finlay, who straightened up on hearing his name. He'd only just turned to face the onrushing Kitty when she leapt up and threw her arms around his neck and shoulders, hanging on in an affectionate hug. Although initially taken aback, as soon as he realised who she was he smiled warmly and wrapped his arms around her, bearing her weight as if she was little more than a toddler.

"Not so tight, Sammy," she gasped. "I can hardly breath."

"Sorry, Kitty."

He put her down and she thumped his arm playfully for the crushing hug. He pretended that she'd hurt him but she laughed because his troll blood made his muscles like rock. If she'd hit him too hard she would have hurt her own hand. He grinned, took another sip of beer and shrugged. Although he was always a little lost for words around her, the sparkle in his eyes said more to Kitty than any lengthy speech could have done.

"Where have you been?" she asked. "I haven't seen you in ages."

"Working away, mostly." He rubbed at his chin while he thought for a moment, the coarse bristles rasping loudly. "And there was some family trouble with my Uncle Sean."

"Families are crap." Kitty knew this from first experience — her step-father had abused her to the point of making her run away from home nearly four years ago. Although she'd plucked up the courage to phone her mum last year to tell her she was all right, she'd refused to go home and hadn't let her mum know she was living in York. She'd never thought to mention she was at university now.

"Yeah." Finlay nodded. "Crap's about right."

"Tell you what," Kitty said. "Why don't you come and meet a friend of mine. We're sitting down the far end."

"Well, I don't—"

"Look, he hasn't bitten my head off yet, so I think he's okay."

She took his arm and dragged him with her and in spite of his size he let her do so, grabbing his beer off the bar as they moved away. Kitty hugged his arm as she led him along.

"Art, this is Sam," she said when they reached their table. "He's a great friend of mine. Sam, this is Art. He's a student at the university."

Art slowly stood and extended his hand with a reluctance that suggested he did so for Kitty's sake rather than anything remotely approaching interest or enthusiasm. Finlay shook it in an equally reluctant manner, barely grasping the offered hand in his big mitt. Kitty's company was clearly too precious a thing to share.

However, the moment their hands touched, an odd,

barely perceptible, spark passed between them. Finlay felt a sense of something familiar about the young man, but he had difficulty nailing down exactly what it could be. He held the grip longer than he should, sniffing deeply, too, as he tried to chase down the memory. Kitty nudged him to let go after a couple of moments.

Finlay sat on the stool across the table from Art and gave him a wary look before drinking half his remaining beer. He turned to look at Kitty and smiled, but it wasn't as natural as it had been a few minutes earlier.

"What's the matter with you, two?" she asked. "Is this the wake following the funeral of friendliness?"

She stared at each of them in turn, waiting for a response. Art glared at the big man all the more but the latter simply finished his second pint and stood up.

"I need a pee," Finlay said and sauntered to the gents.

"Is there something going on I don't understand?" Kitty stared into Art's eyes but he looked away.

"It's nothing." He became more uncomfortable the longer Kitty stared at him. "Sometimes, it's like... you know...?" He had no idea where his line of explanation was heading and stood up. "I need to go, too."

Finlay was just finishing up when Art walked in and he tried to push past the younger man without making eye contact. He didn't like the guy but he couldn't say anything for Kitty's sake.

"I think we need to talk," Art said.

"I've got nothing to say." Finlay stopped, waiting for him to move.

"But I have!" Art grabbed Finlay's arm and even through the material of his jacket the big man sensed the same familiarity. This time, though, the young man's heightened emotions made it stronger and Finlay's memories began falling into place.

He stared into Art's eyes with dawning recognition. "I

know you! You're..."

"Shit! I'd hoped it wouldn't come to this, with you being Kitty's friend." Art didn't attempt to hide his clear pretence. He let go of Finlay's arm and adopted a pose like he was ready to fight. Finlay would have laughed if the little guy didn't suddenly scare him in a way he couldn't put a finger on.

"I don't want to hurt you," Finlay lied in return. He struggled with an intense desire to pound this guy to a pulp in spite of only meeting him a few minutes earlier. "You have no idea know how strong I am."

"That hardly matters when I can do this."

Art raised his arms and his face twisted in fierce rage. A bolt of magical power shot from his open palms and struck Finlay in the face with such force it knocked him the length of the room. The small of his back crashed into the hand basin on the far wall and it smashed into large pieces. His head struck the large mirror on the wall above the basin and the minute fragments it shattered into glistened as they fell.

Art kept up the magical force for a few seconds, crushing Finlay's head into the wall, holding him in place, his eyes wide, enjoying the pain he inflicted. When he released the spell, Finlay slumped to the floor, his face a complete mess, blood oozing from cuts to the back and side of his already swollen head. An eight inch piece of the ceramic basin protruded from his back, blood oozing steadily from the wound.

Smiling at his handiwork, Art breathed heavily a few times with the adrenalin rush. He could feel his heart pounding in his chest and he looked down at his hands, admiring the weapons they had become. He left the gents, cast a spell to lock the door and returned to Kitty.

"Hey," he said. "How about we grab something to eat?"

"Where's Finlay?"

"Said he had to be somewhere." Art looked around innocently as he finished his drink. "Didn't he come through here?"

"No."

"Must have gone out the back way."

Kitty nodded as she finished her own drink, grabbing her bag as she stood, a little frown of concern wrinkling her brow. "I thought he was in a funny mood."

Art smiled — it had been easier than he'd expected. "Fish and chips?"

The Faerie Realm

In spite of working with Bishop and Pope on a number of occasions, thereby learning much about the nature of magic and the supernatural, Tench had difficulty getting his head around the actuality of stepping through a Faerie gateway into the Realm of the Fae — it felt so alien. But as Pope had tried to explain, this wasn't a different planet orbiting another star, this was a whole new plane of existence. Science would never be able to explain it.

This, of course, was a problem for a man who liked to know the why of everything. Tench could get his mind to accept speculative ideas and concepts like hyperspace, wormholes, parallel universes and branching time streams, but this was something that defied classification.

It was, well... supernatural. Though even that seemed more like a simple, convenient label to attach to the unknowable rather than an attempt at an explanation.

They had stepped through the gateway onto a large balcony near the top of Ealvun's huge castle. From up here the Fae Lord was afforded a view of most of his domain. Tench had to force himself not to go over to the balcony and simply stare. The sun alone was fascinating — a huge orb that lit up the thriving, green landscape like a normal sunny day back home, but not only was it about twenty times the apparent diameter of Earth's sun, it was possible to look upon it without being blinded.

In the valley below was the aftermath of a huge party.

Thousands of naked or near-naked creatures slept in all manner of poses; alone, in pairs or in groups. Midsummer celebrations had been lengthy, incredibly drunken, highly debauched and the party-goers were now sleeping off the worst of the effects.

Bishop looked at Tench's astonished expression, understanding exactly how he felt. The strangeness of the Faerie realm was still novel to her, even though it had been over three hundred years since her first visit. But there was business to be undertaken and none of them had the time to gawp.

"What do you want, Ealvun?" Pope asked. He looked around, taking in his immediate surroundings, ignoring the scenery but weighing up the people on the balcony, assessing the situation. As well as those who'd come through the Fae doorway — Ealvun's guards included — there were just two others. Kealin, the Lord's champion, he'd met years earlier, even bested in combat, but the youth was someone he'd never seen before. Although Pope thought of him as a youth, it was always extremely difficult to tell how old the Fae young were. He could have been anywhere from fifteen to forty.

"As I just mentioned, I have information pertinent to your investigation," Ealvun said, his eyes narrowing as he searched for the right phrasing. "However, although the knowledge I shall impart has a connection to those deaths, neither I nor any other Fae has any direct involvement."

"None of you are involved but you bring us here anyway?" Bishop was a little exasperated. "What kind of weird Faerie game is this?"

"This is no game." Ealvun bowed his head a tiny fraction and clasped his hands behind his back as if unable to trust them to remain free. "A mistake has been made that I need your help in putting right."

Pope raised his brows. "Do I detect an apology for some kind of wrong you've committed?"

"It is nothing of the kind." Ealvun looked between Bishop and Pope. "I am neither admitting any wrongdoing nor apologising. I'm simply stating that I wish to correct a mistake that has been made."

"Sounds like lawyer-speak to me," Tench said. He'd pulled himself out of his glassy-eyed stare and his manner was professional again. Mostly.

Ealvun looked at Tench with disdain. As far as the Lord was concerned, a mortal without power was of little consequence. Yet he indulged him nonetheless. "It may surprise you to learn that some of the top law firms in your world are run by lesser Fae."

"I don't care what games you people get up to," Tench said. "I need straight answers not hypothetical wordplay. What do you know about the killing?"

"Tell me, mortal," Ealvun said in a tone that would normally have been reserved for addressing a particularly irritating child. "Is such a blunt approach regarded as a positive skill in your barbaric society?"

"I have a killer to catch, preferably before he kills again. I don't have time to waste on nonsense." Tench glared at Ealvun. "Tell us what you know."

Ealvun bristled, his hands now by his sides again, clenched with barely suppressed fury. His guards became more alert, checking their swords were free in their scabbards.

"Take it steady, Tench," Bishop said, concern edging her words. "You don't have jurisdiction here and Lord Ealvun is offering help of his own free will."

"Which, you've got to admit, is a first for any Fae," Pope quipped.

"Josh!" Bishop fired a glance at Pope then turned to Ealvun. "I apologise for the uncalled for attitude of my friends."

Ealvun's smile was strained. "I understand that the newcomer is unaware of the conventions and protocols involved. However..." He turned to face Pope who simply returned the look without contrition.

"I apologise, Lord Ealvun," Tench said. He'd been forced to play office politics plenty of times and this appeared to be a more pretentious version of that. "I clearly overstepped the mark and ask your forgiveness, but I would appreciate if we could expedite matters somewhat."

Ealvun's expression softened slightly as he slightly nodded to Tench — a bare acknowledgement of the apology — before casting a glance over his shoulder. "Kealin. If you please."

The Lord's champion, wearing one sword on his hip, carrying another in his hand, holding it by its scabbard, stepped forward, drawing the youth along with him, grasped by the elbow. The young man was clearly unhappy at being treated this way and shrugged off Kealin's hold.

Bishop, Pope and Tench looked the young Fae over. His clothing was shabby compared to the splendour of the Lord and his champion. His loose-fitting shirt was open to the waist, revealing an intricate burn scar on his hairless chest — the mark of a vicious branding. It looked long enough healed that it must have been done when he was a very young child.

"This... is Coruban," Ealvun said. "Once the killer of the five Wiccan women is found, Coruban will be the one who deals with the culprit."

"This killer is your mistake?" Bishop was astonished. "You said no Fae was directly responsible."

"The killer is not Fae." Ealvun was curt but he avoided their eyes.

"Yet his magical signature has a strong Faerie element," Pope said. Although the Fae could not lie, nothing forced them to tell the whole truth and Pope sensed that more was being hidden than explained.

"Now, wait a minute," Tench interjected, his directness surfacing again. "When the killer is caught he will be arrested and brought to trial. I have no idea how things work here, but the killer is in our world and British justice doesn't involve killing without a trial."

Ealvun laughed. "Do you really think a powerful wizard can be controlled by incarceration within an ordinary prison? Coruban must find him before his power has the chance to grow even greater."

Bishop turned to Pope. "We can't just hunt and kill him like a wild animal, Josh."

"Why not?" Pope asked. "He's already shown us that he'll kill for his own aims. He's like a bear who wanders into a small town and starts killing people — he's got to be destroyed for the safety of the community. You said yourself that he might be far more powerful than you." Pope stared at her, waiting for her response, but Bishop didn't have an answer and looked away.

"I insist that we hunt the killer by the book," Tench said, trying to get everyone's attention. "This is my investigation and it's my responsibility to stop him. If you want to help, that's appreciated, but we have to pool our resources, not turn it into a travesty of justice. My reputation, and that of the British police, is at stake."

Ealvun clapped slowly. "Bravo, mortal. A fine speech. However, I'd like us all to view matters from a more realistic perspective."

"By the book!" Tench exclaimed.

"We will," Coruban spoke for the first time, his youthful voice almost musical. "But the volume we hunt him by is *The Book of Concurrence*." He looked towards

Ealvun who gave a reluctant, almost imperceptible, nod.

"What is he talking about?" Tench looked at the two magicians, quizzically.

"It's an agreement that dates back almost three millennia," Pope said. "It details procedures for dealing with certain situations, like the kind we have here. Where incidents occur that cross boundaries between the major realms they must adhere to the guidelines laid out in *The Book of Concurrence*."

"Why have I never even heard of it?" Tench asked. "I'm an officer of the law."

"It's hardly common knowledge, Tench," Bishop replied. "It's not like it comes into use every day. There are a few people in authority on Earth who know all the details."

"A government department?" Tench was floundering like a man who had no idea of the truth in these words.

"Hardly. There's no Ministry of Magic."

Tench balled his fists. For a moment he looked like he was going to explode. "Did someone throw out the rulebook when I wasn't looking?"

"If it makes you any happier," Pope said. "Call the Chief Inspector and mention *The Book of Concurrence*. He'll tell you what you should do."

"Bloody hell! There's nothing about the book in your files."

"Your superiors can't tell you everything, Tench," Bishop said.

"We have files?" Pope asked, looking at Bishop.

"Doesn't everyone?" she replied. He raised his eyebrows, shrugged and dismissed it. For now.

There was a brief silence as everyone took stock. Tench looked at each of them and breathed deeply to get his emotions under control. Not only was he in a weird supernatural world that he once thought only existed in children's stories, he was on the trail of a powerful wizard who would have to be killed, possibly in cold blood, in order to stop him committing any further murders.

"Just a minute," Bishop said. "Why do you need our help? Why can't you rectify this mistake yourselves?"

"Do you think we haven't made the attempt?" Ealvun replied. "Unfortunately, success has not been forthcoming and we must accept that our pride must be put aside. We've tried to locate him but he uses his magical powers to hide from our gaze."

Bishop nodded. "I had the same problem."

"Do you have anything concrete we can use?" Pope asked.

"All we have is his name," Ealvun replied, as if it was hardly worth mentioning.

"And...?" Tench pulled out a notebook and an expensive pen.

"The young man you're looking for is called Arthur Stuart Morris Oswald Drax." Ealvun stated.

Pope's eyes almost bulged from their sockets as the significance sank in, his jaw dropping for a moment. "No!" he yelled and leaped forward to grab the front of Ealvun's tunic. "You bastard!"

The guards pulled Pope off their Lord and made to kill him, but Ealvun stopped them doing so with a simple raised hand. Although Pope struggled fiercely against their grip, they didn't release him.

"Josh, what is it?" Bishop asked. Something niggled at the back of her mind, something she sensed was important.

"Arthur Drax was the child we rescued from Ealvun's clutches back in 1957."

"The one he intended to trade for the changeling?" She lifted her hand to her mouth — it all fell into place. "Oh my god!"

"Exactly! He'll be twenty one now and midsummer's eve has just passed." Pope looked at Ealvun with all the evil he could muster. "Our host must have cast some kind of Fae spell on the child before we rescued him. This was his backup plan."

"No wonder he has such a strong strand of Fae magic in his signature," Bishop said.

Pope seethed, straining at the guards who held him. "That spell must have affected him as he grew, giving him magical ability, turning his head, warping his mind and judgement. Now it's coming to fruition, Arthur Drax has gained more power than he could ever have imagined. But it's made a killer out of him in the process."

"As we already discussed," Ealvun said, squirming a little. "It's a mistake we need help rectifying."

"Bloody hell!" Bishop stepped forward and slapped him across the face with every ounce of strength her body could muster.

Without a moment's thought, Kealin drew his weapon and lunged at her.

The Killer's Trail

It doesn't matter how powerful a magician is, when someone lunges at them unexpectedly and swiftly with a sharp, pointy object there's little they can do to bring up any magical defences in time.

Bishop began to dodge the sword but immediately knew she wouldn't be able to avoid the blade; the best she could do was hope to minimise the damage by attempting to roll with the strike. However, the sword was mere inches from piercing her flesh when it fell from Kealin's hand and hit the stone floor with a clatter, barely missing her leg on the way down.

Tench had reacted with amazing speed and brought his police truncheon down hard on the champion's wrist, hitting just the right spot to cause maximum pain. He followed this with a powerful left hook to Kealin's jaw and the champion's head snapped to one side. Tench's wiry frame didn't have a lot of weight on it but he knew how to use it to maximum effect. Those who judged Tench only on appearances were often surprised by the effectiveness of his actions.

The blow would have instantly knocked a normal man unconscious but the champion simply staggered back, a little stunned. Tench took the opportunity to swap his truncheon to his left hand, grab the fallen sword and point it at his opponent, almost pressing it into the Fae's chest.

"Don't move..." Tench had been on the verge of

calling Kealin "son" but he realised the Fae swordsman was probably centuries older than him at the least.

"You bested my champion," Ealvun said. "You must deliver the killing blow."

"Bugger that!" Tench threw down the weapon, well away from Kealin. "I'm not killing an unarmed man."

Kealin pulled the other sword from its scabbard and his eyes glinted with a cold light. "Hardly unarmed."

"Put away that sword!" Ealvun spat. "It is not yours to use. You have already been bested; do not also bring shame upon my house."

For a moment Kealin was a tense keg of rage on the verge of exploding and a few long seconds passed in which it looked like he might disobey his master. Then he abruptly pulled himself together, sheathed the sword, turned to Ealvun and bowed his head. "Yes, my Lord."

Ealvun glowered at him. "Anything further and your days as champion will be numbered." He nodded at his guards and they released their hold on Pope. "Now, where were we?"

"We were about to kill you for the harm you heaped upon the Drax child," Pope growled. For the moment he kept a tight rein on his urge to attack.

"Ah, more threats. How tedious." Ealvun turned to Tench. "I think we have more pressing matters, don't you, Inspector?"

Tench nodded. "As fascinating as this malarkey is, I need to get back to York and pick up this Arthur Drax."

"I want this arse-wipe to pay for what he did," Pope said, jerking his thumb at the Fae Lord. "I should have killed him back in 1957. He's just as responsible for those women's deaths as Drax."

"Really?" Ealvun folded his arms across his chest. "Look not at the women he killed but the type of magic he used. Might you not ask how he came into that power and what may have triggered it? Could it not have been prevented?" He turned his head to stare at Bishop.

She stepped back under Ealvun's dark gaze as if his questions had struck her a physical blow. Her knees became weak. "Oh my god...!"

"What?" Pope asked, grabbing her arm to give her support.

"The earth gem," she replied, her words barely audible. "I put it around his neck for protection but it must have triggered an affinity for earth magic and his power then developed far too quickly." Bishop looked into Pope's eyes with tears forming in her own. "It's my fault!"

"You may have triggered Drax's magical ability, but you're not responsible for his actions." Pope held Bishop's face in his hands, firmly but reassuringly. "The evil his deeds contain came from within."

He glared at Ealvun again. "Or another place entirely."

"I still gave him the power he used to commit an evil act."

"But that was not your intent." Pope could sense every twist of her emotions; he understood what she was going through. "Your only thought was to protect the child."

"Well..." Her tears eased a little. Pope's words began to get through to her. She could see the sense in what he said but it wasn't that easy.

"We use our magic in the best way we can," Pope continued. "We can't see every twist and turn in the road. We can't know what others will make of the good we try to do."

"But I still feel responsible." Bishop sniffed.

"Then it's time to put it right." Pope spoke through gritted teeth and wiped Bishop's tears away with his thumbs before moving back a step. She nodded her readiness, though she was far from happy.

Ealvun gestured with his hands towards the nearby wall of the castle, to which the balcony was attached. It opened up, furling back on itself as the one in the church hall had done, opening another Fae gateway. He nodded to his champion who gave the sheathed sword to Coruban.

"Only use it as instructed," Kealin hissed, narrowing his eyes.

Coruban smirked as he pulled the sword from its scabbard for a moment to examine the blade, testing its weight and balance. He then followed Bishop, Pope and Tench as they walked towards the gateway, re-sheathing it as he went.

Just before he stepped through, Pope turned back. "I'll not forget your part in this, Ealvun."

The Fae Lord lowered his head a little and gave the wizard a dark stare. The look of loathing was reciprocated for a moment before Pope turned away and passed through the Faerie door.

They emerged back in the church hall and the gateway closed rapidly behind them. The forensics team were still busy, although the bodies and severed heads had now been removed for their post-mortems.

"Messy..." Coruban said and smiled. He buckled on the sword and checked it hung on his hip in the right manner.

"Would I be wasting my time if I asked you not to wear that weapon in public?" Tench asked. Coruban slapped him on the shoulder and smiled again, but there was a look in his eye that Tench didn't like.

The quartet ignored the stares of the forensics team who looked as though they would burst from their curiosity.

Tench strode quickly towards the exit with an agitated gait and the others following him. Behind the detective, Bishop caught Pope's attention then cocked her head in the policeman's direction with a concerned, questioning look on her face. Pope shrugged and shook his head.

Coruban followed at the back of the group, scanning his surroundings as if bringing up the rear of an army patrol squad. He looked little more than a child in this world but displayed a body language and attitude that suggested much greater experience.

Outside, Mainbrace was drinking tea from the plastic cup of a vacuum flask, standing with a couple of uniformed officers, and when the four emerged from the hall he was caught a little off-guard. He handed the cup to one of the uniforms and turned to face his boss, giving Coruban and his sword a questioning glance in the process.

"Where have you been, sir?" he asked. "You've been gone over an hour. I couldn't get any sense out of the forensics team. They said..."

"Later, sergeant," Tench replied. "Right now I want you to get on the radio and find out the address of Arthur Drax, aged twenty one."

"Yes, sir." Mainbrace opened the door of Tench's car, sat in the passenger seat and pulled out the radio's handset.

"I know where he lived twenty years ago," Pope said while the detective sergeant made the call.

"I'd rather we made certain," Tench said, brusquely. "Our time is valuable and not to be wasted on anything other than police procedure."

Pope had to turn away at Tench's suddenly formal manner. He didn't know whether to be angry or fall about laughing.

"I got the address, sir," Mainbrace said after a moment. He climbed out of the car and held up the piece of paper on which he'd written it.

"Keep an eye on things here, Peter," Tench said and grabbed the note. He turned to the others and motioned for them to get into the car, then pointed at Coruban. "You, get in the front where I can keep an eye on you."

The Fae swordsman was fascinated by the vehicle but became exceedingly nervous every time Tench took a corner at speed, which he took delight in once he'd cottoned on to Coruban's reaction. In the back, Bishop shook her head — at times Tench was no different to all the other cops.

Such was the detective's eagerness to reach Drax's home and give Coruban a scare in the process, the four of them almost missed seeing the large man stumbling along a quiet street, leaning heavily on the wall he walked beside.

"Sam!" yelled Pope just as they were passing.

"Stop the car!" Bishop screamed.

Tench slammed on the brakes. The car's tyres squealed against the road surface and the car fishtailed a little. Pope was out of the vehicle like greased lightning with Bishop only a little behind. They cautiously grabbed Finlay and turned him around so they could get a better look at him.

"Bloody hell, man!" Pope exclaimed. Bishop was momentarily lost for words at what she saw. Finlay's face looked like he'd gone ten rounds with King Kong, his clothing soaked with blood.

"What happened, Sammy?" Bishop finally asked.

"Attacked," Finlay spluttered through his swollen lips. "Kid we... rescued... Changeling..."

"Drax!" Pope said.

Finlay nodded in confirmation then his whole body

slumped — he'd passed out. They helped him slide gently to the ground, laying him out on the pavement.

"He's lost a lot of blood," Bishop said, tears in danger of filling her eyes again.

"Shit!" Pope said. "Don't worry, Sam. We're going to get the bastard."

"I'll call an ambulance," Tench said. He'd left the car but was now making his way back to it.

"No! We can't do that," Pope called out. "Sam has troll blood in him and we don't want the hospital doing any tests."

"What do you suggest?"

"Get him in the back seat of the car and I'll heal him as best I can," Bishop said, pulling herself back from the brink of crying uncontrollably.

Tench stared for a moment. "But—"

Bishop stabbed her index finger towards him emphatically. "Don't you dare say anything about your upholstery!" She turned to Pope and Coruban. "Give me a hand."

Tench went to the boot of his car and pulled out a blanket, spreading it over the back seat just as the other three dragged the big man into the vehicle.

"Are we far from the Drax house?" Bishop asked.

"Just around the corner," Tench replied.

"Must be the same house as before," Pope said.

"Okay, leave me to heal Sammy. You check out the house." Bishop's practical nature took charge and she pulled an earth gem from her pocket, grasped it tightly in her left hand before placing her right on Finlay's forehead. His injuries made it difficult for him to breathe. She pushed her magic into his body, looking for any life threatening injuries in order to deal with those first.

Pope, Tench and Coruban ran around the corner and a number of houses down the street to where the Drax family lived, but when they beat on the door there was no answer.

"Can you smell something?" Pope asked, his nose wrinkling.

Coruban sniffed the air and pulled a face. "Not good."

Tench crouched down near the door, pushing the letter-box open. The smell wafted out more strongly — a mixture of smoke and decay — which made the detective retch, somewhat surprising considering his years of experience.

Closing the letter-box again, Tench took a breath of fresh air to calm his stomach, then rammed his shoulder against the door in the hope of forcing it open. However, the old door was much more solid than it looked and it would take considerable strength to beak it down.

"Allow me," Coruban said and Tench moved to one side. The Fae stepped forward, lifted his right foot and kicked the door in the middle with such force it flew open and slammed into the wall of the narrow hallway, smashing the plaster beneath the floral wallpaper. Tench looked at the Fae youth through newly surprised eyes.

They moved cautiously down the hallway, steeling themselves against a smell so thick they tasted it at the back of their throats when they breathed.

Entering the kitchen, they found it was both the source of the smoke and of the decay. It was hot and rancid in the small room in a way that made the skin crawl with a desperate yearning for a bath.

It was twenty one years since Pope had last seen Morris Drax, Arthur's father, but it was difficult to tell how the years had treated him; it looked like he'd been dead for at least a couple of weeks. Sitting in one of the dining chairs at the kitchen table, his head hung back and his jaw lolled open. His eyes had been burned out of their sockets. Flies buzzed around the corpse, their irritating presence made the scene feel even worse, as if contact with them would pass on the touch of death.

Ethel, Morris's wife, hadn't suffered in quite the same way but had been left to endure a more lingering final fate. She shuffled across the kitchen floor in a hollow, empty trance. Judging by her emaciated look and the dreadful stains on her cotton trousers, she'd been like this for some time. Most surprising was how she managed to keep her body moving in her completely malnourished state.

On the stove, a pan smoked, its contents long burned away to nothing but blackened remains, the gas ring heating up the room.

"Drax probably hasn't been here for a while," Tench said. "I need to call this in and get an ambulance for the wife." He moved out of the kitchen to check the other rooms for a phone.

"Who would do something like this to his own parents?" Pope shook his head as he looked at the corpse.

"Perhaps they stood in his way," Coruban said. "Parents are not important."

"You think not?" Pope looked at the Fae youth through suspicious eyes.

"You should know."

"Someone's been feeding you gossip."

"It's not difficult to search Fae archives and discover information about Shadow Dominion royalty." The two held each other's gaze for a few moments.

"I never knew my parents." Pope paused, looked away. "There were times I dreamed of killing them for the life they gave me, had they been alive, but I would never have made them suffer."

"In my experience, parents exist to make our lives a living hell." Coruban wiped his finger across the table, picking up some of the greasy soot that had been deposited there.

"Really?" Pope watched him closely. "Tell me more."

"My father hates me. My mother gave me up twenty one years ago." Coruban rubbed his fingers together to rid them of the soot. "I've been an outcast ever since you took me from here and returned me to the Fae realm. I remember biting your flesh as you carried me."

"You were the child Ealvun intended to swap with Arthur Drax?"

"Indeed." He indicated the scar on his chest. "They branded me shortly after I returned."

"And you remember that, too?"

"Every agonising second."

"Damn!" Pope cringed. No child — even one of the Fae — should ever be treated in such a manner. He reached out to put a comforting hand on the young Fae's shoulder but he slapped the hand away. Pope nodded. "What does the symbol mean?"

"Unwanted."

Pope became thoughtful. Ealvun had a lot to answer for — screwing with the lives of two children, causing both such pain in the process. But it couldn't be coincidence that Coruban was the one chosen to accompany them.

"Why are you here?"

"Lord Ealvun told you," Coruban said.

"I know your purpose, but why specifically you?"

"The Lord has given me the chance to redeem myself in his eyes. Perhaps he will then acknowledge me as his son."

Pope's eyes flew wide. "Your his...? But... Ah, forget it."

"What's going on here?" Bishop demanded as she entered the kitchen, her face screwed up against the heat and stench, her eyes red and watering.

Pope turned to face her. "How's Sam?"

"He'll be fine, eventually, but never mind that." Bishop stepped towards Ethel. "Why haven't you done anything about this poor woman?"

"What can we do?" Pope spread his arms wide in exasperation. "What will happen if we break Drax's spell?"

"You have a point," Bishop breathed. "Leave her to me."

She walked over to the woman, put her hand on the dry, almost papery skin of her forehead and closed her eyes. She reached out with her magical senses and attempted to reach inside the mind of the poor woman. After a few minutes she opened her eyes wide and broke contact, staring at Ethel in horror.

"Nothing," she said. "Nothing at all."

"What do you mean?"

"There's no sign of her conscious mind inside her head."

"Can it be brought back?"

"I have no idea." Bishop turned away and switched off the gas ring. "I've never come across anything like this."

"Damn!" Pope exclaimed. "We have to find Drax quickly."

Coruban looked at them both then walked over to Morris's corpse. He stood behind the chair it sat in, placing his hands on either side of his head. In a similar action to Bishop's, Coruban closed his eyes and used his Fae senses in the working of a spell.

"I cannot detect him," he said after a few moments, breaking contact with the corpse. "I cannot find a connection to the killer. He could be anywhere."

"And we have no idea what he's planning," Pope said.

The sound of heavy, uneven footfalls turned their

attention to the doorway and Finlay's large frame appeared from the hallway. He leaned on the door jamb for support, still very weak.

"It's worse than that," he said. "The bastard has Kitty with him."

"Cute Couple"

The music sounded pretty loud in Art's small living room, but it wasn't easy to listen to Blondie's *Parallel Lines* without cranking up the volume. It was the kind of record that almost demanded that the sound be turned up and Kitty was in the mood for Debbie Harry and the gang to let it all hang out.

Art returned from the kitchen and passed Kitty a coke, shouting to her as he did so. "Sorry, I don't have any beer." She grabbed the can from him and shrugged to indicate it didn't matter.

"One way or another..." she sang, keeping up with the record, then did a little seated jig in her place on the sofa. She stripped the ring-pull from the can and tossed it into a nearby bin. She downed a mouthful with a noisy slurp, mostly disguised by the music.

Art turned it down before sitting beside her. "I'm surprised you came."

"Why?" She looked at him like he'd just broken wind.

"A girl alone in a strange man's flat."

"Ooh, scary." Kitty laughed. "I wouldn't have come if I couldn't take care of myself."

"Isn't that what you all say?" Art looked down at his can. He held it in both hands to let it cool his fingers. "Women always say they can look after themselves. Until the axe murderer cleaves their head from their shoulders."

"Are you trying to tell me you're an axe murderer?"

Kitty looked shocked, her gaze intense. "I've never met one before."

Art appeared uncomfortable, avoiding her gaze. "Of course not!" he said, a little loudly.

"I'm kidding," Kitty said and nudged him with her elbow. "But I'll break both your thumbs if you are. See how you wield your axe, then." She laughed.

Art wriggled his thumbs, still aware of some residual pain, then smiled self-consciously at Kitty. Her eyes twinkled as she took another sip from the can.

"You seem suddenly tense, nervous about something..." she said. Then her eyes widened. "Oh... Hey, if you think you're going to get lucky, forget it. I never shag on the first date."

Art's face went bright red. "I... well... I... no..."

Kitty laughed. "Not used to the liberated woman, Art?"

"Well..." He took a long drink from his can then suddenly burped. "Bugger."

Kitty laughed again and stood up. "Is it okay if I look around?" She had to raise her voice over the sound of the music.

"Yeah, I guess so."

She raised a curious eyebrow at him but didn't say anything. As she examined the bookshelves, the pile of records stacked nearby and the other bits and pieces, she looked over at Art and tried to match him with the stuff that filled the room. Somehow he didn't quite fit any of it, like someone else had made the choices for him.

He sat with his head down, presenting a different front to his earlier, confident self. Now he was a little meeker, seemingly smaller, subtly changed. Even his hair seemed to have taken on a new shade. Something about him made her feel like she'd picked up the wrong coat from the pub, but failed to understand why it didn't fit.

She laughed out loud at her ludicrous thoughts.

Art looked at her oddly. "What?"

"Nothing," Kitty replied. "Just me being daft."

Reaching under one of the sofa cushions, Art pulled out a tobacco tin. "Do you want a joint?"

"I don't smoke." She eyed the tin with distaste.

"You don't know what you're missing." He grinned leerily.

"It's not that. If you had space cakes I'd have one of those," she said. "I haven't smoked for years."

Art shrugged and Kitty turned away while he rolled the joint. She wished he wouldn't do it in front of her as it would only bring back the old cravings, but she couldn't stop him doing what he wanted in his own flat.

She picked up a framed photograph from the top of a small portable television. It showed two people in their early twenties, clearly an item from the way they held their arms around each other.

"Cute couple," she said, waving the photo for Art to see.

"Oh, yeah..." he replied, trying to light the roll-up. He puffed a couple of times and the excess cigarette paper flared up and nearly took his hair off. "They're my cousins."

"Really? They look pretty cosy."

"Well, he's my cousin and she's his bird." Art sucked in the smoke and began relaxing again. His whole demeanour shifted back to how he'd been when they were having a laugh in the pub. He took another long drag on the joint and slouched down in the sofa.

"What are they called?"

"Them?" Art screwed up his face in thought. "He's... Morris and she's Ethel."

Kitty nodded, put the photo back and looked around some more. On a nearby shelf was a chipped ceramic bowl that puzzled her. It wasn't the bowl itself but the contents — it was filled with beads, bangles and other assorted, cheap jewelry, including a large, green gem. While it wasn't unheard of for men to wear such items, it really didn't seem Art's style. Then it dawned on her that they probably belonged to a former girlfriend and it was none of her business.

She looked over at Art and it seemed like he was more interested in the joint than he was in her company. She was surprised by how much that bothered her.

"I need a pee," she said.

"Down there, at the end," Art said, talking around the joint between his lips. He waved vaguely to indicate a small corridor to his right.

As she sauntered down the short passage, looking around, she became aware of a faint, but unpleasant smell she hadn't noticed in the living room. She'd have just put it down to the odour of student living if something else hadn't also caught her attention.

A large cupboard was set into the left wall of the passage and a magic symbol had been carved, very roughly, into the door's gloss paint. Most people passing it would never have noticed and certainly wouldn't have known what it represented, but Kitty had been studying magic with Bishop and Pope for three years, which included learning a huge range of symbols. This rough carving was the earth magic mark for safekeeping. It meant the door was magically locked.

It also meant that Art was far more than he seemed. The mixed messages she'd been getting from him suddenly made a lot more sense and a dark feeling of dread began to creep upon her.

Kitty looked over her shoulder but Art was staring straight ahead and took no notice of her. Taking a felt-tip pen out of her pocket she drew her own symbol — one that was designed to negate the power of the one scratched into the door.

It didn't matter that Kitty had no magical ability of her own; symbols had their own magic that, if used properly, could give similar results as spells, within reason. Of course, if Art had infused the carved symbol with additional magic she'd never be able to negate it. That, of course, assumed he was a magician rather than a symbol user like her.

She checked on Art again, glancing at him quickly, then finished drawing her symbol. A slight change in the air, somewhat like the hum of a fridge cutting out — noticed when it's gone — told her the symbol had done the trick; the cupboard door almost appeared to relax in its frame. Kitty pulled on the handle with a slow, steady pressure but the forces pushing on the door from within were suddenly released in a motion that made her jump.

Something large and heavy fell out and onto the floor with a cringe-making impact, followed quickly by a second, which turned out to be rather unpleasant corpses that now filled the flat with a stench previously held at bay by the closed cupboard door.

She screamed, unable to help herself before clamping her hand over her mouth.

One of the bodies had landed face up. In spite of the bloating and decay, it was easily recognisable as the young man in the photo she'd recently looked at.

Kitty gave another little yelp as Art came up behind her, grabbed her by her upper arm and yanked her around. He pressed his face close to hers, all effects of the weed now gone, and the evil in his eyes caused her to cower in fear.

"I really wish you hadn't done that," he said, spitting out his spent joint.

Find Kitty

"Do you mean he's kidnapped her?" Bishop asked.

"No," Finlay said, wincing from the effort of talking. Although Bishop had done a great job healing him past the worst, she didn't have time to finish the job just yet and his face was still incredibly sore. "They were having a drink in the pub."

"What, like friends?" Pope asked.

"Yeah. I knew something was wrong. I couldn't put my finger on it until it was too late. Bastard attacked me in the bogs with a magical blast." He touched his face tenderly. "I've never been hit so hard in my life."

Bishop faced Pope and grabbed his arm urgently. "We've got to find her, Josh. She doesn't know the danger she's in."

"Let's hope it stays like that a while longer," Pope said. He pricked his thumb on a carpet tack from his pocket, squeezing some blood out. When he was sure he had enough, he bent down and drew a circle on the grimy, lino floor tiles. He squeezed some more and let a drop fall into the centre of the circle, speaking in his strange tongue as he did so.

"*Braench al deffer tan* Drax."

The drop hit the floor, formed into a mist then took on the shape of a ribbon, which would normally lead him to the focus of the spell. But instead of winding a trail out of the door, the magical ribbon twisted about itself and collapsed; the spell was finished without success. Pope looked up and shook his head, every bit as worried as Bishop looked.

"Can you track down Kitty?" Bishop asked.

"The spell would never get past the protective charm she always wears — the one you gave her."

"Damn!" Bishop said. "Protection is such a double edged blade." The charm prevented them from finding Kitty but it was unlikely to be powerful enough to keep her safe from direct contact with Drax.

"You killed those people and moved into their flat!" Kitty yelled. "Why would you do such a thing?"

"Why not?" A wild smugness played across Art's face, giving him an evil but almost pantomime look. He held the green gem in in his hand and drew on the energy it contained. Kitty now realised she should have recognised it earlier — it was the kind of gem that Bishop used. Once depleted, Art tossed the stone to one side and it fell behind the sofa. "I have the power to do whatever I want. I don't have to answer to anyone's false moral code. No one tells Asmo Drax what to do."

"Well, sod you!" Kitty regretted her earlier claim that she could look after herself but she couldn't let him sense that. She twisted her arm out of his grip and used the motion to bring her opposite arm around to land a hard, sharp blow on his jaw with the heel of her hand. He staggered back in shock, into the small living room, and she quickly followed, keeping her attack momentum going.

Art raised his arm to cast a spell but Kitty was faster and delivered a powerful kick to his abdomen followed by another to his head when he doubled up from the first blow. He fell backwards onto the floor, blood flowing from his nose, but no sooner had the bleeding started than it stopped.

He lifted his hand again, but Kitty grabbed it, twisting fiercely, slamming it into the arm of the sofa in one fluid movement. She put her weight behind the move and Art screamed out when the bone broke with a sickening snap. Kitty had no time to react — she had to keep up her attack until she'd disabled him enough to feel safe. He was clearly a wizard but she had no way of telling how powerful he was. She didn't want to find out the hard way and needed to keep him from casting a spell.

Kitty kicked him in the head again. Twice. But now he raised his other hand and all Kitty could do was stamp down on it, crushing and breaking the fingers. She surprised herself with the ferocity of her attack but she'd lived on the streets for a while and knew what it was like to have to fight off unwanted attention. She was damned sure she wasn't going to end up like the couple Art had stuffed in the cupboard.

What astounded her more was that, in spite of her best efforts, Art was still conscious. His magical abilities must make him more resilient than normal or allow him to heal almost instantly.

"Let's see how tough you really are," she yelled and booted him really hard in the testicles. That hit the mark and Art dry-retched, gasping for breath, so she delivered another kick to the head which finally knocked him unconscious.

"Bloody hell!" Kitty put her hands on her knees and took a series of deep breaths, allowing her heart to slow down a little. However, she knew she couldn't relax and had to get out of there.

She grabbed her bag and made for the door but as soon as she tried the handle she knew there was no getting out that way. Not only was it locked with no key in sight, it would be impossible to kick down from the inside.

Kitty rushed to the windows but they refused to budge; stuck shut with many layers of paint built up over the years. It would take an age to pry them open. She needed something she could smash through the whole window. The height of the drop was a worry but she had to escape.

She turned around to look for something suitable but gasped in surprise. Art was conscious, already on his feet and incredibly angry. He raised his hands before him while Kitty watched in astonishment, caught with nowhere to run and too far to attack in time. His hand and other arm healed quickly before her eyes, with popping, grinding noises that sounded agonisingly worse than the original breaks. He simply grinned and looked at her with venom filled eyes.

"You're about to regret the whole of your pathetic little life," he said and pointed his hands towards her.

"Use *their* blood," Coruban said and pointed at the woman and her dead husband.

Pope looked at the Fae then at Drax's parents, He raised an eyebrow, nodded and a grim smile settled on his lips. "That might just work. Faye, get me a clean cup, will you?"

Bishop started looking through the cupboards as Pope stepped over to the woman then stuck the tack into the base of her thumb. Because she was so dehydrated, he had to press quite deeply before he drew any blood, but thankfully her trance meant she was oblivious to any pain.

Coruban watched with his arms folded, his eyes eagerly wide. He licked his lips without thinking. Whatever went through his mind, he clearly had no love for humans.

"What the hell are you doing?!" Tench bellowed as he returned to the kitchen.

"I need her blood to help me locate Drax," Pope said.

"A close friend is in danger so we need to find him quickly," Bishop added, holding the cup she'd just found while Pope squeezed a little blood into it.

"Is this really necessary?" Tench's hands clenched and opened a few times and he fought his renewed agitation. Whenever they pulled this kind of stunt to perform their magic he felt he should be arresting them instead of working with them. His mind told him they were working for good but his heart fought it every inch of the way.

"Did you call the Chief Inspector about *The Book of Concurrence*?" Bishop asked.

"Yes!" Tench snapped. He couldn't meet her eyes.

"Then you know that we've got to do whatever it takes." Bishop moved directly in front of his face and he met her gaze for a short second. "We're doing no real harm but we might just save someone's life."

Pope had already moved over to the corpse, looking him over for a minute. "If you want to help, Tench, find something to wrap around Ethel's wound."

Tench began searching the drawers and Pope dropped to his knees beside the corpse. He pulled out a small pen-knife and stuck the blade into the dead man's ankle.

"Why his foot?" Bishop asked as she knelt down ready with the cup.

"It'll be difficult getting blood from a long-dead

corpse, but hopefully gravity will have gathered enough at the lowest point of the body."

With no heart to pump it, the blood oozed out slowly, thickly and reluctantly, but Bishop was able to gather a little. "Enough?" she asked after a moment.

"Yeah, thanks." Both magicians stood up again.

Tench watched closely as he wrapped a clean tea-towel around Ethel's hand. While some magic clearly had its uses, this kind of thing gave him the creeps.

Pope took the cup from Bishop, stirring the viscous blood mixture with his finger before going through the spell's procedure again. This time, as soon as Pope spoke the words and the blood drop hit the floor, a ribbon of red mist formed inside the new blood circle, searched for a direction, then shot out of the kitchen door, down the hallway and into the street. Bishop, Pope and Coruban were instantly running through the house like rats up a drainpipe.

Tench looked around bewildered for a moment and Finlay shrugged at him. He finished tying the knot in the tea-towel, then trotted out of the house himself. However, when he arrived in the street there was no sign of the trio or the mist ribbon.

"Damn!"

Art was a powerful wizard for such a young age, but he'd had no time to develop any refinement to his magic. Trying to target Kitty as she leapt and dodged about the room was like a boxer trying to type with his gloves on.

Kitty was glad of his inexperience — she'd completely wrong-footed him with her first dodge and keeping on the move made her a hard target even in such a confined space. But she knew that sooner or later he'd get lucky or she'd become exhausted. There was only so far a person could go on fitness and adrenalin.

Almost everything in the room was smashed, bent or torn. Plaster and light fittings hung loosely from the ceiling, the TV was caved in and the sofa upturned.

Art readied another blast and tried to work out where Kitty was going to end with her current move and let rip the biggest spell he'd fired so far. Fortunately, Kitty anticipated his plan and slid to the floor, letting the blast go through the space she would have otherwise occupied. The energy slammed into the wall with such force it tore a hole a yard across through the wood and plasterboard partition.

Kitty leapt to her feet and ducked through the hole, finding herself in the flat's bedroom. Plaster was scattered everywhere and dust filled the air. She pressed her back against the wall beside the opening and tried to catch her breath without breathing in too much dust. If Art had any sense he'd be cautious about coming through the gap, which might buy her a little time to think.

Whatever went through the young wizard's mind, thoughts of caution were not in the mix for he stuck his head through the break in the wall almost immediately. Kitty attacked in an instant and punched him in the side of the head with a perfectly timed strike that caused something to pop in his jaw.

"You bitch!" Drax snarled through his dislocation and pulled his head back. In the lull that followed, Kitty faintly heard the sounds of him healing himself.

Quickly looking around the room, she saw something poking out from under the bed. When she grabbed it and found it was a cricket bat she grinned and moved next to the hole again, readying the bat — this would deliver a mighty blow. She'd never played cricket but she was sure that her lack of stroke technique wouldn't matter.

Art stuck his head through as expected and Kitty swung the bat with all the force she could muster, hoping to hit his head for six, but instead of knocking it from his shoulders it struck some kind of invisible shield. She backed away until she was stopped by the junction of the bed and the room's window and could only watch helplessly as he entered the room.

Once through the hole and standing erect again, Drax dropped the shield and prepared to strike again. But as he built his power for the blast, his features began to change, unable to maintain the facade any longer. Gone was the handsome man she'd previously known; in his place was a short, pudgy guy whose hair was already thinning, making him look older than his real age, yet he still had the same captivating green eyes. This was the true face of the man — an unpleasant, physical weakling who wielded power most men couldn't even dream of.

"Art, stop," Kitty pleaded. She almost felt pity for the poor little guy. Almost.

"Call me Asmo!" As Drax shrank three inches in height, so his anger and madness appeared more concentrated. "I'm Asmo Drax!"

"Okay... Asmo." She desperately tried to keep her true feelings from showing on her face. "Why are you trying to kill me? I thought you liked me."

"Whatever gave you that idea? I was hoping for a shag but killing you will be much more fun."

"I'm not dead yet, you bastard."

"Ha! You think a cheap cricket bat can stand against the power of the Earth?"

Art raised his hands and in the half second it took him to prepare his spell Kitty dropped the bat then snatched a pillow from the nearby bed and held it in front of her. The crazy wizard let rip a massive blast of energy that hit her full on and although the pillow reduced the direct impact to her body, the overall force still pushed her clean through the bedroom window.

Coruban proved to be fleet of foot and, following Pope's mist trail, reached the large, three-story house ahead of Bishop and Pope who lagged behind by about thirty yards. They hadn't had to run more than a half dozen streets, thankfully, but were still too late to prevent Drax's final attack on Kitty.

As Coruban dashed across the road towards the house the ribbon identified, a window in the top story shattered explosively above his head and Kitty flew through the air amid a cloud of wood splinters and glass shards.

Cornered

"Coruban! Catch her!" Pope yelled, his voice loud and commanding.

Without breaking his stride, the Fae timed his leap to perfection and plucked Kitty from the air before landing amongst a shower of broken glass with an impact that would have broken the legs of a normal man. He deposited her on her feet and brushed a few fragments of glass off his clothing before Bishop and Pope reached them.

"Kitty! Are you okay?" Bishop grabbed the teenager's shoulders to look her over. There appeared to be little wrong other than a few minor cuts and bruises. Although bewildered by her fortuitous rescue, Kitty quickly shook it off.

"Never mind me, Asmo's gone insane!" she yelled. "He killed two people and tried to kill me." She was still holding the pillow and gripped it so hard her knuckles turned white.

"Asmo?" Pope asked.

"Well, his name's Art but he flipped and started calling himself Asmo. I should explain..."

"We know who he is, Kitty," Pope said and picked a couple of splinters from the girl's hair. He didn't always show his concern for her in demonstrative ways, but she always liked the little things he did.

Kitty began to smile when she caught sight of something and looked up at the broken window. "Look!

There he is!"

They all whipped their heads around to see that Drax was poking his head through the opening, but as soon as they spotted him he disappeared back inside.

Coruban immediately dashed over and leapt onto the roof of the ground floor bay window then jumped up again to grab the sill directly below the gaping hole. He quickly pulled himself through the frame, mindful of the glass shards edging it like teeth, and disappeared into the top storey flat.

Unable to leap like the young Fae, Pope ran into the house through the front door, hardly pausing as he slammed it open. Bishop paused, uncertain, and looked at Kitty who nodded to her.

"I'm okay," the teenager said. "Go get the bastard."

Bishop followed Pope into the house and raced up the stairs to the top floor where she caught up with him just as he burst into the flat by shoulder-barging the door.

Coruban, his sword drawn, had cornered Drax in the wrecked living room and the two were facing each other off. Pope pulled out his penknife ready to draw blood should his magic be needed and Bishop prepared her earth magic reserves.

"Take it easy, Drax," Pope said, his free hand raised in a calming gesture.

"You think I'm afraid of you?" Drax said. His brave words were not matched by his body language.

"We know about the five dead girls, about your parents. We're here to stop you killing any more."

Drax was a little taken aback by this — he hadn't expected them to connect him to those crimes so quickly. He considered the scene for a few seconds, flicking his angry gaze between his opponents. He appeared to come to a decision then quickly raised his hands.

"No one can stop me," he growled.

Bishop sensed the build-up of energy. "Watch out!"

"Wait!" Coruban yelled, but Drax took no notice and unleashed a powerful magical blast that made them flinch.

His target, though, was not any of his would-be captors, but the floor in front of his feet, through which he blasted a three-foot wide hole with edges ragged with the splintered ends of joists and floorboards. In spite of this, Drax jumped through it anyway, directly into the flat below, landing clumsily on a pile of unopened boxes that, from their labels, appeared to contain all manner of electrical goods. In fact, the whole flat was crammed with boxes of different sizes but Drax had no interest in them and shot towards the door as soon as he got his feet onto solid floor again.

Coruban leapt through the hole, too. "Drax, wait!" he yelled but the young magician took no notice.

On the floor above, Pope ran back through the door he and Bishop had just entered by and hared down the stairs, hoping to head Drax off but the young wizard was surprisingly fast, diving down the stairs and onto the street before they knew it. By the time the three of them followed him out there was no sign of him. They looked around a little astonished.

"He disappeared," Kitty said. She was sitting on the pavement a few yards away from the front of the house with her back against a lamppost, hugging the pillow she seemed unable to let go.

"Which way did he go?" Pope asked.

"No, I mean he just vanished. Into thin air." She threw her hands up and apart to emphasise her point.

"He used his magic to transport himself away?" Bishop exclaimed. "It took me decades to learn the discipline for that kind of manipulation and this bastard's done it by the age of twenty one."

"Shit!" Pope said. He ground his teeth and looked at Bishop with wide eyes. "We've got to stop him before his powers grow any further." He turned around on the spot with his arms spread wide in exasperation. "Where the hell has he gone?"

"Kitty," Bishop said. "Where exactly was he standing when he disappeared?"

Taking Bishop's hand for support, Kitty struggled to her feet. Now the adrenaline rush was wearing off the soreness of the fight's blows was kicking in, along with the pain of the numerous cuts and bruises she'd sustained. Training had never been like this She smiled at Bishop wearily and moved to a spot on the pavement almost directly in front of the house's door.

"Here," she said and pointed to the ground.

Bishop smiled her thanks and squatted down. She spread her fingers wide, held her hands an inch over the ground, then moved them about to sense where the magical residue was strongest. When she had the exact spot she pressed her hands to the pavement and closed her eyes while the others looked on eagerly. Pope put his hands in his pockets and waited patiently but Coruban still had his sword drawn, sporting a stance that made him look like he'd explode at any minute. He beat at his thigh with his free hand in angry self-rebuke.

Breathing slowly and deeply, Bishop moved her head from side to side in order to scan for the direction Drax's transportation spell had taken him. With each slow swing of her head she refined the search a little more.

"Will this enchantment take long?" Coruban asked, getting something of a grip on his anger. He sheathed his sword with a grating sound.

Pope glared at the Fae. "That depends on whether or not she's interrupted," he whispered.

Kitty clung to Pope's arm, pressed her face against his

shoulder for comfort. He and Bishop always made her feel safe and had done so since they took her in three years earlier after a six month spell of living on the streets. As a little of her tension melted away, she watched the Fae pace up and down, marvelling at his natural grace, even with a little rage coursing though him. Then she suddenly felt embarrassed when she realised she'd forgotten something.

"Thanks," she whispered softly when Coruban came close.

"I beg your pardon?" He stopped pacing to stare at her in a puzzled manner. "For what reason do you give me thanks?"

"You caught me and I'm very grateful for that. You saved my life."

"That is certainly true," Coruban said, nodding. "But I only did so because the Shadow Prince ordered me to. I assumed he needed you alive because you might have pertinent information."

"No," Pope hissed. "I needed her alive because she's a human being and a very dear friend. Now, will you both shut up!"

"Sorry," Kitty whispered, almost inaudibly. Coruban simply glared.

Bishop opened her eyes, took a deep breath and stood up like someone rising from slumber. She turned slowly a little, squinted against the evening sun and pointed. "There!"

They all looked in the direction she indicated and visible in the distance, through the gap between a couple of the nearby buildings, was the unmistakable sight of York Minster.

"The tower?" Pope asked and Bishop nodded.

"Right on the heart of the ley line!" she said.

"What is that place?" Coruban asked, his eyes

darkening.

"York Minster," Kitty said.

"The cathedral? Holy ground?!" The Fae's breathing increased and he fingered the pommel of his sword nervously.

"That's right," Pope said with a smirk. "Too bad."

Coruban ignored the remark. He thrust his hand inside his tunic, reached into a small pocket and pulled out a small charm on a fine silver chain. He drew it over his head so it hung around his neck.

Bishop watched with surprise and interest — the last time she'd seen a charm like this was when she'd encountered Artill and Cerrin in the Minster's crypts twenty one years earlier. They'd each worn one to protect them from the adverse effects of standing on holy ground.

"Can you take us there?" Pope asked, a look of concern on his face. It had already been a long day and he didn't want to ask too much of Bishop.

She sighed but nodded, before concentrating once more. After a moment she waved her hand in front of her in a slow, circular motion and a portal appeared, called up by her earth magic. The strain of the complex spell clearly etched on her whole demeanour.

"Wait here," she said to Kitty.

"No way!" Kitty replied. "You're not leaving me alone until that maniac is out of the way. Besides, you look like death warmed up."

Bishop and Pope looked at each other and she gave in when he nodded. All four of them linked hands and stepped into the portal.

It was a difficult transition with two of the travellers being from different worlds to Bishop and Kitty. The resistance of their own magical natures created forces that tried to pull them apart. Normally Bishop could handle this with a swift transition but there was something else at work here. Something she couldn't get a handle on.

However, before she had the time to analyse the problem, they were through and standing on the roof of the Minster's main tower, over two hundred feet above the ground. As soon as they arrived they saw Drax, thankfully at the opposite side of the roof and seemingly preoccupied.

Unfortunately, Bishop had never opened a portal directly over a ley line's focus before — she'd never had the need to — and she was startled by effect it had. The effort of opening it here, along with the strain of the transition, was far too much for her, draining all of her stored earth energy.

She collapsed to the floor like a trembling rag doll.

The Tower

Bishop had fallen into an uncomfortable position, half propped up against the stone parapet. Kitty dropped to her knees beside her and set her more upright then moved her head very close.

"Faye, are you all right?" she whispered.

"Just dandy!" Bishop hissed, a little more sarcastically than she'd intended, her eyes wildly frantic.

Pope glanced at her but Coruban kept his focus on Drax, who stood with his head bowed at the opposite corner of the tower roof. The central area of the roof was raised a few feet above the main walkway that ran around the perimeter, but not high enough to obstruct the direct line of sight. However, it seemed that so far Drax hadn't noticed their presence, which was fortunate for it gave them a little breathing space. Coruban drew his sword and started moving forward but Pope waved him to stop.

"Not yet," he hissed and the Fae halted his progress. Pope turned back to the two women. "Kitty, see what you can do for Faye."

"Okay." The young woman grasped Bishop's hand and looked into eyes that had never looked so manic. She wasn't sure what she could do, but she searched her mind in the hope of remembering a magic symbol that would do the trick. When Bishop started shaking like someone with uncontrollable hypothermia, Kitty began to fear for the earth witch's life.

"Faye, what's happening?" she asked in a low, urgent

voice.

"Used my last energy on the portal. Never opened onto a ley line before. Earth power is rushing to fill the emptiness. Rushing in..."

"How? We're so far above the ground."

"Stone tower is a conduit." Bishop's eyes moved drunkenly, like she'd been dealt a knockout blow and was still reeling from the effects. "It's too fast!"

"Can't you stop it?"

"No..." Bishop whispered. "Not stop..."

"Faye, you've got to try." Kitty was insistent but her face was filled with fear. "Try to stop it."

"That's just it, you idiot. I don't want to." Suddenly stronger, her personality shifting, she stared at Kitty with a wild fire in her eyes that burned into the teenager's soul then pushed her hands away. Her voice took on the timbre of a demon. "I want to absorb it all!"

"Faye, no..."

Kitty stared down at her friend and reached out her hands again, but she hesitated before touching her. What could she do? She had no magical ability and her study of symbols had never covered anything like this.

"Ah, sod it!" she spat.

With little time for niceties, Kitty swung her arm with all her strength and connected with her friend's face in a loud slap.

"Faye, stop! You're not Drax!" she growled.

Bishop was genuinely surprised by the strike and raised her hand to her stinging cheek. The redness from the slap disappeared almost instantly and she abruptly spoke in dual tones as if fighting for control against a demonic version of herself.

"Don't ever do that..."

       "Hit me again!"

"Do so and I will kill you!"

"Again!"

"No! Do not dare!"

"Again!"

Kitty was taken aback. She'd seen nothing like this in the three years she'd known Bishop, but she knew she had to choose a course of action. She slapped Bishop's face again, then a moment later struck a third time, but when she went for a fourth slap Bishop grabbed her wrist.

"Enough, Kitty," she said and pushed herself into a better sitting position against the wall. "I'm in control again."

"What was that?!" Kitty yelled.

Bishop ground her teeth and looked wild-eyed. "I don't have a bloody clue."

Pope looked at the two of them for a second, still concerned, but Coruban didn't care and only looked at Pope.

"We should strike now," Coruban said. "While he's not aware of us."

Pope gave him a quick glance with cold eyes that told the Fae they were not yet ready. They locked their gazes for a moment before he turned back to his long-time friend.

"Faye, can you do this?" he asked. "I can't manage without you."

"I need time to absorb power," she replied.

"More power?" He looked doubtful.

"Yes." She looked at him with dark eyes. "Is there a problem?"

"This is more than you've ever absorbed before."

"Do you think I don't know." She breathed deeply a couple of times. "I can handle it."

"Faye..."

"Josh, don't piss me off! We have to deal with Drax." Although the features of her seemingly young face were the same, she also now carried the weight of her many years behind her expression.

Pope clenched his jaw to bite off any further words. He tried to ignore Bishop's strange turn of mood and returned his gaze to the beast across the roof.

The commotion of their exchange had alerted Drax to their presence; he lifted his head and looked over with dark power emanating from hate-filled eyes. Static energy had formed his thinning hair into a halo around his head and he pulled his lips into the grin of the insanely evil. He would have been a joke if he wasn't so dangerous.

"I knew you'd come," he shouted. "I'm glad you did. I need you here."

"You want an audience?" Pope asked.

"Ha! No. You will be a true test of my power." His eyes glinted darkly and he licked his lips. "And eventually, my victims."

"Has anyone told you you're full of crap?" Pope said.

"Of course. And every one of them is going to die."

Pope signalled to Coruban. They each began edging along the perimeter of the roof, moving in opposite directions, skirting the central section.

Kitty stood up and spread her arms wide, making sure she caught Drax's attention.

"Kitty, too," he called out. "How lovely. Bitch."

She looked directly at the man who, in the space of a few hours, had taken her emotions on the kind of ride she'd never want to repeat. A calm fury settled over her and her breathing became deep and measured.

"Kitty, no!" Bishop whispered from behind her. She knew Kitty was trying to buy Pope and Coruban time, but she was putting herself in danger.

"Art..." Kitty said, then faltered when Drax's grin was replaced by a snarl and he glared at her even more intently. "Sorry. Asmo, why are you doing this?"

"I won't explain myself to you." Drax roared.

"Okay, but... you could be better than this." Kitty moved to one side as she spoke, putting a little distance between her and Bishop, who was still lying down and hidden from Drax's view. "With all that power you could be anything you want — why would you choose to be such a complete arsehole?"

"Sod you!" Drax released a magical blast far more powerful than any he'd fired earlier, but he telegraphed his actions so clearly that Kitty had no trouble dodging out of the way, although she winced in pain when she landed, still feeling the injuries from her earlier fight.

The blast struck the tower's crenellated battlement just to the right of where Bishop lay, missing her head by less than a foot. The intensity of the magic attack knocked free a large chunk of the wall and a ton of masonry shook the building as it crashed through the Minster's roof below.

Kitty winced. In drawing his fire she hadn't thought through the consequences and hoped that no one on the ground below had been injured by the falling mass of stone and mortar.

Pope glanced at the missing section of wall then at Bishop, who rose to a standing position with the help of the untouched part of the wall, still absorbing earth energy. They exchanged a look. Both knew that Drax could be impossible to defeat but they had to make the effort anyway.

Coruban had little interest in the result of Drax's blast, preferring to concentrate on moving closer to his target, though he had taken careful note of the wizard's actions prior to unleashing the attack. Drax may have had more power, but Coruban had been given better tuition in fighting and tactics. In spite of this, the Fae's advance hadn't been missed by Drax.

"Don't come any closer!" Drax said, pointing at the young swordsman in the highly affected pose of a cheap movie villain. Dangerous, yet pathetic, too. "Just tell me who you are."

"My name is Coruban and Lord Ealvun sent me." He paused and looked at Drax with dark, searching eyes but the wizard had no idea who he referred to. "I have come for you, Arthur Stuart Morris Oswald Drax."

"Don't call me that. My name is Asmo!" Drax fired a small bolt of energy at Coruban but the Fae had quickly read the anticipation and simply raised his sword into its path. More than just a weapon, the Fae magic, with which it had been enchanted, deflected the spell easily.

"Aagh!" Bishop screamed.

The redirected blast glanced off her shoulder and knocked her onto her back. She slid towards the gap in the parapet with no purchase to stop her following the earlier route the masonry took. Thankfully, Kitty's reactions were fast and she leapt over in a tiny fraction of a heart beat to pin Bishop's legs to the ground just as her shoulders slid over the edge.

Pope watched this with rapidly building anger and cut into the base of his thumb, made the blood flow freely and prepared his blood magic.

Kitty, however, was fury personified and as soon as she realised Bishop was safe she leapt to her feet again, vaulted onto the raised central section of roof and rushed towards Drax with a speed she never would have thought possible.

Not registering her rapid approach, Drax simply stared at Coruban with an astonished look across his face that began turning to fear. He was so sure of his power he never expected it to be deflected so easily. He had to think. Get himself together.

Through the silence he became aware of sirens in the streets below. And of rapidly approaching footsteps here on the rooftop.

Drax's lack of concentration was exactly what Kitty needed and she launched herself at him from the edge of the raised roof section. Although he'd begun turning towards the sound of her footsteps, he was too slow and she delivered a powerful kick to the wizard's head in mid-flight, connecting perfectly with jaw breaking precision. He hit the wall behind him with a hard thud, then fell to the ground, stunned. Kitty was on him in a flash, grabbing him in a choking head-lock he was unable to counter in his stunned state.

Pope paused, the blood from his cut collecting in his other hand, and stared, holding off the spell he was preparing. He watched Kitty in astonishment. Could she defeat him without magic? Their instinct had been to fight his magic with their own but maybe Kitty had a simpler solution.

That hope proved to be short-lived when Drax quickly recovered from the kick in spite of being choked, his magic allowing him to bypass the need to breathe, for the moment. He calmly touched Kitty's arm with his fingertips, ignored his lungs' demand for oxygen, and used his earth power. The wizard reached into the young woman's mind, exerted a little basic control and she relaxed her grip.

A little more mental manipulation from Drax made Kitty let go of him completely, enabling him to drag in lungfulls of air and quickly fix his injuries. He stood up grinning. Pope's disappointment was almost tangible.

As the contact between them broke, Kitty staggered back a little, her head light and dizzy. She raised a hand to her forehead and reached with the other to support herself against the parapet.

Drax gathered himself again but with Kitty now clear of the line of sight, Pope took his chance. He threw his handful of blood in Drax's direction and spoke the words of his spell.

"*Braench fe taro ach velostic.*"

Pope's magic took the handful of blood and accelerated the droplets instantly in the direction of the young wizard. They hit his upper body and head with the force of a burst of machine gun fire, making him jerk and spasm briefly, giving him no time to scream in pain. The liquid projectiles tore through him like they were solid bullets and he fell to the floor in a crumpled, bloody heap, his injuries horrendous. His body and face more closely resembled minced beef than anything remotely human.

Kitty's head cleared in the instant of Drax's sudden death and she looked down at the bloody mess. "Bastard!" she growled, kicking his mostly uninjured leg for good measure.

Pope moved to her side, pulled her to him, hugged her protectively, accidentally smearing blood from his hand onto her clothes. "It's over now, thank the Shadows." As Kitty hugged him back she shook with relief.

Coruban moved a little closer to Drax's body, staring down at it in disbelief. "It was I who was meant to deal with the wizard."

"We didn't have the time to fanny about," Pope snarled, a small, satisfied grin on his face. "Just go back to your weird life and tell your boss we fixed his bloody mistake."

"But..."

Pope turned away and walked Kitty over to Bishop, who was on her feet but leaning against the raised roof and supporting one of her arms. The silence felt good — even the sirens were gone.

"Are you all right, Faye?" Pope asked.

Bishop moved her arm and winced. "My shoulder's dislocated."

Without warning, Pope grabbed her arm and twisted, making the joint pop back into its socket, which forced a scream from her and made Kitty look away. Bishop gritted her teeth, screwed her eyes tightly closed then used a little of her earth power to heal the bruising and take away the pain.

She nodded her thanks to Pope. Of all the injuries she could sustain, a dislocation was one of the hardest to heal with magic. It wasn't like knitting together broken bone or repairing torn tissues and a manual manipulation was the simplest way to deal with it in spite of the pain involved.

Coruban looked helplessly at the bloody corpse then gazed at his sword before replacing it in its scabbard with an angry thrust. He turned on his heel and walk away to look across the city through one of the gaps in the parapet.

Into one corner of the roof was set a door, behind which was a stone spiral staircase that led down into the Minster and the only normal exit from the top of the tower. This door abruptly burst open and Tench came through, completely out of breath. It was a long climb up the two hundred and seventy five narrow steps from the base of the tower. As he stood in the open doorway breathing heavily, Mainbrace appeared behind him but stayed on the stairs.

"What the hell... is going on?" he gasped.

"There's a bit of a mess to clear up," Pope replied.

"Did you find the killer? Is he here?"

Pope pointed to the bloody remains at the other side of the tower.

"Stay here, Sergeant," Tench said. "And don't let

anyone else onto the roof." He closed the door behind him then walked over to the mess that was once the killer he'd been hunting. He crouched by the remains, still sucking air in rapid time, and rested bony elbows on bonier knees, pulling a face at what he saw. "Is this really the killer?"

"Definitely!" Kitty called out, her voice determined but shaky. "Bastard tried to kill all of us."

"Drax was too powerful, but we didn't know until it was too late," Bishop said and hung her head.

"It wasn't your fault," Pope said, carefully putting his arm around her shoulders. He understood Bishop well enough to know this would bug her for a long time. Maybe years. She looked at him with tears in her eyes.

"I'm glad it's over," Tench said. "But I have no idea how I'm going to write my report. Or what forensics will make of it."

He examined the remains longer than he really needed to, fascinated by the gore of of Drax's demise. He was still looking closely when, staring directly at him from a shapeless mass that must have been his face, the wizard's eyes flashed open.

"Bloody hell!" Tench yelled and almost jumped out of his skin. He fell on his backside then scrambled backwards, away from the corpse, getting to his feet once he was a few yards away. "The bugger's not dead!"

All heads snapped in the direction of Drax's remains, although none had a direct view but Tench, who backed rapidly away. Disbelief was painted across everyone's face until Drax began pulling himself together again.

He almost oozed upright, blood still dripping from his many wounds, dragging disconnected parts together again with his magic, healing himself faster than even magic should make possible.

Pope removed his arm from around Bishop and

looked at her with a look she'd never seen before. For the first time in the four centuries she'd known him she saw deep, genuine fear in his eyes along with a sense of hopelessness.

"The ley line!" she exclaimed, feeling much the same as her friend. "He's so completely connected to the earth energy of its focus he's practically unstoppable. He might be impossible to kill."

"We must do it, Faye." Pope ground his teeth. "Whatever it takes!"

They watched Drax for a moment then nodded to each other and moved apart. "Blood and Earth," they said as one.

Coruban was fascinated by Drax's new development and smiled naturally for the first time since his birth. He unsheathed his sword again and swung it around in figure of eight movements a few times.

Tench, knowing he was completely out of his depth, backed against the door he'd earlier come through, more fearful than he'd ever been, but Kitty, even though she knew she couldn't match Drax's power, had gone way past the point fear had taken her and was simply determined do whatever she could to help.

Bishop touched the stone parapet and drew even more earth energy into her body. Although she'd already stored more than was normally possible, she crammed in everything she could suck from the ley line until every cell in her body felt like it would burst.

Pope re-opened the cut in his hand and began collecting blood again. Behind him, Kitty picked up a rough piece of rubble the size of a cricket ball, hefting it in her hand.

A dark look spread across Drax's blood-covered face as he pulled in energy more rapidly and in greater quantity than Bishop could. She realised that this is what the dead women had been sacrificed for — he was linked to their dead forms, their spirits, like some kind of add-on batteries.

Drax looked down at his rapidly healing body then at the others again. His vocal chords finally healed and his voice came back to him.

"That bloody well hurt, you bastards!"

Earth Power

"What in Hell's going on?" Tench asked, but no one had the time or inclination to answer him. "How could he survive that?!" He tore his eyes from the recovering wizard and looked at the others. He wanted answers but at the same time was fearful of getting them.

Bishop and Pope were preparing their attack spells, Kitty prowled like a caged cat and Coruban walked towards Drax with a smile on his face, his sword held ready.

Kitty stopped her pacing and watched the Fae swordsman. She had no idea what he was up to but thought that a diversion might help. She threw her chunk of rubble at the rapidly healing wizard, hoping it would strike home and smash the little git's face in.

Although her aim was true, Drax, without taking his eyes off the young Fae, simply batted the rock to one side as if it had the weight of a table-tennis ball. It sailed over the rampart and hit something below with a clatter. Kitty was disappointed but at least Coruban had moved closer to his target.

The wizard pulled more energy from the ley line below, his left hand reaching behind him, touching the stone of the tower directly. With his right he readied another blast, his self-healing halted for the moment.

"Listen to me, wizard," Coruban said calmly and came to a stop.

"Piss off!" Drax snarled. "I'm not interested."

"If you do not hear me out, there will come a day when you will regret what may have been."

"What can you possibly offer me?" Drax's energy crackled about his fingertips like micro lightning bolts. He let it do so for a few moments to show the Fae how much he brimmed with sorcerous forces.

"An opportunity of which you could normally only dream," Coruban continued. "Together, our might would be phenomenal, for I am your brother."

"Liar!" Drax spat. "I have no brother. Besides, you're a Fae, a creature of impossibility. We aren't even of the same reality, let alone related."

"Without my Lord you would be nothing." Coruban paused and the two matched glares. "Using me, Lord Ealvun made you what you are."

"Bollocks! I'm my own man and always will be."

Bishop paused her preparations. Pope glared at her, urging her to continue, but she muttered to him. "Wait, Josh. He may have the means to deal with Drax — we should give him the chance."

"Twenty one years ago I was chosen to take your place," Coruban called out. "When we were infants, Ealvun left me here as a Fae changeling and took you back to the Faerie realm." He paused, watching as Drax returned to the task of healing himself, content for the moment to listen to the Fae.

"I should have been brought up by your parents in order to fulfil my destiny," Coruban went on. "Instead, you were rescued by Bishop of York and the Shadow Prince and I am an outcast among my own kind. My mother was imprisoned on that day and I have not once been allowed to visit her."

"If you're planning to break my heart with your sob-story, forget it." Drax sneered and shook his head. "I know you're here to kill me — this is just a ploy to get me to lower my guard."

"You and I are linked more closely than any brothers of blood," Coruban said. "We are two sides of the same coin, forged by Fae magic."

Drax spread his arms in further demonstration. Earth energy sparked brightly, pulsing along the length of both arms. "This is not Fae magic but the power of the Earth!"

"And mighty it is," the Fae said. "But Lord Ealvun planted the seeds of our magic inside of you when you were but a child. You will know the truth of it if you look within you."

At the other side of the roof, Bishop glanced over to Pope a little guiltily, still holding herself to blame. "Do you have any idea what's happening?"

"I'd say that we've been duped," Pope answered. "Unless I'm reading it wrong."

Drax lowered his arms a little and became thoughtful, looking within. "Fae magic... That explains why Sunday school always made me feel ill." He looked down to his feet as if seeing the cathedral anew. "I can feel the nausea, now, but the earth power suppresses it."

"Lord Ealvun sent me," Coruban said, spreading his own arms wide, the sword held upright, shining brightly. "Not to kill you, but to join forces."

"What do you mean?" Drax raised his arms again, along with his power.

"My Lord and father has been planning this for centuries," Coruban said. "His desire is for the two of us to become as one."

Bishop was genuinely puzzled. "Why has Ealvun been so devious in his plans?"

Pope addressed her but kept slitted eyes on the Fae. "Most likely he's being circumspect so he doesn't draw unwanted retribution."

Coruban's heightened Fae hearing brought their

muttered words to his ears and he cast his gaze at Pope, smirking at his reasoning. Knowing this wouldn't help them.

"Ah..." Bishop said with increasing realisation. "If his plan goes wrong he can claim that Coruban is a rogue, unhappy with being an outcast." Pope nodded.

In the light of so much power building, Kitty felt a little helpless and she moved slowly over to stand with Tench. The detective looked pleased to have the company in light of way things were currently shaping up.

"Why?" Drax asked. "Why would he want you to join forces with me?"

"Together we can defeat and kill Bishop and Pope," Coruban replied.

"Shit!" Bishop said through gritted teeth, already gathering up more earth power as quickly as she could, preparing again the spell that she'd just paused. Pope looked at her, waiting for her lead.

"Like I need anyone's help for that." Drax shook his head and laughed coldly.

"Yet still they live." Coruban's words were flat, not critical or sarcastic.

"For now," Drax said. "Don't you see? I need them here to help me push my powers to their limit."

"But such is your naivete, you have now told them of your plan."

"And you think that makes a difference? They'll be compelled to fight me anyway. They're bloody idiots, like you."

Bishop and Pope glanced at each other again, uncomfortable, now knowing how children feel when adults talk about them when they're still in the room.

"Together we will become supremely powerful. We can serve our Lord Ealvun and I will be recognised as his son." Coruban's voice began to take on an edge of desperation. "You must take the sword."

"I am nobody's puppet!" Drax shouted. "I don't need your toy!"

The wizard pointed at Coruban, firing a powerful, sustained blast at the Fae and the latter barely raised the protective sword in time. The magical blast fractured and scattered in all directions and the others dived behind the raised roof section for protection.

Seeing the way the sword shielded Coruban, Drax changed tactic and tightened the focus of his blast, specifically concentrating on the sword itself, pouring everything he had into a dazzlingly ferocious beam. The weapon first began to glow then to soften. The intense power of the earth wore down the Fae magic the sword contained until all but the hilt was destroyed. With nothing in the way, the blast hit the young Fae fully in the chest.

Drax's expression turned from one of anger to a look of dark pleasure as the Fae screamed in agony now he was no longer able to protect himself. Although the magical force struck Coruban hard, he remained in place like a butterfly pinned on display, the beam both blasting and holding him, torturing every part of his body, slowly crushing him.

"No!" he gasped, barely able to force out his words. "I told you... we are linked! You have doomed us, foolish mortal..."

The forces that consumed Coruban also protected his life force, after a fashion, though the balance was in favour of slow, consuming destruction. Then something unexpected happened — those same energies reflected back to Drax in a feedback loop that began to consume him, too. He desperately tried to stop his own beam of energy but the connection was unbreakable, taking on a life of its own. It drew on the ley line's power directly, like syphoning a bath of water. Drax screamed in agony with no idea how to shut down his own out-of-control power.

Bishop could feel the earth energy being sucked from the ley line like a tornado tearing at the landscape. It was building incredibly fast, faster than she'd ever known — she knew that the resulting havoc would be immense if they didn't do something immediately. She shouted a single word at Pope.

"Containment!"

Drawing all the additional energy she could from the edge of the maelstrom, Bishop began chanting one of her impromptu lines.

"Earth Spirits, aid my fight."

At the same time, Pope closed his hands around the blood he'd gathered and voiced a repetitive chant in his strange, guttural tongue. *"Braench ach ferran sferkol fo tumus."*

Bishop's spell developed first and a sphere of energy formed in the air in front of her, from a combination of the spell chant and the way she pictured the handling of such primal forces. She picked up the pace of her chanting to keep the sphere stable.

Pope opened his hands, increasing the tempo of his own chant, too. As his palms moved apart, a sphere of blood floated between them, defying gravity. He spread his hands wider still and the blood sphere shifted, growing larger, a little translucent, like a heave soap bubble inflating. A bubble that rippled and pulsed.

The two magicians controlled the growth of their respective spheres to ensure they matched in size, their eyes flicking back and forth as they controlled base forces that would destroy each other given the chance.

When the two spheres were equal, Bishop and Pope guided them towards each other. They pushed through each other, fighting the whole time, until they overlapped so closely they became as one — a sphere of blood and earth magic that threatened to burst apart if they relaxed concentration for the smallest of moments. Both magicians shuddered as they fought against the natural resistance of the other's individual magic. Although not normally given to being paired, the constant instability in the spheres worked in their favour, becoming far more than a simple addition of two separate energy values.

They continued chanting and the new sphere grew quickly to a size of about twenty five feet before they moved it with their will towards Drax and Coruban, who were unable to offer any kind of resistance as the blood and earth magic surrounded them.

The forces unleashed by Drax were instantly cut off from the outside world, the only sign of them being the dazzling light that now emanated from the sphere and which grew more intense with every moment. The surface of the sphere danced with tendrils of vivid orange and pink energy as it struggled to contain such immense forces.

Until now Drax's energies had increased steadily, but he lost any semblance of control and an abrupt surge of feedback caused a violent release of energy within the sphere. It expanded rapidly by a few feet before Bishop and Pope were able to establish a new equilibrium on their containment spells. They had no idea what was happening inside but stopped their chanting. They now controlled the blood and earth sphere through strength of will alone.

As well as the light it emitted, heat also began leaking through the barrier, which increased rapidly and to such an extent that a nearby flagpole smouldered for a moment before bursting into flames.

Tench and Kitty were able to take shelter from the

rising heat by ducking behind the raised part of the roof, but the two magicians could only accept the damage it did to their exposed flesh. It felt like they were standing before a small star.

"We'll have to open the top of the sphere," Bishop shouted to Pope.

"Okay," Pope replied. "I'll count down from three, right?"

"Right."

"Three... Two... One... Now!"

A hole opened in the top of the sphere about a yard across and the forces within blasted up, changing the shape of the containment shell into a huge teardrop. Power discharged immediately, shooting vertically; an intense beam of magical energy slicing through the atmosphere like a laser shooting into space. The sudden release instantly heated up the air around the beam like a lightning bolt and there was an immediate, deafening thunderclap that reverberated about the historic city below.

The outpouring continued for just a few seconds then died out in an instant. With no forces for it to contain, the magical spells collapsed at once, leaving Bishop and Pope struggling to see — the evening light almost dark in comparison to the dazzling spectacle they'd just witnessed.

The area of roof where the blood and earth containment globe had been, now glowed red with its heat, the lead melted in places. Within it, all that was left of Coruban and Drax were two piles of ash. There was a shocked silence for a few seconds as if the whole world had paused after such a monumental event, then gentle evening birdsong and distant traffic brought a welcome sense of normality.

The sun set in the north west and a very light, cooling

breeze played over their burnt and blistering skin.

"I can't believe we did it," Bishop said through cracked lips. She grabbed Pope's hands with the intention of healing them both at the same time, drawing on additional earth energy to do so.

"What did we just witness?" Tench asked of Kitty as he stood up, but she just stared, completely dumbfounded. She thought she knew a lot about magic but after what she'd just witnessed there was clearly so much more she still had to learn. She never imagined anything on this scale was possible. She began to tremble as she looked at her friends with new eyes.

Tench moved as close as he could without stepping onto the hot section of roof and scratched his head. "What the hell will I say to my superiors...?"

Bishop let go of Pope's hands. The healing was mostly done but their exposed skin would be tender for a few days. They looked like pink British holiday makers who'd been out in the Spanish sun for too long.

"You'll have to come down to the station and make a statement," Tench said, turning round.

Pope shrugged. "Why?"

"We have to explain the two burned bodies," Tench replied and gestured to the piles of ash.

Bishop closed her eyes in concentration and, after muttering a little spell to herself, used a little more earth magic to lift the ashes from the roof surface and into the strengthening wind, which caught them and blew them across the rooftops of York.

"What bodies?"

Tench opened his mouth to speak, his face a picture of annoyance, but without any evidence there was nothing he could do. He shut his mouth again without uttering a word.

"It's been good working with you, Tench," Pope said

and held out his hand. The detective stared at it for a moment before shaking it and giving a reluctant smile.

"At least you stopped the killer," he said, nodding. "I guess we got justice for the people he killed."

"In the end, Drax's own power killed him," Bishop said. "We just stopped it levelling the city."

"And," Pope added, "we also stopped Ealvun's nasty little plan, whatever it might have been." He looked over at Venus, visible in the darkening sky near the horizon, blowing out his cheeks in relief. "At least, I hope we did."

Bishop walked over to Kitty who had squatted against the tower's parapet hugging her knees. She looked lost and uncertain and a tear ran down her cheek.

"Oh, Kitty!" Bishop said as she knelt down and hugged the girl. "It's over, now. There's nothing more that Drax can do."

Kitty raised her face and looked into Bishop's eyes. "What are you?" she whispered. She looked away, terrified.

Bishop stood up and pulled Kitty to her feet. "We'll talk through this at home."

She formed a portal and she, Pope and Kitty stepped through, leaving Tench alone on the tower roof.

The detective looked around, sighed and approached the door behind which his sergeant still stood. "Well, Chief Inspector, it was like this..." he rehearsed. Then he paused, remembered that his superior knew all about the supernatural and smiled. Perhaps there'd be no need for paperwork on this one.

The sky darkened into night and the wind dropped and for a moment all was still about the Minster tower.

Then a small whirlwind flitted about the roof, gathering a tiny amount of dust and ash...

Back in the flat Drax had appropriated, the green gem slipped through a gap between two floorboards behind the sofa. In the space between the floor and the ceiling below, it rested against the brick inner wall of the old house. It glowed feebly with the last traces of its energy.

Part Five

Further Arrivals

Grainger and Lassiter

2011, spring

"What?!" Bishop was appalled and confused. It was like her friend had spoken a foreign language she was unfamiliar with.

"You don't meant to, obviously," Kitty said, "but you're each a lens that focuses my attention on my mortality and all my frailties."

"Since when does Kitty Spender have frailties?" Pope's voice was filled with genuine astonishment. "Compared to most people—"

"That's the trouble," Kitty snapped. "I'm not around 'most people'. I mix with those who seem like Gods and Titans in comparison. I battle demons and monsters and others who would do the world harm by supernatural means."

She paused and walked away a few feet, her back to the others. She gathered her thoughts as she ran her fingers through her hair, pulling together the stray strands.

"You three are the best friends anyone could wish for," she said, her back still to them. "But I wanted something more. Some friends who were more like 'most people'."

"And that's where you've been these last few years?" Bishop asked. "Making friends?"

"Oh, I tried," Kitty replied. "But it's impossible to

form close friendships when you have to lie about who you are and what you do. Hell, I couldn't even tell them how I lost my eye."

"You don't need to lie to us," Finlay said.

"No," Kitty whispered then turned to face them again. "But you three are the only true friends I have."

"Isn't that enough?" Finlay asked. He looked puzzled. "Seems more than enough to me."

Kitty stepped closer and took one of his big hands in hers. "A short time ago I realised it wasn't the number or the quality of the friends, but who you are. Or what you are, might be a better way to put it."

"We are who we are," Pope said, disconcerted by Kitty's words.

"Of course, but each of you will outlive me and forget me."

"No!" Finlay said.

"Never!" Bishop exclaimed.

Pope didn't respond straight away but drew a deep breath as he considered his words. "Kitty, I'm over two thousand two hundred years old. I've met and forgotten a lot of people in that time, but I always remember the friends I made. There's not a single one of them I didn't wish to live a longer life, even by a little, but the burden of loss is something we all have to bear at some time." He paused and bore into her single eye with a look of heartfelt love.

"When it happens, the burden of your passing will be one of the greatest I've had to bear, but the bright light of your memory will sustain me through the dark times that follow."

Kitty sniffed and a tear rand down her cheek. "Bloody hell, Josh. You don't half talk some shit."

A sob broke at the back of Finlay's throat and he turned away to hide his emotions, never comfortable with putting them on display. Bishop swallowed her own feelings down, trying to get them under control. Kitty wiped the wetness from her face with the sleeve of her jacket and took a deep breath.

"So, what's the plan?" she asked.

"The real question that needs answering," Pope said, trying to break the mood. "Is whether you still like the same crappy music?"

"Hey!" Kitty responded, laughing through newly forming tears. She hit Pope on his upper arm. "There's nothing wrong with Duran Duran."

Bishop laughed with her own eyes filling up, then hugged Kitty tightly. "I'm so sorry, Kitty," she whispered. Kitty hugged her back without replying.

"Yeah, sorry," Finlay said. He shrugged then thrust his hands into his pockets, blowing a series of short breaths to aid his self control.

Kitty broke from her hug with Bishop. "Look, I'm going to get old. Just don't treat me like I'm bloody senile, okay?"

They smiled their agreement, then Finlay's body abruptly tensed.

"What?" Kitty asked.

Bishop abruptly whipped around and looked towards the fireplace. Finlay sniffed the air and looked that way, too.

"Another visitor?" Pope asked.

"Feels like it," Bishop replied. She turned to Kitty. "This is what we sensed before you arrived."

"Friend or foe?" Kitty asked.

"So far arrivals have been friendly," Pope said. "But..." He fiddled with the tack in his pocket.

Finlay shrugged and scowled. "Best not to assume anything."

They surrounded the area in front of the fire in a wide

arc just as the warping began. It made Kitty feel nauseated and she closed her eye, but the effect continued even with it tightly shut, indicating it was directly neurological rather than visual.

Then at a moment in time none of them could have pinpointed, a middle-aged priest stood before the fire — his presence having come upon them like a timid aunt shuffling around a wedding reception.

For a few seconds he gathered his wits then thrust his hands into his jacket pockets as if reaching for weapons. He pulled out a crucifix and a bottle of holy water, one held in each hand.

"Grainger!" Finlay exclaimed.

"Put those away," Bishop said. "No one here means you any harm."

"Someone must," the priest hissed. "Or I wouldn't have been brought here."

"You have a point," Pope agreed. "But we still have no idea who or why."

"Then I'll keep the tools of my trade at the ready, if you don't mind."

Father Luke Grainger frowned as he looked around the room with his hands trembling. He wiped them on the already shiny lapels of his jacket, juggling the items he held in order to do so. For a priest who'd experienced the supernatural on numerous occasions, he never found it any easier to deal with. When he'd joined the priesthood decades earlier, he thought tales of supernatural entities and magic were scare stories, so it came as a huge shock when he discovered their existence was real.

"I really don't like the way this is shaping up," Bishop said as she mentally checked off everyone now in the room. In spite of Grainger being a familiar face, the atmosphere in the room held a nervous edge.

Without warning Grainger threw up, heaving noisily as he did so. He only just managed to avoid splashing the others as the vile-smelling vomit hit the carpet with a distinctive splat.

"Jesus, Grainger," Kitty said. "Was that necessary?"

"Never fails," Finlay said, returning to the bar. He wrinkled his sensitive nose and scowled at Grainger, who wiped his mouth on a white handkerchief. "You know it's Father Luke because of the smell he brings."

"Is this some kind of reunion I knew nothing about?" Grainger asked, ignoring the harsh remarks.

"If it is," Bishop replied, "you're not the only one not to receive an invitation."

Grainger put his handkerchief away and looked down at the vomit on the carpet. "I'll clean it up. Where's the landlady?"

Pope looked around the group and everyone suddenly felt a little stupid. "Yes, where *is* she?"

When Bishop and Pope looked at Finlay he shrugged.

"Did you not think to check?" Bishop asked.

Finlay raised his hands defensively. "It isn't right to snoop around someone's home."

"What if she's dead?!" Bishop faced up to him.

"So? Searching for her won't help."

"What if she's dying, you idiot?"

"Josh, control her will you?!" Finlay said. Kitty sucked a breath through her teeth and Grainger put his hand to his mouth. Bishop stormed over to the big man.

"Oh, shit!" Pope exclaimed. "You're on your own, my friend."

Bishop gathered her energies and Finlay set himself in a defensive pose.

"Stop!" Morton shouted. He appeared from the shadows and positioned himself at a little distance from the group. Bishop simmered, waiting for the chance to deal with Finlay. "As much as I would welcome your company in the afterlife, it would be a terrible waste of your lives if you were to kill each other, now." He looked hard at both of them. "As you were asking, the landlady is fast asleep. In the cellar."

"What?!" said Kitty.

"For twenty four hours?" Bishop said, turning on Morton. "Why didn't you tell us sooner? We need to make sure she's all right."

Pope began moving towards the bar but stopped when Kitty spoke.

"Wait!" she said. "The ghost could be leading us into a trap."

"Are we not already in a trap?" Grainger regarded Kitty with surprise. "I have met Mr. Morton's ghost in here before and I have no reason to think he'd mean us harm."

"He's right, Kitty," Finlay said. "We all know Archie."

"In fact," Grainger added, "I'd say his trustworthiness is far greater than most of the church-goers I know, more's the pity."

Morton looked a little surprised but said nothing.

With attention diverted away from him, Finlay turned to Bishop and whispered almost inaudibly. "Sorry."

Pope turned away again. "Never mind all that, we still need to—"

"We've got another one coming through," Bishop said, interrupting his line of thought.

They all stepped back and formed an uneven semicircle around the materialisation spot once more. Again, they were left waiting for the moment of appearance and they stood still, hardly daring to breathe. Although they were greater in number, implying more safety, the tension in the room had increased in far greater proportion.

"Can I ask you a question, Joshua?" Grainger asked.

"Of course you can, Father."

"Was it you who sent Inspector Dobson to me for a gallon of holy water?"

"Bloody hell!" Pope exclaimed. "I'd forgotten all about the poor bugger. He's probably wondering where the hell we are."

"I take it you intended the errand as a ruse to delay him?"

"Yeah. We had a demon to deal with and I didn't want him getting in the way."

"Ah..."

The warping of the space in front of the fire stopped the discussion instantly and a tall man appeared, dressed in a dark suit, tie and overcoat, along with an immaculate top-hat that made him appear taller still.

The new arrival presented an image that immediately brought to mind the role of a sombre undertaker, which was fortunate, for such was his chosen profession. His small, family business provided funeral services for the deceased from all walks of life, including those of a supernatural background when the situation required it.

"Lassiter!" almost everyone said in unison. For reasons no one really knew, none of them had an idea what his first name might be, if he even had one.

Like the others, Lassiter was a little disorientated by his sudden displacement and stepped back unsteadily. Unfortunately, he placed his immaculately shod right foot into the patch of vomit on the carpet. He spoke in an exasperated stage whisper.

"Of all the unpleasantness I've had to endure in my time as an undertaker, I never once stepped into the contents of someone's stomach spread upon the floor of a tawdry public house."

"Looks like this is your lucky day," Pope said. "I'd give

anything for a new experience."

"Excuse me," said Morton. "I'd rather you didn't refer to this fine establishment as 'tawdry'."

Lassiter rolled his eyes and turned away from the ghost as if the opinions of the dead man were of no consequence. He stared at Grainger who cringed under the tall man's gaze.

"I was going to clean it up," the priest said. "But we all became distracted. Things are a little tense, Lassiter."

"That's hardly surprising, Luke," Lassiter said. "Looking at the members of our group I assume you've all come to the same unfortunate conclusion as to why we are here?"

Kitty ground her teeth in anger but they all nodded, except for the ghost, who looked completely baffled. Morton turned to face the others.

"What conclusion?" he interjected. "Is there something here that I should be made aware of?"

Lassiter took in Morton's mode of dress, regarding the old fashioned nature of it with disdain. He returned his gaze to those he was familiar with and raised an eyebrow.

"Pub ghost," Kitty said.

Satisfied, Lassiter turned back to Morton. "Imagine, if you will, the most evil person possible."

"Like the Ripper?"

"Indeed. Now imagine that same person has a magical power to rival anything ever known in this world. A power that enables him to do virtually anything he wishes."

Morton looked uncertain but nodded anyway.

"That man happens to be a decidedly unpleasant wizard by the name of Asmo Drax."

Almost as one, the group drew in breath at the mention of the name. Kitty touched her eye-patch subconsciously and Finlay clenched his fists so hard his knuckles popped.

Morton looked around nervously, confused. "What does that have to do with us?"

"Not you," Lassiter said, his voice deep and hypnotic. "Some years ago, the six of us were very fortunate to defeat this monster. We were certain that never again would he pose a threat."

"Defeated or not," Pope said. "It appears that he's returned from the grave."

"And he more than likely wants revenge," Bishop said.

Sandra

"How can it be possible?" Kitty asked. "We all saw him go into the ground."

"I'm sure Archie would agree with me here; that's not necessarily an end point," Bishop said and Morton nodded, somewhat unnecessarily. "Besides, who else links the six of us? Who else would want revenge for what we did to him?"

Pope was solemn. "You're right. And he clearly has the power to reach from the grave."

"Pigs' bollocks!" Finlay whirled around and punched the wall with his right hand, shattering the plaster and brickwork as if he'd struck it with a sledgehammer.

"Now, Samuel, I think it would be far better if we each keep a civilised, level head," Grainger said. "If we don't over-react we might—"

"Over-react?!" Finlay spread his arms wide in exasperation, dust and debris flying from his hand, along with a few drops of blood from the broken skin of his knuckles. "That evil bastard is going to kill us. He'll probably torture us first, knowing the way his sick mind works."

"It's hardly an excuse..."

"That's enough! I can't believe you're bickering," Bishop said. "We won't get out of this trap without working together and if we fight among ourselves we've gone half way towards handing him victory." The others stared at her with varying degrees of disbelief — it wasn't long since she'd tried to pick a fight with Finlay herself. "I know how that sounds but we've still got to pull together."

Morton looked puzzled. "Just a moment. If you defeated this Drax fellow, how is he able to trap you like this?"

"That's what we need to work out, sunshine," Kitty replied.

The group looked at each other warily, hoping that someone would be able to offer up a suggestion that might help their predicament. When it seemed that nothing was forthcoming, Morton spoke again.

"If I may share a thought," he said and when no one appeared to object he continued. "If you analyse the events that occurred when you defeated him, perhaps you'll find something that will explain why he's been able to return and trap you."

"At last, one among us with a level head," Lassiter said. "Along with a perfectly good plan we should undertake at once."

Bishop almost chuckled and said, "very droll." Lassiter looked at her quizzically. She shrugged and didn't pursue it.

"It's easy for Morton to stay calm," Finlay exclaimed. "He's got nothing to lose."

"You'd be surprised," said Pope.

Bishop grabbed a seat at one of the larger tables and the others did the same, some a little more reluctantly than others. The gravity of the situation demanded an organised approach, but in spite of knowing they should talk about it they sat in silence, each of them hoping that someone else would lead off the discussion.

"While we're all being moody," Grainger said, rising from his seat, "I'll clean up the mess I made earlier."

"Not before time," Finlay murmured.

Grainger took off his jacket and went behind the bar, rattling bottles and glasses on the shelves as he looked for the things he needed. A few moments later he emerged with a bucket of soapy water and a roll of paper towel. Near the fireplace he got down on his knees to deal with the vomit. Everyone watched him work until Lassiter spoke once more.

"How long has everyone been here?" he asked. "As the last to arrive, perhaps you could bring me up to speed?" He pointed to the broken window with his thumb and raised an eyebrow.

"Sam's been here a full day," Bishop said. "But the rest of us arrived in the last few hours. The window is Josh's handiwork."

"I tried to bust us out," Pope said. "We've tried three times with no success."

"Drax is too bloody powerful," Finlay said and the group fell silent again.

The clatter of Grainger's bucket drew their attention towards him again. He'd finished cleaning up the vomit and he now took the bucket and soggy paper away to the toilets. When he returned a few moments later the mood around the table was still as dark. He grabbed his jacket and took his seat again.

"If Drax simply wanted to kill us he'd have picked us off one by one," Pope said. "I think we've been trapped here because he wants something from us."

"Do you have any idea what it might be?" Lassiter asked. He removed his top hat and placed it on the table.

"Doesn't matter," Finlay said. "He'll get what he wants then kill us anyway."

"That is very possible, Samuel." Lassiter sighed gently; he always seemed to do so when speaking with Finlay, as though the big man's existence perpetually bothered him. "But while we're able to think and plan, we have an extremely good chance of coming up with a solution that may well save our skins."

"But what is it he wants?"

"If we knew, we'd likely not be having this conversation."

The pub was silent for a moment while everyone stared blankly and rummaged through their thoughts. Behind most of their eyes was a clear sense of dread at the idea of having to deal with Drax once more. Grainger shook his head and checked his pockets.

"You defeated him once, though," Morton said, still a little way away from the group.

"That was down to preparation and luck," Pope said. "This time, Drax has rigged the deck in his favour. If we hope to have any chance, whatever plan we devise needs to be a solid one and not waiver."

Finlay's breathing picked up its pace and he clenched his fists. Kitty grabbed his forearm in an attempt to placate him but he shrugged her off and thumped the table. "We haven't got a hope in hell."

"It sounds as if you've already given up, Samuel," Lassiter declared. "Will you simply lie down, go to sleep and let this man trample your body to dust?"

"Sleep!" Bishop sat upright. "Damn! We forgot about the poor landlady." She leapt to her feet. "Where's the entrance to the cellar, Morton?"

"Behind the bar," the ghost replied. "There's a trapdoor."

Bishop dashed behind the counter and immediately saw the hatch set flush with the floor. She pulled on its large brass ring to hoist it open. "Give me a hand will you, Sam?" she said, descending the steps and flipping the light switch.

Brightly lit, the cellar was clean and well-managed. It smelled faintly of bleach and was filled with a varied range of barrels, crates and bottles, all stored on heavy-duty shelving.

The cellar's brick-built, arched ceiling were a clear indication of the building's mediaeval origins and hinted at the history of the place. In one alcove sat the bones of an ancient skeleton, sealed behind a heavy pane of glass. They reputedly belonged to a debtor walled up for centuries before being discovered and put on display to those customers willing to pay a little extra for the privilege of seeing the macabre sight. The rest of the place had been scrubbed clean and the brickwork re-pointed a couple of decades earlier.

Finlay and Bishop found the landlady nestled behind a large stack of crates. She was a large woman, sprawled in an old garden chair in a rather ungainly fashion. She snored loudly with her head hanging over the back and her bottom in danger of sliding off the seat.

Pope and Morton had also entered the cellar, but while Morton moved to a position beside the sleeping woman, Pope moved over to where a chute led up to the outside trapdoor, through which the beer would be delivered from the pavement on the street above. Unfortunately, his hopes of escape were dashed once more as he felt the invisible barrier that prevented him from entering the alcove below the trapdoor. The barrier came down in line with the outer wall of the building above.

Bishop ignored Pope's actions — she felt the woman's pulse and rubbed her arm. "She's freezing. Can you get her upstairs, Sam?"

Finlay took a moment to think of the best way to approach his task then crouched down and hoisted the woman over his shoulder in one smooth movement. Her snoring barely faltered, other than a sudden release of breath as she was settled into place. He climbed the steep steps easily but took care not to harm her on the trapdoor entrance. Without his strength, they would have struggled to get her out of the cellar.

Although Finlay was uncomfortable about going into the pub's private quarters, Bishop insisted that he carry the woman all the way up to one of the bedrooms on the pub's first floor. He carefully placed her onto the bed, laying her down as easily as if she were a child, then he immediately backed away. Everyone crowded into the room as Bishop wrapped her in the quilt.

She knelt beside the bed then turned to look at Morton. "Do you know her name?"

"Sandra Tindall." The ghost's look was one of curious concern. "I hope she's none the worse for her ordeal."

Bishop reached into her shirt and lifted one of the earth gems from around her neck. She laid it on the exposed flesh between the landlady's ample breasts, then reached under the quilt to grasp one of the woman's hands in both of hers. Bishop closed her eyes.

"Sandra, I need you to let me in. Do you understand?"

There was no response, of course, but Bishop continued with her magic, pushing the tendrils of her extended senses into the sleeping woman. She moved those feelers through her body, fixing some minor aches and pains caused by sleeping so long in the basement chair, then tried to reach into her mind to wake her.

As she worked away, Bishop's pattern of breathing shifted and changed, until it matched that of Sandra. The landlady twitched as if dreaming then spoke a single word, "No!"

Bishop still searched with her senses as she spoke to the others. "She's been put under a sleep enchantment."

Kitty clenched her fist. "Bloody Drax!"

"Shouldn't she have recovered by now?" Pope asked.

"Drax's enchantment ties her directly to the barrier that surrounds the pub," Bishop replied. "Her ownership of the pub strengthens the links and feeds the barrier."

"That's one hell of a powerful binding force." Pope looked between Bishop and Sandra with a mixture of disbelief and concern. "Tread carefully, Faye."

"Oh, no..." Bishop's tone abruptly changed. "Drax is still maintaining the link — I can sense him... He's trying to... He's..."

"What is it, Faye?" Kitty asked.

Bishop pulled her senses back, opened her eyes and released Sandra's hand angrily. "He broke the bloody link. I was so close to finding him."

With the connection broken, Sandra's eyes fluttered open and she screamed at all the strangers in her bedroom. Then she threw off the quilt, thrust her hand under her pillow and pulled out a butcher's cleaver she clearly kept there for such eventualities.

"What the hell are you doing in my bedroom?!" she yelled, waving the weapon a little weakly.

Kitty moved quickly and used her years of martial arts training to disarm Sandra before she had time to react. The landlady scooted backwards across the bed, trying to get away from them. Her eyes darted from one to another without knowing where to settle. She shivered badly. "Why am I so cold?"

"We found you in your cellar," Bishop explained. "You'd been down there for over a day, put into a trance by a highly dangerous man."

"What? Who would do that?" Sandra asked.

"Asmo Drax," Pope said.

"Never heard of him."

"I'd be surprised if you had." Pope clenched his jaw with determination. He looked at Bishop then turned to the others, his back to Sandra. "Time to take the battle to

Drax."

"How on Earth do we reach him?" Kitty asked. "In case you've forgotten, we're trapped here."

"In order to keep Sandra under the sleep enchantment and maintain the connection between her and the barrier, Drax has to be positioned within it," Bishop said. "He's hiding somewhere in this building."

Tea and Troubles

"Damn!" Finlay said. A look of helplessness washed over his face.

Kitty almost snarled. "He's bloody playing with us."

Everyone looked from one to another and those nearest the open doorway shifted nervously away from it. Finlay kicked the door closed with the toe of his boot.

"That won't help," Bishop said.

"It makes me feel better." Finlay folded his big arms.

"Will someone tell me what the bloody hell is going on?!" Sandra moved forward on the bed and beat on Pope's back a couple of times in frustration but she stopped as soon as he turned to face her. "This is my pub and home and you people are swanning around as if it's yours. I'd like to know what gives you the right to do as you please."

Grainger stepped forward, his hands spread in an appeasing gesture. "Sandra, can I suggest that you calm down?"

Her eyes narrowed. "You... you're a priest. Shouldn't you know better than to break in?"

"We haven't broken in, I can assure you."

"If I find that you've been drinking my beer without paying, so help me I'll give you what for." She started beating at Pope again. "Just tell me what the hell's happening."

Pope grabbed her wrists to stop her flailing arms and get her attention. It worked for a moment, then she pulled free of his grasp and sat in the centre of the bed with her arms folded, a petulant look on her face.

"Perhaps I can get a word in, now." Pope glared at Sandra, who avoided his gaze. "Asmo Drax has trapped us here. He cast a magical binding spell—"

"Sod off!" She glowered under her brows at him. "Now you're taking the piss. There's no such thing."

"Just listen, will you?" Kitty yelled and moved as if she was about to slap the landlady.

"Wait, Kitty," Bishop said. Once she was sure her friend wasn't going to interfere she held out her hand, palm upwards. "Watch this."

Bishop's face set into a look of concentration as she focused her magical energies and muttered a small spell under he breath. A moment later a small ball of light appeared above her hand and rose towards the ceiling, taking on the shape of a bird as it did so. Before it touched the oak beams, Bishop waved her hand and it disappeared.

"Oh, my God...!" Sandra exclaimed. "I must be dreaming."

"I wish that was true," Kitty said. "I wish we were all dreaming."

"This isn't like the magic on the telly, is it?"

"It's not a conjuring trick," Bishop said. "My magic comes from the power of the earth and York is an ancient city with a lot of earth energy."

"Bloody hell!" Sandra slumped on the bed. From her changing expressions and confused eyes, it was clear she struggled with these new ideas and for a moment it looked like she might just break down completely.

Changing her approach, Kitty sat beside her on the bed and took her hand. "We're not all magicians, Sandra, just Faye and Josh, really. But we've got to stop Drax and we probably need your help to do it."

Sandra took in a deep breath and shuddered, still feeling the cold of the cellar. "So where the hell is he? I'd like to give him a piece of my mind."

"I don't think you understand," Pope said. "Drax is an incredibly powerful wizard."

"You keep saying that. So?"

"His magic isn't about calling up pretty balls of light." He threw an apologetic look over to Bishop. "Confronting him is the last thing you want to do. Last time we battled him we were lucky to get out alive, let alone defeat him."

"But he *can* be beaten?"

"So we thought at the time," Lassiter said. "Yet here we are, fifteen years later, and Drax has captured us all with, as yet, unknown intent. Though it's unlikely he's throwing a birthday party."

Sandra stared at the undertaker for a few moments as if trying to make sense of his strange look. Then she climbed off the bed. "Well, as my old mother used to say, 'Fortune favours the brave'." She opened the door and walked out of the room. "Besides, I'm dying for a cup of tea."

Bishop looked at Pope who grinned back at her.

"I like her," he said.

Bishop nodded. "And she's right. Cowering like this we're just playing into Drax's hands. He could be hoping our fear will defeat us."

"Sod that!" Kitty said. "We've got to do something. Anything."

"Well, I for one would love a strong cup of tea," Father Grainger said. "While we formulate a plan, of course."

Fifteen minute later they were sitting around the kitchen table drinking tea. Sandra cast her gaze at the varied group.

"Do you have a plan?" she asked.

"If we told you..." Pope said.

"Josh!" Bishop hissed at him. "We don't have time for your misplaced levity."

"No, you're right." The others stared at him, expecting more. He shrugged. "I've got nothing."

"Can't we just find him and kill him?" Sandra asked. "We have strength in numbers."

"We've killed him twice before," Bishop said. "He's remarkably resistant to death."

"Whatever we come up with needs to be powerful, permanent and something we can bring about quickly," Pope said. "If we give him too much time to react he'll defeat us easily."

"You said he was hiding in the building..." Sandra prompted.

"There's no point looking for him until we have a plan."

"We can't make a plan until we figure out what went wrong last time," Kitty said. "We don't want to screw up again."

Bishop sat forward, eager to keep the momentum going. "All right, let's go back to the beginning. We knew it all hinged on that artefact of his, the Ellen-Maegen."

"Yeah..." Kitty rubbed at the scars on her face again.

"Where does everyone fit in?" Morton hadn't spoken in quite some time but this was his original idea they'd returned to.

"You think *you* can solve it?" Finlay asked.

"No... I simply think that my outside point of view may be able to cast a different perspective on matters."

"That won't hurt, I guess," Bishop said as they all looked at him thoughtfully.

"Besides," Morton said. "I happen to be caught up in this trap as much as you so I'd like to be as fully informed as the rest of you in case this Drax's plans might also harm me."

"Mr. Morton has a valid point," Lassiter said. "He should be aware of all the facts in order that he can be as prepared as we." No one disagreed.

"You mentioned an artefact," Sandra said. "What was it?"

"The Ellen-Maegen was his source of power," Bishop replied. "Like a battery for all the energy his powerful magic needed. But so much more, too. It was very personal to the way he operated."

"So we needed a plan to deal with him," Pope said.

"You wanted to kill him?" Sandra stared at Pope with wide eyes.

"We wanted to destroy him!" Pope ground his teeth and clenched his fists as he spoke. "We had to stop him before his power grew beyond our ability to do so."

"You must understand that none of us were happy with the plan," Grainger added, somewhat surprised by Pope's passion. "Taking a life, no matter the reason, is not something any civilised person should consider lightly." Agitated, he crossed himself and continued gravely. "However, in this instance we could see no alternative."

"Faye and I had to bring in enough people with the right skills to make it work," Pope said. "And it's not like we could put a card in a newsagents' window."

"It scared the life out of me." Finlay clasped his hands together to stop them shaking. "Still does."

"Then why do it?" Sandra asked.

"We had no choice." The big man downed his mug of

hot tea in a single gulp like it was only lukewarm.

"Precisely the conclusion to which each of us came," Lassiter said. "Joshua involved me because he knew I always keep a supply of wood soaking in holy water. Father Luke and I used some of it to construct a coffin specifically designed to hold the wizard, in the hope that he could be defeated and placed inside."

"We lined it with lead, engraved with scripture and the text of numerous binding spells," Grainger whispered. "Just to be certain. I also consecrated the ground of a specially chosen spot where Samuel dug a grave twenty feet deep."

Bishop looked at the table and rubbed her thumbnail along the wood grain. "I wish it was as simple as we're making it sound," she mused.

BLOOD AND EARTH

Part Six

Innocent Victim

BLOOD AND EARTH

The Whispers in the Wind

1981

Malcolm was sure he felt the wind that year. Naturally, he assumed it was his imagination for, as a ghost, he'd never felt so much as the hint of a breeze before. But as the year went on there was no mistaking it — the wind cut through him like a knife.

Although the sensation was somewhat hard to define, the wind itself felt warm and moist, like a brisk breeze following a hot summer shower. Part of him welcomed feelings he hadn't experienced for over four hundred years, but there were undertones that agitated his dead nerves with distress, his ghostly spine a quivering column of fear and loss. His teeth were set on edge throughout his short stays in York.

He was relieved that the curse placed upon him caused him to travel beyond the city, for once outside the old, mediaeval walls the effects of the paranormal wind died swiftly away. For six days out of seven he was free of its effects, but with each return trip he dreaded the sight of the old walls more and more.

Malcolm noticed, too, that the wind cut through him even when the air was still and even on the windiest of days the breeze he felt moved counter to the shifting of the atmosphere.

He probably should have said something — Bishop and Pope would likely have listened to him — but the longer he kept quiet, the harder it was to voice the fears that grew a little stronger with each circuit that brought him back to the city.

For want of a better phrase, he hoped it would all blow over.

1982

Bishop first sensed the paranormal oddness the following year, when she detected a barely perceptible corruption of the earth power along the ley line. She had no idea what could be causing the problem and simply put it down to natural fluctuations. Ley lines could be temperamental at the best of times — even powerful ones like the line in York — affected by long-term weather patterns, shifts in the Earth's magnetic field and even Sun-storms. But as the corruption continued unabated and even grew in strength, slowly over time, Bishop knew that this was not a natural phenomenon. Unfortunately, she couldn't pin down its cause. Her every attempt to do so felt more like chasing chickens blindfolded than properly directed spell casting.

It was months before she felt comfortable enough to broach the subject with Pope as he sat in the living room, which felt cold in spite of the fire in the grate with weak autumn light struggling through the windows. His first reaction was simply to nod thoughtfully, completely unfazed by the idea.

"You already know about the ley line corruption?" Bishop asked.

Pope pursed his lips before speaking. "Of course not. But there's something going on in the city. I just haven't been able to put my finger on exactly what it is."

"I thought I was imagining it."

Pope nodded and smirked. "Seems like neither of us wanted to discuss it."

"Could that be part of its effect?"

"Hm... Maybe." Pope frowned. "It feels weird talking about it even now we've begun."

Bishop shivered as if an icy wind had suddenly blown through the room. "I don't understand how you know about it when it feels like a problem with the ley line."

"It's not the ley line I'm sensing." Pope sat up straighter in his chair. "There's an odd vibration — a kind of resonance — in the confinement spell that keeps me in York. I've never sensed anything like it before."

"You think there's a connection to you being trapped in the city?"

"It doesn't feel like that. More like something else is having an effect on both." He scratched at the stubble on his jaw. "As far as I can tell, it doesn't extend beyond the walls."

They both became silent and thoughtful for a long time before Pope's snoring announced that he'd fallen asleep.

The next day they tried a spell that mixed each of their magical abilities, but even with this combined power they could find no solution to what the cause might be. Frustrated, they resolved to return to the problem another time.

1984

It seemed that the whole of Britain watched the news of the fire in the York Minster. Certainly, for many of the City's residents it felt like a personal tragedy and teams of firefighters fought the blaze for hours before finally bringing it under control.

Bishop and Pope climbed through an attic skylight and perched on the roof of their house to watch the fire, just a few hundred yards away. They were up-wind of the Minster so they were in no danger from stray sparks, but it felt that the supernatural edge to the breeze was particularly biting that night. The two looked at each other but neither needed to speak the thoughts that went through their minds.

The official cause of the fire was lightning and that certainly may have been the case. The two magicians investigated as best they could, hampered by various branches of local and national authorities, but they could find no evidence then or later that lightning hadn't triggered the blaze.

However, their feelings told them another tale, particularly when, in the months following the fire, the wind in the city had returned to normal.

Pope was sure that whatever it had been must have come to a head on the night of the fire and it was now over, but Bishop had a nagging feeling that wasn't the case. Although she wouldn't have wished it so, she was proved right at the end of September when the unnerving wind returned, now a little darker than it had previously been.

By the time Christmas came around, even York's general population were picking up on a strange feeling they couldn't adequately describe, even if they'd wanted to, which most people didn't. Some put the tension it created down to the political turmoil sweeping through Britain, a reasoning that wasn't without credibility. But in such a politically bland city, anything short of full-scale, nationwide revolution washed over the population with little impact.

Though they had no idea what it was and never talked about it, they knew that something was wrong and steadily growing worse.

1985

Felthrop Market had been abuzz with speculation for months. While most of those prone to magical influences weren't quite sensitive enough to detect the original wind, when it returned months after the Minster fire, practically all of the stall holders and customers knew that something darkly supernatural was abroad in the city.

Many of them fancied they could hear the faintest of voices carried on the air, particularly when they were down-wind of the Minster, and Old Matty, a market regular, coined the phrase, "the whispers on the wind". The speculation amongst the community members focused on the mood of the whispers and the creepy nature of the wind in the city.

Unfortunately, not one of them could make out what was being said and those with a little more grounding to their nature suggested it could simply be a trick of the street acoustics. But the longer it went on, the more convinced they became that the whispers were real and that they were a portent of something sinister on the horizon.

Such was their concern that on the spring equinox a deputation of them sought out Faye Bishop and asked her advice, worried that the city was in danger. She'd never before realised how much of the supernatural community looked to her and Pope as unofficial protectors and leaders, so she felt particularly bad when she was unable to offer any substantial help or guidance.

The people of York would simply have to live with this uncomfortable feeling and the whispers on the wind.

Some of the more sensitive folk left the city for good.

1994

No one was sure if the problem with the wind died away slowly over time or everyone simply got used to it as the years passed by, but by the turn of the decade there appeared to be no sign of the strangeness on the wind.

It was a little surprising, then, that in 1994, the wind whipped up by a particularly bad storm had all the hallmarks of the previous troubles and a sense of whispering dread settled on the city.

That particular night it had taken Bishop a few hours of tossing and turning before she'd eventually managed to get to sleep, only to be woken a couple of hours later by the sense of something she'd hoped never to detect again.

She bolted from her bed and rushed to Pope's room, barging in without knocking — something she rarely did, such was their respect for each other's privacy.

He was already sitting up in bed as if waiting for her arrival. "What's going on, Faye? I have no idea why I woke, but I'm pretty sure it can't be anything good." Pope always fell to sleep readily and slept very soundly so Bishop was surprised by his alertness.

"Definitely not." Bishop breathed heavily and put her hand over her rapidly beating heart. "This is the worst thing you could imagine."

"I have a pretty good imagination. Just tell me."

She took a couple of deep breaths. "Drax is back. I recognise his magical signature."

Pope looked at her, stunned. Their eyes locked and he knew there was no point asking if she was sure.

"How is that bloody possible?" he asked. "He was dust on the wind when we last finished with him. He should be in Hell."

"All I can think is there must be something here that acts as a link, that anchors him to the real world." Bishop paused. "I think I know what it is. The gem I gave him as an infant, the one left behind on the Minster tower when he died — it's missing."

"We should have destroyed it." Pope scratched at his chin in thought. "Can you get a fix on him?"

Bishop sat on the corner of Pope's bed and closed her eyes. She pushed out her magical senses and frowned with concentration. After a few minutes she opened them and shook her head, fear edged her gaze.

Downstairs the phone began to ring.

Pope leapt from the bed forgetting he was naked, but raced downstairs in spite of this. Whoever called them in the middle of the night must have had an urgent need to do so; not many people had their number.

He snatched the receiver from its cradle and spoke his name.

"Oh, Josh," the person at the other end wailed. "Am I glad to hear your voice."

"What's the matter, Kitty? Are you in trouble?"

"I... I had a really awful nightmare." She paused. For a moment she felt stupid calling all the way from Africa about a dream. "Only, it was much more than that. I don't really know how to describe it. Like a premonition, I suppose."

"Let me guess - Drax?" Pope clenched his jaw.

"How the hell could you know that?"

"We felt the same disturbance," Pope replied. "Faye even identified his magical signature."

"What does it mean?"

"That he's somehow come back from the dead." He ground his teeth as he spoke.

"Damn!" Kitty spat. For a moment Pope could hear

her breathing hard. "I'm coming home."

"Kitty, there's no need for that."

"Oh, yes!" she spat. "I want to help. I want to be there when you take the bastard down again."

Artefact

1996

Bishop and Pope had no idea that Kitty had left the house, let alone where she was heading, but she'd had enough of going round in circles and discussing everything to death. They'd talked and talked but never actually did anything about the problem. Even though they'd tracked down where Drax lived, they seemed reluctant to make a move. Someone had to make the first move and Kitty had decided it would be her.

The motorbike she'd taken to riding in the last two years since returning to Britain, caressed the road with its muted power, sounding more like a tiger purring than a mechanical beast. The roads she knew so well seemed happy to help her on her way and it only took her minutes to reach her destination.

She parked the bike at the top of the lane, removed her helmet and took a pair of night-vision binoculars out of her bag. As she scanned the house from the line of trees that surrounded its extensive lawns, she wondered who he'd killed this time in order to take possession of the place.

Satisfied there was no sign of any physical security measures, she put away the binoculars and double-checked the other items she'd brought with her, transferring a couple of them to the pockets of her leather jacket. The items were a mixture of defensive and offensive charms and amulets.

Kitty proceeded cautiously, her boots crunching lightly on the twigs and dead leaves beneath the trees as she skirted the perimeter of the property. She needed to make her way around to the back of the large house — the front was too brightly illuminated by the full moon.

She paused in the shadow of an old stable that now looked as if it was used as a workshop of some kind, but she had neither the time nor the interest in finding out the details of its purpose. She continued on and into the shadows at the rear of the property.

She slipped on a pair of half moon glasses, the lenses of which had been replaced by specially crafted crystals that gave her the ability to identify the presence of earth magic. As soon as she lifted her head to look through the crystal lenses, she saw the clear signature of protective spells on each of the ground floor windows and doors. Breaking in through any of these would alert Drax instantly. Kitty shifted her gaze to the first floor windows in the hope of spotting something there.

She smiled to herself — a couple of the windows were unprotected, presumably because they were impossible to climb up to. Or so Drax had thought.

On the far left of the building's rear was a balcony area that no doubt acted as a sun deck in the height of summer and Kitty mounted the steps up to it. The door that led inside was covered by a protective spell but she wasn't interested in that. She used the balcony railing to climb onto the roof then crept across to where the two unprotected windows were situated.

Swinging her legs over the edge of the roof, glad of her loose-fitting jeans, Kitty gripped the rain gutter tightly and lowered herself slowly until she could reach out with her toes and touch the windowsill. She pulled out a knife and released the catch of the old sash windows before sliding up the lower portion. Seconds later she was in.

However, now she was here she realised she didn't know exactly what she was looking for, but none of them did. They'd managed to work out that Drax had manufactured some kind of artefact he used as both a storage for earth power — like Bishop's earth gems — and an efficient conduit to the power of the ley line, something her friend had so far been unable to achieve, apparently.

Kitty padded through the rooms of the first floor as quietly a her boots would allow. She would have preferred to have taken them off but they were nicely weighted for kicking, should she be forced into doing so.

The sounds of someone snoring came from behind one of the doors and Kitty pressed her ear to it to make sure. Whoever was inside was sawing logs with a vengeance. Most likely Drax. And if his artefact was so precious to him it was likely he'd keep it close by while he slept.

She pulled a length of strong fishing line from an inside pocket and secured it across the doorway at a height of about four feet, using a couple of small screw hooks she'd also brought with her. She tested the tension with a finger before ducking beneath it and opening the bedroom door as silently as she could. Whoever had previously owned the house had kept it well maintained — the hinges were completely silent.

Drax slept alone in a large double-bed, lying on his back, illuminated by the moonlight coming through the window. His snoring was so loud it disturbed the surface of the water in the glass on the bedside table, sitting next to which was a stone cylinder about twice the size of a large bean tin. For the most part it looked like a portion of a small stone column, but as Kitty drew closer she could see it more clearly.

It was a simple looking object - an ancient granite cylinder eight inches in length and four in diameter with magical symbols engraved on its surface in a spiral design, mostly earth symbols but small Fae symbols had been added among the main design. Drilled through the cylinder's axis was a hole about an inch in diameter.

The artefact looked more like a cheap door-stop than a device of power. But when she looked through her crystal lenses she saw the symbols picked out in an intense, eerie blue light. This was definitely the device she was looking for. She stared down the central hole and saw that something was attached inside, halfway down its length, but though she could see a faint green glint, she couldn't make out what the object was and didn't have the time to investigate.

For a moment Kitty was held by the sight of the seemingly helpless Drax — glowing with magical light when viewed through the lenses — and she had to fight the urge to drive her knife into his heart. He'd recovered from being blasted to dust, so a simple stabbing would mean nothing to him.

Kitty briefly thought back to that day on the Minster's tower and the immense amount of power in use had scared her. It had been a long time before she'd been able to look at Bishop and Pope with friendly eyes again. Then she pushed away those thoughts and brought her mind back to the task at hand.

She grabbed the stone artefact, tucked under her arm like a rugby ball and headed back towards the door with swift and silent movements. She'd made it halfway across the room when the snoring stopped. Without turning to check, she put her head down and ran towards the room's entrance like a rugby forward driving for the try line. The moment she was through the opening she turned left along the corridor and headed for where she hoped the stairs would be.

Drax had roused as soon as he'd realised someone had touched the Ellen-Maegen, the artefact Kitty now carried. As he'd shot out of bed he only just caught a glimpse of someone fleeing the room. He immediately ran in pursuit, only to find that something struck his neck at the doorway — he'd hit the fishing line strung across the doorway. His feet swung forward like a pendulum and he landed on his back, cracking his head on the floor as he hit. A little stunned, he took a few moments to pick himself up.

Kitty was surprised that she hadn't already been blasted by Drax's powerful magic, remembering her last encounter with him, but she didn't look back as she thundered down the stairs, barely able to see in the dark house, and she stumbled as the steps took a sharp right on a small landing. She tried to recover but her momentum was too great and she fell to the floor of the large hallway.

Before she hit the ground, she managed to tuck herself into a ball and roll with the momentum, bringing herself to her feet as if she'd planned it that way all along. But just when it seemed she had a clear run to the front door, Drax materialised in front of her, barring her way.

Without pausing, she took the artefact from under her arm and slammed it into Drax's face. He staggered back a little and Kitty hit him with more blows and kicks, attempting to keep them as random as possible so he wouldn't be able to anticipate any kind of pattern.

In spite of her non-stop movement, she managed to get her bag into a position in front of her, thrust the artefact into it and pull out a small device that looked like a large glass marble, about the size of a golf ball. She immediately threw it at Drax.

The magician batted it away with the back of his hand — at least that was his intention. The glass sphere had a thin shell that broke on contact, the magical contents of which clung to his hand like a limpet.

It was a special ur-charm constructed from air magic that Kitty had bought some time ago for a premium price, but it was worth it to see what was now happening to Drax. The spell, now triggered, surrounded Drax completely with a thin film of hard vacuum, sucking the air from his lungs in the process. His eyes bulged and threatened to burst from their sockets. Kitty grinned to see him suddenly so helpless.

Then he lunged at her, totally unexpectedly, ignoring the effects of the ur-charm, and she was caught off-guard, such was her pleasure at seeing his discomfort. One hand latched onto her throat, the other clawed at her face before she could move to defend herself, but it only took her half a second to bring up her knee and drive it forcefully into his testicles.

Drax's whole body convulsed and he clawed at her face with unpleasantly long nails that took skin from her forehead and cheek but worse, gouged out her left eye in a sudden, agonising movement. Ignoring the burning pain that shot through her, she pushed him away and fled the house before he could recover.

Twenty minutes later Kitty was back at the house belonging to Bishop and Pope — the only place she'd ever called home — surprising herself with how she'd managed to ride the bike home with only one eye, in the dark and losing blood. She collapsed through the front door and into the house's hallway with a clatter that resounded through the whole building. She lay on her back on the floor, groped with her hand to check the artefact was in her bag then gave in to the exhaustion and pain.

Bishop found her a few short moments later, woken from her bed by the sound Kitty had made. Turning on the light, she was initially unsure of the extent of Kitty's injuries — a piece of torn-off shirt material appeared to have been applied to an injury to her eye.

"Kitty!" Bishop exclaimed. "What have you done to yourself?" She rushed to her friend's side and it was then she realised the material had been wadded into the eye socket itself and that the eye was completely missing. She pulled the other woman to her, attempting to cradle her head, trying to heal her. Kitty pushed her away.

"Never mind that," Kitty replied, a little breathless, trying to grin around the pain at her accomplishment. She fumbled with her bag but struggled with her coordination and failed to open it. After a moment she thrust the whole bag at Bishop, who grabbed it in reaction rather than with any desire to do so. "I got hold of Drax's artefact. We can destroy it!"

"No," Pope said, descending the stairs. "He'd only make another."

Bishop's interest in the artefact was almost non-existent and she lay the bag on the floor again before returning her attention to her friend's injury. She pulled the blood-soaked material from Kitty's eye socket. It looked a mess and the gouged flesh around the orifice added to the gruesome sight. Even with centuries of experience and all the dreadful sights she'd seen, Bishop couldn't help but grimace with a sharp intake of breath.

Pope entered the hallway and came to stand by them. He nudged the bag with the toe of his bare bare right foot, feeling the weight of the object inside. "That's really it?"

"Sure is." Kitty looked up at Pope with her one remaining eye. "What do you suggest?"

"Use it to bait a trap."

"Works for me," Kitty said then lay down so Bishop could begin the healing process.

The Abandoned Factory

They chose an abandoned factory down by the river because they knew things would get messy — it always seemed to be the way of things when dealing with Drax, as Kitty's injury had demonstrated. And even though Bishop had been able to heal the wounds in and around the eye socket, regenerating the eye itself was beyond her powers.

It had taken two extremely nervous days of planning and hard work to get to the point where they all felt confident they had a chance of defeating him. Slim though that chance was, they had to take what they could and make the most of it.

As soon as they realised they could use Drax's artefact to bait a trap, Bishop had placed it into a lead-lined box covered in magical symbols that were designed to keep its contents hidden from any probing spells. Even if the prying magician had incredible power, enchantments could always be used to conceal things from them if applied in the right way.

They could have left it inside the box forever, but knew it would only be a matter of time before Drax made another one or attacked them anyway — he was still a dangerously powerful magician without it. Besides, baiting a trap gave them the chance to call the shots.

Bishop discovered an earth gem embedded at the centre of the artefact and she quickly sensed it was the one she'd used on him as a child. She wanted to remove it and destroy it, but the last thing they needed was for Drax to detect their tampering.

Now, in the dusty gloom of the abandoned factory, six of them waited for Drax to appear. They'd removed the artefact from its box a couple of hours earlier and lingered in the shadows, hiding behind the factory's rusting machinery. Drax would have sensed the object the moment it was removed from the box but was likely formulating a plan of his own. It was to be expected. And they had to be ready for anything.

Bishop had already cast her sensory net wide, using power from the nearby ley line to extend her senses to a half-mile around the factory, wanting to get as much advanced warning as possible. The wait seemed to go on for ever, but at last she picked up his magical signature as he entered the periphery, walking towards the factory, presumably to save his magical power.

She signalled for people to start getting ready and Finlay took the chance for a last minute pee against the back wall of the factory.

Drax didn't try to hide his approach; his confidence in his own abilities prevented him from caring. He wanted his artefact, he was prepared for the confrontation and he feared no one. It was hard for a person to feel fear when they were seemingly impossible to kill.

Bishop, Pope and the rest of their party were not without fear; in fact they were pretty terrified, in the main. Even the two magicians, long-lived as they were, were not immortal and the fear of death was just as strong in them as any of the others. However, they were confident their preparations would help them win out if they worked together as planned. Kitty's main concern wasn't the fear she felt but the worry that she might die before she got the chance to pay him back with interest.

Five minutes later Bishop signalled to the others and

spoke in a loud whisper. "He's here."

In spite of their planning they were still taken aback when he entered the factory, for none of them expected the insurance he brought with him in the shape of a young hostage. They all shifted nervously.

The girl was no more than ten years old and filled with more terror than anyone of that age should ever have to endure. Her cheeks were wet with tears as she sobbed continuously. Her T-shirt, shorts and pink hoodie were dirty; her knees grazed where she must have fallen down recently, the blood dry and scabbing.

The group had chosen the location well — far enough away from innocent bystanders with enough room to get serious with Drax, they had expected to begin the altercation as soon as he arrived. They'd tried not to underestimate his abilities or overestimate their own chances of success. Every scenario they could think of had been thoroughly discussed. Yet still they hadn't foreseen the poor child caught in the middle. They had assumed his arrogance would simply bring him here for a direct confrontation. But even unbridled self-confidence needed some kind of safety net.

Drax forced the girl to lead the way as the pair entered the building and walked across the dusty floor. She wore a silver collar attached to a silver chain, the other end of which Drax held firmly as he followed a few paces behind her, keeping the chain just less than taut. As soon as they saw how she was tethered, each member of the waiting team knew that one tug on the chain meant the girl would die. There would be some kind of release catch attached to the chain that would trigger a killing spell in the collar far quicker than any of them could react.

"Damn!" Pope whispered from the shadows. "This changes everything."

"No it doesn't," Kitty rasped back, touching the fresh bandage over her left eye socket. "I didn't lose an eye getting hold of this artefact to give it back at the first sign of trouble." She gripped the artefact tightly and stared at it as if she wanted to use it to cave in Drax's skull.

"We cannot let an innocent child die," Grainger said.

Lassiter nodded in agreement; his stare fixed each of the others in turn. "As much as I wish to see the end of Drax, I'll not be part of any plan that involves the death of this child."

Finlay breathed heavily at the new uncertainty. Drax scared him more than anything else he'd ever experienced and there was plenty of scary creatures that came from the realm of the Fae. He'd agreed to be part of the plan because there was a good chance it would succeed, but now the plan had been undermined and uncertainty had come into play. "We've got to take him out."

"I agree," Kitty said. "One life or millions...?"

"Kitty!" Grainger admonished. Pope held up his hand for silence as he looked out into the huge room.

Drax and the child reached the centre of the factory floor and he told her to stop. He looked around and smiled, feeling confident and in control, sensing the presence of the others.

A relatively small man, Drax's slight build and thinning hair gave the impression he was far less dangerous than he really was. His soft face had a timid quality, completely at odds with his killer nature and immense earth power.

"I know you're here, Kitty," he said. "And that you have friends with you again, for all the good that will do." He paused, waiting for a response, then continued when none came. "This is simple; the Ellen-Maegen for little Amber's life. There will be no tricks for a fair exchange." The girl let out a gentle sob, her hands, by her side, were trembling.

"What do we do?" Finlay whispered.

He, Grainger and Lassiter looked to Bishop and Pope while Kitty watched Drax and seethed. The two magicians exchanged a look and considered their thoughts a moment, both knowing they had to decide on something quickly.

"Just get ready to move," Bishop said. She rose, gathered her courage and charged her earth power to its maximum level. "You'll know when."

Catching Kitty by surprise, Bishop took the artefact from her hand quite easily and strode out of cover towards Drax and the girl. Kitty gasped and moved to stop her friend but Pope grabbed her firmly and held her back.

"Have faith, Kitty."

Grainger looked at Pope in astonishment, surprised by the unexpected phrase.

"You'd better be right," Kitty said.

Bishop's spine was on edge and she felt the tension thicken in the dusty air as she strode forward with the artefact in her hands. She held it in front of her so Drax could clearly see there was no trick, that the object was genuine.

Drax licked his lips at the sight of the artefact, trying hard to keep his eyes on Bishop and not stare at the stone cylinder. He pulled the chain a little tighter and Amber gasped, further terrified.

"Stop right there," Drax ordered when he felt that Bishop had approached close enough, but she took an extra couple of steps before doing so. "I said stop!"

"Okay, okay," Bishop said. "Just let the girl go."

She was almost close enough to dash the few paces and snatch the child up, but the presence of the collar and chain made that idea an impossible wish. She felt every bit of the frustration it caused and dare not even look at Amber's scared face in case it distracted her from the task at hand.

"Put the artefact on the floor and back away. Only then will I free her."

Bishop looked nervously into Drax's smug eyes and nodded. He could be lying about the child's release but what other choice did she have? Her mind worked like a steam train — fearful of Drax's proximity and worried she was going to screw everything up.

She casually took another step forward as she crouched to place the artefact on the floor, which brought her within two yards of the child. She closed her eyes and ground her teeth as she stood the artefact on one of its flat ends. For a second she paused and turned her attention to the earth power within her.

Letting go of the stone object with a dramatic spreading of her arms, Bishop used the motion to disguise the creation of a portal, flat to the floor, that encircled her, the artefact and the girl. As Bishop got swiftly to her feet she also raised her arms in a grand gesture that lifted the portal upwards in a fraction of a second so they were engulfed and gone before Drax had a chance to react. He was left holding the end of a dangling piece of silver chain, cropped cleanly by the passing of the portal's edge, a growing look of fury on his face.

"Now!" Pope shouted and a sudden flurry of activity erupted with Drax as its focus. Finlay threw a huge mallet, Pope blasted him with sprays of bullet-like blood droplets and Kitty fired round after round of iron slugs from a pair of revolvers. None of this would kill him or do any permanent harm, but it would keep him busy until Bishop returned and they were a complete team again. In the shadows, Grainger and Lassiter muttered religious incantations and scattered holy water about in the hope it would disrupt the Fae magic that made up part of Drax's nature.

Drax's indignant fury was rapidly replaced by confusion and for a moment he knew fear.

Elsewhere, in the snug home of Maggie Trimble, the other end of the portal connection opened. Maggie almost dropped her teacup at the sudden appearance of the visitors, but having worked as assistant and housekeeper for the two magicians for four decades — and a witness to all manner of strange things — the surprise wasn't as intense or long-lasting as it might otherwise have been.

Bishop was instantly into action and caught the girl as she collapsed from the shock of the translocation. She didn't actually faint but it was all a bit too much and she looked more terrified than when she was in the factory with Drax. As Bishop held her she tried to examine the silver collar but the girl was beginning to fight back.

"Maggie," Bishop said. "This is a pretty desperate situation and I need you to hug her so she doesn't move."

Maggie moved into place, kneeling on the floor and wrapping her arms around the terrified girl from behind.

"Don't worry, pet," she whispered into the girl's ear. "Faye is very clever and is going to help you. She'll take off the nasty collar in no time, but she needs you to be very still and very brave. What's your name?"

"Amber," she breathed, hardly daring to speak.

"You're doing great, Amber," Maggie said. "I don't think I've ever seen a girl as brave as you. When the collar is gone we'll have a drink of milk and a delicious piece of cake. Does that sound good?"

Amber whispered, "Yes."

Bishop let their conversation wash over her as she concentrated on the collar's mechanism, careful not to pull on the short length of chain and trigger the spell.

She sucked in breath through her teeth a couple of times at the unpleasant nature of the device but it wasn't long before she had the measure of it.

She pulled a crystal from her pocket and used it to score a line across the width of the collar, muttering under her breath as she did so. The line glowed with an orange light for a moment and Bishop continued to whisper her impromptu words, willing the spell to work quickly.

With a bright flash of light, the collar sprang open along the score line and Bishop removed it instantly, throwing it across the room where it bounced off the wall and landed on the floor. It immediately turned red hot, the silver partly melting, and set fire to the rug it rested on.

Bishop leapt to her feet, grabbed a vase of flowers and dumped the water over the flames. "Sorry, Maggie."

"That doesn't matter," Maggie said. "Not now this precious little thing is all right." She hugged the girl to her tightly and Amber let go of her terror and cried heartbreakingly. "Okay, pet. You're safe, now. Let it all out."

"Make sure she's okay and contact her parents. I have to go."

Bishop scooped up Drax's artefact from Maggie's floor, opened another portal and returned to the abandoned factory.

The battle with Drax wasn't going particularly well. He looked a little battered from their first assault — the loss of his hostage put him completely on the back foot — but he'd soon raised a defensive shield around himself a few metres in diameter. Now, neither Kitty nor Finlay could get close enough to engage with him physically.

Pope's attempts to break down the barrier were having no success, either. The vials of blood he shattered against the invisible wall enabled him to unleash powerful magic, but it did little more than make the shield flare momentarily.

In the plus column, at least Drax wasn't making any attacks of his own, as that would mean lowering his defences, but it quickly became obvious to everyone that he was simply biding his time for the right opening.

He noticed Bishop's return and when he saw the artefact he visibly brightened, like a caring mother at the sight of a lost child being returned. His concentration faltered slightly but not enough that he dropped his shield.

"Give it to me!" Drax demanded.

"Come and get it," Bishop invited. She held out the artefact tauntingly.

Drax moved forward a step before halting. It would be a mistake to get drawn into anything that wasn't on his own terms. He stepped back, laughed and began to gather his magical energies. "Time to get serious."

"Indeed," Bishop said and quickly checked that the others were on board before she looked at Finlay, who nodded to her.

She instantly formed a portal around him and transported him inside the shield behind Drax, relieved that she'd been able to make it happen. The fool had neglected to isolate the base of the shield from the ground. Before the wizard could react, the big man punched him in the back of the neck, stunning him enough to make the shield drop and allowing the others to move in.

As Drax collapsed from the blow, Finlay grabbed him and pinned his arms to his body with a crushing bear hug. He lifted him clear of the ground to take away any direct connection to the energy of the earth. Kitty moved in and kept Drax stunned with repeated blows to his body, paralysing nerves and maintaining his helplessness. A few of her blows missed their mark because fighting with one eye was still pretty new to her, but she landed more than enough to prevent even Drax's unnatural physiology from recovering before the next blow came.

Drax writhed but could not break Finlay's powerful grip. Nor could he land a kick on Kitty, who easily managed to dodge his attempts to do so.

Pope pulled out a larger vial of blood, unstoppered it and poured it over Drax's head. As it ran down the wizard's face he blinked it out of his eyes and glared at Pope who enjoyed the reaction. It was a pleasure to see genuine fear on the man's face.

Pope chanted in his strange tongue and triggered all the energy the blood contained, then placed his hands on Drax's bloody, jerking head. There was a momentary jolt like a surge of lightning and Drax went limp, his mind blasted as if he'd been subjected to a dangerous level of electro-shock therapy. Pope's hands were blistered and smoking.

"We don't have much time," he said, trying to ignore the pain in his hands.

Bishop helped Lassiter and Grainger wheel over the trolley on which an open, heavy coffin had been placed. Constructed of wood, long soaked in holy water, it had then been lined with lead, into which had been inscribed all kinds of entrapment symbols, along with holy scripture designed to trap and hold its occupant.

As the coffin moved, the holy water that filled it threatened to spill over but they hardly lost any of it until Finlay eased Drax's body into the coffin and the displaced water sloshed over the edge.

Even in his mind-shocked state Drax screamed at the touch of the water. The reaction was far greater than it should have been, which suggested that when he'd brought himself back from the dead he'd used and incorporated the natural power of Coruban, the Fae swordsman he'd died alongside, linked as they had been by the actions of the Fae Lord, Ealvun.

Ignoring the screams, and the rapidly reviving struggles, they worked together to get the lid in place with Finlay holding it down with his great strength.

"Wait!" Bishop said. "We left out the artefact."

Pope grabbed it from her, lifted the lid just enough to slip it inside then slammed it closed again.

As they secured it with bolts, padlocks and chains of iron and silver, Grainger read aloud from a small, ancient, religious tome he always carried with him, performing the ritual that sealed the coffin spiritually, too. As he neared completion, the scratching from inside the coffin ceased and they knew they had succeeded in vanquishing Drax.

They stood for a moment in silence, barely able to believe their success.

BLOOD AND EARTH

Part Seven

Blood and Earth

Eyes Open

2011, spring

"Well, we thought we'd beaten him," Bishop said and hung her head. "But obviously not."

"Oh, my god!" Sandra said, her eyes wide, her mouth agape. "What a bloody awful coincidence."

They'd all hung on Bishop's words, still seated at the kitchen table, even though most of them had been in the factory that day. Now they turned their attention to Sandra, puzzled by her words.

Pope leaned forward. "Whenever Drax is involved, things are rarely down to coincidence."

"You know something?" Bishop asked.

The colour had drained from Sandra's face and her hands shook. She looked nervously at the group, flicking her eyes across each of them as they stared at her before lowering them to look at her trembling fingers, but not really seeing them.

"Amber..." She bit her lip and tried to control her breathing, fiddling with her empty cup as she did so. "That poor mite was my niece, my sister's kid."

"Was?" Bishop reached over and held Sandra's hand, helping calm the shakes.

"Amber was never the same after her disappearance. Now I can see the why of it, I'm not surprised." Sandra paused to take in an unsteady breath and picked at imagined crumbs on the table with her free hand. "She was only gone for a few hours, but afterwards she'd changed completely. She had nightmares all the time and weird visions that made her unstable. Mentally, I mean."

"Oh my god! If I'd known, I could have helped her..." Bishop looked at the others for any indication they might have known something, but drew only blank expressions.

"I think she was beyond help," Sandra said. The tears began welling up in her eyes.

"Was she taken into care?" Grainger asked.

"Janey, my sister, refused. Scared of letting her out of her sight, I reckon. But it affected her so badly the doctors had to treat her for depression. I tried my best to help her but we lived too far away to call round every day." She pulled a tissue from a box on the side counter and blew her nose. She screwed it up tightly then took another she didn't use, but held onto it anyway.

"One time, Amber woke up in the middle of the night. It was only a couple of months after she'd gone missing." Sandra took in another deep breath and started slowly ripping the second tissue into ragged strips. "Janey and her husband must have been unaware of the poor thing creeping around, even when she filled the house with gas from the cooker." Bishop once again put her hands on Sandra's in a comforting way but the landlady drew them back before she continued. "She must have known exactly what she was doing when she struck the match. They were all killed in the explosion."

"Oh my god!" Kitty exclaimed, which drew admonishing stares from both Grainger and Lassiter. She rolled her eye and looked away from them.

Morton had positioned himself in the corner of the kitchen and hung onto everything Sandra said. He seemed fascinated by the details she shared. Almost eager.

"I remember dealing with the family's cremation

arrangements," Lassiter said.

"Their ashes are still upstairs in my bedroom," Sandra whispered.

Lassiter's deep voice shifting into a softer, more undertaker mode. "It was impossible to recognise the child and I'm afraid I made no connection to the girl Drax had used so terribly."

Pope shrugged, his eyes a little moist. "We thought we'd fixed everything. Why didn't I think of the girl?"

"It's easy to forget about the fallout," Grainger said. "I should also have followed up and checked on her spiritual well-being."

"We can all take a share of the blame." Bishop whispered. "But we know where the real fault lies and we need to do something about him."

"Whatever you need from me, just let me know," Sandra said, leaning hard on the table with her forearms, her fists clenched tightly. She looked at the others with fire burning behind her welling tears. "This arsehole is going to pay for what he did to my darling Amber."

They each returned her gaze with fresh determination marking their expressions. The effects of fear could only remain active for so long before the mind became a little immune to them.

"Right, let's find where Drax is hiding," Kitty said.

"Not without a plan," Pope cautioned. "At least, not without knowing what he wants from us."

"Indeed, but what *does* he want?" Lassiter asked.

"He could just be pissing us about," Kitty replied. "Having a bit of sick fun before he polishes us off."

"Are you missing something important?" Morton asked returning to the room. They all turned his way. He'd been quiet for some time and they were a little surprised by sound of his voice.

"Mr. Morton is most likely right," Lassiter said. "If

only for the fact that if it were otherwise we would already have the solution for which we search. Perhaps if we itemise everything we know about Drax and our previous dealings with him we may be able to come up with something far more constructive."

"I'll get us a flip-chart," Finlay mocked.

"Now, now, Samuel," Grainger said. "Lassiter is simply attempting to be methodical. As much as we all fear Drax, and rightly so in my opinion, we have defeated him once and I'm sure we can do so again."

"Ha! We were as lucky as hell."

"No, Samuel. We acted as a team and that's where our strength lies."

"Well said, Father," Sandra said, looking at him with hope in her eyes. "You must be a very brave man."

"If I'm honest," Grainger said. "Every time I become mixed up in something magical or of a supernatural nature it scares me witless. But what frightens me more is the state of my soul if I don't do what's required of me."

Sandra stared at Bishop. "Can't you just do what you did last time?"

"The difference between now and then," Bishop explained, "Is that we had the artefact, the source of his power, which gave us an advantage."

"And we did everything right," Finlay said. "We buried him with the bloody thing. He should never have escaped."

"Wait, if he was buried with the source of his power, wouldn't he have used it to escape?" Sandra asked.

"Under normal circumstances, yes," Bishop agreed. "But the lead lining of his coffin cut him off from any contact with the earth. I know we said the artefact was his source of power, but it's really a conduit through which he could draw energy from the earth."

"What, like ley line power?" Sandra felt she was

getting a handle on things.

"Exactly like that. What do you know about ley lines?"

"I watched a series on the telly about all kinds of spooky happenings and mumbo-jumbo." For a moment she faltered over what she'd just said then continued. "There's even supposed to be a ley line here in York that goes through the Minster. Is that really true?"

"It exists all right. While there is a lot of mumbo-jumbo on TV," Bishop grinned, "not in this instance."

"Clearly not." Sandra stared into Bishop's eyes and the latter answered the unspoken question with a nod. Magic and the supernatural were far more significant than Sandra could imagine.

"Wait," Kitty said. "I think we're getting to the heart of the matter. Drax should never have been able to get out, especially with his artefact by his side, so something must have gone wrong with the process. Maybe with the coffin." She looked at Lassiter and Grainger with a cold edge to her eye.

"Although I fully understand why you think we may be at fault, Kitty," Lassiter responded. "The reason Father Luke and I worked together on the coffin was to ensure neither one of us made a mistake or overlooked any vital detail. The coffin was sound." He sipped from his cup to cover his obvious annoyance and looked at Grainger who nodded in agreement.

"Then it must be something else," Kitty said.

"I remember we were all so eager to close the coffin lid on Drax we nearly forgot the artefact altogether," Bishop said.

"Oh, yeah..." Finlay exclaimed, nodding. "Josh had to open it up again and slip it inside."

Pope made an embarrassed clicking sound with his tongue and all eyes turned to him. He smiled weakly and gave a long, embarrassed shrug. "Actually, I didn't."

"But we all saw you, Joshua," Lassiter said.

"Slight of hand. Sorry."

There was a shocked silence for a few seconds while everyone took in the significance of this revelation. They all sat back in their chairs, a little stunned, somewhat betrayed. Morton, however, became massively interested in this unexpected development and moved forward, staring intently at Pope.

Bishop's initial surprise turned quickly to fury and she stood up, strode around to where Pope was sitting and yelled at him. "What the hell, Josh? You've had it all this time?"

"Calm down, Faye." Pope stood up to placate her. "I thought it would be okay. He should have been completely disconnected from it."

"We had to be sure we dealt with him for good!"

"I needed to examine it." His nostrils flared to match his widening eyes.

"You bastard!" Bishop slapped him hard across the face. "Sometimes I don't know you at all."

"Ow! I think you knocked a tooth loose."

"I'd knock your brains loose, too, if we didn't need you to help us get out of the mess you've landed us in."

"Why the hell did you take it?" Kitty demanded. "I nearly lost my life getting it from Drax. I *did* lose an eye."

"What good would it do you?" Bishop raged. "It channels earth magic and you're a blood magician."

"There are ways..." Pope spread his hands. "I hoped I could use the power it channels to break my entrapment."

"Nothing will ever break that," Bishop said. "After this stunt you deserve it."

"What entrapment?" Sandra asked.

"I've been trapped within the walls of the city since the current ones were established in the thirteenth century," Pope said. "They act like a giant confinement circle and I have no idea who was responsible."

"Just how old *are* you?" Sandra looked at him closely, trying to get his measure.

"If I've calculated it correctly, about two thousand two hundred years. But most of the early centuries are a blur. Things were pretty boring back then."

Sandra became a little thoughtful. "When I took over this pub, the previous owner told me a tale of a man who'd supposedly been drinking here for centuries. I thought he was taking the piss."

"No, that'll be me."

"Although this news is hardly pleasing, at least we now know what Drax wants from us." Lassiter's sombre voice underlined the fact that the knowledge gave them little comfort.

"I understand why you'd want it, Joshua," Grainger said. "But what did you do with the artefact?"

For a moment Pope held the priest's gaze and almost didn't reply to the question. "I took it home to study, of course."

"I knew it!" Archie Morton fist-pumped the air, grinned then pointed at the group. "I knew you'd give away its location if I gave you the time to do so."

"What the hell are you talking about?" Finlay's confusion played across his face as he looked from Morton standing beside him to the rest of the group.

"Don't be so dumb, Finlay," Kitty said from his other side.

Finlay jumped up and pulled back his fist as if about to punch Kitty, then quickly twisted the arm about and grabbed for Morton with his huge hand.

The ploy worked and Finlay grabbed the lapel of his jacket, which turned out not to be ghostly in the least. Unfortunately, Morton was too fast for him and he wriggled out of the garment, ripping the buttons off in the process. Before anyone had time to react, he raised a shield around himself and laughed.

"You won't get the chance to defeat me this time," he said.

Morton passed his hand in front of his face and it distorted into another form entirely. His body warped and shrank at the same time. It wasn't long before they were faced with the true appearance of Asmo Drax, a slight, balding man of about fifty, with a blob of a nose and striking green eyes. For a moment his ears took on a pointed appearance before settling into a more normal shape. The clothes designed to match Morton's normal attire faded and revealed Drax's real garb — grubby-looking T-shirt and jeans. Considering the power he wielded, his ability to self-heal didn't extend to maintaining a youthful appearance.

He gloated. "Forgive my smugness, but you were all so easily trapped. I expected more from you, Pope; you must have known I'd be back for the Ellen-Maegen."

With that, he turned on his heel, dashed out of the room and ran down the stairs, his shield pulled tightly around him. Almost as one, the group thundered after him.

"I'm going to kill him!" Sandra yelled and raised the meat cleaver aloft.

Kitty was a little surprised at the reappearance of the blade. "Join the queue, lady."

In the pub's main room, Drax stood in front of the fire, waiting for them, grinning still. Sandra threw the cleaver as soon as she was near enough to do so, but even though her aim was good, the shield protected him from its deadly edge and gripped the metal for a moment. Then the blade abruptly shot upwards with such a force it embedded into one of the ceiling's beams halfway along its length.

Drax looked up at the cleaver and laughed. "I'm going to enjoy thinking of you all rotting in here. Please don't be quick about it."

The air about him twisted and warped and in the time between blinks he was no longer there.

"Thank God for that!" Pope said.

A Trap Within a Trap

"What in heaven's name do you mean?" Grainger stared at Pope with a confused look on his face but most of the others didn't appear to be at all surprised.

"Look, we don't have much time for explanations," Pope said. "When Drax fails to find the artefact he'll come back here and he'll be pretty pissed off."

Sandra was as puzzled as the priest. "Just tell us, will you?! I hate being kept in the dark in my own pub."

Lassiter studied the place where Drax had disappeared. "I think it would be for the better if everyone's moving at the same speed."

"Okay, but I'll have to make it quick. We'll need to work fast before he returns." Pope looked at Grainger and Sandra.

"I couldn't say anything or he'd have known I was onto him, but I had an idea who Morton really was almost from the start. I've known the real ghost, on and off, for a long time. When Faye said that Drax was hiding in the building that confirmed it."

"Hiding in plain sight," Bishop said, a look of irritation on her face.

Sandra and Grainger still appeared to be none the wiser and Pope waited for the connection to be made. After a moment where nothing seemed to be happening, he continued.

"We know there are many ghosts that haunt this building, so why was Morton the only ghost trapped in here? He'd also want to hide in a way that meant he could keep an eye on us and we knew he's able to change his appearance at will."

Grainger's face quickly brightened as the pieces fell into place, then he became serious again, looked at the others and shook his head. "You all suspected Morton? I had no idea."

"You're far too trusting, Luke." Lassiter smiled kindly — a look not entirely suited to his countenance. "Although I must admit I didn't immediately figure it out."

"I only worked it out because of his smell," Finlay said. "Ghosts don't smell of anything and Drax has a very distinctive scent."

"But..." Grainger looked exasperated.

"None of us dare say anything," Bishop said. "We didn't want to tip him off that we knew."

"Indeed," added Lassiter. "The last thing we wanted was to battle Drax without preparation."

Finlay scratched his head. "I don't understand why you told him where the artefact is?"

"He didn't," Bishop said. "He told Drax where he'd taken it after the burial. I assume it's somewhere else entirely, now."

Pope grinned. "Of course."

"But why not tell us?" Finlay asked. "We could have helped."

"My plan relies on you all knowing as little as possible." Pope looked at them with a hint of apology in his eyes. "You can't tell him what you don't know."

Bishop looked like she was about to slap Pope again. "You still shouldn't have taken the artefact."

"Faye!" Kitty interjected. "As much as I want to brain the idiot myself, we don't have the time to squabble. We know it's Josh's fault but we still need to deal with Drax."

She turned on Pope. "And this time it needs to be permanent."

"Wait. Why didn't you give him the location earlier?" Sandra asked. "Why drag it out?"

"It had to feel like it cropped up naturally," Pope said. "If Drax realised I knew who he was he'd suspect a trap."

"Why didn't he just force it out of you?" Sandra asked.

"He wouldn't have known which of us had it," Bishop replied, trying to calm herself. "He'd probably have enjoyed torturing all of us, but this way would have been quicker."

Pope looked her in the eye, breathing heavily. He'd had fifteen years to make himself ready for the day this came out but he never imagined it being in such a manner. "We need to prepare for Drax's return."

Bishop nodded in agreement. "But when this is done, you and I are going to have words." She pointed to the floor in front of the fire. "We need to create a confinement circle there," she said.

"Are you sure?" Kitty asked. "We're already in a confinement circle of sorts."

"It's tricky, but not impossible." Bishop frowned. "However, Josh is right — we don't have much time. Sandra, we've got to take up your carpet. I need to draw the circle on the boards."

"Bloody hell," Sandra said. "I only had it laid a couple of months ago. Still, if it helps you defeat that bastard... do whatever you need."

"Sam..."

"I'm on it." Finlay turned and crouched down. "You want me to rip the carpet up, right?"

"No, you fool," Bishop said. "Find the sharpest knife you can and cut out a large, neat square. When the circle is done we need to replace the carpet so the trap is hidden from view."

She turned to the priest as Finlay headed to the kitchen.

"Father, can you bless a gallon of water for me?"

Grainger nodded. "Of course."

"I'll get you a bucket," Sandra said. She didn't know why it was needed but assumed these people knew what they were doing and if speed was important there was no time to ask for explanations. Grainger followed her behind the bar.

Pope moved close to Bishop and whispered in her ear. "There's one guaranteed way to break Drax's confinement spell."

Bishop pulled back and looked at him with horror. "We are *not* sacrificing Sandra in order to save our own hides," she hissed. "If we cross that line we might as well let Drax win now."

Pope turned and stormed across the room. He knew he really ought to stop himself voicing these big picture perspectives, particularly as he knew she was right. They'd already lost Amber and her parents to Drax and they had to stop him killing any more, no matter how indirectly he did so.

Finlay came back sucking his thumb, the knife he'd found in his other hand. Pope laughed. "I'm guessing it's more than a little sharp."

"Ha bloody ha."

"Whatever you do, don't cut through the boards," Bishop said. "We've only got one shot at this and we've got to make it count."

"Give me some credit, Faye." Finlay looked at the carpet to work out where he'd make the cuts.

Lassiter created space for Finlay by moving some of the tables and chairs closer to the walls. He had an air of quiet deliberation as he set to the task, picking up each piece carefully as if the thought of dragging furniture was complete anathema to him. There was strength and urgency to his movements, at odds with his calm, immaculately-dressed appearance.

Finlay cut through the carpet and underlay as if they were rice paper. He quickly had them rolled up to one side and the floorboards, blackened by the passage of time, uncovered.

Bishop pulled her stick of white pastel from her pocket, dropped to her knees and started to draw a circle on the boards. The oil pastel worked better than school chalk because it was more resistant to smudging. Making the sticks herself meant Bishop could include her own earth-based ingredients, such as local limestone, which enhanced the power of any earth symbol drawn.

She centred the circle on the spot in front of the fire where each of them had appeared. Because she wanted to be sure that Drax materialised inside the circle when he returned, she made it larger than she normally would. A dozen people could easily fit within it. As she drew closer to the fireplace, she broke out in a sweat not entirely caused by the heat, though she battled through her fear.

When the circle was complete she looked up at Pope. "Which direction is North?"

He thought for a moment then pointed towards the chimney breast.

"That makes sense," Bishop said.

She now drew a pentagram within the circle, orientated so that one of its vertices pointed in the direction of the fire. She then drew a simple figure of a man upside down, relative to North, in the centre of the pentagram. She looked at the small stub of pastel that remained before returning it to her pocket.

Bishop stood up and beckoned everyone closer.

"Right, I need you all to space out around the circle and touch it lightly with your right forefinger. Then will yourself into the circle," she said. "Make sure you don't smudge the line."

She positioned herself at the southern segment of the circle and the others arranged themselves around the circumference. Each of them squatted down and did as Bishop requested. She drew on her reserves of magical earth power and forced it all into the circle. There was an audible crackle as the energy settled in place and the tang of ozone prickled the insides of their nostrils.

On a sign from Bishop, they withdrew their fingers and stood up. The magician was suddenly light-headed and staggered back, falling against one of the tables. She struggled for breath and Pope moved over to supported her.

"I'm all right," Bishop gasped. "But I used everything I had to activate the circle." Pope helped her to a chair where she cradled her head in her hands and breathed deeply.

"What's the holy water for?" Pope asked, mindful that Drax could return at any second.

"Soak the square of carpet with it and replace it very carefully. We don't want the lines to smudge. Put the underlay out of sight somewhere."

They did as she asked, spreading around the square of wet carpet and gripping it tightly in order to lower it carefully and vertically onto the magically marked floor. There was a lot of calling back and forth as the group guided each other while positioning it. Once it was down it overlapped in a couple of places but they couldn't drag it into perfect position because the pastel lines could be broken and the power released.

"Now, can someone get me some chocolate?" Bishop asked. "Please."

Sandra grabbed a handful of Snickers bars from behind the counter and placed them on the table next to

Bishop.

"I'll never understand why some people like to eat chocolate with their beer," the landlady said. "But you've got to cater to weird tastes in this business."

Bishop tore into the snack bars with a ferocity normally seen in someone who'd not eaten for a month. Her sugar levels were dangerously low, which the chocolate would restore, but her magical reserves would remain depleted.

"He's coming back," she mumbled around a mouthful of peanut and chocolate, pleased she had just enough power left to make make use of her heightened senses.

Everyone backed away from the area in front of the fire and prepared themselves as best they were able. Sandra had grabbed the large blade Finlay had used to cut the carpet and held it at the ready.

Drax reappeared as quickly as he'd previously vanished. Although they all expected him, the moment of materialisation still took them by surprise and a few of them gasped involuntarily.

"You lying cretin!" Drax snarled, looking hard at Pope, his fury seemed out of place on his pathetic countenance. "You knew it wasn't there."

"I never said it was." Pope smirked. "But you will go jumping to conclusions. I hope you didn't make a mess of my rooms."

"Tell me where it is!"

"And spoil the fun of you trying to find out?" Pope folded his arms and his smile became wider.

Drax looked around at the group circling him. "You were expecting me back."

"Of course." Pope continued to smile. "It was inevitable once you realised it wasn't there."

"You won't look so happy when I've torn off your arms and legs."

"I'd really like to see you try."

His anger increasing further, Drax stepped forward, hit the invisible wall of the containment circle and staggered back a couple of steps. An initial reaction of complete surprise swiftly turned into a rage he barely managed to contain. After a few moments he reached out cautiously and moved his hands across the interior of the barrier's invisible surface, not quite touching it but sensing its energy.

"I should have realised you'd try something of the sort," he said, irate condescension playing across his features. "But such a waste of time. I presume it's drawn beneath the carpet."

No one responded to Drax's glare so he squatted down and touched the carpet with the flat of his hand. The enraged confidence on his face was instantly replaced by an expression of pain at the touch of the holy water soaked into the carpet. He withdrew his hand as if he'd received a high-voltage shock.

"Agh! You flea-bitten mongrels!" He rose, wiped the holy water from his hand on the seat of his trousers and paced around the perimeter of the circle, his feet squelching with every step. "When I break free you're each going to die. Very slowly. Very painfully."

"Yeah, yeah," Pope said, waving his hand dismissively. "Then you'll never find your precious artefact."

"In that case," Drax said, looking directly at Pope, "you can watch as I kill each of your friends."

"Like I care."

Sandra was shocked to hear the way Pope spoke but was equally surprised to see it had no effect on the others, each of whom watched the proceedings calmly.

"Then I'll begin with the pitiful Miss Bishop." His voice grew colder with every word.

Bishop swallowed the mouthful of chocolate bar she

was chewing and shook her head. "You have no idea how little Pope cares for any of us," she said. "It's true, we work together and spend a lot of time in each other's company, but what other options do we have? We know of no one else that matches our ages."

Drax ceased his pacing and glared at Bishop. "You think your pathetic drivel will stop me? It won't take me long to free myself."

"Hey, knock yourself out," Bishop said. "Please."

Drax gathered himself inside the circle. He drew his power into a focus and fired a bolt of energy towards Bishop. It hit the invisible confinement limit, rebounded and spiralled around the inside of the cylindrical column. After a few seconds it petered out and Drax was left more outraged than ever.

He again gathered his power into a focus.

"I think we're going to be here all day," Kitty said to no one in particular.

"We should have ordered in pizza," Pope said. In spite of her anger at him, Bishop couldn't stop herself smiling.

"I have some frozen ones in the kitchen," Sandra offered.

Pope raised an eyebrow at her. "A freezer is good for many things, but pizza isn't one of them."

Drax ignored them and used his power to create a defensive shield around himself. He slowly expanded its size and Pope looked nervously at Bishop who shook her head and gestured for him to keep calm. In spite of Drax's concentration, he saw the exchange and grinned. He pushed out the size of the shield until it met with the confinement circle.

There was an enormous flash of light and Drax's shield backfired, shrinking suddenly and quickly, threatening to crush him with its force. He dispersed it as quickly as he was able but not before a couple of ribs cracked with audible pops and his face became bruised. He sniffed and wiped a drop of blood from his nose with the back of his hand.

Drax gathered his power yet again, but before he could do anything he began hopping about in pain, yelling as if he'd stepped in scalding water.

"I have a strong suspicion," Lassiter said with the hint of a wicked grin upon his lips, "that the shoes you're wearing are not as waterproof as you might like them to be. Perhaps you should be gracious in defeat and surrender to us. For as long as we have the strength and will to do so, we shall not cease in our efforts to prevent you killing another living soul."

"Spare me your patronising verbosity, Lassiter," Drax snarled, trying to ignore the pain in his feet. He slowly levitated himself two inches above the soaking carpet and removed his shoes while still floating then discarded them. His feet looked painfully red but he quickly healed them as he hovered.

"Why don't you just kill him?" Sandra asked.

"Like that hasn't occurred to us," Finlay said.

"Samuel, please," Grainger said. "Remember, Sandra doesn't understand the workings of magic. It's understandable she wants answers."

"Ah, yes. Sandra Tindall..." Drax's words dripped with fresh malice, heightened by the pain in his feet. "Your pretty little niece gave me the focus to begin my escape, opened up the gap I needed, as it were."

"What? How? Why her?" Sandra asked, her large chest heaving.

"Why? She was convenient and susceptible to my magic." Drax appeared to be taking great pleasure in relating this. "As for the how — I created a permanent link in her mind. You never know when these things will come in useful. Unfortunately, her pathetic little mind wasn't up to the strain—"

"You bastard!" Sandra screamed and rushed towards him with the knife held high. Everyone started to move but Kitty reacted quickest and wrestled Sandra to the ground face first, disarming her for a second time.

"You can't respond to his goading, Sandra," Kitty said as she sat astride the landlady, pushing her face into the carpet and twisting her arm up her back. "If you break the circle you'll release him and he'll kill us all."

"You could have explained that in the first place," Sandra said around the distortions of her squashed face. "I don't know anything about this mumbo-jumbo of yours. Now get off me!"

As Kitty climbed off Sandra, Bishop looked around the room and realised the group was in danger of fragmenting. Even from inside the confinement circle, Drax still influenced them with his manipulative use of fear.

"Come on," Bishop said. "Keep your minds on the problem before us." She went to each of them in turn and gave them an encouraging touch on the arm or a pat on the shoulder, like a coach giving a half-time pep-talk. She helped Sandra get to her feet and gave her a positive hug before turning to the others again.

"Now, do we think we can kill Drax outright, or at least incapacitate him long enough to deal with him for good?"

"He's spent," Kitty said, standing close to the circle with her hands on her hips. She stared into Drax's eyes and let every ounce of her loathing show on her scarred face. "He has nothing else in his little bag of tricks. He's completely out of ideas."

"Oh, Kitty, Kitty, Kitty," Drax smirked, shaking his head. "How wrong you are. I've been saving it for just the right occasion, but I have something special for you."

Kitty's hands dropped to her sides as his gaze bore into her, pushing back her hate-filled confidence. Drax reached into a pocket and pulled out a small jar. Astonished, Kitty stepped backwards when he raised it for everyone to see its contents — a single eye floated in preserving fluid. Drax waved his hand and the eye swivelled around to look directly at Kitty as if still alive.

"Damn!" She lifted her hand to the eye-patch and moved a little further away.

"Yes, indeed. Have you missed it?" For a man trapped in a magical prison, he looked remarkably sure of himself.

"No, don't! Please..."

"Finlay!" Pope said and the big man moved towards Kitty.

He wrapped his arms around her to prevent her breaking the circle and Drax gestured again. This time Kitty contorted with agony-induced spasms and tore off the eye-patch as if that would somehow help. The socket, although healed and inert for fifteen years, now oozed blood.

Her friends gathered around her with no idea what to do while Drax looked on and laughed.

Kitty

Kitty's piercing screams were both extremely shrill and deeply haunting — enough to give even the most hardened person chills. For her friends, the sound also emphasised how little they were able to do. The only way to stop Kitty's pain was to take the eye from Drax, but to do so would result in the collapsing of the magical barrier and the release of the powerful wizard.

Bishop grabbed Kitty by the shoulders and tried to get her attention but it was like trying to reason with an enraged bull elephant intent on wreaking havoc. The jerks and spasms were beyond Bishop's ability to overcome and she was thankful that Finlay had hold of her friend, though even his strength was being put to the test.

"Kitty, you must listen to me," Bishop said and slapped her hard across the face, causing a few drops of the oozing blood to fall to the floor. "You have to pay attention to what I tell you."

"Help me, Faye!" Kitty screamed through clenched teeth. "You've got to bloody well help me."

Bishop looked around at the others. Finlay shrugged his brows, Sandra was bewildered and scared, Grainger and Lassiter were praying and Pope gripped her shoulder for moral support. In his confinement circle, Drax laughed; both at their helplessness and the pain he was inflicting on Kitty. Each time they met it seemed she would be on the receiving end of severe pain of one kind or another.

Bishop returned her attention to her one-eyed friend and put her hands on either side of her head.

"Kitty, you've got to block him out. Whatever connection Drax has formed, you've got to fight it. Do whatever you must to sever that link."

"I can't, Faye, I can't. It hurts so much." She shook her head against Bishop's hands. "How can I fight his magic?"

"Kitty, eighty percent of magical ability is simply the use of re-directed willpower. Use your years of martial arts training to focus."

"Oh my god, I can't think. I can't do it." She screamed again and writhed in agony with such force that Finlay was forced to lay her on the floor he was so worried she'd hurt herself. The others came close and helped hold Kitty down to prevent her coming to harm.

"Stop the pain! Please! Kill me if you must."

Pope stood up, stared intently at Drax and composed himself to do what was necessary, breathing hard and fast to fire himself up. He took the knife from where it had landed when Kitty had disarmed Sandra. Although the landlady was bearing up remarkably well, Kitty's distress showed what her niece must have gone through before she killed her family. As Pope raised the knife, Bishop registered what he was doing.

"Josh, no!" she cried.

"I'll hate myself tomorrow, but she wants this, Faye." He hardened himself. "She wants us to end her pain."

Grainger and Lassiter turned from Kitty and looked at each other. They dropped their heads in unison with nothing to say.

Kitty unexpectedly stopped screaming and her body went limp. She breathed heavily but otherwise appeared to be unharmed. Everyone eased their hold on her, watching closely. Bishop looked over at Drax who shrugged. He looked far too smug to be doing anything other than scheming.

Bishop hardened her gaze. "Keep hold!"

Drax gestured instantly and Kitty broke free of everyone's relaxed hold, leaping to her feet like her feline namesake. She shook her head as if clearing it of cobwebs. There was a dark look to her single good eye that none of them had seen before and they quickly tried to grab her again.

Kitty moved like a woman possessed, which effectively she was, and punched Bishop in the face before elbowing Pope on the return action. Finlay moved in quickly and went to grab her again but she was far too fast and rained a number of blows on him before he had a chance to react. They did little harm to his tough body but they kept him off balance while she edged towards the confinement circle. Even with Drax controlling her actions, her many years of martial arts training shone through.

"Stop her!" Bishop yelled.

Pope took the knife he still held and stabbed downward with it and into the toe of Kitty's boot, pinning it to the floor but he held it in place because it wasn't anchored securely enough. Finlay saw this, dropped to his knees and hammered on the end of the handle with his fist, driving it further through the carpet and into the floorboards beneath. Such was Drax's control of Kitty she didn't register the pain and only realised what had happened when she discovered she couldn't move her foot.

Lassiter picked up a stool. "Forgive me, Kitty," he said and smacked her across the head with it. The impact sounded sickening and although she wasn't in control of her body, it knocked her out nevertheless and she hit the floor like a side of beef.

Her sudden lapse into unconsciousness sent a jolt of unexpected, powerful feedback right at Drax and he doubled over as the pain struck though him. He very nearly dropped the glass jar he held, fumbling with it a few seconds before taking a firm hold once more, still levitating above the carpet. He stared at the eye in deep concentration before gathering his powers and will for another assault.

"You're going to wish you'd never done that." Drax gestured with his free hand and it became instantly clear that the connection was unbreakable in spite of Kitty's unconscious state.

Kitty's arm moved with lightning speed and pulled out the knife as if from butter. Before anyone could react, let alone stop her, the knife was in Finlay's arm and he let go of her in reflex, which gave Kitty the opportunity to pounce to her feet once more.

"Knocking her out may have been a bad move," Bishop said. "Now she's unable to fight Drax's connection."

They grabbed Kitty and held on as best they could but her strength had become super-charged and they knew they wouldn't be able to restrain her for long. Grainger ran behind the bar, quickly filled the bucket he'd used earlier with more water and blessed it as rapidly as possible. He threw the holy water over Kitty, soaking everyone in the process.

Though Kitty had no Fae magic or blood in her, the link to Drax fed back to him again. The wizard screamed, blasted backwards against the far side of the containment circle by the surprising strength of the backlash. His levitation faltered for a moment and one of his feet touched the wet carpet. Once more he reacted in pain and for the moment his attention turned away from those who'd trapped him.

Kitty shook her head and became lucid again, thanks to the cold, holy water and the broken link — a temporary respite from the pain inflicted upon her. She limped over to Pope and punched him in the face.

"Does everyone want a go?" he yelled.

"This is your fault, you bloody idiot!" Kitty screamed. "If you'd placed the Ellen-Maegen in the coffin he'd never have escaped and I wouldn't be his plaything."

"We're all well aware of my stupidity," Pope said, checking his jaw was still in one piece. "What we need is a way of defeating the toss-mongrel."

"What if we can't? What if he'll always have dominance over us?" She paused but there was no answer, no comment. "Do you know what that artefact contains? Why Drax needs it so desperately?" She glared at Pope, furious with him. "It contains a vital piece of his soul, set into the earth gem at its centre."

The others looked at one another in astonishment.

"I... should have destroyed it," Pope said in a whisper.

"Even if we manage to kill or dispose of him in some way, the artefact will bring him back. It's his insurance policy. He's going to defeat us and you — you, Joshua Pope — are the bloody reason it will happen."

Pope spread his arms and looked at Kitty but the words of reassurance he wanted to deliver wouldn't come. They didn't even exist. Within the circle, Drax had recovered and was watching the exchange intently.

"Kitty Spender," Drax said. "I never knew you had such knowledge and insight. I've clearly underestimated you over the years and I find myself rather intrigued. Perhaps the two of us could...?"

"Go to hell, Drax," Kitty spat.

"I could make you do it."

"But you wouldn't." She glowered at him, blood still

seeping from her empty socket. "Even you know how sad it would be to force someone to love you. It would never provide the boost your inflated ego needs."

"Attempting to anger me is a little unwise considering the current situation. As you said, I have the edge."

"But not the artefact. If you're so smart and powerful, why can't you use your power to work out its location? Why do you even need us?"

"Because Pope has hidden it from my senses and I would need to be within a hundred feet to detect it precisely. Now, I need you to do this..." Drax stared at the eye in the jar and gestured again.

Kitty whirled around, grabbed Pope's head between her hands and held on tightly. She was unable to let go and before he could pull her hands free Pope slumped to his knees. Within the circle, Drax closed his eyes and concentrated with all his might. Kitty was a conduit to Pope and she stared at her hands in disbelief. They held up Pope who hung limply from the neck down like a rag doll.

Finlay, still bleeding badly from his wound, moved behind Pope and ignored the pain as he grabbed Kitty's wrists.

"Finlay, don't!" Bishop warned. "You'll kill them both if you break the contact. He's using his connection with Kitty to read Pope's mind and find where the artefact is."

"Do we have any other option, Faye?" Lassiter asked. "We cannot let Drax gain this information from Pope."

Unfortunately, before they had made a decision, Drax broke the contact and Kitty released Pope's head, completely horrified by her part in this. He slumped to the floor completely exhausted. She stared at her hands, then, filled with loathing, turned to face Drax, who smiled and gloated.

"Thank you," he said. "I'd like to stay but I have

something to recover."

"You bloody bastard!" Kitty said.

"I shall miss our intelligent repartee, Miss Spender."

Drax drew on his power again. He concentrated intently, searching with his supernatural senses, using the information he'd drawn from Pope's mind, and smiled. He promptly vanished.

Kitty swayed for a moment then collapsed to the floor and stopped breathing.

Blood

Bishop rushed to Kitty's side. "Someone check Josh."

"I'm fine," Pope said. "I've just never been mind-raped before. I don't recommend it."

"Does anyone know CPR?" Bishop asked. "I don't have any power left to heal her."

Lassiter stepped forward, dropped to his knees, arranged Kitty in the recovery position and began chest compressions. "I will need to take turns with someone else every few minutes," he said as he counted his downward thrusts.

"I'll help," Sandra said. "If you show me what to do."

Bishop left them to it and helped Pope to his feet. His arms and legs shook as he stood up. "What are we going to do, Josh?"

"You need to break the link between Kitty and her eye."

"I can't. I don't have the power to create a circle strong enough," Bishop said. "I used up all my stored reserves and this trap has cut me off completely."

"Then I'll have to break the containment trap with blood," Pope said. He looked around at the group. "I think I can gather enough to do it."

Grainger and Lassiter looked at him with concern. They viewed blood magic as a dark art and didn't like its use at the best of times. In unskilled hands it had a regular tendency to corrupt the wielder. Even though to Pope it was a way of life, they still disliked the practice.

"Don't worry, fellers. Lesser of two evils, after all." Pope almost winked, but now was not the time to tease them as he regularly liked to do.

"Wait," Grainger said. "What about Drax? Now he knows where his artefact is he'll be unstoppable."

Pope grinned. "Drax may have greater power than me, but I've been around the block far more often than him — he's not the only one who can set traps. I'll explain once we've helped Kitty."

Pope went behind the bar and started rummaging around. "Sandra, I'm looking for a couple of large jugs..."

"This isn't the time to get personal," she joked. She'd taken over from Lassiter and her not insubstantial bosom was bouncing with the compressions she was applying. Then she glanced up, a little abashed. "Sorry, I'm too used to the punters' banter. In the kitchen — the cupboard over the sink." She smiled at Lassiter uncomfortably as Pope rushed up the stairs but the undertaker's deadpan face gave nothing away.

Pope found the jugs quickly enough then rummaged around the drawers until he had a number of small, sharp knives and a pile of freshly laundered tea-towels. He lit one of the gas burners on the stove and sterilised each knife in turn before wrapping them in one of the clean cloths. Then he took a little time rummaging in Sandra's bedroom until he found the additional item he needed.

Back in the bar, he laid everything out on a table, pulled a bottle of vodka from its optic measure and prepared to do the bloodletting.

"I might as well go first," Finlay offered. "Seeing as I'm already bleeding." He released the pressure he'd been applying to the wound and blood dripped freely into one of the jugs. After a moment Pope swapped over the jugs and a little blood oozed into that one, too.

"I have to make sure the same mix is in each," he

explained, but the part troll gave him a look that suggested he needed no explanation. After a moment he gave Finlay the nod and the big man stopped the bleeding by applying pressure again.

Bishop stepped up and bared her arm. "Will it work."

"It's the best chance we have." Pope looked into her eyes and a brief moment of tension passed between them before Bishop rolled up her sleeve.

Pope sloshed some vodka onto one of the cloths and cleaned the crook of Bishop's elbow, then he used one of the knives to make a small cut, puncturing the vein. The blood flowed freely and again Pope collected a little in each jug. He tied the cloth about her arm when they were done and she drew in breath as the alcohol in the vodka stung the cut.

Grainger and Lassiter took their turns, though the latter wanted assurances on the sterility of the knives used and Pope was forced to tell him how he'd prepared them before he'd even bare his arm.

Once Pope added some of his own blood to the mix, each jug was about a third full. He turned to Sandra who got Lassiter to take over chest compressions again before coming over with a worried look on her face.

"I'm afraid I need more of your blood than I took from the others," Pope said. "The confinement spell on the pub was created with a strong, direct connection to you and it's the only way I can break it."

"Yeah, okay," Sandra said, steeling herself with a hefty breath. "Whatever I've got to do to help you get Drax. This is for my family." Pope smiled briefly at her and got her to sit down at the table. She looked like she was going to be sick as she stared at the knife while Pope cleaned her arm, but she swallowed hard and gave the go-ahead with a nod of her head and a clenching of her teeth. Pope made the cut and she closed her eyes and turned away.

The first of Sandra's blood flowed into one jug's mix and the pub shook gently for a few seconds, as if a particularly heavy truck had just driven by outside. Bishop looked at Pope with concerned expectation. The tremor was a encouraging sign that the blood magic might actually work.

Pope switched the jugs regularly to keep the two mixtures even, but as the level in each rose to the two-thirds mark he became a little worried.

"How will you know when you have enough?" Sandra asked. Pope's anxiety disturbed her and she watched the flowing liquid with rising apprehension. She abruptly yawned without being able to stop herself.

"I'm attuned to the blood," he replied, silently willing each drop to be the last. "I'll know when there's enough."

"But it's taking more than you expected, isn't it?" Sandra's breathing was a little forced.

"I'm afraid so. Do you want me to stop?"

"I want you to stop that evil monster. Do what you need, Mr. Pope." Her voice became a little slurred and she looked weary, rapidly deteriorating. "Do whatever you need..." Her eyes fluttered and closed. She went limp in the chair.

"Josh, what's wrong?" Bishop asked. She moved behind Sandra and held her upright in the chair while Pope continued the blood-letting. Her frustration was clearly evident.

"The remnants of the sleep spell are taking over again," Pope said, switching the jugs once more. "We'll have to act quickly once the confinement is broken."

The blood continued to flow and each jug was over three-quarters full before Pope declared that he'd taken enough. The pub shook again, this time with the force of a minor earthquake. Glasses and bottles rattled on the shelves behind the bar and one of the bar stools fell over. The mirror behind the bar cracked down the middle.

Bishop quickly wrapped Sandra's arm and checked her pulse. "She's fading."

Pope quickly opened the final item he'd brought down — the small casket containing Amber's ashes — and tipped half of the dusty remains into each of the jugs, stirring each one carefully with one of the knives.

"We've got to do this now," Pope said, satisfied with the mixtures. "Listen carefully.

"Sam, peel back the carpet and don't disturb Faye's symbols whatever you do. Lassiter, Father Grainger — as soon as the carpet is clear get Kitty into the circle and hold her upright in the centre. Faye, you and Sam do the same with Sandra. You all need to take up as little space as possible because I need to be able to walk around the internal perimeter. Okay?"

Everyone nodded at him. No one raised any questions.

"Good, now go!"

Everything went so fluidly they were grouped in the circle within ten seconds. Pope stepped into it with a jug of mixed blood in each hand and as he did so another, longer tremor shook the pub, again a little more intense.

He immediately started pacing around the inside edge in an anti-clockwise direction, keeping within the limits of the magic outline. He steadily poured the blood and ashes mixture from the jug in his right hand so it fell to the floor in a thick splatter outside the pastel ring. He chanted as the liquid flowed.

"*Pel braench ach malod fo ta dovelan.*

"*Pel braench ach malod totad Drax ta vod.*

"*Pel braench ach restichas ordut fo chad.*

"*Pel braench ach ta libech cagos heroch.*"

As Pope finished his circuit, the last of the mixture

from the first jug completed the bloody circle on the floor and a play of energy raced around it a few times to seal its force. The building shook even more strongly and a picture fell from the wall. Sandra's breathing weakened and became erratic.

Suddenly, the ghost of a young girl appeared, flickering in and out of existence. Each of them recognised her scared face as that of Amber as they'd very briefly known her fifteen years earlier. For a moment they could not take their eyes from her but none of them said anything.

Pope turned and walked in the opposite direction. This time he poured the blood from the second jug so it landed inside Bishop's pastel line, taking care not to step in the red liquid.

"*Pel braench ach ta libech cagos heroch.*
"*Pel braench ach restichas ordut fo chad.*
"*Pel braench ach malod totad Drax ta vod.*
"*Pel braench ach malod fo ta dovelan.*"

When the second loop of blood was complete the effect was devastating. Pope had set powerful, opposing forces in motion and they competed for control of the pub. Still holding the two jugs, he wrapped his arms around the group and urged them to hang on as crackling energy shot around the bloody circles in contrary directions.

The whole building rocked and rattled to its foundations. Cracks formed in the plaster on the walls and a whirlwind arose outside the protective circle, tossing pieces of heavy wooden furniture around like they were nothing more than polystyrene replicas, wrenching the bar fittings off in the process.

Amber's ghost appeared again, now here, now there, jumping about the pub's main room in a seemingly random fashion.

The outer circle of blood began to bubble and burn and everyone who'd had their blood taken experienced a fiery agony in the wound. They couldn't help but scream. Although unconscious, Sandra broke into a sweat in spite of her skin temperature dropping a few degrees. Her breathing was weak and ragged but at least it was there. They fought the pains and clung onto the hope her tenuous grasp on life gave them.

Then it was done.

The tremor ended like someone had slammed on the brakes. The wind stopped, the dust began to settle and the remains of the window Pope had pulverised earlier fell to the ground in a pile of shattered glass and wood.

Amber's ghost screamed piercingly then vanished.

They smiled and sighed with relief rather than pleasure — they were all still alive. With the possible exception of Kitty, who was still not breathing.

Earth

Pope quickly broke the blood circles with his foot and the world rushed in to strike Bishop hard, like an intravenous rush of pure adrenalin and caffeine. It affected her in exactly the same way whenever she'd found herself cut off from the earth for any length of time. She fell to her knees with relief, somewhat drunk on the revitalising connection with the planet's energy.

Lassiter and Grainger laid Kitty on the floor again and the undertaker continued with compressions. "I don't know how long her body can survive this treatment."

Pope placed the two jugs onto one of the tables while Finlay took Sandra to one side of the room and made her as comfortable as he could. Her breathing was weak and ragged. She looked dangerously pale.

Bishop crawled towards the pub door and Pope rushed over to help her but she waved him away. Instead he opened the pub door wide and held it open, further proof that his blood magic had broken Drax's entrapment spell. As if the opening of the door was some kind of signal, the ghosts that regularly haunted the pub returned, rushing past Pope in varying degrees of transparency, including the real ghost of Archie Morton, who immediately went to the side of the rapidly fading Sandra and hovered there looking worried.

Outside, it was already growing light and the city was waking up. A woman passed by on her way to work and gave Bishop a disgusted look as the magician dragged herself through the pub door.

She placed her hand on the cold flagstone of the doorstep and made a direct connection with the earth once more, sucking in air with the thrill of this second rush. The pub was located very close to the York ley line so it was a simple task for Bishop to reach through the earth and tap directly into the power she needed, re-energising her whole body as she did so.

Bishop drew on the earth energy as if quenching a week-long thirst. The wound on her arm sealed and healed instantly, her eyes became brighter and more alert, refreshed like dew on a spring morning. Centuries of weariness dropped from her bones. After a few minutes she stood and went over to Kitty.

"Leave her, please," she said. Lassiter stopped the compressions and backed away, rubbing at the stiffness in his hands.

Bishop pulled the pastel stub from her pocket and drew a plain circle on the carpet around her friend. She touched the line with her finger and charged it with most of the energy she'd just taken in.

As soon as the protective circle was active, Kitty sucked in air like someone who'd just been saved from drowning. She coughed and wheezed for a while before pulling out a handkerchief and spitting something green and gruesome into it.

"Kitty, are you all right?" Bishop asked. Kitty felt her eye socket gingerly but the bleeding had stopped. She pulled a spare eye patch from her pocket and put it in place before looking up at her friend, panting like she'd just run a mile.

"I could murder a pint," she said and Bishop grinned. Lassiter and Grainger looked on with little humour on their faces but clear signs of relief. The priest took out a handkerchief and mopped his brow.

"For now you need to stay in the circle until we work out how to deal with Drax permanently."

"That could take forever." Kitty's breathing was calming down already but her face turned into a grimace.

She undid the lace of her boot and pulled it off, revealing a sock soaked in blood, which she also removed. The knife Pope had stuck through her foot had gone through cleanly enough so there'd be no permanent damage but the blood still oozed from the wound. She ripped a couple of strips of cloth from her shirt and wadded them up, then removed her other boot and sock and used the sock to tie the wadded material against the top and bottom of her damaged foot.

"Faye!" Finlay called over from the other side of the room.

He was crouched over Sandra's still form and he looked worried and more than a little helpless. The landlady's skin had lost all of its colour and her breathing was now so shallow that Bishop didn't need a close inspection to know she didn't have long to live. She needed to do something quickly but she couldn't keep drawing on the ley line power from the doorstep, it took too long.

Bishop stood up, moved into some free space and used the last of her energy to open a portal to transport her home.

Long ago, she'd arranged her workshop in such a way that she'd quickly be able to find what she needed in emergencies such as this. Shelves containing important items and magical supplies were well-ordered and close at hand. From bottles of potions to powdered minerals in jars and even rocks and sacks of soil, everything she might use had been prepared in advance and she regularly maintained the supply.

Right now, Bishop simply needed a means of

recharging her energy swiftly and grabbed a green gem from one of the shelves. She absorbed the earth power she'd previously placed into it, stored inside its crystal structure like a magical power cell. She threw it onto the workbench as soon as it was depleted, ready for recharging later.

Refreshed again, she took a couple of similar gems attached to copper chains and hung them around her neck before stuffing a couple of plastic bags into her pockets. They contained powdered substances she often added to her spells for strength and stability. Finally, she grabbed three brass and granite pendants, opened another portal and returned to the pub.

She threw one of the pendants to Finlay who placed it around his neck and put his hand over it, pressing the metal and stone to his chest. The blood instantly stopped flowing from his wounded arm and the cut began to heal. The pendants were a recent idea Bishop had developed, into each of which she'd stored specific healing spells along with enough earth energy to make them work.

She took the other two pendants over to Sandra, hung them around her neck and activated them. There was always a danger that using two such spells at the same time would over-stimulate a person's natural healing mechanisms but Sandra was so far gone that a single spell wouldn't be enough.

"Will they work?" Pope asked. Although he knew that Bishop's magic was powerful, there was also a limit to how much damage — magical or physical — a body could take before it was beyond the scope of recovery.

"Drax entwined Sandra into his perverted magic to such a degree that she may not make it," Bishop whispered. "All we can do now is hope."

"And pray," Grainger added, kneeling by the unconscious woman's side.

"We don't have time for that, Father." Pope rose from the chair. "I need you to come with me. You too, Sam." He looked at Bishop. "You up to it?"

She took a deep breath then nodded. Normally, she would have attempted to heal Sandra herself but they had another, more pressing matter to attend to. A crazy, powerful wizard with the urge to kill them all, to be precise.

"I shall pray in your stead, Luke," Lassiter said. He knelt by Sandra's body and clasped his hands together. His lips moved soundlessly.

"Wait," Kitty urged from within her protective circle. "What are you doing? You can't leave me. What if Drax comes back?"

The Hill on the Wolds

"Don't worry, Kitty," Pope said. "Drax is caught in a trap I created some time ago."

Everyone looked at him, their curiosity briefly piqued by this new revelation. Bishop, already unhappy with him, became angry once again, but the others a little less so. Although no one spoke it was clear they were all waiting for him to continue. He looked them over and knew that a proper explanation was necessary if he hoped to get them on his side once more.

"When I discovered that his artefact couldn't help me, I decided to use it as bait on the off-chance that he ever escaped.

"Off-chance?!" Bishop snapped.

Pope ignored her and carried on. "I coated it in my own blood for months before doing so in order to hide its exact whereabouts."

"But why didn't you tell us?" Kitty asked.

"I needed to be sure he'd come through me so I'd know when the trap was sprung." Pope paused. "I couldn't risk any of you knowing its location. I've trained my mind to be very specific about the information I revealed to him. I needed Drax to believe he'd forced the location from me without him discovering the trap I'd laid. Sorry."

Grainger nodded as if it all made sense and Finlay shrugged like it was all the explanation he needed from his friend. Kitty and Bishop were less convinced, judging by the dark looks on their faces.

"I know this doesn't fix all the things I've done, but can we not worry about that until later?" He looked at each of them with pleading eyes. "Right now I need to deal with the vermin in my trap."

Bishop sighed and nodded. "Where's the trap located?"

"First, we need to go somewhere else if we're to defeat Drax for good." Pope looked into Bishop's eyes and she nodded. "You know the old mill about two miles south down the river? There's a company there now that mixes concrete."

"Miller's Aggregates," Finlay said, testing his newly healed arm. "Our firm uses their concrete."

"I know it well enough," Bishop said, which meant she'd be able to open a portal there.

Pope stepped closer to her and beckoned over Grainger and Finlay.

"Have I ever mentioned how much I hate travelling this way?" Grainger said.

Finlay clapped him on the shoulder for reassurance. "Every time, Father. Every time."

"How long do you have, Josh?" Bishop asked, referring to the amount of time he could remain outside the city walls.

"Forty-seven minutes," Pope replied. "It should be plenty of time."

"If nothing goes wrong."

Bishop drew on more earth energy and created a portal in the space in front of her. Linking hands, the four of them stepped through and seconds later they were in the busy, dusty yard of Miller's Aggregates, the workday just beginning.

The sound of heavy machinery came from inside a number of large industrial sheds that defined one side of the yard's perimeter. Standing on the opposite side were a number of huge bays, each filled with different grades of sand or gravel. Mixer lorries, tipper trucks and payload feeders thundered back and forth, stirring up the dust.

"Oy, you!"

They turned at the sound of the unfamiliar voice and saw a man hurrying towards them, wearing a hard hat and a reflective vest with the word "foreman" printed on it. In his left hand he carried a clipboard and pen and he shook his right hand at them in a somewhat pantomime fashion.

"You can't come in here without a hard-hat."

"Hey, Mike," Finlay said. "These are my friends." Most people in the local construction industry knew Finlay because of his size and strength, but he'd also had enough dealings with the people at Miller's to be on first name terms with the foreman.

"We need some concrete, Mike," Pope said.

"You still need a hard-hat." Mike looked from one to another. "As you well know, Sam. The guy on the gate shouldn't have even let you in, never mind the fact that he did so without giving you hats."

Pope looked into the foreman's eyes and held his gaze for a moment. He thrust his hand into his pocket, pricked his thumb on the ever-present carpet tack and smeared a drop of blood on Mike's forehead.

"*Braench ach mentum ſo lictach,*" he said, unlocking something in the man's mind. "Forget the hard hats. Take us to where you mix the concrete."

"Of course, sir," Mike said, his eyes having taken on a glassy look. "Which grade did you have in mind?"

"It needs to be the hardest, most durable you have."

Mike nodded. "Follow me."

He walked towards a building flanked by silos and beneath which mixer lorries were being filled. The noise of the machinery grew louder as they approached. When they reached the building Pope looked into the foreman's eyes again.

"Mike, you're to do exactly what Sam and Father Luke tell you," he said.

"Of course, sir," the foreman said.

"Which is the chute our concrete will come from?" Bishop asked. Pope smiled — he so rarely had to explain the fine details of his plans to her.

Mike pointed. "That one, number seven."

"Thanks." Bishop took a good look at the chute and its relation to the surrounding area in order to commit it to memory.

Pope turned to Finlay and Grainger. "Father, I need you to bless the water they use to make the concrete. Sam, make sure nothing goes wrong. Give me a call when the concrete is ready."

"How much do you need?" Finlay asked.

"Oh, good point," Pope said and thought for a moment while he did a mental calculation. "About thirty cubic yards."

"We work in cubic metres these days," Mike said, clearly trying to be helpful.

"Okay, thirty cubic metres, then. Tell you what, let's make it fifty for good measure."

Mike seemed pleased at that and climbed a narrow flight of steps into the building. Finlay was about to follow when Bishop handed the two plastic bags to him.

"Add the contents of both bags to the mix," she said. "But take care — one is powdered iron, the other contains ground rocks taken from a confluence of ley lines." Finlay took the bags gingerly — he was always a little wary of magical materials but powdered iron could be pretty dangerous to the troll side of him if he wasn't careful with it.

"Come on, Faye," Pope said. "We don't have much time and we need to go to Far Tree Farm over on the Wolds."

"The place the three witches were killed twenty years ago?"

"That's right. It's been deserted ever since." He looked additionally serious for a moment. "Can you remember it?"

"Of course."

It had been another case on which the two magicians had been consulted by the police in the hope of apprehending the killer. Inspector Tench was still on the force and because of his dealings with paranormal matters, the Humberside authority had brought him in because they'd run out of ideas. He, in turn, had called on Bishop and Pope once he realised that genuine magic was involved. The regular detective in charge was under pressure from his superiors because one of the dead women was the sister of a local magistrate.

After the case was resolved — they'd tracked the killer down in a couple of hours — stories of disease contamination had kept people away from the farm. However, to make absolutely sure people stayed away, Pope had bought the land and installed bio-hazard signs along the perimeter fence.

Bishop now opened another portal, which took her and Pope directly to the farm. She followed him as he rushed up the gentle slope behind the derelict barn. There was little of Pope's available time remaining and they had to make the most of what they had.

The top of the hill was barren — nothing grew in the dusty, chalky soil for a hundred yards in a rough circle around the summit where a well had been sunk many years earlier. It was this shaft that Pope headed towards.

The well was dry and always would be, situated at the

top of a chalk hill — it hadn't been created with the intention of providing water. After the killer had been apprehended, Pope and Bishop had discovered the well was half filled with the bones from numerous sacrifices, which were mostly animal remains but some had definitely been human. The authorities removed the bones for evidence and re-burial. Analysis had suggested the sacrifices had been taking place for at least fifty years. Whatever the witches had been up to at the farm, there was a chance the killer may well have been justified in his actions. But even under prolonged interrogation and mind manipulation from Pope, he'd not spoken about why he'd killed them.

Pope stopped about thirty yards away from the summit and turned to Bishop when she caught up.

"I hate this place," Bishop said. "The earth is dead."

"Why do you think I chose it," Pope said. "I cleaned up the well and installed a power circle at the bottom made of blood gold."

"That must have taken a lot of visits."

"Yeah. I came here during those months I had some of my freedom time spare."

"Impressive. I presume the gold is intended to act as an ever-lasting confinement circle?" Bishop couldn't help nodding and smiling. It wasn't often that Pope surprised her with something new, but she had to admit that this was pretty neat in spite of her anger towards him.

"Exactly." Pope smiled. He'd put a lot of work into this plan and was pleased it now seemed to be justified.

"I suppose the Ellen-Maegen has been sitting at the bottom of the well for years, waiting for Drax to snare himself."

Pope nodded and moved closer to the well. "Don't look over the edge."

Bishop glared. "Really? You think I'm stupid enough

to break the confinement circle?"

"Sorry. Look it's just..."

"Forget it. What now?"

"We wait for the concrete." Pope put his hands on his hips and stared at the hole. The temptation to peer down it was surprisingly strong.

"I know you're up there, Pope." Drax's voice carried up the shaft of the well, sounding echoey and unreal. "I can sense the vile stench of your half-breed aura and it makes me want to vomit. When I get free, I'm going to torture you and your friends for years."

Bishop looked surprised. Pope didn't exactly broadcast his mixed parentage to all and sundry, so Drax's knowledge of it was unexpected. She shuddered.

"The concrete is just an insurance, right?" Bishop asked.

"Well, almost," Pope said. "But the holy water in the concrete will sever his connections to Sandra and Kitty. Your additions will enhance that protection and fuse his power in place."

He paused. "But there is another reason we need the concrete. Without it he'll escape."

"What? No one can break free of a gold confinement circle."

"But it's power isn't infinite. If he's able to levitate high enough, he'll eventually reach a point where the strength of the confinement has faded enough for him to escape."

"That's never occurred to me," Bishop mused. "All the magic circles I've ever seen have been indoors."

"Exactly! The height is restricted by the ceiling above. But I must admit I only realised this once I'd installed the gold ring." Pope gave a wry smile. "Based on what I've seen you accomplish, I estimate that with his abilities and strength it will take him eight hours to reach the point where he could escape."

Levitation proved to be a struggle for all magicians. They might be able to case fireballs or transport themselves across the world but lifting themselves even an inch off the ground took a lot of energy and constant concentration for even the most powerful. If a magician wanted to rise further they could only do so by adding to their elevation incrementally. Most found that their limit was only a few inches.

"Your estimates are way off the mark," Drax said and laughed. "In eight hours I will have escaped, imprisoned you both and gone after your friends." From the altered timbre of his voice they could tell he wasn't far from the top of the well.

"Damn!" Pope stared at Bishop. He'd underestimated how quickly Drax would be able to levitate up the shaft. He pulled his phone from his pocket and stared at it, willing it to ring.

If the concrete wasn't ready very quickly, Drax would make good on his promise to torture them.

Battle to the Last

Bishop gripped his arm. "Don't start worrying just yet, Josh."

Pope looked at her then looked at the phone before speaking through clenched teeth. "I'm going to call Sam." He keyed in the number and it rang for about twenty seconds before the connection was made.

"Hello, Grainger speaking," the answering voice said.

"Luke, where's Sam? Is something wrong?" Pope glanced over to the top of the well.

"There's a little difficulty with the feed mechanism," Grainger replied. "Sam's trying to free it as we speak. He assures me it won't take long."

Pope checked his internal clock. "Tell him to make it sharp. I have less than thirty minutes to make this happen."

He closed the phone and turned to Bishop. "The bloody feed mechanism's jammed." He stared at the phone as if he wanted to hurl it far away but thrust it into his pocket. "Bloody hell!"

"What on earth's the matter with you?" She grabbed his shoulders. "I've never seen you like this."

"I..." Pope stepped away from her. "You have every right to be mad at me — I really blew it this time."

"Josh..."

"But you can't know how furious I am with myself. I'm amazed at how stupid I am and yet I still managed to live for more than two thousand years. My arrogance is greater than Drax's..."

"Just stop it, now!" Bishop stepped forward and slapped his face. "You're like a teenager having a temper tantrum."

Pope seethed but his barely controlled fury wasn't caused by Bishop's slap or words. Inside, he boiled with all he'd failed to acknowledge to himself over every year, every decade, every century of his life. It came to the surface, unbidden, and for a moment he was sure he was going to weep. Or explode.

"Do I need to slap you until you get your bloody act together?" Bishop asked. "We don't have time for this. If you want to feel sorry for yourself, do it when we've defeated Drax."

"Time's running out and the fat lady's about to sing."

"Then stuff a sock in her bloody cake-hole and hide her sheet music." She paused and looked him in the eye. "We all make mistakes and screw things up; it doesn't mean we can't fix them."

Pope lifted his head and took a deep breath. He looked hard at Bishop, over at the well, then back to her. He smiled. "Thank god you're my friend."

They both turned to face the well in time to see Drax's head rise slowly over the lip of the hole. For a moment the waves of self-doubt washed over Pope again and he collapsed to his knees. He knew that a faint connection still existed between him and Drax and the latter was using it to manipulate Pope's mood. Although he felt like he was falling into a pit of darkness, he pulled himself to his feet, his eyes damp with tears of despair.

Bishop squeezed Pope's arm again for additional encouragement and Pope's spirits lifted. The gentle touch of a true friend grounded him and gave him hope. They looked at each other then stepped away with renewed determination. Drax nudged himself a little higher, a little strain on his face from his efforts to levitate at his current rate.

"Your little melodrama almost brought a tear to my eye," he said. "But I cannot spare the effort for hysterics. I can see why you've never conquered the world."

"What?!" Bishop looked a little bewildered. "You think we have any interest in that?"

"Why else develop so much power?"

"Occasionally we have to stop megalomaniacs like you," Pope said.

"You have no big plans for your life? How pathetic. You deserve to be ground into animal feed then shat onto the fields."

"Now listen..." Bishop began but her words were halted by Pope's unexpected belly laugh. She'd never known a man whose moods could change so much so quickly.

"Thank you, Drax," Pope said after a few seconds. "I needed to hear your whiny ramblings to help me gain a little perspective."

"Do you really think you have a chance against my power?"

"What you need to ask yourself," Pope said, his mind becoming refreshingly clear, "Is can you hope to win out against two people who have survived for well over two and a half millennia between them?"

"We shall soon see." Even the strain on Drax's face couldn't hide his smugness.

"I think not." Pope looked at Bishop who nodded almost imperceptibly. "We will defeat you before you've risen high enough to escape."

"Not when I'm already high enough to do this!" He gestured with his right hand and clicked his fingers.

Bishop and Pope turned slowly to look behind them. They'd felt, rather than heard, the arrival of someone new and were astonished to see a familiar face striding up the hill.

Coruban, the Fae swordsman, had been dead for more than thirty years, yet he approached them with murderous purpose showing clearly in his body language, his sword gripped tightly in his hand.

"Spirit?" Pope whispered.

"Definitely!" Bishop replied in a similar tone.

However, in spite of his form being somewhat ghostly in appearance, his sword looked real enough. The weapon had originally been created to bind the young Fae and Drax together, but that uniting had taken a form neither had anticipated. Coruban's spirit now appeared to be at Drax's beck and call.

Pope and Bishop exchanged a look. They were both unarmed and had no means to physically defend themselves but they couldn't flee the location as they had to hold on until they got the call from Finlay.

Bishop felt uncomfortable on the dead hill — somewhat separated from the earth like being trapped inside the pub — but tried to ignore the feeling as she pulled the power from one of her gems into her body. As soon as the gem was depleted she drew some of that energy into a tight focus and muttered a spell under her breath. A blast of power shot from her hands and struck Coruban's spirit form directly in his torso.

She half expected the blast to have no effect on the ghost, but the Fae shattered into half a dozen pieces like he was made of glass. His sword fell to the ground without striking a blow.

Behind the two magicians, Drax chuckled and gestured again. The six pieces of the spirit Fae rapidly morphed and grew into Coruban copies, each with their own sword. For a moment they stood in place as if gaining their bearings then began to advance on them.

Bishop quickly blasted one of them and then another, but this time they didn't shatter they were simply knocked back and as soon as they landed they picked themselves up and advanced again.

"I can't keep doing this, Josh," Bishop hissed. Her earth power would quickly run out.

Pope leapt forward and grabbed the original sword from where it lay on the ground, but as soon as he did so he screamed and dropped it again — the whole sword was made of silver and his hand was ablaze with searing pain.

He used his other hand to rip the front from the rest of his T-shirt and he wrapped it around the sword's handle. With this weapon in his undamaged hand he approached the nearest of the advancing Corubans.

The copy fought sluggishly and was easily dispatched with a swift blow that cleaved its head from its shoulders, but it only stayed down for as long as it took for the parts to recombine, by which time Pope was already fighting with the second one. Bishop blasted a couple more of them further down the slope to give them more time but she'd depleted her current power and was forced to draw on the energy stored in the last of the gems.

"I can't use any more energy on them, Josh," she said.

Unfortunately, the Corubans kept coming and the two magicians knew it was only a matter of time before they wore them down. Worse was that Pope knew he was down to his last ten minutes.

He dropped the sword, pulled out his knife and cut into his injured hand. The blood pooled quickly in his cupped palm, but the copies drew closer as he waited for enough of the red liquid to gather.

When he threw the blood and muttered his Shadow Dominion words, the blood droplets blasted forward like a huge fan of shotgun pellets, hitting each of the

Corubans with such force that they broke into tiny fragments that fell to the ground, seemingly spent.

But Drax wasn't finished and he gestured yet again, though the strain caused his levitation to falter. This time, his magic caused all the fragments to gather together as if drawn by some spiritual magnetic force. As they coalesced, they took on the form of Coruban once again but this time he was a giant of more than twenty feet in height. As the last piece fell into place, a giant sword grew from his hand and the strange spirit stared at it in pleasure, the old Fae symbol glowing brightly on his forehead. The giant tested the massive sword's weight, swirling it around with a sound like that of a wind turbine.

Pope threw his phone to Bishop and grabbed the sword in his uninjured hand. "I'll hold it off as long as I can."

Drax had now risen high enough to be completely clear of the well opening and he laughed in spite of the intense concentration that contorted his face. The blood-covered artefact was tucked under his left arm and he made another motion with his right.

Pope's sword arm was abruptly no longer under his control and he swiped at Bishop with a swift stroke that would have taken her head off her shoulders if she hadn't ducked in time.

"What the hell, Josh?"

"I can't control it!" he yelled. "And I can't let go." He thrust with the blade again and Bishop only just managed to dodge once more.

Then the phone rang as the giant Coruban lumbered up to the top of the hill. It raised its huge sword to strike and Pope did the same with his.

"Sod this!" Bishop shouted and kicked Pope in the balls. Whatever part of Bishop's body his stroke had intended to hit, it missed completely and the sword's blade sunk into the ground a short way as Pope collapsed to his knees.

As soon as she'd kicked him she raced between the legs of the giant Fae spirit and the path of the giant sword stroke followed her, gouging out a huge piece of the ground and hacking through the giant's own leg with the unchecked momentum. It immediately collapsed backwards down the hill and almost fell onto Bishop as it did so but she leapt out of the way, sprawling onto the dusty earth and winding herself a little.

As she picked herself up she answered the still ringing phone. "Yes?" She listened as Finlay told her they were ready.

"Okay, Josh, this is it." She began the preparations of making a portal.

"Wait!" Pope shouted. "Just a few seconds." His left hand still gripped the sword and was beyond his control, trying to pull the weapon from the ground. So he forced his injured right hand into an inside pocket of his jacket and pull out a small electrical device with a single button on it.

Drax was in the process of recombining the giant with its severed leg when Pope pressed the button and the explosive device he'd planted inside the artefact went off. Drax and the Ellen Maegen were sufficiently blown to pieces that the magician's control of his magic was gone in an instant. His remains slid down the interior of the confinement column, leaving no trace as they did so. They landed at the bottom of the well with a disgusting, yet satisfying, squelch.

The giant Coruban collapsed and vanished immediately but Pope now kept his grip on the sword intentionally, ready for anything further that might come their way.

"Now, Faye," he said.

She gathered the energy she'd earlier drawn from the gem and concentrated. This portal would have to be far more precise than usual and she couldn't rush the preparations. It also had to be a two-way portal, something she didn't often have a need for, normally using them to travel only one way. Sweat beaded her brow as she intensified her concentration.

Pope looked on, desperately wanting to urge Bishop to hurry, but he knew he couldn't break her concentration. He just needed to hope that Drax couldn't pull himself back together quickly enough.

Bishop took a deep breath and opened a portal directly over the top of the well, making sure it was small enough to be inside the confinement barrier. The other gateway opened below the mixer chute at Miller's Concrete and Finlay's voice over the phone told them that the portal was aligned.

"Let it go, Sam!" Bishop yelled into the phone.

Holy water concrete shot straight out of the portal and down the well in an incredibly satisfying rush. It splattered at the bottom and the noise of it filling the column rose in pitch as the level inside drew nearer the top. The flow of concrete continued as if never ending but they were able to breathe more easily. They'd at last trapped Drax and his artefact together. Or the remains of them, at least.

"We did it, Josh."

"Yeah, I guess." He slumped a little, feeling the strain.

Bishop looked at his burned hand. "Tell me — why didn't you blow Drax up sooner?"

"I only had one chance to do so." Pope winced as he looked at his own injury. "If I'd detonated the bomb too early he might have regenerated before we dumped the concrete on him. This way the holy water and concrete together will stop him reforming."

Bishop nodded but didn't say anything. She couldn't fault his reasoning.

"Oh, gotta go..." Pope felt his internal clock counting down the last few seconds of his time outside of the York walls and he vanished with a small popping of air. Surprisingly, the sword had gone with him.

The concrete filled up the well and began to rise above the top, confined by the power of the gold circle. She decided that was enough and immediately closed the portal.

She took a brief moment to look across across the Wolds. It was peaceful, not a soul in sight, the only thing disturbing it the tinny voice that came from Pope's phone.

"It's okay, Sammy," she said into the device. "We got the bastard."

She closed the connection and heaved a sigh of relief. Then she simply stood, staring at her feet, feeling she'd forgotten something vitally important.

"Oh, damn!" she exclaimed, looking up. "Sandra!"

Return to the Pub

Bishop drew on more of her internal energy and opened another portal. Seconds later she was back in the pub. Lassiter and Sandra were still where they'd been before she left. Kitty was still in her protective circle but appeared to have gone to sleep. Bishop noticed that Lassiter had closed the curtains over the gaping window to prevent people looking in.

What astonished her more than anything was the huge number of ghosts that now filled the pub, drawn back here since they were no longer banished by the barrier Drax had erected. More arrived all the time until they were moving about one another like tightly packed shoals of fish. There were far more than the twenty seven Finlay claimed haunted the place. Among their number was the real ghost of Archie Morton who hovered near Sandra looking extremely concerned at her lack of wellbeing.

Bishop immediately went over to where the landlady lay on the floor. The woman was so pale and drained she looked as if she would expire at any moment. Lassiter broke off his praying and looked up at Bishop with a questioning look.

"We did it, Lassiter," she said. "Drax is trapped in a confinement circle, encased in concrete."

Lassiter nodded then looked down at Sandra.

"Why has she failed to recover, Faye?" he asked. He stood up and his knees popped like firecrackers. "I thought your healing pendants would have restored her to normal."

"She was too far gone for that," Bishop said. "They simply kept her alive until I could get back here. I need to perform something far more powerful. Just give me a moment."

She returned to the doorstep and pulled in more power from the ley line. The flow was slower than she expected and she realised that exhaustion was taking its toll on her. But she had to hold on for Sandra's sake. The sound of boots thundering along the pavement caught her attention and when she looked up she saw Pope racing along the street towards her. He'd just run the half mile from home, which was where he always appeared when forced back to the city at the end of his monthly time.

He stopped right before her and rested his hands on his knees while he got his breath back. The last day had taken it out of both of them.

"Where's the sword?" Bishop asked, referring to the silver Fae weapon.

"Safe at home," Pope gasped in reply. "I thought you might need this." He pulled an object out of his pocket and handed it to Bishop — another of her earth gems.

"Thank god," Bishop said and snatched it from his hand. She drew on the power quickly, topping up the energy she'd already been able to draw from the line. "I need your help with Sandra."

Back inside, she knelt by Sandra's side and placed her left hand over the still weeping wound in the crook of her elbow. Pope rolled his jacket sleeve up and picked the scab off his own wound then held his arm out so Bishop could place her right hand over it, becoming a conduit between the two of them.

As soon as the link was made, Sandra stopped

breathing and it seemed that her fight for life was over. Morton crouched by her side and stared down at her. He looked less substantial than his fake counterpart had been.

Bishop closed her eyes and quickly fell into a trance, gripping both arms tightly, triggering the connection between the three of them. Pope groaned with the discomfort of the transfer and Bishop's skin rippled and pulsed as life energy moved from him and into Sandra.

Both Pope and Bishop had to fight the urge to stop the process. Life energy is such a precious thing that everyone's body reacts against an attempt to interfere with it. The landlady's skin took on some colour but still she wasn't breathing. Bishop's own body laboured with the effort of forcing air into her lungs but she still managed to mutter under her breath. "Come on, Sandra, come on."

Then Pope passed out and Bishop knew she could take no more from him. She opened her eyes and released her grip on him but carried on for a few moments pushing her own energy into Sandra. Unfortunately, Sandra still didn't breathe and lay deathly motionless. Bishop hung her head and stopped in fear of passing out herself — she was so sure she'd be able to help her.

"An unfortunate state of affairs ," Lassiter said. "Yet another innocent victim of Drax's evil. She tried so hard to put her family tragedy behind her. But then her husband died a year ago and this pub became her life."

Bishop looked at him as if she was mulling over his words in her mind. "Of course!" she said, slapping her forehead. "Help me get her outside. Quickly!"

Before they could move, every ghost in the room shrunk back from them, pushing against the walls as if by an invisible force. A few of them vanished or left the pub completely, but most were held in complete terror by something Bishop couldn't sense. Morton was torn between fleeing and staying near to the landlady.

"No!" he cried, his ghostly embodiment filled with fury. "You cannot have her!"

With that a new presence materialised — a dark ghost with little proper form, which hovered over Sandra, shifting and changing in a menacing way. More of the other ghosts left and this new arrival seemed to laugh at the fear it generated.

"The earth is dark, here," it hissed. "It suits me well."

Bishop felt there was something almost familiar about this apparition. "Do I know you?"

It laughed again but didn't answer. Instead, it reached down towards Sandra and pulled on her arm with an almost smoke-like appendage. But rather than connecting with her physical being it took hold of her inner spirit and was already beginning to draw it from her body.

"Help her, please!" Morton cried from a little way away but the dark ghost hissed at him and he moved further away.

From the way Morton had clung to Sandra's side since returning to the pub, it was clear that he thought the world of the landlady and he wanted to protect her from harm. But the dark spirit had other plans and clearly wanted Sandra's soul for himself.

Bishop leapt to her feet and searched her pockets for something suitable, but she had nothing that would help.

"Can I do anything?" Lassiter asked and Bishop turned on him.

"Do you have a crucifix?" she said. "Or a bible?"

Lassiter reached into his inside pocket and pulled out a small, well-worn copy of the new testament, a gold-leaf crucifix embossed into the front of the leather binding.

He passed it to Bishop.

The dark ghost redoubled its effort, hoping to complete his task before she could work anything on him but Bishop stepped forward, pushed the front of the bible into the forehead of the ghost. Unfortunately, nothing happened.

"The ghost of a Christian will not be harmed by such things, nor that of an unbeliever," Lassiter said and took the bible back from Bishop.

Then Amber's ghost appeared, clear and fragile-looking, staring at her aunt with concern. She watched as the dark spirit pulled Sandra's spirit a little further from her body.

"Help us," Bishop pleaded with the child's ghost. "Help your Aunt Sandra. Please, Amber."

The young ghost looked at Bishop as if seeing her for the first time then moved over to the dark ghost, placing her small hand into its form to get its attention. It turned as if to face her and the girl's eyes widened but not through fear. Her determination to save her aunt gave her a strength the other ghosts lacked and she plunged her other hand into its vapour-like form.

The dark shape lost even more structure and writhed against the interference of the young ghost's innocence. It tried to pull itself free of her touch but it was like she held on with barbed hooks.

"Leave Aunt Sandra alone!" Amber yelled and pushed further into the dark ghost. It writhed in even greater distress and attempted to fight back, but the girl moved her arms wide as if trying to rip the grim form apart. The action, however, caused a backlash of pain to her own ghostly body.

She screamed and vanished, but took the malevolent spirit with her.

Sandra's spirit drifted gently back into her body and

Morton clasped his translucent hands in joy.

"Come on, Lassiter!" Bishop said. "We can still save her."

Struggling a little, the two of them carried her by her shoulders and feet, out through the door of the pub and rested her on the pavement, ignoring the looks of the passing public.

Bishop placed her hand on Sandra's chest just over her heart and sent a surge of energy into the organ. There was a reactive spasm from Sandra's body but she hadn't recovered.

The earth witch gripped the pendant around her neck and tried again. She gathered her power, drew the last of the reserves from the gem and forcing everything she had into the woman. If this didn't do it nothing would. Sandra's body jerked and shook with the strength of the surge and Bishop's hand almost slipped from the woman's chest.

For a moment she had a strange vision of Sandra's spirit shackled to the pub with an immense chain and an echo of Drax's spirit caressed the chain as if it was his last contact with the world. Suddenly it became clear — she had to break this chain or Drax would find a way to use this tenuous echo to break himself free, no matter how long it took to do so.

Bishop reached into Sandra with her heightened earth senses and sought out the exact location the chain was connected to her spirit. After a few moments of searching she wasn't surprised to find it was tethered to her heart. No wonder she couldn't revive the woman. But not only was it anchored here, Drax's echo held it in place with a tenuous yet firm hand.

She could sense him holding on, this delicate link of earth power keeping his hopes alive; his hopes of returning once more to plague all of their lives. In spite of the sense of dread Bishop felt, she gathered her will like never before, knowing that she would get no more chances.

With an intense surge of her last traces of energy, she blasted both the chain and the hand free and restarted Sandra's heart. At least, that was her intention.

Her head spun. She had nothing left with which to try again and she slumped down on the pavement, rested her head and closed her suddenly sleepy eyes, unsure if she saw Drax's spirit disappear or if she heard someone draw in a great lungful of air.

On the hill at Far Tree Farm, the ground shook with an unexpected tremor and the setting concrete settled into the well shaft with a little more finality.

Bishop woke a little later inside the pub, propped in one of the chairs alongside Sandra, who was looking much better than Bishop felt. They smiled weakly at each other and tears filled Sandra's eyes. She reached over and gripped Bishop's hand as tightly as she was able.

"Thank you," she whispered. Bishop smiled and returned the grip.

Bishop used the brief contact to gently reach out with her magical senses and check Sandra over. Along the way she helped the healing process a little more but worked her tendrils through to the landlady's heart, a little afraid of what she might find there. Thankfully, the organ was clear of any link to Drax but it showed signs of the strain of the last couple of days.

Although Bishop had little energy to spare, she spent it on healing the woman's heart and set it beating in a more relaxed rhythm. As she let go of the woman's hand,

Sandra gave out a brief, "Oh!"

Then she asked a question, gently. "Did I imagine it or did I see my lovely Amber?"

"She helped save you." Bishop didn't elaborate further.

Pope had also recovered and was standing beside Lassiter with a pint in his hand. Both were relieved to see Bishop come round. Kitty was sitting on the floor looking tense — her injured foot was still bleeding a little — but she managed a warm smile for her friend.

"You did it, Faye," Pope said.

"Not me. We all beat him."

"Faye, do you think you could tell me why we had to take Sandra outside to bring her round?" Lassiter asked.

"You said it yourself, the pub was her life," Bishop said. "This place is a magical nexus and Drax used that aspect to create a connection I had to break. It worked through Sandra and wouldn't release her while she remained inside." Lassiter nodded and almost smiled.

"Mr. Pope," Sandra said. "Could you tell me something? I thought you said you were trapped within the city walls and it was impossible to leave."

"It is," Pope said. "Except for ten hours and sixteen minutes every lunar month." He looked around at the others. "Though I cut it a bit fine this time."

"Faye?" Kitty asked, a note of desperation in her voice. "Please?"

"Oh, sorry," Bishop said. She beckoned to Pope and he helped her over to where Kitty was sitting. Bishop wiped away part of the pastel line and broke the protective circle surrounding Kitty. It was always safest when the person who created it did so.

Kitty held her breath for a moment but when it was clear the link to Drax no longer existed she heaved a huge sigh of relief.

"About time!" Kitty said, rising cautiously to her feet. "I'm dying for a pee." She limped quickly towards the toilets.

Bishop leaned on Pope, exhausted. "I think I'm going to sleep for a week," she said.

"Really?" Pope said. "I thought we could paint the town red to celebrate."

Bishop pulled back and gave him an icy stare. "I don't want to see the inside of a pub ever again."

"That's a shame," Sandra said. "You're welcome here any time you want."

A strange snorting noise sounded and it was a moment before Bishop realised it was coming from her pocket. She pulled out Pope's phone and the sound became much clearer, resolving into the pig grunting that only meant one caller. "It must be Dobson," she said and handed it over.

Pope grinned and answered the call. "Inspector Dobson! Where were you when Faye and I dealt with that demon yesterday?"

Bishop rolled her eyes while Pope waited for Dobson to speak then shook her head and began to laugh. Her earlier anger at him was already mostly gone.

"I'll tell you what we've been doing," Pope said into the phone. "We've been busy saving the world, we have... Well, you've got to move fast to keep up with us."

Tears running down her face, Bishop now shook with a fit of almost silent, but hysterical laughter.

ACKNOWLEDGMENTS

Thanks must go to all those who have been very supportive during my time of writing this novel, especially my wonderful partner, June.

I'd also like to thank my former agents from Smart Talent, Kelly Marshall and Sidney Coe, who gave such valuable feedback during the early drafts of this novel.

Thanks, too, to the members of the York Screenwriters Guild who were keen to read more about the characters I created here.

ABOUT THE AUTHOR

Steve Ince is a writer, artist, game designer, consultant and speaker with many years of development and writing experience, working in a freelance capacity with a variety of clients across the globe.

Steve gained a nomination for Excellence in Writing at the Game Developers Choice Awards in 2004 for Broken Sword: The Sleeping Dragon and received a second nomination in 2008 from the Writers' Guild of Great Britain for his writing on So Blonde.

Steve's book, Writing for Video Games, was published by A&C Black and has sold throughout the world, sometimes used as a text in game writing courses.

Regularly invited to speak at conferences around the world, Steve enjoys sharing his knowledge and experience.

His short film, Payment, was released a couple of years ago to critical acclaim.

Blood and Earth is his first urban fantasy novel.

MILFORD COMMUNITY LIBRARY
Village Hall

2 Park Road
Milford on Sea
Hants SO41 0QU

Printed in Great Britain
by Amazon

70117351R00246